TERMS OF USE

TERMS OF USE

SCOTT ALLAN MORRISON

THOMAS & MERCER

Published by Thomas & Mercer, Seattle

www.apub.com

Amazon, the Amazon logo, and Thomas & Mercer are trademarks of Amazon.com, Inc., or its affiliates.

Hardcover ISBN-13: 9781503951501
Hardcover ISBN-10: 1503951502

ISBN-13: 9781503946897
ISBN-10: 1503946894

Cover design by Cyanotype Book Architects

Printed in the United States of America

For Martha

"Don't Be Evil."

*—Google co-founders Larry Page and
Sergey Brin*

-1-

Sergio Mansour marveled at the giant eyeball staring back at him from his computer display. He leaned closer to the tiny 3-D camera perched atop the monitor until his brown iris and sparkling pupil popped from the screen in electrifying detail. On any other morning, he would have been exhausted after working through the night. But this was the moment of truth and Sergio felt curiously wired, as if all the synapses in his brain were firing in rapid succession. He could have dismantled his computer, piece by piece, and then put it back together again, just for the fun of it. It had to be the dopamine.

He clicked his mouse and captured a frozen image of his eye in the computer's memory. In an instant, the picture began to flutter, each pixel on the screen momentarily blurring, adjusting, and resetting based on complex pattern-recognition software churning away in a rack of computers in the cooling room down the hall. A tiny round icon in the top right corner of the monitor blinked steadily as the servers processed each of the twenty million pixels in the image. As the seconds ticked by, the number of fluttering pixels declined until tens of thousands, and then just hundreds, remained in flux. After a long 7.9 seconds, the three-dimensional photo of his eye locked into place and the flashing icon steadied with a beep.

```
>>BETA USER

>>IDENTITY APPROVED
```

"Yes!" cried Sergio, as he sprang off his stool and pumped his fist.

Finally. Seven months of complex programming, false starts, and frustrating errors had paid off. He was well on his way to one of the most important achievements of his career—a virtually foolproof user-identification system that would catapult Circles, already the world's biggest social network, into the stratosphere.

Sergio craned his neck to survey Circles' highly secured research lab. A spartan assemblage of engineering workstations, linoleum floors, and artificial light, the big room in the heart of the lab was home to a dozen or so colleagues. But it was eerily quiet for nine o'clock on a weekday morning.

He bounced along a row of closed office doors on the far wall. "Anyone here?" he called out as he made his way down the line, peeking in each unit's narrow window as he passed. He reached the end of the row and shook his head in disbelief as he looked back at the empty offices. Not even one person to share the news with?

A heavy sigh escaped him. It had been too long since his last eureka moment, that instant when countless lines of artfully woven code clicked for the first time, transforming fanciful notions into amazing new technologies. It had not been lost on him, or his bosses, that many of the biggest innovations to come out of Circles Labs, the company's R&D unit, in the past few years were the work of colleagues half his age. The gap between him and the new generation of coders had hit home when he became the first Circles employee to turn fifty and one twenty-something coworker thought it would be fun to bust Sergio's balls by giving him a bottle of Old Grand-Dad bourbon for his birthday.

The thought of it still irked him. Oh sure, he had plenty of gray in his beard, but that only added a touch of distinction as far as he was concerned. He still had a full head of chestnut hair and he could out-ski or out-surf most of his young colleagues. More importantly, his mind remained as razor-sharp as ever.

Sergio made his way down the back hall and checked the cooling room, a thirty-by-forty-foot vault stuffed with rack upon rack of powerful servers, each one brimming with tangled cables and flashing LED lights. Not a soul in sight. He wandered into the lab's empty conference suite just as the massive arm of a construction crane swung past the windows. Down below stood the concrete skeleton of Circles' new wing, still about five months from completion. He pressed his head to the glass and smiled with satisfaction.

The new wing was just one more reason to believe the social network's best days lay ahead. Naysayers were quick to declare that Circles had peaked, but they didn't know about China yet, nor could they have any inkling of the boost the company would get from his inexpensive iris scanner. Built with a high-definition 3-D camera instead of the conventional but very costly infrared-light technology, the scanner would likely become the de facto security standard at Circles within two to three years. The software and programmable chip would be ready within six months; then the computer companies and cell phone makers would jump on board. They loved new products that spurred consumer demand and drove up prices. And they'd never buck the most powerful Internet company on the planet, not if Circles gave them the technology to protect the social network's two-and-a-half billion users from cybercrooks bent on committing fraud, identity theft, and online reputation crimes.

Once his 3-D iris scanner was built into every new cell phone, tablet, and laptop that rolled off assembly lines, Circles could expand into dozens of new activities. People would trust the social network to bank, get a mortgage, trade stocks, pay their taxes, and maybe even one day vote—all without concern for their privacy or the safety of their personal information. Maybe, just maybe, Sergio's big breakthrough would help keep his run going a little bit longer. *Help the team win and they will love you for it.*

Sergio stepped back from the window and caught a reflection of his disheveled self. He tossed his hair back and tucked in the tails of his light green Hugo Boss Oxford shirt. T-shirts, shorts, and sandals were all accepted attire at Circles, but if he was going to wear a collar, he might as well look the part. He exited the conference room, walked up the hall, and stopped at the kitchenette. He opened the fridge and pulled out a bottle of Veuve Clicquot, one of several kept on hand for these impromptu occasions. It was his moment to celebrate, even if he had to do it alone.

Sergio returned to his stool and set a plastic flute amongst the camera parts, laptop computers, and tiny tools scattered across his workbench. He popped the cork and held the bottle at arm's length as bubbly spilled to the floor. Wiping his hand on his jeans, he poured himself a healthy tipple and solemnly lifted his glass to a framed photo hanging on the wall. The late Circles founder, Johnny Weiss; Sergio; and several senior staff stood beaming on the balcony of the New York Stock Exchange. They were about to ring the opening bell and watch Circles shares trade on Wall Street for the very first time. They were all about to become millionaires.

A muted ring brought Sergio back to the moment. The landline on his workbench announced an incoming call from George Verneek, the company's security chief and a close friend. *He never uses the phone,* Sergio thought, *unless . . .*

"Yeah?"

"We got one," said the familiar voice. "And it looks bad. He's been poking around for at least a month. I could use your help."

Sergio set down the flute and leaned forward on his workbench. He lifted his head and stared at the giant eyeball peering out from the computer monitor. The eye, only moments ago a source of celebration and excitement, now seemed to be mocking him. He had gotten too far ahead of himself; a utopian future free of intruders and cybercriminals would have to wait. Circles was under attack.

-2-

Sinon leaned forward to scrutinize the data flowing across his dual computer screens. His face shone brightly in the cool blue glow of the monitors, the only source of light in the chilly room. He preferred working with the lights off; darkness provided an illusory but comforting cloak of anonymity.

Sinon nervously massaged his mouse and silently prayed he had not gotten too aggressive. A few minutes had passed since he'd ratcheted up his attack and so far he'd seen no indication Circles had discovered he was siphoning data from the company's network. Any novice hacker knew a company like Circles had security thresholds for a wide range of online activities. Post too many photos, send out too many buddy requests, or download too much data and Circles' security software would automatically alert staff that something might be amiss. At the present rate, Sinon was stealing the equivalent of 470 hours of streaming video every hour, but he wasn't sure—nobody outside of Circles' security team could really be certain—exactly how far he could push without stumbling over one of the company's trip wires. This little game of cat and mouse was the most nerve-racking part of his attack.

Gaining a foothold within Circles' network had been easier than he expected. The company was among the most sophisticated Internet giants in the world, but they were powerless to guard against human error—all it took was one gullible employee to fall for an email scam and cough up a critical password. Naive employees were the bane of all security officers.

Password in hand, Sinon passed himself off as the bonehead employee and used the unsuspecting staffer's machine as his home base within Circles. He installed a handful of special programs—his digital toolkit—that enabled him to probe, identify, and map out all the computers on the company's vast network. Then he rolled out snooping software that let him roam the company's virtual hallways, watching employees come and go as they punched in their user names and passwords. Within a couple of months, Sinon had free run of just about all of Circles' computers by pretending to be the very people who were supposed to use them. It had been slow and tedious work, but there was no other way.

A jolt of adrenaline coursed through Sinon as he once again punched at his keyboard and watched intently as the flow of data from Circles picked up speed in tiny increments. The urgency of the situation demanded that he tap the keys a few times more, even as the nervous tingling in his fingertips warned him he was pushing his luck. Years of playing these games had taught him to trust his instincts, even when trying to outwit a soulless piece of software.

By day, he was a respected security contractor who helped Air Force Intelligence, the Department of Energy, and the Defense Department defend against attacks by the very best computer minds China and Russia could throw at the US. The work was frustrating, eye-opening, and ultimately enthralling once he learned to think like his opponents—the data they sought, the software they used, the tactics they preferred. He often found himself marveling at his opponents' creativity, skill, persistence, and occasionally, sense of humor. It had occurred to him that he spent his days—and often entire nights—watching master artists at work.

But now he was one of the artists—a master of deception. In history books, Sinon was the Greek warrior who tricked the Trojans into wheeling the giant wooden horse into their city. In shadowy chat rooms where computer geeks, script kiddies, and organized criminal gangs traded information, data, and services on the fringes of the Internet, Sinon was the brazen hacker who'd pulled off a legendary attack on the Pentagon, scoring detailed blueprints for several of the US military's next-generation weapons systems. He promptly sold those plans to the first person who deposited three million dollars into a Swiss bank account. The shadowy buyer did not know the account belonged to the US Treasury, or that the plans were specifically drawn up and released to Sinon in order to sow disinformation among geopolitical rivals. As far as the online underworld knew, he was one of them.

Sinon toyed with his mouse as he made mental calculations. The tingling in his fingertips was more acute than usual, a reminder he was not merely testing government defenses.

He grasped the bright red rubber ball on the desk and began squeezing it with his left hand, expending nervous energy each time he clenched and released his fist. This was for real. Any miscalculation could destroy his career and land him in jail. But he couldn't stop now, not after stealing the crucial algorithmic keys that unlocked much of the encrypted Circles data he'd already downloaded. As he began to decipher that information, he spotted a disturbing pattern, one so outrageously audacious that he couldn't quite believe it. He needed more proof, evidence still locked away within Circles' network.

Sinon tapped the keyboard again, commanding his worldwide network of computers to suck data from Circles at an ever-faster rate. The nerves in his fingertips were screaming now and he pumped the squeeze ball faster. He was taking a huge risk, but he had no choice. At the current rate, it would take five more days to transfer all the data he'd seized. That would be too late; the election would be over by then.

-3-

Sergio stepped to the outer edge of the glass elevator and looked over the sun-splashed atrium that soared to the top of Circles' seven-story San Francisco headquarters. He barely noticed the open floors zip past as he dropped to the main entrance below. George was one of the top security experts in the valley; he'd never confronted an attack he couldn't handle. But the stress in his voice and the curtness of his words said it all. Trouble waited below.

The elevator fell past the ground floor and its doors opened to the basement seconds later. Sergio stepped into the cavernous room that served as the company's operational nerve center. Daylight shone through a ribbon of street-level windows set high along one of the walls. Ventilation ducts, cable conduits, and colorful light fixtures seemed to float over clusters of workstations scattered across the open floor.

Something wasn't right. The keyboard clicks, idle banter, and laughter that usually filled the room were absent. Employees huddled in small groups, either at someone's desk or by the kitchenette on the far wall. He noted several of his "missing" lab colleagues mingling with coworkers, exchanging whispers as they craned their necks toward the security bunker.

Heads turned toward Sergio as he crossed the basement, and he dutifully nodded whenever he met a colleague's glance. He stepped inside the bunker, a utilitarian room the size of a squash court separated from the rest of the basement by a large glass wall flanked by two doors that were always wide open. Security ninjas hunched over their Apple desktops, pecking furiously on their keyboards. They were surrounded by at least a dozen colleagues from the network operations team who had crammed inside to follow the action. Front and center sat George, an affable and gregarious character with captivating blue eyes, a scruffy beard, and a corpulent frame. The security chief's gaze was locked on a row of LED monitors hanging from the ceiling above the glass partition. The screens, filled with graphs, pie charts, and maps displaying data traffic patterns and network performance metrics, were awash in red light.

"Someone tripped an alarm," George said to Sergio. "We isolated the breach and, odd thing, our hacker has been quietly downloading data for about a month and then all of a sudden he steps it up." George chomped down on his lower lip, a sure sign he felt tremendous strain.

Sergio was surprised to see Dan Prederick standing over George's shoulder. An Internet industry veteran who'd taken over as chief executive after Johnny Weiss' sudden passing, Prederick sported a toothy smile, aviator glasses, and a full head of bushy hair worn long enough to cover his oversized ears. The overall effect was goofy and it had prompted a lot of jokes when he first joined the company. That quickly changed after a mid-level manager made a crack about Prederick's ears during a company softball game. Prederick, who gamely agreed to wear a cap that exposed his ears, appeared to laugh it off, but it was not lost on anyone that the manager was never again seen in the company's hallways. No one ever mentioned Prederick's jutting ears after that. Next to Prederick stood Victor Ko, a Chinese-born engineer Prederick had brought on board to run Circles Labs.

Their arrivals were controversial, for it was widely understood they had a mandate to put profits first, a focus entirely at odds with the breezy user-centric culture that Weiss had instilled in the company. George, like Sergio and most other old timers, had nothing but disdain for Prederick and Ko. Neither of them had ever responded to an alarm.

Sergio studied the overhead screens, trying to get a handle on the situation. He was no longer part of Circles' security team, but for years he'd worked closely with George to build what was widely considered the Internet's most complex and robust self-defense system. It was a virtual fortress with multiple layers of defense protecting all the sensitive personal information users had entrusted to Circles, as well as the company's most critical data and trade secrets. Each barrier was designed to delay intruders as long as possible, giving George and his team enough time to detect and thwart any attack.

What made Circles' security software so special was its ability to track every update, comment, photo, and buddy request that users posted on the site—over fifty billion read-and-write actions every single day. The software meticulously monitored every employee keystroke, how much power the company's twelve million computers were using, how much disk space was occupied, as well as the amount of data moving through Circles' digital pipes. Any traffic or sudden spike of activity outside normal parameters was immediately flagged as suspicious, setting off alarms in the security bunker.

Sergio's pulse picked up a beat or two. The amount of data flowing out of Circles' network was abnormally high for nine thirty on a Friday morning.

Sergio ran through his mental checklist. It'd been a while since he'd been on the front lines. "Where's it going?" he asked, as he slipped past Ko and leaned over George's shoulder.

"We've identified twenty-seven IP addresses, in Romania," replied George.

Sergio knew those twenty-seven nodes were merely the outer edge of a vast underground network of computers that had been secretly commandeered by hackers. Tucked away in living rooms, classrooms, and corporate data centers around the world, those computers formed a communications chain that bounced hackers' commands from country to country, making it extremely difficult for Circles to trace an attack back to its source.

Sergio looked up. The flashing overhead screens showed outgoing traffic had just spiked another notch or two.

"Where are the files being sent from?" asked Sergio.

"We've isolated fifty-one machines across our network." George spoke in succinct clips. Unnecessary details only got in the way at times like this. "Our hacker rotated, sending bursts of traffic from one machine at a time. Then he started sending bigger bursts from all fifty-one machines at once." George turned to look up at Sergio. He had never seen him so perplexed. "It's like our hacker was suddenly in a hurry."

"Okay. Okay," said Sergio. So far, it was all pretty standard. "What's he got?"

George shook his head. "Dunno. Looks like the hacker encrypted everything."

Sergio nodded. Intruders typically copied the data they wanted to steal and encrypted it before slowly siphoning it off in small increments. That way, even when a company discovered its network had been breached, it was next to impossible to figure out exactly what had been stolen.

"Have you traced internal traffic to the fifty-one nodes?" asked Sergio, struggling to figure out what made this attack so interesting to Prederick and Ko.

Ko's reedy voice sliced through the bunker. "We've already been through this, Sergio."

Sergio spun toward Ko. "I haven't," he blurted out, a bit more forcefully than intended. Keyboards fell silent and murmurs faded. Sergio understood he'd crossed a line.

Ko took a single step forward and the room waited in silence. A few engineers stole furtive glances in Ko's direction, but most looked away from the Labs' chief, who had a sharp chin, arching eyebrows, and a dagger-like widow's peak. His intimidating mien was compounded by the fact that he wasn't shy about speaking his mind, no matter whose toes he stepped on or whose feelings might be hurt.

Ko lifted his chin, making it appear like he was looking down at Sergio. "Our crack security team," he said, nodding at George, "has discovered a massive amount of traffic between the fifty-one nodes and Labs. Imagine that."

George shuffled awkwardly in his chair and cleared his throat. "Traffic patterns to the fifty-one machines suggest the intruder has used them to collect user data, financial material . . ." He paused a beat and tilted his head toward Ko. "And possibly files from Labs."

George's words rattled around Sergio's brain for an instant. The idea that someone had breached the most highly secured part of Circles' network was pretty far-fetched. Only a small team of Circles' top R&D people had access rights to the Labs subnet where Circles kept its critical source code, software prototypes, and research data—all the sensitive proprietary data that enabled Circles to keep its competitive edge. Sergio's 3-D iris scanner was in there, too. It was all encrypted and useless to anyone who didn't have the keys, but the mere fact they were having this discussion was a big black eye for George.

Ko's voice filled the room. "So glad we have people like you protecting us."

All eyes turned to George and the room waited for his reaction. Sergio watched his friend's jaw muscles tighten and his hands, big as bear paws, momentarily curl into massive fists before releasing. George reached into the fish bowl of Peanut M&M's on his desk, pulled out a handful, and stuffed them into his mouth. Everyone held their breath and the sound of George chomping on his candy filled the room. Sergio exhaled quietly, relieved by his friend's restraint. There was no upside to picking a fight with Ko.

"Let's dangle this guy for a bit," offered Sergio. "Let's see if we can figure out what he's accessed and where all this data is going."

"We cut him off now," said Ko in a firm voice.

Sergio pointed to the center screen on which George had isolated the suspect stream of data flowing from the fifty-one computers. "At the current rate, it will take this guy three to four days to transfer all the data he's copied to those machines."

Sergio was pushing his luck. Allowing an attack to continue was controversial, but secretly monitoring an intruder might be the best way to turn the tables. If they could figure which parts of the network the attacker had broken into they'd have a reasonable idea what data had been compromised. It was also Circles' only real chance of tracking the attacker back to his location. "Let's follow this guy for one hour and see what we find," said Sergio.

"*You* no longer run Labs," Ko countered, his eyes locked on the overhead LED monitors. George's ragged asthmatic breathing filled the otherwise silent bunker. Then Ko's voice commanded the void. "I said, cut him off . . . Now!"

Sergio bit his tongue and steadied himself, pausing to make sure he spoke his next words calmly and with no hint of aggression. "We will lose him for good if we do that. We'll never figure out what he's been taking."

"We don't need him getting any more than he's already stolen," countered Ko.

"We have an obligation to our users and shareholders to figure out what he's taken."

Ko pried himself away from the overhead monitors and turned to Sergio. "I don't give a fuck about that and . . . neither . . . should . . . you," he said, barking his words in half-beats as he jabbed his index finger at Sergio.

Ko turned to Prederick and raised an expectant eyebrow, waiting for the CEO to put an end to the debate. Prederick would not overrule

Ko—he hadn't done so yet, not once in the two years since Prederick had put him in charge of Labs. It had been a huge blow to Sergio, who was research chief at the time. He'd kept his title, but he now reported to Ko as part of Prederick's corporate reorganization. And Ko hadn't merely assumed an administrative or oversight role, he actively worked with dozens of twenty-something engineers on next-generation projects written in new languages like Navajo and Boomslang—all while refusing to work with Sergio or the rest of the old guard.

Prederick nodded to George. "Cut him off," he said softly.

George cast Sergio an apologetic glance as he typed in a series of commands blocking all traffic to and from the Romanian computers receiving the stolen data. He also isolated the fifty-one Circles' machines, ensuring the attacker couldn't access them from another IP address. "Done," he said, tapping the ENTER key on his keyboard.

Within seconds the room filled with a cacophony of beeps, chimes, and dings, all warning signs that Ko had made the wrong choice.

-4-

The message flashed across Sinon's screen:

>>COMMUNICATION ABORTED

"Damn!" Sinon blurted, as he pounded his fist on the desk. He chided himself for not paying heed to his twitchy fingers. His desperation had almost certainly caused him to trip an alarm and expose his attack. He gave the desk a second more measured thump to vent his frustration.

His displeasure was tempered by the grim satisfaction of knowing he'd just made life pretty damn miserable for Circles. He opened a new browser window and typed in the address for Circles' home page.

The page popped up immediately, as expected. Sinon waited fifteen seconds and tried again. This time the page loaded much more slowly. The third time should be the charm. He reentered the address:

>>ERROR 404

>>THIS PAGE CANNOT BE FOUND

Just as he thought. The digital land mines he'd planted within Circles' network had detonated. The booby traps were set to communicate with his computer every thirty seconds. If they did not receive a reply—meaning his connection to Circles had been severed—the digital land mines would detonate and wreak havoc on the network.

Sinon couldn't be entirely sure what would happen once the booby traps went off. All the user accounts stored in the Twin Falls and Leavelin data centers would be wiped out. Circles had backups for that data, but taking Twin Falls and Leavelin offline would put immense and unpredictable stress on other parts of the network, most likely creating a domino effect. Millions of users would notice the crash within the next few minutes and tens of thousands of them would no doubt fire off angry tweets, blog posts, and emails to anyone who cared. The national media would catch wind of this within ten minutes and TV broadcasters would squeeze word of the crash into their next news cycles.

A wry smile spread across Sinon's face as he paused to consider the chaos that must be taking hold within Circles. He couldn't be sure, but he allowed himself to imagine that Victor Ko was right in the middle of all the confusion. Still, as satisfying as that might be, it was little consolation. Sinon had been cut off short of his goal; now his only hope was that his little act of sabotage would stir things up just enough to help him reach it.

-5-

Liu Ting Wei looked at the incoming number and frowned as he pressed the phone to his ear. "Yes?"

"The shipment goes out tomorrow," said the caller.

Liu closed his eyes and released a deep sigh. "Two days early?"

The voice on the other end of the line was unmoved. "I need it by four in the afternoon."

Liu looked up at the kitchen clock. "Very well," he said curtly. "I will see you then."

Liu cursed his bad fortune. His meeting with the governor would have to wait. Worst of all, his portly frame would object to the trip for several days afterward. He pulled out a bowl and served himself a helping of Cheerios, a Western favorite he'd grown to love during his many years of travel outside China. Moving to the dining room table, he shoveled spoonful after spoonful into his mouth as he woke up his laptop to catch the latest news before bed. He also kept one ear trained on the local TV news blaring from the living room of his ornate twenty-second-story penthouse.

Liu's appetite for news was voracious and self-serving. As director of the government-owned Baotou Jingyuan Rare Earth High-Tech

Company, he was keenly aware his firm could be battered by, or greatly benefit from, national political developments, technology trends, macroeconomic issues, and distant geopolitical events like the contentious presidential campaign nearing its culmination halfway around the world.

Local websites had little of interest so he moved on to CNN, the *New York Times* and the *Washington Post*, sites that were inaccessible to the great majority of Chinese. Liu's position afforded him many privileges, one of which was that his keystrokes were routed around—or more precisely through—the Great Firewall of China, a vast digital system that blocked traffic from websites containing unfiltered news, subversive commentary, and obscene content that authorities deemed detrimental to Chinese values and political stability.

The widget on his laptop screen told him it would barely hit twenty-nine degrees Fahrenheit tomorrow in Baotou, the grim industrial outpost he'd called home for the past twenty-five years. He typed in *Shanghai* and the on-screen widget brought a satisfied smile to his face. It would reach sixty-two degrees there the following afternoon, a welcome but all too short respite from the gloomy fall weather that had blanketed Baotou for the past month.

He moved to the living room, just as a cute correspondent appeared on TV. Behind her loomed the White House, Liu's cue to pay attention. "And in the US, the presidential race is coming down to the last few days . . ." she began.

Liu watched intently as a headshot of his old friend Richard Diebolt appeared on the screen. Diebolt had defied the odds and come back from ten points down in the past three months. He was now locked in a statistical dead heat, with the finish line only a few days away; several polls even put the Republican standard-bearer ahead of Democratic rival Ian Lester for the first time. Diebolt had all the momentum, the reporter concluded, and it increasingly looked like it was his election to lose.

Liu bowed his head. He wished he could be happy for Diebolt, but Liu always knew this day might come, the point at which they found themselves on opposite sides, torn apart by nationalism, corporate rivalry, and simple greed. It was the moment two longtime friends became enemies.

-6-

Sergio stepped up behind Julian Cahill, who sat at his station in the center of Circles' network operations pod. Clusters of bright red flashes lit up the computer screens in front of them. Each burst of red light was accompanied by a high-pitched beep signaling that a server somewhere on Circles' network had failed. Cahill, responsible for keeping the company's entire system operating smoothly, looked up to Sergio and spoke in a dry, understated voice. "We have a problem."

Sergio had seen it all before, but this time somehow it felt different. The timing, mere minutes after Ko had ordered George to pull the plug on the hacker, couldn't have been a mere coincidence. For a fraction of a second, Sergio allowed himself to gloat.

Cahill rose from his chair, raised an arm over his head, and snapped his fingers to make sure he had the full attention of the nine-man network operations team seated around him just outside the security bunker.

"Hundreds of servers down at Twin Falls," he called out across the cavernous basement.

The piercing cacophony of beeps gathered pace until their discordant notes melded into a steady screech that sounded like a heart monitor hooked up to a person in the throes of death. Cahill corrected himself in a more urgent tone. "Make that thousands." His eyes grew wider as he stared at the screen. "Tens of thousands. Twin Falls is crashing."

Cahill dropped into his seat and began hammering out commands, his focus shifting rapid fire between his twitchy fingers and the flashing alarms on his monitor. He reached for the phone as he issued commands to his team. Then he turned to Cody Kimble, a fresh-faced engineer who only months earlier had graduated from Stanford University. "Kimble," he barked. "Let's reboot."

The rookie engineer froze in place, his startled gaze locked onto Cahill. "Come on, Kimble. Today."

The words jolted Kimble out of his stupor. His eyes darted to the ceiling and his lips moved quickly but silently, as if running through the recovery protocol for emergencies like this one. Sergio had never met the young engineer before, but he knew Kimble was about to be tested. This would be his chance to prove he had the chops to deal with an emergency—or not.

Kimble lowered his head and fell into a desperate pattern, striking his keyboard in furious fashion and then stopping to scan his monitor for verification that his commands were working. Each brief flurry of action was followed by another hopeful pause. The entire room understood that failure at this juncture meant millions of people would be unable to use their Circles accounts—an embarrassing and expensive black mark for the company. For engineers like Sergio and Cahill, staying online 99.999 percent of the time was a point of pride. For the suits, downtime meant lost advertising dollars, irrecoverable revenue that reached into the millions with each passing minute.

Those around Kimble held their collective breath, waiting for some sign—a flash of green lights, a respite from the steady screech of alarms, a relieved smile—showing that the rookie had the situation under control.

Instead, a low groan escaped Kimble's lips. The furrow in his brow grew more pronounced as Circles' network monitoring software indicated the number of inaccessible boxes at the company's Twin Falls data center—color-coded red instead of the usual green—continued to mount. Cahill brought some relief when he killed the awful screech of alarms with a few keyboard strokes.

"Kimble," snapped Cahill. "What the fuck's happening?"

Kimble looked up from his screen with distress in his eyes. "They're not rebooting."

"I can see that," Cahill said flatly. "Why not?"

"It's not me," Kimble protested. "I didn't do anything." The color faded from Kimble's face and his gaze morphed into a vacant stare.

"Kimble," barked Cahill. "Get a grip. We need you to stay focused."

Sergio could tell it was already too late. The youngster just sat there with a glazed-over look, shaking his head slowly. He was rattled—more than rattled. He had buckled.

Sergio looked to Cahill, who responded with a silent nod. Sergio came up behind Kimble and placed a gentle hand on his shoulder. "Kimble," he said quietly. "Time for a break. I'll take over."

Kimble's head drooped as he exhaled a deep breath. Sergio gave his shoulder a squeeze. "We need you to get up."

Sergio took Kimble's seat and began to scroll through screen after screen of Kimble's commands. The rookie engineer had followed emergency protocols by the book and his syntax was good. Kimble had not been the issue. Something was seriously wrong.

A voice from the other side of the pod broke the silence. "Leavelin is crashing too."

Sergio's fingers froze on the keyboard. Twin Falls and Leavelin each housed more than a million servers, making them the largest data centers in Circles' network. Losing them both simultaneously would be devastating. He shuddered at the possibilities. Tens of millions of Circles users were about to go dark—and it would be much worse if any other data centers went down as well.

Cahill stood stoically at his desk, a landline in one ear and a cell phone pressed against the other. His eyes narrowed as he listened to reports from the field. "Manual reboots at Twin Falls and Leavelin have failed," he announced to the room. He hesitated before continuing. "The servers have been wiped clean."

An uneasy hush crept across the cavernous basement. Scores of employees looked up from their screens and shared uncertain exchanges with each other. Maybe they were looking for guidance, or perhaps reassurance. Sergio felt Cahill's stare, but he could offer nothing in return. Sergio had never heard of an entire data center being wiped clean, let alone two. They were in uncharted territory.

The rustle of cotton and a big heaving groan broke the silent spell. George had moved his big frame into the doorway between the security bunker and the network operations pod. He wheezed as he held out one meaty arm into each room, like a cop directing traffic. "Listen up," he commanded, alternating his gaze between the two teams. "Disaster recovery is in effect."

His words jump-started the paralyzed basement. The network and security guys had trained for these moments; George had just reminded them of that fact. Keyboard clatter and breathless murmurs filled the basement once again as the security chief barked out commands with a calm, professional demeanor. Sergio smiled inwardly. His good friend, who only moments before had been badgered by Ko, was back in command. Circles would get through this.

George jabbed a finger at Sergio and another engineer. "And I need you guys to run integrity checks on everything—HR, finance, procurement . . . every database, web server, and storage rack we have."

Ko emerged from the second security bunker door. Behind him followed Prederick, wearing the bewildered expression of someone who'd never seen shit hit the fan before. Ko stepped up to George. "What's your assessment?"

"Hours, maybe days. Depends on the damage."

Ko's face darkened. "I want a full audit on all traffic in and out of Labs," he said to George. "And you better hope for the best." He spun around and nodded at Prederick. Then they marched across the basement and disappeared up the stairs.

Sergio clapped his hands, drawing attention away from George. "Okay," he called out across the room. "Let's get to it. We have a lot of work ahead of us." He walked his friend into the bunker. "Don't worry," he said. "We'll deal with Ko later."

George snorted as they sat down to work. "If he doesn't deal with me first."

Minutes blurred into hours as the network operations and security teams toiled in concert, triaging the damage and working to reboot crashed servers, restore lost data, and repair damaged programs. Figuring out what the hacker had stolen was a job for another day. Sergio labored well into the afternoon running integrity checks on Circles' human resources and finance software, tedious and time-consuming work that nonetheless had to get done.

The only murmur of excitement came when George discovered the hacker's signature on one of the fifty-one Circles computers he'd commandeered to transmit stolen data. The hacker had left it in a file the security team would surely check, almost like he was leaving a phone number or email address on a Post-it Note. It was a simple yet cryptic calling card: "S . . . N."

The discovery baffled Sergio and the rest of the team. The last thing a data thief wanted to do was draw attention. This guy had worked carefully to avoid detection for more than a month, and now he was leaving clues? Some hackers left calling cards out of sheer ego, others like the hacktivist group Anonymous did so to make political statements. This one felt different. The attacker had stolen huge amounts of data and then had gone out of his way to trash hundreds of thousands of servers and knock Circles sideways, even for a few hours. It was as if the attacker wanted to publicly embarrass Circles. If that was the case, well then, this was personal.

CIRCLES CRASHES AFTER SOFTWARE GLITCH

SAN FRANCISCO (AP)—More than 10 million Circles users across the western US were unable to log in to their accounts Friday after the social network suffered a software glitch that knocked out servers at two key data centers.

A person familiar with the situation said the disruption occurred during a routine maintenance operation, although the exact cause of the problem was not immediately known.

A company spokesman declined to comment on the cause of the outage, but said Circles' staff was investigating the circumstances that led to the outage. The spokesman said the company was working to restore service as soon as possible.

It wasn't immediately clear how many users were affected, but blog posts and comments on Twitter suggested
the outage was widespread across the western US. Sam
Rolland, founder of the influential DailyDose tech blog,
wrote that the crash appeared to be the company's largest outage ever.

The impact of the service disruption was magnified by
the variety of services the social network provides to its
users, including messaging, video chat services, search,
and shopping. Internet giants like Google and Amazon
have experienced similar outages over the years, but the
last known service disruption at Circles happened more
than six years ago.

-8-

Richard Diebolt peered out from behind the curtain and caught a glimpse of the twelve thousand energetic supporters who awaited him. This was one of the biggest crowds yet, and he reveled in the intoxicating rush that pulsed within as he prepared to go on stage.

"Richard Diebolt is going to fight for your rights. He's gonna make sure your future is bright and the future of your children even brighter!" the emcee bellowed, as the crowd roared in approval.

"Richard Diebolt is proud that he's no Washington insider. He's a businessman who knows how the private sector works. He's been the CEO of Diebolt Incorporated for ten years, but at heart he's a family man who lives each and every day by the traditional values that have made America strong. He'll fight for the middle class, and he'll stand up for America!"

The crowd's cheer rose to a deafening level. Diebolt's campaign manager slipped beside him and handed him the latest Colorado poll numbers. He was *up* three points on his Democratic rival, Ian Lester. Earlier in the campaign, Nathan Aaron used to hand him encouraging notes from key supporters right before he went on stage. Now that momentum had swung in Diebolt's favor, Aaron saved the best poll numbers for his stage appearances. Earlier in the year, his candidacy was all but dead in the water, and Diebolt still had trouble believing polls that put him in the lead.

There was little doubt his shift on China had been the masterstroke. Lester's hard line on the People's Republic had been a winner on two counts: it had tapped into the electorate's wariness of China, and it had made Diebolt look soft in comparison. So he did what any smart politician would—he outflanked Lester as aggressively as possible. If Lester was going to be tough on China, Diebolt had to be downright hawkish.

Right-wing commentators immediately took note of Diebolt's new China stance and corporate cash began to roll in. Conservative voters, many of whom were unemployed and looking for someone to blame, were not far behind. Before long, Diebolt's campaign had become the hottest trending topic on social media, fueling an outpouring of support that seemed to feed on itself. It was like some kind of virus, or at least that's how Aaron put it.

"And now, without further ado, I give you . . . Richard Diebolt," the emcee said, Diebolt's name rolling off his tongue as if he were introducing a heavyweight boxer before a championship bout in Vegas.

A burst of light splashed down on Diebolt and followed him across the stage to the podium. Bryan Adams' edgy and aggressive "We're Gonna Win" blared from overhead loudspeakers.

The crowd reverberated in thunderous approval. Winning was infectious and they had caught the bug. Diebolt just loved moments like this.

"Hello, Denver!" he called out, as he waved to voters, pointed at well-wishers he recognized, and shook hands with contributors whose donations had secured them front row seats. He clasped his hands, held them overhead, and pumped them in a triumphant display of confidence. The audience volunteered one last burst of vigorous applause.

"It's great to be here in Denver. My name is Richard Diebolt and I want to be your next president."

Diebolt flipped into cruise control. He'd given the speech so many times it had become second nature to him. Biographical details: family man, businessman, a man of God. Check. A defender of liberty, family values, and free enterprise. Good. Strong on national security, uncompromising on terrorism, and tough on immigration. Done. But not all was well. Times were tough, jobs scarce, and the debt was ballooning out of control. The list. He'd fight for the little guy. He'd lower taxes and cut regulations. More oil exploration. Next. And most of all, no one was better prepared to take on China, the biggest threat to America's prosperity and superpower status.

The audience erupted in approval. Their hatred—and fear—of China was palpable. The financial crisis that began in 2008 had proven far more painful than anyone dared to predict. Corporate profits soared and the stock market had rebounded to new highs, but good jobs remained scarce, wage increases were minimal, and overall economic data showed more Americans than ever were being left behind. Toss in concerns about the debt and anxiety over rising health care costs, and voters had good reason to worry about the future.

Meanwhile, China's economy surged ahead as it captured an ever-growing share of the global manufacturing sector. Its affluent citizens were becoming the market of choice for manufacturers around the world, tipping the balance away from the US. China took away jobs and stole US corporate secrets. It had massive reserves of US Treasuries with which it could fund the greatest infrastructure spending spree the world had ever seen. Its army and air force had expanded rapidly, while its navy was building a fleet of aircraft carriers and nuclear submarines to assert itself on the world stage. China was the biggest threat to the future prosperity of the United States, and Diebolt made damn sure to exploit that fear.

". . . and I will never compromise on the security and future prosperity of these United States of America, so help me God. Thank you all. Thank you." Diebolt waved his arms in triumph as the crowd cheered. "And may God bless America!"

-9-

By late afternoon, Circles had moved past the immediate crisis. More than two million servers at Twin Falls and Leavelin had been wiped clean by the attacker, and it would take days of on-site repairs to bring them back online. But in the meantime, Circles' network and security engineers had redirected traffic away from the damaged data centers and optimized system workloads. Circles' network remained degraded, but most users wouldn't notice.

Sergio had done his bit; the integrity checks on Circles' human resources and finance software had uncovered no evidence those systems were compromised. He was just about to ask George for a new task when the security chief spun around and addressed his team. "Why don't you guys go grab something to eat?" he suggested. "Let's take advantage of the calm, just in case we get hit again."

A murmur of agreement filled the bunker. The team could be in and out of the company cafeteria in ten minutes flat, even less if they had to rush back. The first group of three shuffled out of the room when George looked over to Sergio. "Sergio? I can handle things for a few minutes."

It wasn't like George to coddle his team. Hell, he'd prefer they ate at their desks so they never left their workstations. That kind of suggestion—leave me all alone in the company's nerve center—would've normally sparked his suspicion had it come from anyone but George. Sergio mulled the offer before deciding he could take advantage of the quiet to rest his aching head and soothe his puffy eyes. He'd been staring at the screen too long; more than anything else, he needed a few minutes of downtime.

"Nah, I'm not hungry. I need a power nap," he replied to George, who in turn made a show of rolling his eyes. Sergio called out to Ritchie Eckhardt, who was headed for the door, "Pick me up a tuna wrap or something, Ritchie."

Voices faded and keyboards went silent as the room emptied. Sergio unlatched the lock of his swivel chair and eased backward until he settled into a comfortable recline. His head fell against the headrest and his closed eyes shut out the world, however fleetingly. He didn't care if people sniggered about his naps. They helped him relax, recharge, and often brainstorm. He couldn't begin to count the times he awoke from a short nap to magically discover the answer to the vexing question of the moment or challenge of the day. It didn't make much sense, but it worked and he couldn't argue with success.

Sergio tried to make sense of the day's very curious events. The attacker was undoubtedly highly sophisticated, and yet he'd made a couple of amateur mistakes. Why did he suddenly increase his download speed when he'd been successfully stealing data for over a month? A good hacker was patient; everybody knew that. And why blow up two data centers? Sergio pondered his questions for a few minutes and then consciously released them into the black fog rapidly enveloping his mind. The answers, he hoped, would come to him soon enough.

Sergio's eyelids suddenly snapped open and a flood of fluorescent light overpowered his senses. He squeezed his eyelids shut, but he knew sleep was no longer possible. He couldn't be sure how long he'd dozed. Five minutes? Ten? The room was silent save for the clicks of a single keyboard. Sergio opened his eyes and tilted his head toward George's desk, just in time to see his friend slump in his chair and insert a thumb drive into a USB plug in the computer tower under his desk. Then George began slapping at his keyboard.

Sergio froze, shocked to see George break a cardinal security rule. Thumb drives were strictly forbidden. The policy, standard for most major corporations, was designed to thwart theft or minimize the chance that an employee might introduce a virus or other malicious software into the system. USB ports on all Circles' computers had been rendered inoperative by a digital lock designed by George's team. But if anyone could disable that lock, it would be George.

"Hey!" Sergio barked in a low growl.

George's head snapped around and Sergio instantly saw the fear in his eyes. Sergio tried to project a severe and disapproving glare but his confusion made that difficult. He was torn between outrage at George's actions, concern for his panicked buddy, and anger for having been put in such a position.

"One tuna wrap and a granola bar for dessert!" Eckhardt announced as he breezed into the room.

Eckhardt maneuvered his way past George, dropped a brown paper bag on Sergio's desk, and continued to his chair. Sergio stared icily as George surreptitiously snatched the thumb drive from his computer. Others filed back into the room, but Sergio ignored them as he punched out an instant message to his friend.

"WTF?"

Sergio saw the three letters pop up on his friend's screen. George turned back and gave Sergio a conspiratorial wink while raising his outstretched index finger to his lips. *Shhhhhh.* Then he stood, stretched his arms outward, and announced he was going to take a leak. George buried his fist in the bowl of M&M's, pulled out a handful, and tossed one up in the air, catching it in his mouth as he strolled out of the room.

Sergio sat in a daze, unsure what to do. Turning George in would be the end of the road for him. On the other hand, Sergio's own job and reputation—not to mention a chunk of unvested stock options—would be on the line if it was ever revealed he'd done nothing to stop George.

Sergio jumped up just as George entered the restroom on the far side of the basement. Sergio walked briskly across the floor, his mind whirling with all sorts of reasons that would explain what he'd just seen. He pushed open the door, stepped up to the urinal next to George, and challenged him with an angry stare.

"Just what the fuck do you think you're doing?" he whispered, as he unzipped.

George shot him an annoyed look and muttered: "Not now." Then he zipped up and pulled away from the urinal.

Still aiming with his right hand, Sergio reached for George's shoulder with his left. George spun around and batted Sergio's hand to the side. Eyes lit up and lips gnarled in anger, he jabbed Sergio with his finger. "I said *not now*," he growled. Then he pointed to the gap under the toilet stall doors. They were not alone. By the time Sergio pulled his eyes away from the stalls George was already half way to the door.

Sergio returned to the bunker, unsure what to do. He and George had joined the company at about the same time and worked side by side, moving up the ranks together, for the better part of fifteen years. They'd even shared an apartment during the early days and spent their weekends riding mountain bikes and drinking too much beer. Sergio couldn't just turn in his good friend, not without confronting him first.

But George did not leave his desk again for the rest of the day. Not once during the next several hours did he look in Sergio's direction and, as the outside light faded, Sergio came to the sinking conclusion he'd waited too long. If he was going to report George at that point, he'd have a hard time explaining why he hadn't acted the second he saw his friend break protocol. By failing to immediately report the incident, Sergio had tacitly become complicit.

At six thirty in the afternoon, the jig was up. George and Julian had mopped up most of the mess, and they insisted the day crew head home. George looked straight at Sergio and announced he'd stay with the night shift, just in case. Sergio knew his friend had no intention of answering questions—not until he was ready.

-10-

Prederick propped himself against his mahogany desk, facing the door, legs apart, and arms across his chest. He said nothing as Ko strolled into Prederick's second-floor office and stood in the center of the spacious room. The soft light and baronial furniture in the CEO's inner sanctum was a stark contrast to the open utilitarian decor in the rest of the building. Prederick pushed off from his desk, walked past Ko, and slammed the door.

"What the fuck is going on?" Prederick's voice was raw and his face felt flush. "Is this China fucking with us? This is not what we agreed to."

Ko folded his tall frame into the leather sofa and crossed one leg over the other. He studied Prederick dispassionately. "You start throwing around accusations like that and we could lose everything we've worked for over the last two years."

"Doesn't the timing seem odd to you?" Prederick threw up his arms. "For Christ sake, we're three days away from approval and now this?"

"Circles has waited over a decade to get into China and you want to rock the boat now? Calling China out would be a huge mistake even if this were a Chinese attack."

Prederick glared at Ko, frustrated by his CTO's inscrutable air, but fully aware he was right. "Any suggestions?"

Prederick had relied on Ko's advice many times since hiring him two years earlier. At the time, Prederick was under immense pressure to prove he'd been the right choice to lead Circles, which was still reeling from the death of founder Weiss nine months before. The intelligent, energetic, and charming founder had been the guiding force at Circles. He'd developed the company's strategic vision, encouraged employees to break rules, and even managed to convince impatient Wall Street investors that Circles' long-term potential was far too great to be sacrificed in the pursuit of short-term profits. Employees, analysts, and the media had openly questioned whether Circles could survive his death.

A handful of Wall Street hedge funds saw opportunity in Weiss' death. They'd invested billions of dollars in Circles, and the time had come to extract their return. Cravenly exploiting family fault lines, they quickly took control of the voting shares and board seats that Weiss had left to his new wife, parents, and siblings. Within six months, the syndicate of investors appointed Prederick as CEO and tied his compensation to very aggressive financial targets. Achieving those targets would require bold leaps and big gambles, so when Ko came along offering innovative technologies and key contacts in China, Prederick was all ears. Ko quickly put together a plan to crack the Chinese market, a breakthrough that would propel Circles' user base to new heights and drive revenue growth for the next decade. Prederick, in return, offered Ko access to the company's deep pockets and global network, a platform that was apparently large enough to accommodate Ko's outsized ego.

"Let me make some calls," Ko said. "If this attack came from China, my friends will know. We'll deal with it then."

Prederick scowled. "Did they break into Labs?"

"They?" Ko arched one eyebrow. "How can you be so sure this wasn't some kid in Estonia?"

Prederick seethed. He hated Ko's cocky attitude. "Was Labs compromised?"

Ko nodded. "But I'm not sure to what degree."

"The auto-censoring code?"

Ko nodded again. "We have to assume so."

Prederick spun around and threw his head back, his hands on his hips. He held still for a moment, gazing up at the ceiling, and considered the possibilities. Ko's automatic-censoring software had been one of the key reasons Prederick had brought him into the company. It was probably the only reason Chinese authorities were prepared to let Circles operate on the mainland.

Ko's remarkably sophisticated software would let Circles block Chinese users from sending or receiving any content that ran afoul of the country's strict censorship laws, whether it be pornography, religious material, or politically sensitive information. The software filtered every update, message, photo, and video uploaded to Circles and made instantaneous decisions about what was acceptable or not based on parameters selected by Communist Party officials. Any inappropriate content could be deleted, without affecting the overall flow of data traffic. Americans and other users outside China would be unaffected. They'd still be free to say what they wanted, but anything deemed inappropriate would be scrubbed from Circles pages viewed in China.

Prederick felt a pang of guilt about the deal he and Ko had struck, but only a very small pang. Censorship was a fact of life in China and its citizens were used to limits placed on their freedom. On the other hand, Circles would almost overnight become the biggest communications conduit between China and the rest of the world. Despite agreeing to abide by China's strict censorship laws, Circles could still play a key role in breaking down the barriers between East and West.

The strategy was certain to cause controversy. Yahoo and Google had previously taken a lot of heat for trying to have it both ways in

China. Circles would inevitably face the same public-relations storm once word of its auto-censoring software got out. But Prederick was determined to put off that day for as long as possible, hopefully long enough to build a sizeable user base in China. By that time, Prederick would have collected his bonuses and cashed out his stock options. But he hadn't expected this turn of events.

"Let's just suppose for a minute it was China," said Prederick. "We'd have to assume they now have our censoring software. And if they have it, the next logical step would be for them to adapt and deploy it to police all Internet activity within the Great Firewall. And if that really is the game, China's authorities now have no incentive to allow Circles entry into their market."

"Perhaps," countered Ko. "But there's another possibility. What if the attacker's goal is to either blackmail us or shame us by exposing the censoring software?"

Prederick froze. Ko's second suggestion would be a disaster, one that could force Circles to pull back from China before it even signed up its first Chinese user. Atoning for past sins was one thing, but trying to dismiss a sin one was about to commit was another matter entirely.

Prederick leveled his gaze at Ko. "We need to be very sure about this. We're not going down this road if . . ."

The first heavy notes of Chopin's *Funeral March* filled the room. Annoyed by the interruption, Prederick glanced at the unfamiliar number flashing on his mobile phone. His instinct was to let the call go to voicemail, but something made him reconsider. This was no normal day.

"Prederick here," he snapped.

"Sir, this is Michael Harton, on the security team," the caller announced.

"And?"

"We completed much of the audit, sir." Harton's voice wavered. "I think you should see it."

"You want *me* to look at the audit?" Prederick turned to Ko with a curious frown on his face. "Where's George Verneek?"

"In the bunker, sir."

Prederick said nothing, his silence prompting Harton to continue.

"Well, sir," Harton hesitated. "It looks like George is holding out on us."

Sergio stepped through the front door of his tony Russian Hill condo. He draped his jacket on a hook and caught a glimpse of himself in the hall mirror. His hair was tousled again and his rumpled shirt hung to his hips, but he was most bothered by the dark circles of exhaustion seared into the skin beneath his eyes.

"You look like shit," he said to his reflection.

He poured himself a shot of Gran Centenario and fell into the black leather couch in his living room. A big screen TV hung on the wall in front of him; the shelves behind him overflowed with tech manuals and souvenirs from Mexico and Lebanon. Outside, the distant lights of Sausalito shimmered across San Francisco Bay as the rotating beacon atop Alcatraz's lighthouse announced itself at five-second intervals. Farther west stood the Golden Gate Bridge, the arch of its elegant span glittering at the mouth of the bay.

Sergio took a sip of tequila and pressed his hand into the side of his face. It had been one of the most stressful days he could remember. And that was even before George's little stunt. Sergio downed the rest of his shot and fought off the urge to pour another. Maybe he was getting too old. He had been the consummate team player at Circles, a leader who mentored young employees, rolled up his sleeves alongside them, and generously shared any credit due. Two years earlier he couldn't have imagined doing anything else. But Circles had changed since Prederick and Ko arrived. The billions of people who used Circles were no longer important, much less the employees. All that mattered was squeezing every penny of profit they could from the company. Could it be time to cash in and move on?

He reached for the remote and turned on the TV. Anything to push the day's events from his mind. Frenzied election coverage filled the screen on every channel. Diebolt and Lester—a choice between two narcissistic and self-serving candidates who'd achieve absolutely nothing of note. The election couldn't be over soon enough.

Sergio's watch beeped. It was seven thirty. He went upstairs to shower. The soapy warm water washed away the stress of the day, and he felt his body tingle in anticipation of his date with Malina. She was gorgeous—soft auburn hair, beautiful face, and smoky hazel eyes.

Sergio rinsed off and dried himself in front of the mirror. He turned sideways to examine his profile, then leaned in to study his face. His soft brown eyes were as sparkly as ever, his Roman nose was ageless, and his olive complexion remained wrinkle-free. He pulled away and stroked the salt-and-pepper stubble on his chin; it was the perfect five o'clock shadow. Then he cocked his head and slowly reached for the jagged scar where his left earlobe used to be.

Sergio drew in a deep breath and expelled a burst of nervous energy with a *whoosh*. He'd never dated someone like Malina before. Other than the gold diggers who glommed onto him at parties, Sergio pretty much stuck to women within the tech community. It was convenient and easy, and there was always something to talk about. He had long ago admitted to himself that he was a little too into coding. Nothing turned his crank as much as algorithms, those magical mathematical formulas that return the right search results, recommend new Circles members to befriend, or find the best airline tickets—all in milliseconds.

Malina, on the other hand, was definitely no starry-eyed techie eager to make an impression. That was pretty obvious from the moment they'd met a week ago at an invitation-only sneak preview of the new Woody Allen movie. He'd spotted her the second she stepped through the lobby doors and took a chance when he realized she was still alone when the lights went up at the end of the movie. He'd maneuvered himself next to her on the way out, caught her eye, and smiled.

"Fantastic, huh?"

She regarded him for a moment. "Definitely good, but I'm still waiting for him to top *Match Point*."

"Ahhhhh." He nodded with approval. "Nothing can measure up to the perfect film."

"But a girl can still dream. Can't she?"

"If you must. I prefer to enjoy them as they come."

She frowned, but Sergio sensed it was more of a pout and more than likely not even a real pout. "Would you like to go next door and grab a drink?" he asked.

She pulled over to the wall, placed her hands on her hips, and addressed him with a playful grin. "I have to tell you, I've never had anyone try to pick me up in a movie theater before. It's most unusual."

She resumed walking and Sergio fell in beside her again.

"Is this your regular MO?" she asked, with a single arched eyebrow.

"Excuse me?"

"Tell me you don't make a habit of this . . ."

"Ouch," he said with a chuckle. Feisty. He liked that. "Are you trying to make me feel as insecure as Woody Allen?"

"I could do much better than that," she countered, her grin now more mischievous than playful.

Sergio laughed, harder this time. "Please, you've done enough already." He moved to the side of the lobby and stopped. She paused beside him.

"So, how about that drink?"

"I don't even know your name."

"Oh, sorry," he stammered. "I'm Sergio."

Her eyebrow shot up again. "Just Sergio?"

"Mansour," he quickly added. "Sergio Mansour."

She studied him carefully, her eyes narrowing slightly before revealing a flash of decision. "I can't right now," she said, reaching into her purse. "But anyone who likes Woody Allen can't be all that bad."

She pulled out a business card. "Here," she said, handing it to him. "I work the day shift this week, starting at six. Business picks up pretty quickly so you'd better call early if you want to reach me." With a quick smile and a wink, she turned to leave.

Sergio massaged the card with his fingers as he watched her walk away. She was practically out the lobby doors before he looked at the card. Dr. Malina Olson. Emergency Medicine. San Francisco General Hospital.

He read the words several times, trying to gather his thoughts. Malina was totally out of his league, but there was no denying he felt irresistibly drawn to this beautiful, spirited woman. Maybe he liked the idea that she was tough; she had to be to work in an emergency room. Or perhaps it was her quirkiness; after all, it was the age of cell phones, instant messaging, and social networks, and she still gave out her number with a business card. But in his gut, Sergio knew there was more to his attraction than that. Deep down, there was no ignoring the vague but all-too-real sense that Malina Olson could challenge him like no woman had before.

-12-

The driver eased the town car past warehouse piers along San Francisco's Embarcadero. Prederick sat in the back with Francis Wynan, the company's PR chief, prepping for the CNN interview. The attack had disrupted service for tens of millions of Circles users across the western US, most of whom were unable to access their accounts for about six hours. It was ugly to be sure, but Prederick was thankful the fallout hadn't been more widespread or longer lasting. The bigger issue was the online chatter suggesting the crash had been caused by an attack. Those "rumors" ran counter to the company's official line. It was his job to quash them.

Prederick, Ko, and Wynan had discussed the pros and cons of doubling down on a lie. The company's immediate priority was to convince users their personal data was safe from hackers. Users also wanted to be reassured they would not be similarly inconvenienced in the future. Anything less than that would be bad for business. If word of the attack eventually did leak, Circles could always say they were withholding the truth until they had sorted through all the details. The decision to lie had taken no more than a few seconds.

The limo rolled up to the front of CNN's studios, and Prederick and Wynan dashed into the lobby. They were met by a bubbly young production assistant, who led them to reporter Elizabeth Tanev in the studio.

Prederick had done hundreds of interviews with mainstream news anchors and reporters. Most of them didn't know squat about technology and that made it easy to steamroll them. Today would be no different. He extended his hand as he strolled up to Tanev, a statuesque blonde with riveting blue eyes. He concluded she was even hotter in person that she looked on TV. They took their places on the set as a voice among the cameras began counting down. "Live in five, four, three, two, one."

Tanev burst into a smile as she addressed the camera. "We're here with Dan Prederick, CEO of Circles, the world's biggest social network. Circles was in the news today after an internal programming mistake disrupted service at two data centers in the western US, leaving as many as one hundred million users unable to access their accounts. So Mr. Prederick, what happened?"

"Well, first of all, Elizabeth, I want to thank you for having me on today. I always love getting the chance to speak directly to our users. And let me just say that we don't know for sure how many users were affected today. But I'd suggest to you the hundred million figure floating around is a grossly inflated number."

Prederick turned away from Tanev and looked directly into the camera. It was time for a little humble pie. "We were frankly quite embarrassed by the outage this afternoon, but it just shows you how hard it is to do what we do. We have the best engineers building the best system to deliver the best services to all of our users—and we still occasionally make mistakes. Given the complexity of our network, sometimes even a small mistake can have big consequences."

"So, what exactly went wrong?"

"Right, so I could take you into the weeds but I think I'd bore you half to death. We were upgrading some software and we failed to notice a small bug in time. The good news is that our crack team managed to restore service in a few short hours."

"There have been some blog reports saying Circles suffered a cyber-attack."

"Nonsense," said Prederick, dismissing the question with a wave of his hand. "We have the most sophisticated and secure network on the planet, and I'd like to take this moment to assure our users that their personal data, their photos, credit card details, bank account information—whatever they've entrusted to us—is completely safe and was not in any way compromised by this glitch."

Prederick's gaze drifted stage left to Wynan, who wore a smirk on his face.

"What about people who point out that the disruption underscores how much users now depend on Circles? I mean, some people were really put out by the crash. They couldn't communicate with friends, get money, shop . . ."

"Well, let's not blow this out of proportion. This was a one-off event. Remember that we have gone many years since the last time this happened. Hurricanes cause much greater disruption to people's lives and they come along far more frequently."

Wynan held up his hand, index and middle fingers extended in a victory signal. Two minutes. Time for Prederick to dial up his pitch.

"But aren't users . . ." began Tanev, before Prederick interrupted.

"Let's not—excuse me, Elizabeth." He paused in a show of contrition. "Let's not get down on the Internet because of one isolated event. The Internet is one of the most transformative technologies the world has ever seen. It connects people, it entertains them, it gives them information to make better decisions, it empowers people politically, and it gives them a voice personally. The Internet is the great equalizer. Circles is at the heart of this transformation, and I am confident we will continue to be so for many years to come."

Prederick's rhetorical flourish left Tanev struggling for a response. He could see she had not been expecting it, although she should have if she'd done her homework. He recycled the same old lines practically every time he sat down for an interview.

Tanev swiveled to her left and looked into camera two. "Dan Prederick, CEO of Circles. Thank you."

Prederick eased off the stool, sneaking a peek at Tanev's lithe body. That couldn't have gone any better, he mused. Softball questions and a megaphone he could exploit to the fullest.

"Thanks, Elizabeth," he said, as he stared deeply into her blue eyes. "That was a great interview."

-13-

Sergio locked his Range Rover and set off down the sidewalk in the city's squalid Tenderloin district. He passed a solicitous transvestite, sidestepped a couple of homeless men camped on the pavement, and crossed to the other side of the street to avoid an agitated man yelling at unseen tormentors. When he reached the end of the block, he knocked on a thick wooden door at the corner. A small window in the center of the door swung open and a pair of severe eyes gave Sergio the once-over.

"I have a reservation. The name is Sergio," he said.

The bouncer nodded, unbolted the door, and ushered Sergio into the dimly lit club. A hostess escorted him past the heavy oak bar and led him toward a curtained booth that reminded him of the confessionals his parents used to frequent on Sundays. He spied Malina through the half-opened curtain, her girl-next-door beauty apparent in the glow of her phone. He pulled the curtain apart and slid into the booth with a beaming smile on his face.

"Is this my competition for the night?" he asked, pointing to her phone.

She locked her hazel eyes on him. "Think you're up to the challenge?"

Sergio chuckled. "That depends. Are you an addict?"

"I manage to keep it under control," she replied, as she laid her phone on the table. She crossed her arms in front of her and lifted her chin, ever so slightly, before she spoke. "So I heard you guys had some big crash today."

Sergio's heart skipped. She'd checked out his profile. It was easy enough with his name. There were only two other Sergio Mansours on Circles and they both lived in Spain. As far as he was concerned, it was a sign she was interested.

"Tell me about it," he groaned. "What a day." The attack, and George's odd behavior, was the last thing he wanted to talk about. He fixed his gaze on Malina and squeezed out a smile. "The worst part was not knowing whether I'd be able to see you tonight."

"Are you trying to tell me you might have picked a few billion strangers over me?"

Sergio chuckled. "You must have days like that, too."

Malina nodded knowingly. "Every now and then."

"Well, I can't wait to hear about them." He waved at a passing server. "Two Cazadores Reposado, please."

"How did you know I like tequila?" Malina asked once the server walked away.

"A lucky guess," he said with a wink.

Malina eyeballed Sergio. "So what happened today?"

Sergio drew in a big breath and released a big sigh. "Oh, it was just some bonehead engineer who screwed up while we were upgrading our e-commerce software," he said, avoiding Malina's stare. "He didn't troubleshoot it correctly and boom—that's all it takes."

She leaned forward and gave him a conspiratorial glance. "I read somewhere that Circles was hacked."

"Nah." He waved off her suggestion. "There's always someone saying that whenever we or anyone else has a crash. I guess people really get angry when they can't get into their accounts."

Malina scrunched her face into a grimace and looked away. Sergio bowed his head, sensing what was coming.

"I wouldn't know . . ." Malina's words lingered. "I don't do Circles."

"Oh?" he said, trying to scrub any hint of judgment from his reply. His media training came in handy whenever he had to defend social media to holdouts like Malina.

Malina looked uncomfortable, even a bit jumpy, as she struggled for words. "It takes so much time and . . ." She stiffened in her seat before continuing. "It's *creepy*."

"Creepy?" Sergio pulled back in his seat.

"People need to be more private about their personal lives. I can't believe people want to put their entire lives up on the web." Malina frowned. "It's dangerous," she said, taking the time to enunciate each syllable. "These big Internet companies know so much about us, and we've seen over and over that all that information is not adequately secured. Circles users are sitting ducks for identity thieves, fraudsters, stalkers . . ." Her voice dropped. "There are a lot of bad people out there, you know?"

Sergio forced a laugh. He could humor her, but she was smart enough to see right through that. "Wow, you're a real conspiracy buff," he finally replied. If this was not meant to be, then they might as well get it over with sooner rather than later. "You realize that's a bunch of crap, don't you? Sure, our users choose to share personal information. But we keep it all under heavy lock and key. No one who isn't supposed to see that data ever sees it."

Malina scoffed. "I don't care how much you want that to be true, but it just isn't. Nothing is one hundred percent safe." She looked down, avoiding his gaze. The frown remained frozen on her face.

Sergio was undeterred. "A hundred percent? No. But do you know that we have two-and-a-half-billion users, eighty-five percent of whom use Circles every day, and we only had about fourteen thousand suspicious actions last year?" He pulled out a pen and began drawing tiny diagrams on a napkin, illustrating with concentric circles how Circles' multilayered defenses worked. His voice continued to rise as the words spilled out of his mouth ever faster. He'd delivered the pitch hundreds of times to cynical journalists over the years; he knew it by heart. "That works out to a success rate of 99.999 percent," he said, making sure to accentuate each of the nines. "Do you realize how hard it is to do that?"

Malina looked away, her lips pursed.

"What?" he asked. He felt oddly embarrassed; maybe he'd been a tad aggressive. "Was that too much?"

"Look," she said, meeting his eyes once again. "I didn't come here to argue about your job. Sorry."

"No," he replied. "I'm the one who should be sorry. I guess I got a bit defensive."

The server parted the curtain and set down their drinks. Malina reached for her glass and raised it for a toast. "A peace offering," she said.

They both took sips, put down their glasses, and shared a long awkward moment. Sergio jumped at the first thing to cross his mind. "What made you want to be a doctor?"

"Remember that TV show, *St. Elsewhere*?" Malina's eyes lit up and she relaxed her shoulders. "I remember watching it as a kid. I knew way back then that I wanted to help people."

It didn't escape Sergio that the downtrodden reputation of the TV show's fictional St. Eligius hospital was similar to SF General, the regional go-to trauma center where Malina worked. "But why emergency medicine? I thought that was something doctors did as training and then moved on to private practice or some sort of specialty."

"Emergency medicine is a specialty," she explained. "All my colleagues thought I was nuts. It's incredibly stressful and there are times when it's emotionally devastating. But I get such an adrenaline rush when a patient comes into the ER and my team and I are all that stand between them living or dying. I couldn't imagine doing any other job."

"You must see some pretty wild stuff," he suggested.

Malina looked up to the ceiling in thought. "I remember one guy who fell off a ladder and hit his head. He was in and out of consciousness.

He couldn't move one side of his body and one of his pupils was dilated. And he was vomiting. I was pretty sure he had a subdural hematoma." She paused and tapped her head. "Sorry," she continued, "he was bleeding inside his skull. But we didn't have time to verify. His symptoms were so bad that I just had to go for it."

"What do you mean, 'go for it'?" Sergio leaned forward, morbidly fascinated.

"I drilled a hole in his skull." Malina pressed a pointed finger to the side of her head. "We're not supposed to do that kind of thing in the ER, but I didn't think he'd make it to surgery."

"And?"

"And blood came spurting out, a lot of it, like an oil gusher. That guy probably wouldn't have lasted five more minutes if I hadn't done that."

"Holy shit," he said, the words slipping from his mouth before he realized it.

Malina continued unprompted. "Then there was this lady a few years back who tried to kill herself. She got really drunk and threw herself off a balcony. Except she didn't hit the ground. She landed on a wrought iron fence and one of the spikes went right through her neck." Malina's eyes grew wide as she pointed to one side of her neck and then the other, indicating how the woman impaled herself.

"She came in to the ER with the rod still in her neck. We were stunned she was alive but it turned out the rod missed her spinal column, her trachea, her esophagus, and her carotid arteries." She paused, her wonderment still apparent. "I mean what are the odds of that? And this was someone who wanted to kill herself."

"So she made it?"

"It took a lot of surgery, but yes. About six months later, she came into the ER to thank us for saving her life. And the best part was that her miraculous luck was not lost on her. The last I heard she was working at a shelter for the homeless."

Sergio couldn't quite believe his ears. "You mean Shine Memorial?"

Malina's mouth fell open. She started to speak, before abruptly stopping herself.

Sergio leaned in, his curiosity too great to resist. "Are you talking about Juanita?"

Malina pitched forward until their noses nearly touched. "You *know* her?"

"She's now the housekeeper for the Deacon at Shine," he said, stunned by the coincidence. He'd never felt right asking Juanita how she got those awful scars. "I teach computer classes there, for disadvantaged kids and families. Some homeless people, too," he explained. "Juanita is great."

Malina's gaze softened. "I guess I didn't imagine you as the volunteering type," she said quietly.

Sergio sat back. "What do you mean?"

"Oh, I don't know," she said, waving her hands in front of her. "I shouldn't have said that."

She looked down as she fidgeted with her shot glass.

"I was a poor kid once," he finally said. "And I guess my life could have turned out very differently if not for all the teachers and mentors who took an interest and showed me the way forward." He reached for his tequila. "Now I can make a difference. I guess you could call it my way of saving lives."

She looked up, her eyes full of apology, and raised her glass for another toast. "To saving lives," she said, as their glasses clinked. Sergio nodded, tossed back his shot, and lowered the glass to the table.

"So where do you get a name like Mansour?" she asked in between sips. "You certainly look like a Sergio, but you don't look like a Mansour."

"My great-grandfather emigrated from Lebanon to Mexico in the early 1900s. Hundreds of thousands of Christian Lebanese fled the country back then to escape the oppressive Ottoman Empire. He married a Mexican girl, so I guess you could say I'm one-eighth Lebanese."

"When did your family move north?"

"My parents came in the fifties. They worked the fields and ended up in a small town outside Fresno."

"Are they still there?"

"They're dead." Sergio reached for his glass. It was empty.

"Sorry."

"It was a long time ago."

"Any siblings?"

"Emilio, my younger brother. I raised him after my mother died."

"That must have been tough."

"It was, believe me," he said with a chuckle. "I had just received a scholarship to UC Berkeley when she died, but I had to defer a year so I could make some money to support us. After that year, they told me I'd lose the scholarship if I didn't accept it."

"So what did you do?"

"I didn't want to throw away my ticket, our ticket, out of poverty, so I went to Berkeley, got a room off-campus, and moved both of us into it. I put Emilio in junior high and did my best to keep him in line."

"That was incredibly unselfish. Where is he now?"

Sergio's face tightened as he shifted in his seat. "Back in Fresno."

Malina pressed forward, her inquisitive tone now more tentative. "Are you guys close?"

"It's been a while since we spoke." Sergio's voice trailed off as he drifted back in time. "More than twenty years, I guess."

"I'm sorry. I didn't mean to pry."

He shrugged. "It's . . . complicated."

Malina waited for him to continue, her curious eyes asking the question her lips would not. But there was no easy way to explain why Emilio had shut him out, despite Sergio's countless phone calls, birthday greetings, and Christmas cards over the years.

He toyed with his glass until he forced those memories aside. "What about your family?"

"It's just me, my mom, and dad. Well, my stepdad. My father died when I was seven." She tossed the rest of the tequila down her throat. "Death is very much a part of life."

Something about Malina's expression told him she was ready to move on, but he couldn't help himself. "Death is so much more a part of *your* life," he ventured.

"Excuse me?" She let the shot glass thump down on the table.

"I mean, you must see a lot of it at work. I don't know how you do it."

"Do what?"

"How do you deal with it?" His head hung low. "I mean, stories like Juanita's are great, but I'm sure they're the exception."

She nodded somberly.

"So doesn't that get to you? How do you cope?"

"How else? You go on emotional autopilot. You try to close yourself off. But really, you're just bottling it up and sticking a cork in it. And you hope like hell that you're in a good place when the cork comes flying out." She smiled sheepishly.

"Really?"

She shrugged. "We all do it to some degree. I'm sure you do, too."

"Me?" he said, pulling back in surprise.

"Don't you?" She let the question hang in the air for a moment. "What about your brother? I bet you haven't talked about him in years, have you?"

Sergio looked down. "No," he began. "But that doesn't mean—"

"No, it doesn't," she interrupted. "It doesn't mean anything really, other than the fact that you've bottled it up. And there's nothing wrong with that," she continued. "We all try to bury the painful stuff."

The curtain flew open and the server reappeared. Sergio exhaled, grateful for the distraction. He ordered another round and a few tapas, and quickly steered the conversation toward her favorite restaurants. Soon they moved on to foreign cuisines and exotic destinations. After that, they dabbled in politics. It all flowed effortlessly from one subject to the next as the hours passed in the shelter of their private confessional. The tumult of the day faded in memory as Sergio sank back into his seat and allowed himself to be hypnotized by Malina's eyes. He couldn't get enough of her expressive eyes—the way they spoke to him, one minute sparkling with intelligence, the next warm with compassion, and then oozing sensuality. Malina came from a different background, worked in a different world, and lived a very different life, and yet the past few hours with her had been so comfortable, so genuine. He couldn't remember the last time he'd shared himself with anyone on such an intimate level.

"So I have a confession to make," she said.

Sergio leaned forward. "I like confessions," he whispered. "Is it sordid and seamy? Or more of the garden variety type?"

She propped her elbows on the table, rested her chin on her clenched fists, and leveled her eyes to his. "I almost didn't come tonight."

Sergio allowed himself a hearty laugh. "Why not?"

Malina sipped her drink, her gaze fixed on Sergio. "When I Googled you and realized who you were, I was kind of put off."

"You mean my job? All that creepy stuff?"

Malina nodded as she ran a finger along the rim of her glass. "That and the fact that all I ever hear and read about you hotshot techie guys, frankly, doesn't sound that appealing. You're all supposed to be greedy, sexist, and self-absorbed jerks who think the world is your oyster."

"There is definitely no shortage of assholes in tech," he said. "But most of us are not like that."

"Oh really?" She leaned back and rested her palms on the table. "And what are *most* of you like?"

"Mostly, it's young people, in their twenties and thirties, with all the immaturity and insecurities that implies. I can't really speak for the business side, but most of the engineers at Circles just want to write code and play video games. There will always be guys who get big heads, but I see it as part of my job to keep that to a minimum at Circles."

"So you're kind of like a den mother, is that it?"

Sergio laughed. He'd never thought of himself like that.

Malina perked up. "You know, I was a bit of a gamer myself, back in the day."

"Oh, yeah?"

"Why so surprised?"

Sergio shrugged. "You don't exactly seem like the nerdy type. What games?"

"Super Mario Brothers, Donkey Kong," she said, with a soft chuckle. "They were all the rage when I was in high school. I used to play for hours."

"I was more of a Doom guy."

"Back then, *every* guy was a Doom guy."

Their eyes met as they shared a laugh. For a split second, Sergio thought he saw desire in her eyes. And just as quickly, the look was gone.

"It's funny," she continued. "I don't think I've played since I started medical school. There was just no time. And then life has a way of taking over." She turned to look through the opening in the curtain, letting her words linger and her mind wander.

"So why did you come?" he asked softly.

Malina's eyes snapped back to his, only now they were glassy and moist. "I can't really explain it," she said, shifting in her seat. "It would have been extremely shallow of me to reject you simply because of your job." She looked down and drew in a deep breath. "Something told me I'd regret it if I didn't come."

Sergio sat quietly, reluctant to intrude on her private thoughts. It was as if he'd come close to pulling the cork, and now certainly wasn't the time for that. After a long pause, he cleared his throat. "Do you regret coming?"

"No," she said quickly, looking up as she wiped the corner of her eye. "I'm very happy I came." A warm smile spread across her face and she placed her hand on his. "There's so much more to you than I expected."

Sergio cocked his head and nodded stiffly in mock approval, the way an English Lord might acknowledge fine tea. "You don't say," he intoned. "Such as?"

"Like your volunteer work," she said quietly, before adding, "and the way you helped your brother like that."

"Don't forget, I'm a den mother, too," he needled.

Malina laughed with a wink. "You get points for that, as well."

"You're very generous. But I *am* a bit of a geek, if you must know," Sergio said with a wince.

"Maybe. But you're more intelligent than nerdy. And I think you're one of those optimists who really do want to make the world a better place. You care too much about what you do to be in it solely for the money." She gave him a sultry look. "Plus, you're pretty handsome for a nerd."

Sergio chuckled. "I'm supposed to take that in the best of ways, right?"

"Time will tell, won't it?"

Minutes later, Sergio opened the passenger door of his Range Rover for Malina. She stepped forward and placed her hand on the edge of the door, just next to his. He hesitated, not sure if she was inviting him closer. He couldn't remember the last time he was so nervous with a woman. Excruciating seconds passed as he worked up the resolve to kiss her. What if he was wrong? Then, in a moment of decisiveness, he pressed forward with pursed lips, just as she turned to get into the car. His kiss landed forcefully on her right ear, his nose jamming into her temple in the process.

"Oh!" she cried out as she cupped her ear. Then she burst into laughter. "I'm going to assume that was *not* one of your smoother moves," she said.

Sergio rubbed his nose. "Sorry," he said timidly. "I guess I miscalculated."

Malina reached for his hand and brought her face close to his. He felt her gaze bore into him with a soft intensity that excited him like never before. "Sergio, I like you. A lot. You don't need to calculate anything. Just be yourself. Okay?"

Sergio nodded with embarrassment and Malina tilted her head slightly upward, inviting him in a second time. He moved closer, this time more slowly and with his eyes wide open. She closed hers and Sergio pressed forward, their lips meeting in a delicate kiss.

"Mmmmm. Nice," he murmured, pulling back to look at Malina.

"Uh-huh." A naughty smile crept across her face. "I've been looking forward to that."

The ring of Sergio's phone shattered the mood. He quickly reached into his pocket, hoping to silence his phone before the moment passed. He jabbed the device with his thumb several times, but the ringing continued. He pulled the phone from his coat to turn it off, only to notice the call was from Prederick. That couldn't be good.

"Sorry, I have to take this." His eyes pleaded with her. "Work."

Malina nodded with a hint of disappointment.

He smiled at her as he lifted the phone to his ear. "Yeah?"

"George is dead."

-14-

Sergio flew along the wide streets of San Francisco's South of Market district, zigzagging east and south to avoid as many red lights as possible. The words kept searing his ears—*George is dead, George is dead*—as his brain struggled to process the notion that his closest friend was gone. Murdered. In his garage. Sergio felt a raging headache coming on.

He passed under Interstate 80, skirted AT&T Park, and turned south into Mission Bay, a once decrepit warehouse district razed lot by lot to make way for modern office buildings, luxury condos, and a massive research hospital. From a distance he could see the seven-story-high frosted *C* etched into the modern glass cube that was the company's headquarters. He drove past the concrete skeleton of Circles' new wing and pulled into the executive parking lot. He swiped his ID card at the security doors and bolted up to Prederick's office.

"So what happened?" Sergio demanded as he barged in. Prederick sat at his desk; Ko was on the sofa.

"Sergio . . ." Prederick rose, somber-faced. "I'm very sorry for . . ."

"What happened?"

Ko stood up. "George left rather abruptly at about eight thirty, leaving

Eckhardt to tie up loose ends during the night. One hour later we received a call from the police."

"Do they know who did it?"

Ko shook his head.

"Who found him?"

"Susan."

Sergio felt sick to his stomach as he imagined the shock and grief George's wife must be going through.

"Was it a robbery?" he asked.

"The killer cleaned out his pockets and ripped up his car, but the police don't think it was a robbery," said Ko, his delivery matter-of-fact.

"Why not?"

"Sergio . . ." Prederick stepped forward, anguish etched into his face. "George was shot several times . . . six times in all. The police said the wounds appeared to have been inflicted to cause maximum pain. The killer shot him in the knees, the elbows, the groin. And then he was killed with a shot to the head." Prederick wrung his hands together and lowered his gaze to the floor. "Sergio, they think he was tortured before he was killed."

A blinding flash of light ripped through Sergio's head, and he was transported back to the dirt road of his childhood, like he was reliving it one more time. There were those angry men, the bright headlights, and the bloody body in the dirt. Sergio's stomach churned violently; he felt as though he might vomit. Shuddering with revulsion and fear, he looked to Prederick. "But why?" he protested.

"The police want to question you," Ko announced. "You should expect a call or a visit from them soon enough."

The throbbing in his head grew stronger and he raised his hand to shield his eyes from the fluorescent sheen overhead. His brain screamed with anger and fear. Sergio struggled to control himself.

Ko exchanged a quick glance with Prederick before he continued. "Did you see him tonight?"

Sergio closed his eyes and massaged his temples. "I was on a date," he mumbled. *Is Ko questioning me?*

"I know you knew George a long time," continued Ko. "Did you trust him?"

Trust him? Sergio looked up at Ko and searched his eyes for . . . compassion? Understanding? Ko did not oblige. His steely gaze gave away nothing other than his usual relentless intensity.

"He never gave me any reason to doubt him," replied Sergio.

Ko shook his head and pursed his lips in disapproval. "This afternoon George plugged a thumb drive into his machine and downloaded company data . . . *proprietary* company data." He spoke in a quiet, measured tone. "It goes against policy, to say the very least, wouldn't you agree?"

Sergio mustered a stoic gaze to mask his rising apprehension. "How do you know he did that?"

"The logs confirm it," said Ko, referring to software that automatically records all activity on the network, much like the black boxes on airliners that aviation officials depend on when investigating plane crashes.

"Jesus Christ! Our system practically implodes and you waste time auditing our security chief?" The ferocity of his outburst took Sergio by surprise. He wrestled to control his growing sense of foreboding. "George lived for this company," he said, torn between his loyalty to his friend and his duty to Circles. "He would never do that."

Ko rolled his eyes. "Say what you will. It won't change the facts."

"What did he download?"

Ko started toward Sergio. "That's not important—"

"The hell it isn't," snapped Sergio. He thrust his arm out, jabbing at the air between them with a pointed index finger. "You're accusing our security chief, a man who gave his career to this company, who was just *murdered* . . . What the hell are you accusing him of anyway?"

Ko dismissed the question with a flick of his wrist. "Did you see George download the files? Or were you in any other way aware of what he was up to?"

It was now clear the conversation wasn't about George. "Hell no," replied Sergio.

Ko's voice turned terse. "Then explain why you were messaging George at precisely the moment he was the copying files? 'WTF?' An odd message given the situation, don't you think?"

Sergio looked to Prederick, who sat on the edge of his desk with his arms crossed. He appeared as uncomfortable with the situation as Ko seemed to relish it. Sergio couldn't decide if they were playing a good cop/bad cop game or whether Ko really was calling the shots.

"An odd coincidence, I guess." He made sure to maintain eye contact as he told his lie. "I saw George give a tiny fist pump and I wanted to know what he was all jacked about. I figured he'd tracked the intruder or something like that. He just waved me off and I let it go. I didn't see a flash drive, but then I wasn't looking for one."

Ko scrutinized him for a full ten seconds, cocking his head first to the left and then the right, as he weighed Sergio's response. It was one of Ko's many annoying habits, one that prompted Circles' engineers to joke that Ko was wound up so tightly he often couldn't think straight.

"I will ask you this one time. Do you have the thumb drive George stored those files on? If you do and hand it over now, all will be forgotten. If you hold out on me, I will destroy you."

Sergio spun to Prederick and tried to summon all the phony indignation he could. "Are you going to allow this? Are you going to let him question me like this, *accuse* me like this?" Sergio glared at Prederick, then shifted his eyes to Ko for a brief moment before settling on Prederick once again. "Well?"

Prederick looked to the wall. "Just answer the question."

Sergio shook his head and shot Ko an angry sneer. "Anything else?" he asked, turning for the door. He didn't wait for an answer.

-15-

Sinon rubbed his face and stretched his arms over his head. He stifled a yawn and forced apart his eyelids; four shimmering computer screens floated before him until his watery eyes locked into focus. Then there were just two side-by-side LED monitors.

He checked the time. Circles had probably emerged from crisis mode by this point and traffic patterns would be returning to normal levels—a volume of activity that would help disguise the next phase of his attack.

He hunched over his keyboard and began randomly selecting targets from a long list of computers he'd previously hacked. He felt a guilty pleasure as he typed in commands to assume control over a cluster of servers at Mexico's Figueroa Enterprises. At his command, the compromised computers sent out discreet electronic messages across the Internet to hundreds of thousands of other machines around the world. These too had all been previously infected with malicious software, turning them into a vast network of unwitting "zombie" computers ensnared for the sole purpose of doing whatever Sinon asked them to do.

Sinon imagined all those computers, some in corporate cubicles, but most in small businesses, home offices, and student dorms, quietly whirring into action without their owners suspecting anything was amiss.

On Sinon's command, the zombies began pinging ports—digital doorways within Circles' network—that Sinon had surreptitiously pried and left open during the past several months. It was plan B, just in case his attack was cut off and he needed to regain access.

Circles monitoring software would be on high alert given his earlier attack and Sinon knew it wouldn't even be out of the question for the company's security team to actually eyeball any incoming traffic that did not fit normal patterns. But that had been dealt with when he reprogrammed the company's security software when he first broke in. The company's scanners were no longer able to see that he had opened the ports. More importantly, he had disguised his attack so it would look like legitimate Internet traffic to Circles' security team.

Sinon leaned back in his chair, patiently waiting for one of his commandeered computers to break through. Within a couple of minutes, his screen filled up with scores of prompts signaling that his network of zombie computers had opened communications channels that delivered Sinon straight back inside Circles' network.

His first target was George Verneek's machine. He punched in Verneek's user name and password.

>>ACCESS DENIED

>>PASSWORD DOES NOT MATCH USERNAME

Sinon's second attempt netted the same response. He tried to log in as Victor Ko and also failed. When he couldn't sign on as Dan Prederick, Sinon understood the company had changed all its employee passwords.

Sinon nodded in grudging approval. Circles was operating on a worst-case scenario basis and correctly assumed he'd penetrated multiple accounts. They also figured he'd try to get back in. Forcing all employees to select new passwords was the best way to deal with that. It was a setback he'd hoped to avoid, but knew was likely. It was time to move on to plan C.

-16-

Sergio stormed across the basement with no specific destination in mind. He veered left to avoid a cluster of desks and found himself staring into the employee kitchenette. The pounding in his head had given way to a low-grade headache. Sergio needed a strong coffee, aspirin, and some time to think.

He pawed at the switch inside the door and unleashed a flood of fluorescent light across the kitchenette. A startled figure jumped from his seat in the corner. It was Ethan Burrard, a Labs team colleague who worked nights to minimize his interaction with the rest of the staff. Burrard had a thin face accentuated by a cleft chin, pouty lips that were too big for his mouth, and a shiny forehead that anchored a wispy tuft of brown hair perched atop his head. He wore a Nick Cave & The Bad Seeds T-shirt and a pair of jeans, the same clothes he wore every Friday.

"What are you doing down here?" Sergio asked.

Burrard ignored the question. "Did you hear about Verneek? Got fucked up. I heard it was execution style," he said excitedly.

"Burrard, anyone tell you you're an asshole sometimes?"

"I'm just saying, karma is a bitch."

"Karma?" Sergio clenched his jaw. He knew better than to react to Burrard, who was widely recognized as brilliant but slightly off kilter. Few could match his command of the complex algorithms at the heart of Circles' network, but nature's lottery had denied Burrard the capacity to successfully navigate social situations. Sergio moved to the counter, put a pod of Colombian brew into the coffeemaker, and grabbed four aspirins from the first-aid cabinet.

Burrard toyed with the small piece of circuit board he wore on a chain around his neck. "You might not believe in karma, but I certainly don't believe in coincidences."

Sergio spun around. "What are you talking about?"

"The audit showed the attacker hacked several accounts to roam the network," said Burrard. "One of those was George's, so they had to take a closer look at him, just in case. That's when they discovered he was stealing files."

One of the great mysteries about Burrard was that despite his reticence to engage colleagues, he was always the first to know what was going on at the company. Most of the staff believed that was because Burrard and Ko had worked together for many years. Sergio didn't buy into that theory. He'd seen Burrard and Ko interact in Labs for the past two years and neither of them showed any interest in being friendly to each other.

"Next thing we know, George gets hauled onto the carpet in Prederick's office," Burrard said, his words spilling from his mouth. "Ko was there, too, and they posted a security guard outside the door. There's lots of shouting. Then George storms out and leaves. That's when they searched his belongings."

"Are you saying Prederick and Ko had something to do with George's murder?" Sergio could hardly believe he was asking such a question.

"No, that's not what I'm saying. George was up to something, that's pretty clear." Burrard twitched and his elbows flapped away from his body, an indication that anxiety was beginning to get to him. "And now he's dead. That's all I'm saying. If that's not real bad karma, I don't know what is."

Sergio kept quiet; egging Burrard on when he was excited would only rile him up even more.

"Word is you are on their radar as well," added Burrard.

Sergio thought he saw a thin, almost imperceptible, smile on his colleague's face. "Word is? What do you mean, 'word is'? *Whose* word?"

"Ko's," came the reply. "He ordered an audit on your account."

Burrard's words landed like a body blow, sucking the wind out of Sergio's gut and leaving him grasping for words. "An audit? For what?"

"Anything unusual. You know the drill," said Burrard, his eyes now locked on to a spot about a foot over Sergio's right shoulder.

Sergio slumped into a chair, feeling dazed. He knew the drill. Audits were conducted any time an employee was suspected of theft, corporate espionage, spying on users, or breaching protocol in any other way. The audit would reveal nothing more than his poorly-timed message to George, but the mere fact that the audit had been ordered sent a loud message to the rest of the staff: Stay away from Mansour. He was tainted and should expect no help from any colleagues. It was Sergio's turn to stare at the floor, unwilling to face Burrard.

Sergio finally broke the silence. "Why would they do that?" His words sounded feeble and defensive.

Burrard lowered his hands and tucked in his elbows, a sign his anxiety was ebbing. "You and Verneek were good friends," he said with a crooked smile.

Sergio couldn't decide if Burrard enjoyed watching him squirm or whether his colleague truly didn't understand how one ought to act in these circumstances. Hell, Sergio wasn't sure himself. He leaned forward, rested his elbows on his knees, and pressed his face into his hands. It had been a serious mistake to send that instant message. Or maybe the mistake was to trust his friend.

After all, everyone has a price. Maybe someone had met George's. Could his hatred of Prederick and Ko have trumped his loyalty to Circles? It wouldn't be the first time an insider turned on his employer. But no sane man would use his own account and password for an attack, particularly on his own company. Under any other circumstances, the logical conclusion was that George's account had been commandeered by the attacker. Except George had plugged that thumb drive into his computer and downloaded a bunch of files. He'd squandered all his credibility with that stunt.

Sergio pulled his head out of his hands and looked to Burrard. "Do you think George could have turned?" It would have been an unthinkable question only twenty-four hours earlier.

Burrard spun away. The smile on his face was gone. "George is old news. The question now is whether you turned with him."

-17-

Sergio leaned against the back wall of the elevator as the doors slid shut. The pounding in his head had returned, a steady backbeat to the scattered thoughts colliding in his brain. *Karma.* Burrard's word kept coming back to him and it seemed a little more eerie each time it crept into his mind. Sergio replayed the day's events and tried to reconcile them with George's execution-style murder in his garage. It was surely the first murder in the well-to-do St. Francis Wood neighborhood in years. Sergio wasn't so sure he believed in coincidences either.

He stepped out on the top floor, skirted a small cluster of desks, and stopped in front of a heavy steel door painted fire-engine red. His eyes drifted to a card scanner on the wall as he wondered if Ko had cut off his access to Labs. He held his breath as he swiped his Circles ID badge, exhaling with relief only after the door's powerful magnetic lock released with a click. He swung the door open and stepped into a hallway the size of a large closet with heavy steel doors at either end. The first door swung shut with a thunk. Alone in the passageway, he looked to the overhead security camera, mindful that Prederick and Ko could—and probably were—monitoring his movements through streaming video feeds delivered to their computers. Sergio barely noticed the fuzzy crackling sound piped in through a wall speaker, one of several installed along the lab's perimeter that emitted white noise to prevent people outside from overhearing, inadvertently or otherwise, sensitive conversations inside.

The company's obsessive penchant for security was deeply engrained at Circles and the indoctrination of new employees began on day one. Newbies were encouraged to protect the company and their own futures by keeping a tight lid on everything they saw at Circles. And if the positive message wasn't convincing enough, the orientation team made sure to tell stories about former employees who were sued for leaking company information. Everyone had heard of the marketing executive who got canned after his wife was overheard at a party gossiping about Circles' difficult relationship with a key advertiser.

Outsiders and spouses weren't the only dangers. Employees were strictly forbidden to discuss projects with any colleagues who weren't part of their team. Each group existed as a separate cell, working on a need-to-know basis, much like a spy agency. Some employees were hired to work on key projects, but the assignments were so sensitive the staffers could not be told what they were until after they had accepted. Company documents bore digital watermarks, making any leak easy to trace to specific individuals. It was rumored that undercover security agents patrolled popular bars near headquarters to listen for any shop-talk that might violate the rules. The company never admitted this, but it made no attempt to deny it either.

Nowhere was security more tightly controlled than in Labs. The R&D unit took up much of the seventh floor, separated from the rest of the building by two-foot-thick reinforced concrete walls, floors, and ceiling. Labs had a separate ventilation system, its own power system, and a dedicated computer network accessible only to Labs team members and possibly, Sergio surmised, Prederick, too.

Sergio pulled out his wallet, withdrew a second Circles badge—a credit-card-size ID issued only to the Labs team. He touched it to the card reader next to the inner door and typed a seven-digit password into the keypad. A second magnetic click released the inner portal and Sergio pushed through the final barrier to Labs.

He made his way across the lab, scanning the row of offices as he moved along. He slipped down the back hallway to check the conference room and the server room. Finally, he knocked on doors to the "Gulag" and "Solitary," secure rooms where the most secretive projects were kept isolated from the rest of Labs. Certain that he was alone, Sergio allowed himself to relax. It was the site of his greatest achievements, and he thought of it as a sanctuary of sorts where he could be free of distractions. Tonight it allowed him to escape scrutiny, for there were no closed circuit cameras in the top-secret lab.

Doubling back to his workbench, Sergio felt the sticky floor tug at his shoes. The champagne and flute remained on his workbench, a reminder of how this terrible day had started off in such promising fashion. He jiggled the mouse and brought his laptop to life. An on-screen prompt asked him to create a new password and re-enter it just to be sure. Then he checked the machine's system log and discovered, with no surprise, that it had been wiped clean. Ko would have done so to cover his tracks after auditing his machine. Sergio could safely assume Ko had checked and copied all the program files, the 3-D iris scanner files, his email account, and instant messages. Being audited was like getting a digital enema.

He opened the filing cabinet tucked under his workbench and rummaged through the office supplies, technical manuals, old mobile phones, and business cards. Missing were a half dozen or so USB thumb drives. Fuming at the intrusion, Sergio unplugged the mouse and monitor from his laptop, slipped the computer into a blue messenger bag, and turned for the door.

The elevator floated down the atrium, now bathed in the soft turquoise hue of the building's after-hours lights. Bursts of white light streamed out from work areas on different floors, evidence that some employees still preferred working through the night, even if the all-night hack-athons that were once part of the company's early culture were now a thing of the past. Seconds later, Sergio stepped out of the elevator and walked into the bunker, where he found the night-shift security ninjas breezily cracking jokes. The vibe was all wrong, until Sergio realized that no one had bothered to tell them their boss had just been murdered.

He didn't have the energy, or the will, to break the news. He nodded at the two men and settled into George's chair. Through the reflection in the window, Sergio saw the two ninjas look at each other quizzically. One mouthed a question and the other shrugged. Sergio sat silently for a few minutes, his eyes roaming about George's desk. A bag of chips to quell the munchies. A bottle of TUMS to soothe his stomach. His Peet's coffee mug. A photo of Sergio and George wearing those unbear-ably hot fire-retardant suits after their first race.

"Is there anything we can help with?"

The voice brought Sergio back to the moment. It was one of the security engineers behind him.

"No," replied Sergio without looking around. He pointed to the overhead LED monitors, now flashing bright green. "I just wanted to take a look at the board to see where we're at. Looks good."

"Thanks, sir. George did most of the heavy lifting."

Sergio nodded, his focus still fixed on the overhead monitors. He didn't dare turn around, lest they see in his eyes the maelstrom of grief and anger he'd barely managed to control for the past hour. The pound-ing in his head roared back; he saw the glare of headlights and the bloody body tossed in the dirt. An overwhelming sense of dread threat-ened to swallow him whole.

He looked down from the bright overhead lights; they only fueled the dark images in his mind. He turned away, drawn to George's bowl of M&M's. The cheerful colors captivated him, soothed him. He had never before noticed just how beautiful they were—like those brilliant kaleidoscopes of yesteryear. Ruby red. Vibrant yellow. Rich chocolaty brown. Bright blue. Neon green. Midnight black.

Midnight black? He shook his head and refocused on the bowl. He'd never seen black M&M's before, but sure enough there was a black piece of *something* near the bottom of the bowl. Sergio fought to contain a knowing smile. Could George have been so cheeky? Being summoned to Prederick's office was out of the ordinary, so it stood to reason George would have wanted to hide any evidence of wrongdoing, just to make sure. Best of all, his employees would have expected him to scoop up some M&M's on his way out.

Sergio lifted his arms above his head and a low weary groan escaped his lips. "Wow, what a day," he declared, leaning forward in George's chair. "I'm starving," he added, as he plunged his hand deep into the M&M's. He pushed deeper, causing the hard-shelled candies to rattle against the bowl like pebbles in a rocky surf. Missing on his first try, Sergio spread his fingers and rotated his hand to search for the black item inside. The sugary pebbles scraped the glass; he did not have much time before he drew unwanted attention to himself.

His pinkie brushed across an angular surface. An edge! He dug deeper, prizing a rectangular item from the bottom of the bowl. Pulling it to the surface, he cupped his hand and scooped up the black thumb drive with a handful of candies.

He palmed the device and popped two M&M's in his mouth as he half-turned to the nightshift ninjas. "You guys need anything before I head home?"

-18-

Liu Ting Wei tapped his foot impatiently as his driver nudged the black town car through traffic. Baotou was a small city by Chinese standards—only two million people—but its roadways were always clogged with donkey carts and scooters vying for space among the cars and buses. A handful of glass-and-tile buildings pierced a skyline dominated by blocks of drab low-slung structures. In the distance, beyond the Kundulun River, towering smoke stacks discharged thick plumes of vapor that drifted to the mountains north and east.

For twenty-five years, Liu had fought against the dreariness around him. On this day he wore a crisp navy blue suit, a red silk tie, and black Ferragamo wingtips. With closely cropped gray hair, manicured nails, and a hint of cologne, he projected elegance, wealth, and power. A quick glance at his watch confirmed he was running late. His private jet would wait for him; the shipper in Shanghai would not.

Liu slipped his hand into the leather satchel next to him and caressed the black laptop inside. The stakes could not have been higher. This was a once-in-a-lifetime chance to consolidate China's dominance over the global economy for generations to come. As director of the world's largest rare earth minerals company, Liu would play kingmaker.

China was already the undisputed leader of rare earths, a group of obscure elements critical to the production of high-tech products like semiconductors, cell phones, and TV screens. Without neodymium, lanthanum, and a dozen or so other minerals, much of the consumer technology the world takes for granted would not exist. And without more coveted heavy rare earth minerals like samarium, it would be impossible to make sophisticated weaponry such as cruise missiles, precision-guided bombs, and stealth aircraft.

Liu liked to point out that the term "rare earth minerals" was a bit of a misnomer because they were really not uncommon at all. They could be found in extremely low concentrations throughout the Earth's crust as a byproduct of almost all massive rock formations, but there were few known places where they could be economically mined. And nowhere were rare earths more economical than in the Bayan Obo iron-mining district, some one hundred and twenty kilometers north of Baotou. Scattered across southern China were the more critical heavy rare earth minerals, which, combined with Bayan Obo's massive resources and the country's low regard for environmental regulations, enabled China to claim more than half of the world's estimated rare earth deposits.

But that was merely the starting point for Liu. By perfecting the tedious, expensive, and toxic production processes developed by his mentor, Liu had helped China seize a virtual monopoly on the entire rare earth value chain: mining and refining the ore; transforming it into metal; and ultimately making the high-strength magnets, alloys, and other key products so vital to high-tech manufacturing.

With the Communist Party's blessing, Liu carefully tracked global supply and demand, and controlled exports in order to manipulate the international market. Not long ago, he'd pushed prices so high that US smartphone upstart Modulo had to shut its doors. Now he was flooding the market to drive down prices and scare away private investors in the US, Japan, Germany, and Australia, who for a brief moment thought there was money to be made in rare earths. On the domestic front, he ensured that emerging Chinese electronic manufacturers had priority access to the critical rare earth end products they needed to compete with Western rivals. Liu was arguably the most powerful man in the world that nobody had ever heard of.

The car swung south onto the Baodong Expressway. The airport was now only ten minutes away, traffic permitting. A distinctive ringtone escaped his satchel, an unwelcome reminder of the troubles at Circles. He pulled out a black smartphone; it was untraceable and loaded with voice encryption software. Only one person had the number. He silently scolded himself for believing assurances that Circles' network was bulletproof. Now a massive cyberattack, a rogue employee, and a wayward thumb drive threatened to ruin everything he'd worked so hard for. He pressed the phone to his ear. "Do you have good news?"

The voice at the other end hesitated. "The intruder covered his tracks well," came the reply. "I cannot say whether we've been compromised."

"What about that employee?"

"He is no longer of concern." The scratchy voice paused several seconds before continuing. "But the thumb drive is still missing."

Liu let his silence communicate his displeasure until the scratchy voice continued. "It's possible he had help."

Liu's abdominal muscles contracted as he grit his teeth. He closed his eyes and ran his fingertips into his coarse hair. "Another insider?" he finally asked.

"Yes," came the reply. "And if anyone can make sense of the data, it would be this man."

Liu cursed quietly and cleared his throat. "We cannot afford to take any chances," he said.

"I agree."

"Tell our friend he has more work to do."

-19-

Damon Graves had to put George Verneek in the past. He had work to do. His next mark, this Sergio Mansour, had pulled out of Circles in a silver Range Rover and was now two hundred yards down the street. The four-lane avenue was empty and Graves couldn't risk drawing attention. He couldn't afford any mistakes, not after the mess he'd left in the garage.

The big man should have been a simple kill. George Verneek had given in as soon as he saw the gun. It was only after Graves had bound his hands and feet, and sealed his mouth with duct tape, that Verneek had realized it wasn't a robbery. He'd claimed ignorance, but Graves had recognized the glint of recognition in Verneek's eyes when Graves demanded the thumb drive.

Graves had searched Verneek and his car. Nothing. Then, brandishing his Sig Sauer 9mm pistol, he'd knelt down next to his wild-eyed mark.

"You get one chance," growled Graves. "Where is it?"

Verneek protested through the tape and shook his head vigorously. Graves pressed the tip of the silencer against Verneek's kneecap and squeezed the trigger.

Verneek howled in pain, but through the duct tape his protests sounded like the gurgled cries of someone screaming underwater. Graves waited until Verneek quieted down before peeling back a corner of the tape. Panting uncontrollably, Verneek tried to yell, but Graves quickly pulled the tape tightly across his mouth. Then he aimed the gun at Verneek's other knee and fired.

Verneek's muffled cries of agony carried through the garage, and for a brief instant, Graves feared a neighbor might hear. He covered Verneek's taped mouth with his hand. "You try that again and it only gets worse," he said, glaring down at him. "Understand?"

Head thrown back, Verneek heaved with spasms of pain. Sweat poured from his body.

"Do you understand?" repeated Graves.

Verneek fought off the pain with a clenched jaw. His breathing slowed and he focused his steely gaze on Graves.

"Where is the thumb drive?" Graves asked.

Verneek tossed his head, beckoning Graves to move closer. Graves leaned in and again peeled back the tape from the left side of his mouth. The wounded man cleared his throat and forced a spurt of spittle through his lips. "Fuck you," he whispered.

Graves pulled back and studied the wounded man. The fear was now gone. His eyes were angry, defiant. He knew he was already dead.

The third bullet destroyed Verneek's left elbow. Graves felt no remorse; he was angry now. The fourth shot shattered the right one. It should have been a simple job, but now there was blood everywhere—and no thumb drive. The fifth bullet, to the groin, was fired out of sheer spite. Graves had waited a few minutes, just to make the big man suffer. Then he had fired one more round into Verneek's head.

Graves could not afford to fuck up this next one. Mansour was far enough up the road now, so Graves nosed his Chrysler 300 forward and followed at a distance. Surely Mansour would be more wary—and dangerous—now that one man was dead. But as Graves tailed the Range Rover, it seemed his target was oblivious to any threat. As they moved north from Mission Bay, Mansour stayed within ten miles of the speed limit, stopped at red lights, and signaled well in advance of his turns. He made none of the standard evasive maneuvers designed to flush out a tail. He'd be an easy mark, after all.

A ghostly fog laden with heavy mist enveloped the two vehicles as they moved into the South of Market district, a grid of wide one-way streets lined with old warehouses converted to offices, lofts, and nightclubs. Graves wondered how the two computer geeks could have ended up in his sights. It had never before occurred to him that the greed, envy, and hatred he saw in his line of work also infected Silicon Valley. But why not? Power, money, and egos were all in play here, too, just like in the casinos, mines, and oil fields of the world. It was not his place to assess whether the situation warranted such extreme measures. His sole concern was to take care of business.

It was after midnight when the Range Rover eased into a vacant spot in front of a twenty-four-hour diner on Howard Street. Graves pulled over short of the diner and watched the techie step out of his car with a messenger bag slung over one shoulder. The guy didn't even bother to look around before entering the diner. Clueless. Graves found an empty parking spot on the other side of the broad one-way street. From his vantage point, he saw Mansour settle into a booth, leaving only his head and shoulders visible above the bench backrests. His eyebrows were raised high, as if he were struggling to stay awake. His jaw was clenched and lips pulled tight. He looked haggard, confused, even a little distressed. Whatever was going on, this Mansour guy wasn't coping very well. Graves snorted. Civilians were soft. They lived in their insignificant little worlds full of imaginary dramas. Most of them had no idea what real stress was, let alone how to handle it or go to the limit when necessary.

That's why men like Graves had to carry the load. Do what needed to be done. He had stepped up when his country needed him, and he'd paid the price. Three close friends, dead. Two Purple Hearts, excruciatingly earned. One brief relationship, shattered. And for what? No one had his back when he returned home. His family and friends didn't understand what it was like to go to war. The government had strung him along for benefits, and jobs were impossible to find. Civilians always found some reason to back away: his meager education, his OxyContin habit, or the domestic assault. He had one fallback position and this was it. Luckily, it was very lucrative.

Graves pushed those thoughts from his mind and focused again on the techie. Mansour had won his battle with weariness, or distress, and was now immersed in his laptop. Graves reached for his phone—prepaid with cash—and dialed his contact.

"He's at a diner on Howard."

"And?"

"And he's working on his computer."

"Does he have the thumb drive?"

"Can't see. I'll go grab a coffee . . ."

"No," replied the contact. "If he has it, I'll know soon enough."

-20-

The screen on Sergio's laptop surged to life with a blue flicker and a soft chime. From his favorite booth at the back of the diner, he took in the usual assortment of insomniacs, all lost in the glow of their own machines. The eatery's cozy wooden interior and the owner's willingness to let customers linger for hours made it a popular hangout for urban techies. Irene, the plump middle-age waitress, poured coffee and took his order. A Reuben sandwich with fries. He was starving. Sergio rolled his head in a broad sweeping arc to loosen his neck muscles. He fought to keep his leaden eyelids open. Just a few more hours.

Sergio punched in his password and—just to make sure—booted up a virtual machine, a temporary and untraceable operating system that ran isolated from the rest of his laptop. Then he slipped the thumb drive into a USB port on the side of his laptop.

After a couple of quick taps on his thumbpad, he found three directories had been copied to George's black thumb drive: two contained a single file each and the other held twenty thousand files.

Twenty thousand? He shook his head. How the hell was he supposed to get through that many files? The enormity of the task filled him with doubt. *You are breaking the law. And for what? A dead friend who might have sabotaged the company?*

He reached for the screen, ready to pull the lid shut. He could crush the USB drive, toss it in a Dumpster, and no one would ever know any better. And yet . . . Sergio still couldn't get his head around the idea that George had turned. Few loved their job or were more committed to the company than George. His friend must have had a good reason to copy those files. Nothing else made sense. Sergio stared at the directories on the screen for a long while. His hands trembled and his throat felt dry. He double-clicked the first directory. There would be no turning back.

A long list of files appeared and he quickly clicked the first. The screen filled with a blob of raw data in human readable format, interspersed with dozens of photos of an attractive young Asian woman. He picked out a series of Asian characters, which he copied and ran through an online translator. The young woman's hometown was Beijing. Sergio opened a second file; another beautiful young lady with a series of similar photos. She too was from Beijing. The third lived in Shanghai; the fourth called the southern city of Guangzhou home.

One by one, he ran through dozens of randomly selected profiles, each with images of attractive men and women. By the time he viewed fifty or sixty profiles, Sergio didn't need to open any more to understand what he'd discovered—the profiles of twenty thousand Circles members from mainland China.

He closed his eyes and pressed his fingertips to his temples. It didn't make any sense. The only Chinese profiles he'd seen were the ones Labs whipped up to test the company's soon-to-be-launched mainland China pages. They had run in test mode on a massive bank of Lab servers for the past two months, but after weeks of debugging, Sergio, Ko, and Burrard had deleted them. Circles' Chinese pages were now a series of blank templates, ready to be filled in by new members once the social network opened for business in mainland China. As far as Sergio was concerned, none of these twenty thousand profiles on the USB drive should exist.

An excited voice broke his concentration. "Sergio Mansour?"

He looked up. A young blonde woman in her mid-twenties stood before him, her expression a mixture of awe and excitement. She was attractive and svelte; Sergio would have remembered her if they'd met before.

"Yes?" he said, his focus split between the girl and his computer screen.

"Hi. I thought it was you. Wow. How cool is that?" She stared at him awkwardly for a second. "I just love the new Circles interface. The developers' blog said you led that project."

Sergio stifled a chuckle. He remembered how his own unbridled enthusiasm got the better of him when he was new to Silicon Valley and ran into industry stars like Apple's Steve Jobs or Yahoo's Jerry Yang.

"Thanks," he offered, "but you can't believe everything you read online, you know."

The girl laughed nervously. "I work at a startup called Dinky. We do . . ."

Sergio held up his hands and shook his head. "I don't do business development. I'm sure you've got a great idea but you're going to have to go through Ruben Havelich, our VP of biz dev."

The waitress appeared at the woman's side. Wearing a frown that suggested she didn't approve of the girl bothering Sergio, Irene edged the young woman aside as she placed his order on the table. The woman deflated, forcing a smile that was not quite broad enough to mask her disappointment. "Well, it was nice meeting you."

He nodded silently, took a bite of his sandwich, and refocused on the computer. He pulled up the second folder and opened the single file within. The screen filled with line after line of code he immediately recognized as C, the programming language at the heart of all modern operating systems. He punched in a series of commands, ordering the software to cough up its secrets. Within minutes, he recognized that the program on his screen was a virus designed to latch on to Circles' operating system, and once bound to its host, the virus would attack the social network's monitoring systems. He rubbed his eyes, half hoping he'd open them to discover he was wrong. But there was no denying what he'd found. If this program was actively running on Circles, then every one of the social network's defenses would be meticulously disarmed. This virus not only exploited the cracks in Circles' monitoring systems, it made everything appear normal. It was like an intruder who'd picked the locks and then relocked the doors and closed the blinds behind him so the security guards wouldn't notice anything wrong.

But why? Sergio closed the virus program and opened the third folder. Another program spilled from the USB drive, disgorging itself rapid fire until hundreds of thousands of lines of code scrolled before his eyes. He slapped together a simple program to dissect the code and identify key landmarks within the program. Now it was up to him. Outside stimuli faded as his mind absorbed, processed, and visualized the bits of data each character of code represented. Brain cells fired and bursts of endorphins coursed through his body as his mind transformed strings of text into a massive multi-dimensional diagram of the artificial organism on his screen. Sergio had many times tried to describe the pulsing map of interconnections he built in his mind, but the only example that ever made sense to others was one of those three-dimensional molecular models that high school students first learn about in chemistry. But they were a woeful example as far as he was concerned; the web of dynamic systems he conjured in his mind was far more complex, intricate enough for him to see billions of bits of data coursing through this artificial organism, feeding off, engaging with, and responding to billions of Circles users.

The diner was nearly empty by the time Sergio pulled himself away from the screen. He threw his head back and ran both hands through his hair, shaken by his discovery. Somehow, in all the mess and confusion following the attack, George had tripped over—and copied—highly advanced socialbot software, a program to create and operate fake profiles that looked and acted like real people on Circles. Socialbots were designed to befriend real Circles users and dupe them into divulging their sensitive personal and financial information. There were always some people who—out of vanity or desperation—accepted buddy requests from people they didn't know. Over time, successful socialbots could build networks of thousands of buddies who unwittingly exposed their personal information to the criminals controlling the socialbots.

Circles had for years tried to smoke out computer-generated accounts, but every advance the company made was inevitably trumped by the bad guys. And while some of the code didn't yet make sense, Sergio could tell this socialbot software was far more advanced than any he had ever seen before. It was the work of an expert, crafted with sophisticated logic that was well beyond the capabilities of the programming masses.

Most striking was the way the socialbots tailored invitations to people so it would appear they shared common backgrounds, hobbies, interests, affiliations, and memberships—making unsuspecting users think they had been contacted by a kindred spirit, or a long-lost acquaintance or colleague they couldn't quite recall. These bots chose their targets carefully and then adroitly camouflaged themselves. Sergio heard a rumble in his gut; his stomach felt queasy. Whoever had written this socialbot software was years ahead of the curve. He pushed the Reuben across the table.

Gathering himself, Sergio returned to the profiles he'd opened earlier. Every single photo featured an attractive Chinese person. And they were no mere snapshots either. The images were crisp and clear, as if taken by professional studio photographers. One profile photo in particular caught his attention: a young woman with brilliant black eyes and a cute button nose, her smile sparkling white and her skin texture delicate as a flower. She was flawless—too flawless. The more he stared at her, the more Sergio became convinced he was looking at a digital image generated by the socialbot program George had discovered.

A stab of anger cut into Sergio. Someone had planted advanced socialbot command-and-control software on Circles' network. And that person, or people, had used it to generate at least twenty thousand fake Chinese profiles. Any smart hacker—*if* a hacker could even have pulled this off—would surely have waited until Circles went live in China. Then it would have been much easier to hide all those socialbot profiles among real ones. Sergio shook his head as he settled on the inevitable conclusion. This was an inside job. Someone within Circles was breaking company rules in a big way and putting the social network's reputation on the line. But why? Sergio stewed. If word got out that Circles was scamming its own users, it was game over. Users would flee en masse to other sites and never return. Everything he, George, and Johnny had worked for over the past fifteen years would be lost. Poof. Just like that.

Sergio looked to the ceiling. Few people had the programming chops and security clearances to pull off something like this. A couple of network architects, a few of the guys in Labs, George maybe, Sergio himself . . . and Victor Ko. Sergio sat up straight as the synapses in his brain fired wildly. It would certainly explain Ko's aggressive interest in George's thumb drive. Sergio's jaw tightened as he replayed his confrontation with Ko a few hours earlier. That prick had all but accused him of betraying Circles and, in ordering an audit, Ko had left Sergio's career hanging by a thread.

But why now? Ko had somehow convinced Chinese authorities to let Circles operate in China; this was a huge moment for the company. If Circles could conquer China, its user numbers would soar, advertisers would spend billions of dollars to promote their brands, and investors would drive Circles' share price ever higher. Ko would be the hero who transformed Circles into *THE* social network for the entire world. And he'd be handsomely rewarded for it. So why put all that at risk now?

"What are you up to, Victor?" he murmured.

Sergio barely had enough time to mull his next move when his phone lit up and announced itself with the classic ring of an old rotary phone. It was an incoming call from Ko.

"Victor," he answered in a matter-of-fact voice.

"I'm very disappointed in you, Sergio." Ko's voice was dry.

"Aren't you done already?" Sergio could hear irritation in his voice, but he didn't care. "You audit my account, examine my computer, search my desk, and when you don't find anything, you smear my name. Can't you just leave me alone?"

"A guy your age should be home sleeping at this hour, not rifling through stolen data."

A chill trickled down Sergio's spine. Ko couldn't possibly know, could he? Sergio's eyes found the top right-hand corner of his screen. The Wi-Fi icon was on; his computer had automatically connected to the diner's network. If Ko really was monitoring Sergio's computer, he was screwed. He switched off his Wi-Fi. He didn't know what else to do.

"What the hell are you talking about?" said Sergio, bluffing.

"I'm talking about that thumb drive plugged into your laptop right now."

The words hit Sergio with the force of a body blow. "You put spyware on my machine?"

A soft chuckle filtered through the earpiece. "I gave you your chance, Sergio."

The line fell silent. Sergio's mind raced and his stomach protested, the rumbles growing louder as the seconds passed. "What do you want, Victor?"

"Most of all, I wanted you to be a loyal Circles employee. That would have been best for everyone." Ko sounded cheerful, as if he relished tormenting Sergio.

"I know what's best for me. And for Circles."

"You and George stole company data. How is that best for the company?"

"What you're doing is dangerous. Don't you see that? If it ever gets out that we're running socialbots on the site—"

Ko cut him off. "Now who would let that out?"

Sergio held his tongue.

"You've crossed a line." Ko's easy tone changed abruptly. His voice now seethed with anger. "Trade secret theft will get you ten years in prison. Throw in George and it looks like a conspiracy. That's another count."

Sergio's muscles tightened. The steady foundation upon which he had built his career had just shifted violently. He pulled the phone from his ear and held it unsteadily in front of his face. He planted his elbow on the table to steady his trembling hand. "What do you want?" he asked.

"The thumb drive. Bring it to me now. And your laptop," demanded Ko. "You have ten minutes. If not, we'll press—"

Sergio pressed his finger to his phone, ending the call. He knew the rest of it and it was bad. At best, a data theft indictment would mean the end of his career. He had a very sudden urge to take a drag off a cigarette, a craving he hadn't felt in more than a decade. He recalled the soothing sensation, that tingling buzz he used to get when he first started smoking in his late teens. He looked wistfully around the diner. Smoking wasn't allowed.

The phone rang; another call from Ko. Implicit in his ultimatum was the suggestion he'd cut a deal. At the very least, Ko wouldn't call the police. Sergio let the phone ring as he considered the idea for a moment. It would be foolish to expect any kind of cooperation from Ko. They had been at odds ever since Ko was installed as his boss. Prederick was all that kept them from each other's throats. Sergio turned off his phone; he needed more time to think.

He still had leverage. Word of the socialbots could ruin Circles. Ko would deal, if only to ensure his scheme—or whatever it was—remained a secret. He replayed the conversation in his mind, probing for any hint or slip by Ko that might give Sergio an edge. Then he froze. *A guy your age should be home sleeping.* Ko knew he wasn't at home. The CTO could have traced him through the diner's Internet address. But what if . . . ?

Sergio's eyes darted to the window. The street was quiet, only a passing truck. Cars parked nearest to the diner were empty, but he couldn't see inside the vehicles across the street. He shuffled to the counter and sat on a stool near the window.

The gaunt waiter behind the counter ambled down to Sergio. "Can I help you?"

"Just a glass of water."

"Coming right up," he replied as he turned away. Sergio spun his stool toward the window and scanned the misty street beyond. His eyes swept the street again, and then a third time. No one in sight. Nothing out of the ordinary, even though he didn't have the faintest clue what to look for. A car moved up the street, its high beams slashing through the mist. And then he saw it, inside a gray Chrysler 300 parked across the street. The muscular car had tinted windows, but under the glare of the passing vehicle the Chrysler 300 gave up its secret—the outline of the driver sitting inside. Or was that just the shape of a headrest?

For the first time, Sergio had the awful feeling that his terrible night was about to get much worse. He lifted himself to his feet and leaned forward, his palms placed flat on the counter. He closed his eyes and tried to picture Malina's hazel eyes, at once sparkling and warm. He needed to stay calm.

"You okay?" The skinny waiter regarded him with concern as he slid a glass of water in front of him.

"Yeah, yeah," he replied, with feigned nonchalance. "It's been one of those days."

Sergio returned to his booth and looked out the window. There it was, just within view. If someone was indeed watching him from the Chrysler, they'd made sure to park where they could see him inside the diner. A flurry of palpitations rocked his chest. The sickening sensation reminded him of that awful moment years ago when the corporate jet hit an air pocket and plunged two hundred feet in an instant. He drew in a deep breath, grabbed both sides of the table, and exhaled slowly. He repeated his controlled breathing until his heart resumed its rhythmic beat. Only then did he turn his mind over to the task of dealing with the phantom in the car. After several minutes, he settled on a plan.

Under cover of the booth's walls, Sergio pulled the thumb drive from his computer and put the tiny device in his jeans pocket. He slowly closed the laptop and slipped it into his messenger bag. Holding the bag tightly against his belly, Sergio stood up and ambled toward the back hall of the diner. Anyone watching from outside would assume he was headed to the restroom. Once out of sight, Sergio pushed through the rear door of the diner, crept around the back of the building, and slipped behind a row of Dumpsters in a side alley that opened to the street. Tucked safely behind the metal containers, he inspected the Chrysler directly across the road, but the glare of street lights reflecting off the car's tinted windows made it impossible to see inside. A nauseating stench of grease, coffee grinds, and rotting vegetables spilled out of the Dumpsters and assaulted his nostrils. He cradled the warm laptop in his arms and pressed it to his chest. It was a welcome salve against the damp chill air. He hoped he would not have to wait long.

Sergio squatted between two Dumpsters and leaned his back to the wall so he could rest with only his feet touching the wet pavement. A streetlight near the alley cast a slender angular ray that pierced the darkness around him. A burst of traffic rushed past and within seconds the drone of engines and whoosh of tires faded down the street.

Dizzied by the stench and thrown off balance by his surroundings, Sergio found himself replaying his decisions of the past hours. The day had begun in triumph and he was now on the verge of committing career suicide, not to mention a felony, as he cowered in this squalid alley, hiding from a shadow of a man who might only exist in his overactive imagination. *I must be losing it.* Why not stroll across the street, rap on the Chrysler's window, and sort this out? The rational side of his brain tried to coax him toward the—empty?—car, but his instincts screamed caution and patience. He'd wait a few minutes more.

Just then, the Chrysler's door swung open and a man stepped out on the curb. Backlit by the streetlights, his face was obscured, but his tall, powerful physique was evident despite his windbreaker and loose-fitting jeans. The man's rigid posture and closely cropped hair pointed to a military background. He scanned the empty street as he reached for the small of his back with both hands, as if tucking something into his pants. Sergio had seen that motion in hundreds of murder mystery and spy movies; he knew right then he wanted nothing to do with the shadowy figure across the street.

The man moved along the opposite sidewalk to get a better view into the diner. Sergio sank deeper behind the trash bins as his stalker stepped off the curb to cross the road. The man's footsteps grew heavier as he approached the alley. Then he stopped. Sergio held his breath and strained to hear the sound of the coffee shop door—his cue to make a run for it. Another step, then two more. Something was wrong—the footsteps were getting louder.

The man turned the corner and stopped at the entrance to the dark alley. He stood just a couple of yards away as Sergio crumpled to the pavement to escape the sliver of light from the street. He tucked his head into his arms and held his breath, trying to make himself as small, still, and quiet as possible. He could do nothing about his furiously pounding heart.

The man stepped forward and Sergio watched a shadow slip past on the wet pavement, followed by one, then two, black—combat?—boots. The man's arms were once again tugging at the small of his back, only this time the hulking figure pulled a pistol from his waistband.

Sergio's heart went into overdrive. *Why would anyone want to kill me?* Ko was probably quite capable of many unethical—or even illegal—things, but this was on a whole different level. The man in black slipped past Sergio's field of vision and continued down the alley. Was this the same guy who had killed George? *The killer shot him in the knees, the elbows, the groin. He was tortured before he was killed.* Prederick's words had a far more urgent ring to them now. Sergio fought against the sensation that he was drowning in a wave of panic and dread. This couldn't be real. It didn't make any sense.

He threw his hands to his face, hooking his thumbs under his jaw and digging his fingertips into his forehead and temples. He clawed at his face with slow repetitive motions, trying to soothe his frazzled nerves. He had to get a grip; he needed to think. This *was* real. The man with the gun was still there, down the alley some forty feet beyond the garbage bins. Sergio took a shallow breath and listened until he could no longer hear the man's footsteps. He lifted himself off the pavement and peeked around the Dumpster. The man had turned into the narrow back lane Sergio had just used to escape the diner. Sergio scrambled to his feet and ran for the street. He had fifteen seconds, maybe twenty, before the gunman realized he'd fled the restaurant.

Sergio reached the Range Rover and cursed his earlier parking karma. He was now exposed under the streetlights as he scrambled for his keys in his jacket, acutely aware that everyone in the diner could see him. A shadow moved in the back hallway, no doubt the gunman searching the restrooms. Sergio clutched at his keys and fumbled them, the entire set slipping out of his grasp and tumbling to the street. He dipped down to retrieve them and unlocked the SUV's doors with the fob. A sharp movement inside the coffeehouse caught his attention and his brain registered danger. The gunman raced from the back hallway, crashing into tables and shoving them aside as he rushed to the front door. *Sergio had been spotted.* Just then a young woman turned away from the counter and stepped in front of the gunman as he bolted for the exit. The collision knocked him off stride and sent her to the floor with a scream. An older man stood up to yell; the gaunt waiter behind the counter stared in stunned disbelief.

Sergio had mere seconds to start the car and escape—*unless the gunman pulled out his pistol right there and started shooting.* Sergio tossed his messenger bag on the passenger's seat as he fell into the driver's side. He fired up the engine, yanked on the steering wheel, and slammed his foot on the accelerator, awkwardly launching the SUV forward. Gaining control of the Range Rover, Sergio roared down Howard Street, looking back to see his pursuer run to his car. He'd have a block, maybe a block-and-a-half head start on the gunman, but his SUV was no match for the Chrysler, not if it was one of those STR8s with the Hemi V8 engine.

The three-lane street was empty except for a few scattered cars ahead. Sergio caught them as they slowed for a red light. He tapped his brakes on instinct, but just for a second. He would take his chances with cross traffic. He stomped on the accelerator and blew through the inter-section. Out of the corner of his eye, he saw several headlights coming toward him some fifty feet down the cross street. A few seconds later and he might have been dead.

Sergio pushed the thought from his mind. He'd done what he had to do—put distance between him and his pursuer. But for how long? In his mirror, the Chrysler lurched into motion. Sergio stomped on the accelerator like he was trying to drive it through the floorboard. The Range Rover neared seventy-five miles per hour and the next cross street came up quickly. The second red light was easier than the first, if only because he had already made his choice.

Halfway to the next intersection, he glanced at the speedometer. He was at eighty-five miles per hour, confirmation of what he sensed in his bones—the car was no longer accelerating quickly. He looked in the mir-ror. The Chrysler's headlights shone bigger and brighter in the mist. He hammered the steering wheel with his open palm, urging the car forward.

"Come on. Come on!" he cried.

He flew through a third red light at 7th Street, it too was sequenced to keep cars moving at the twenty-five mile per hour speed limit. If he kept this up, he'd eventually catch up to the earlier cycle of green lights—as long as he didn't crash or get caught. The Chrysler closed quickly, much too quickly. The gunman raced through the red signal at 7th Street, showing as much commitment to catching Sergio as Sergio was investing in his escape attempt. He didn't have much time, maybe just enough to reach San Francisco police headquarters, about a mile away. He'd veer left on 8th Street and pass under the highway. Another left-hand turn and he'd practically be at the station's front door.

The buildings along Howard were a blur as Sergio hit ninety. All he could see were the Chrysler's headlights as they filled his rearview mirror. The gunman was now within a few hundred feet, just a couple of seconds at this speed. Sergio kept his foot pressed on the accelerator until he suddenly realized 8th Street was coming up much faster than he had anticipated. He swerved to the far right lane and braked hard, setting himself up for a wide left turn at about sixty miles per hour. The traffic lights turned green just as Sergio dove into the turn, tires slipping across the intersection. After the rush of Howard, the corner came to him in slow motion. Physics pulled him right as the car moved left. His body strained against the seatbelt as he finessed the steering wheel to maintain his line through the corner without spinning out on the damp pavement. Arms braced, he gripped the wheel tightly as the Range Rover passed within a few inches of the inside corner. The car's momentum carried it across the four lanes of 8th Street before the tires reasserted their grip on the wet road, less than a foot from the parked cars on the opposite side of the street. The glare of the gunman's headlights flooded the interior of Sergio's car and the low roar of the Chrysler's powerful engine filled his ears. He didn't have to look back. The gunman was now almost directly behind him.

Sergio stomped on the accelerator, his eyes shifting from the road and to the mirror just as the gunman lowered his window and thrust a pistol into the wind. Sergio swerved right and left across the four-lane road to make himself a hard target. He blasted through a green light as the Chrysler moved smoothly behind him. Sergio sensed the gunman was being patient, waiting for his moment to strike. *I'm not going to make it to the station.* Ahead he saw Harrison and just beyond was the highway overpass. Swerving to the far right lane, he suddenly understood what he needed to do. It was a desperate move, with one chance to get it right, but he could not see any other way to hold off his charging pursuer.

He eased off the accelerator and allowed the Chrysler to get within a few feet of his rear fender. The gun reappeared from the driver's window and Sergio heard a rapid-fire *clank, clank* of two bullets lodging somewhere in the back of his SUV. The traffic lights ahead turned green and he moved into the intersection as the gunman leveled his weapon once more. Sergio glanced to the left, up the off-ramp that spilled cars from the highway above into the intersection. It was empty and he committed to his plan, waiting for the last possible instant to yank his steering wheel hard to the left. The Range Rover's tires howled in protest as they skidded through the intersection, hurtling the car toward the off-ramp. He froze with his hands on the wheel, watching helplessly as the approaching curb grew to outsized heights. Sergio immediately regretted his decision, fearful his car would come crashing to a halt, or even flip over, as it slammed sideways into the curb. From behind came another screech of tires as the surprised gunman skidded past the exit ramp.

Sergio felt a crucial shift in the Range Rover's momentum. The SUV no longer skidded sideways; it started to push forward once again, up the ramp. He checked his rearview mirror and saw the gunman back his car to the bottom of the ramp and come to a full stop. He threw his arms out the window, pointing his pistol, and Sergio saw three quick flashes. He heard two bullets whiz by; a third lodged somewhere in his car with a *thunk*.

Sergio neared the top of the ramp, with only a dozen yards to go before he could see any oncoming traffic on the highway above. His heartbeat spiked as he realized the dim glow of headlights beyond the horizon was getting brighter. Suddenly, he was awash in the glare of the halogen high beams of an eighteen-wheeler coming at him head on. The truck's brakes locked and its air horn blared as Sergio leaned in and cranked his steering wheel hard to the right, sending the Range Rover careening into a cluster of water-filled safety barrels at the top of the ramp. The steering wheel air bag blew up in his face and drove him back into his seat as the SUV spun around violently. The safety barrels exploded in a massive eruption of water that flew into the night air and splashed across the roadway. His car came to a rest on the highway as the tractor trailer skidded to a halt halfway down the ramp.

Sergio sat dazed for several seconds, unable to get his bearings after the violent whipsawing he'd just suffered. His vision was blurry and his nose throbbed with pain. Blinking and squinting, he soon became aware of the massive, lighted towers of the Bay Bridge floating in the distance. It was oddly quiet and the shimmer of city lights looked beautiful. His head felt woozy and heavy, and he let it fall back onto the headrest.

Somewhere out of the darkness a distant voice called out, "There's a man with a gun on the ramp!"

You're still in danger.

Sergio willed himself to sit up. He faced east on the westbound lanes of Interstate 80, peering into the headlights of several stopped cars. A couple of drivers approached his car with caution, like they were wary of some drunk driver who'd just come up the exit ramp. *The ramp. You are still in danger.* Sergio snapped forward with a jolt and fought off the pain and heaviness in his head. He had to get away from the gun-man on the ramp. *George was tortured.* Sergio reached for the ignition and threw his head back in relief as he heard the Range Rover's engine roar to life. The drivers around him scattered as he spun around with a screech of tires. Sergio let out a giddy, nervous laugh as he gathered speed and disappeared around the first bend in the highway.

-21-

Sergio drove down the first off-ramp he saw and stopped at an intersection tucked under the elevated freeway. By day the Mission Street exit was a bustling crossroads, but it now stood eerily quiet. A lone figure wrapped in blankets slept on the median, protected from the misty drizzle by the imposing roadbed above. A ghostly white van floated past, but its driver paid no heed to the crumpled front end of Sergio's SUV. A police siren wailed in the distance, probably in response to the chaos he'd just left behind.

He released the steering wheel, pulled his hands into his lap, and closed his eyes. His body trembled and his mind was a jumble of sights and sounds: the gun waving in the wind, the roar of the Chrysler, the hulking semi bearing down on him. He opened his eyes to make it stop.

A sudden flash of headlights in the mirror jolted him out of his daze. He punched the accelerator and shot through the red light. Only then did he see a blue Honda come to a halt under the bright streetlamps where he had just stopped. Sergio kept moving. He needed to get off the street.

"Come on," he said, gritting his teeth. "Think!"

He couldn't risk doubling back to the police station. The man in the Chrysler was still out there somewhere. The cops would be looking for him, too. He'd just left the scene of an accident and someone there had surely taken down his license plate number. And if Ko was serious about pressing charges, Sergio might wind up in jail until he could make bail on Monday or Tuesday. Ko would have more than enough time to cover any tracks that needed covering.

Sergio couldn't go home. That would be the first place the gunman would look. And he couldn't chance going to a friend's place. If the man in the Chrysler really was working for Ko, the gunman probably already had a list of his friends. Hotels were too risky. His beat-up Range Rover would surely attract notice.

"Malina." Her name spilled from his lips before he realized it.

He shook his head, dismissing the idea. He racked his brain for several minutes, revisiting his options and quickly knocking them down. Each time, his mind kept circling back to her. She was so new in his life that she wasn't even part of his Circles social graph. Their only link so far was a couple of phone calls he'd made to her hospital, and Ko wouldn't have access to those records. It would only be for tonight, just a few hours until he figured out what to do.

Ten minutes later, Sergio stood in front of the house next to the Claytonia, a sixteen-unit apartment building known in local lore as a Hare Krishna flophouse during the Haight-Ashbury heyday of the late 1960s. Sergio and Malina had laughed only hours earlier when they realized he used to live right next door to her house. He rang the buzzer, waited half a minute, and then rang again.

A pinprick of light appeared through the peephole in the solid oak door and then a dim porch light came on. He heard a woman's muffled voice from behind the door. "Sergio?"

"I need your help."

Several seconds passed before Malina spoke again, her voice sharper than before. "It's two thirty in the morning."

"I really need your help."

"Are you alone?"

"Yes," he said with a nod.

She unlatched two locks and pulled the door open until the security chain snapped taut. Malina peeked through the opening and her mouth dropped open.

"My God. Your face!"

She closed the door, unlatched the chain, and flung open the heavy door. Her thin cotton nightie clung to her athletic body as she reached for his hand and pulled him inside.

"You're shaking," she said. "What happened? Are you all right?"

"I think so. It's been a very strange night."

Malina led him to the kitchen and sat him down on a stool next to the sink. "I'll be back in a minute. Take off that shirt."

He looked down and for the first time noticed a glistening crimson stain on the front of his shirt. In an instant, throbbing pain spread across his face and his eyes watered. He extended his index finger and traced a crooked line along the bridge of his once-straight nose. He moaned in protest. "I think my nose is broken."

"Don't touch it," she said, returning to the kitchen with a red nylon medical bag. She slipped on a pair of latex gloves while he took off his shirt. She ran a dish towel under the hot-water tap and wiped the blood off his face and chest with quick efficient strokes.

"Let me take a look," she said with a professional demeanor and clinical voice. She tilted his head back and delicately probed the outside of his nose. She pulled out a small flashlight from her bag and inspected both nostrils for blockage. "Can you breathe okay?"

He nodded.

She released him. "Good. Looks like it's broken but nothing too serious. We're going to have to give it a few days to let the swelling go down and then we'll see what it looks like." She examined his jaw, cheekbones, and eye sockets for fractures. Then she pressed a stethoscope to his chest and took his pulse before switching on the flashlight once again and shining it into his pupils. She held up three fingers, then two, and finally four. Sergio gave the correct answers.

Malina handed him a bag of ice for his nose. "Here," she said, her voice more relaxed once she was satisfied he wasn't seriously injured. He gently held the ice pack to his nose. It felt cold but refreshingly soothing.

She spun a chair around and sat in front of him, her arms crossed on the backrest. "So what happened? And what does the other guy look like?"

"Not as bad as I do," he replied, forcing a weak smile.

She leaned toward him until they were face to face. "Does this have anything to do with your friend George?"

"I think so," he said. "But I'm not entirely sure."

"So why didn't you go to the police? What are you doing here?"

Sergio froze. He hadn't thought this through and now he wasn't sure what to share with her. "It's complicated."

Malina pulled back. "You already got me out of bed."

Sergio struggled to get a grip on the conflicting impulses clouding his fuzzy mind. It wasn't fair to draw her into whatever mess he was in. How could he even be sure he could trust her? Still, he wanted her help; he *needed* her help, at least to get him through the night. And somewhere deep inside, it didn't feel right to ask for help unless he leveled with her.

He regarded Malina, her eyebrows expectantly raised. Then he began, slowly at first but with building momentum, to retell the events of the past eighteen hours—from the moment he learned of the cyber-attack to the car chase that landed him on Malina's doorstep. "This was the only place I could think of where I'd be safe," he concluded.

Malina studied him carefully, her brow furrowed and lips pressed tightly together.

"Just until tomorrow morning," he quickly added. "Then I'll figure something else out. Please, I need your help."

"So I still don't understand why you didn't go to the police."

"Because I stole data. That's a felony." He covered his mouth with his hand, wondering if he could take back that word. "I also left the scene of an accident. I'd be arrested the second I showed up at a police station. And I'd probably wind up in jail until they arrange a bail hearing early next week."

"Why don't you just tell them what you found?"

"I don't know what I've found." He heard frustration in his voice. "At least, it's not clear to me it's illegal. Irregular, yes. Improper, probably. But illegal? I don't have any proof."

Malina's gaze dropped to the floor, like she was contemplating his story.

He pressed on. "Whatever George stumbled across, it seems rotten enough that whoever is behind it will stop at nothing to avoid getting caught."

She squinted. "To the point of murder?"

Put that way, it did seem far-fetched. Not your typical Silicon Valley storyline. But as much as he clung to the notion that social networking was a powerful force for good, he knew it was already big business—and it had the potential to become much, much bigger.

"Last year our CEO quietly gave financial institutions"—he held up his hands and hooked his fingers like quotation marks—"*greater insight* to their clients' Circles activity so the banks could better target customers. Now Circles users looking to buy a home or a car immediately get unsolicited loan offers from their banks—complete with tailored plans based on their assets. Deals are being worked out with network providers, insurance companies, retailers, carmakers. It's all collated, correlated, and sold. Our lives laid bare."

Malina's jaw tightened. "And you just went along with this?"

Sergio bowed his head. "Circles gets a tiny fraction, less than a quarter of a percent, from every mortgage that banks sell with the help of our user data. That doesn't sound like much, but with roughly two trillion dollars in new mortgages issued annually, we stand to generate five hundred million dollars in new revenue every year if we can funnel ten percent of all US mortgages through the social network."

Disdain was etched into Malina's face.

"The point is, there's a lot of money yet to be made at Circles. Opportunities that are counted in the tens of billions of dollars. People get killed for a lot less, sometimes even a pair of running shoes."

She rose from her chair and stepped back against the counter, facing him. She crossed her arms. "Why did you lie to me?"

His heart sank. "Huh?"

"You told me at the bar tonight that the crash was due to an internal error. Isn't that what you said?" Her tone was cool and composed but her eyes bored into him. "And now you're telling me Circles was attacked."

Sergio looked away for several long seconds. "I couldn't tell you about that then." He was angry at himself for what he was about to say. "Company policy."

"You lied to me," she said again, her voice sharper. "And now you come to me with this crazy story? Why should I believe you?"

Sergio's mouth went dry under her searching gaze. She was the only person he could trust at this moment, but only if she was able to trust him. She had every right to be mad and no good reason to help him, at least none his paralyzed brain could come up with. Eventually, he pieced together the only answer that rang true.

"Because I've told you the truth," he said. "And if I've learned anything about you tonight, it's that you don't shrink from the hard stuff."

He offered her two upturned palms. "So here I am."

-22-

Prederick sat across from Ko, a single lamp on the CTO's desk filling the void between them. The door to Ko's utilitarian office was closed and Prederick felt uncomfortably confined in such close quarters. But it was late at night and Ethan Burrard was almost certainly somewhere out in the main lab.

"Sergio's not coming," said Ko.

Prederick pulled off his glasses and rubbed his eyelids. "So what do you think he wants? Money?" He slipped his glasses back on. "Or do you think Sergio's having second thoughts about the auto-censoring software?"

"It's not the censoring software I'm worried about," said Ko.

"Meaning?"

"Meaning the situation is perhaps a bit more delicate than you realize," replied Ko.

Prederick cleared his throat. "Delicate in what way?"

A low gurgle filled the room, followed by the sharp click of Ko's electric kettle timing out. The CTO stood up, walked over to a small counter, and returned with a bamboo tray. He set it on his desk with a subtle smile. It held a small red clay teapot, three single-serving teacups, a set of utensils, a strainer, and a container full of dry twisted leaves.

"I checked the logs this afternoon. The hacker accessed my account. George followed his trail and discovered an unencrypted copy of a database of Chinese users that I was working on." Prederick saw Ko watching him closely, trying to gauge his reaction as he doled out additional details. "It's . . . awkward."

"We don't have Chinese users yet," Prederick countered. "I might not be able to code like you, but I sure as shit know that much."

Ko picked up a pair of tongs from the tray and carefully dropped gnarled leaves into the teapot. "Like I said, it's awkward."

"Spell it out."

"This is Iron Goddess," he said, holding up a single leaf for Prederick's perusal. "It's a very special Oolong tea from Fujian Province. It is considered one of the world's best teas. They say Oolong sharpens one's thinking skills and improves mental alertness."

Prederick pulled his glasses down his nose and glared at Ko over the rims. "I'd just as soon have Nestle Iced Tea."

Ko lifted the kettle and poured boiling water over the teapot to rinse it. "We've allowed China to run one hundred thousand socialbots on our network."

Prederick felt his jaw fall open, even though he couldn't quite make sense of what Ko was telling him.

"The Chinese insisted on it," Ko added, as he dropped tea leaves into the pot.

"For what?" demanded Prederick.

Ko poured more boiling water into the teapot until it overflowed. Then he put the lid on the pot. "So they can keep tabs on people."

"You mean *spy* on people." Prederick yanked his glasses from his face. "You're telling me that we agreed to let the Chinese authorities spy on our users? Who the hell made that decision?"

Ko stiffened. "I did," he said, with heavy emphasis on the "I."

Prederick sprang to his feet. "Who the fuck gave you the authority? We've spent the last several years trying to convince the public that we don't give our users' data to the NSA or any other agency. And now you strike a deal to do exactly that in China?" Prederick felt his face contort with rage. "If this gets out, Circles is fucked."

Ko tucked in his chin and waited for Prederick to finish yelling. Then he lifted his head. "Don't *you* realize we could never have convinced China to open its doors to us without this concession? I did this because I knew you'd be too gutless to agree. And without China, you can forget about your growth projections, your revenue forecasts, your share price targets, and your bonuses," he snapped. "Let's face it, Dan, I saved you from yourself."

Prederick couldn't quite believe what he was hearing. His CTO had always been quick to recommend, encourage, and at times insist on a specific course of action. But Ko had never pushed this far before; he'd never overstepped the line by openly challenging Prederick's authority. "And if I say 'no' to the spying?"

Ko poured the tea into three small cups. "First, we must wash the leaves. Only then will the flavor of the tea come out." He then emptied the cups, allowing the tea to spill onto the teapot, flow through tiny slits in the tray, and settle in the drain pan below.

"Pouring the tea onto the pot keeps it hot," he said. "As for your question, you can kiss China good-bye. They would be none too pleased. And I wouldn't be surprised if a story leaks out saying we have socialbot software that enables us to spy on our users."

"You bastard," Prederick seethed.

Ko pulled back and held his hands apart, palms open, like a gunslinger showing he was unarmed. "We're on the same side here, Dan. Some tea?"

"You know damn well I don't like tea."

Ko raised the electric kettle once again, but this time he held it high in the air as he poured in a tiny circular motion until the clay pot overflowed. He replaced the lid and squeezed a little more water out of the pot.

"Look, we're not going to operate the socialbots," he said, adopting the persuasive polish of a salesman. "We developed the software in-house only to ensure it won't raise flags or trigger any of our alarms. Once we hand over the socialbot command-and-control software to the Chinese, we'll have plausible deniability. We will be able to assert, in legal documents and sworn statements if necessary, that we do not under any circumstances provide user information to authorities in China."

Prederick looked upward as he rubbed his chin. Plausible deniability. A singularly powerful concept.

"We wouldn't be doing anything that everyone else operating in China isn't already doing. Those are the rules of the game there. And if you want in . . ."

Prederick held up his hand to stop Ko. He'd made his point. Circles needed China much more than China needed Circles. And it would be easy enough to evade responsibility, especially when they were talking about a country as opaque as China. But that did little to ease the sting of Ko's insubordination.

Ko poured more tea, this time moving back and forth between the two cups in a swift fluid motion so they filled simultaneously. "For once, I insist that you join me."

Ko picked up one of the cups and offered it to Prederick. "Pouring tea for someone is a sign of respect. Young people show piety for their elders by offering them a cup of tea. And at work, an employee should be so honored to have the opportunity to serve it to his boss."

Prederick looked long and hard at Ko before he reluctantly held out his hand. He accepted the cup, took a sip, and winced. The tea tasted sour, like he knew it would.

Prederick leaned back in the chair and silently massaged the back of his neck. Circles had just suffered its worst crash ever, one employee was dead, and another was running around with a thumb drive full of data that could sink the company and personally cost him millions of dollars. When he finally spoke, he did so softly.

"So where do we stand with Sergio?"

"I've already locked him out," Ko said, as if he'd been anticipating the question. "He can't get into the building or log on to the network. We just need to make sure he's muzzled before he can raise embarrassing questions about our China strategy, if that's his game."

"We need to call the FBI."

"No," replied Ko. He lifted the teapot and nodded at Prederick's full cup. "We risk losing control of the situation if we bring them in."

Prederick covered his cup with his hand. "We've already lost control. Sergio has a drive full of data that can crush us. And we don't have any idea what he's going to do." He stood and paced in tiny circles. "We need their help. We need to get him in custody." Prederick stopped, faced Ko, and rested his hands on his hips. It was the right decision. "I know the head of the FBI's cyber unit. I trust him a lot more than I trust Sergio."

Ko poured himself another cup. "I don't like it."

"Do you have a better idea?"

Ko took a sip but said nothing.

"We can tell them we've developed all those socialbots to test our latest security software," said Prederick. "They don't need to know any more than that."

Ko set down his cup and gave a single nod. "They don't need to know any more than—"

The familiar somber notes from Prederick's mobile phone filled the room. He studied the incoming number and lifted the handset to his ear. "What is it?"

"It's Harton, in the bunker," blurted the voice at the other end of the line. "You're not going to believe this."

"Believe what?" asked Prederick.

"The Mansour audit. It looks like there is a whole other side to Sergio we never knew. Turns out he's got some pretty unsavory friends, the kind you'd find at the top of a most-wanted list."

-23-

The limo driver raced along the service road and cut under the express-way before doubling back to the vast cargo terminal on the other side of Shanghai Pudong International Airport. Liu checked his watch as he gripped the leather satchel under his right arm. Fifteen minutes before the shipment went out. He couldn't have cut it any closer.

The situation with the United States had grown ominous. American investments in cyberwarfare were starting to pose a real threat to China's expansionist ambitions. Chinese intelligence also predicted the US was poised to dramatically step up military spending in Asia and strengthen defense ties with Taiwan, Thailand, and Malaysia. Even his old friend Diebolt had piled on, surpassing Lester with inflammatory speeches that actively fueled the growing chorus of anti-China sentiment. Worst of all, the Department of Energy had finalized its proposal to stimu-late the US rare earth industry as a counterweight to China. With both houses of Congress unusually unified on this issue, the bill was likely to become law no matter who became president. Liu could not afford to ignore the risk.

The limo glided to a halt outside the Arrow Logistics cargo office. Liu stepped out of the car, his satchel in hand and his daughter's old pink

Hello Kitty daypack slung over his shoulder. Then he dialed his phone. "I'm here."

Moments later a squat man emerged from the employee entrance and waved Liu in. They exchanged silent nods and Liu fell in behind as they marched into a vast warehouse, where row upon row of aluminum shelves towered above them like a giant skeleton reaching for the corrugated roof. Hulking robot cranes rode rails up and down the aisles picking up or depositing pallets and aircraft cargo containers. Workers in forklifts zipped past, but no one took notice of the two men. They entered a small meeting room near the warehouse control center. A single cardboard box sat on a table. Liu noted the shipping address and scribbled down the tracking and serial numbers. He nodded in approval.

The Arrow boss sliced open the carton and removed a new computer from the box. Liu unlatched his satchel and produced his laptop, the same model as the computer from the box. The squat man wrapped the cord, sealed Liu's machine in packing plastic, and cradled it in Styrofoam molds. He put Liu's computer in the box and sealed it with Lenovo packing tape, carefully making sure the company logos on the top layer of tape rested exactly on the logos below. The Arrow manager worked quickly, as if he'd done this many times before. Then he handed Liu the computer from the box.

Liu followed the squat man out into the warehouse and watched him insert the box into a stack of boxes on a plastic pallet. He secured the cardboard boxes to the pallet with blue packing straps and wrapped the entire pallet with clear shrink wrap. Liu looked around; he was surrounded by scores of pallets packed with Lenovo computers, hundreds if not thousands of machines, all wrapped with identical blue bands and clear shrink wrap, all awaiting shipment to the US.

He smiled. There was almost no chance US customs officials would happen upon his particular machine. Bulk X-rays wouldn't reveal anything out of the ordinary. Even close up, the box looked the same as the others. The odds of anything going wrong were infinitesimal and it was far safer than trying to carry the laptop into the US himself. He was important enough in China to be of interest to US officials, but he lacked the diplomatic status necessary to bypass border inspections. He'd been stopped by customs many times in the past; they always insisted on reviewing his computer—and had every right to. He couldn't afford to take a risk like that, not this time.

The Arrow boss turned to Liu and clasped his hands in front of him. "Is everything good?" he asked with an air of finality. He might just as well have said *pay me.*

Liu laid his satchel on the floor and the two men crouched down, each looking past the other to make sure they were alone. Liu slipped the pink daypack off his shoulder and unzipped it to reveal ten bricks of cash, each consisting of one hundred 100-yuan bills—a total of one hundred thousand yuan, or about sixteen thousand dollars. It was chump change considering the billions of dollars at stake.

The Arrow boss bowed his head in a curt nod of gratitude. He took the bag from Liu and gestured toward the exit. The two men walked silently. No questions had been asked and none would have been answered if they had. Liu had one final detail to confirm.

"When will it get there?"

"It's a rush shipment. It should get through US customs by tomorrow afternoon. It will arrive at Circles on Monday morning."

-24-

A thin slice of morning light streaked between the curtains and hit Sergio in the face. He rolled over, half awake, and struggled to get his bearings. Sagging cushions. The sound of running water. The distant clanking of dishes. His throbbing nose.

He opened his eyes. A droning newscaster stared back at him from the TV. He jolted upward, unsure of where he was. Then it hit him. The sofa at Malina's. George was dead. Someone wanted him dead, too. He stared at the ceiling as a deep mournful sigh escaped his lips.

"Good morning." Malina stood in the kitchen doorway, still dressed in her clingy nightgown. Her voice was perky but not quite cheerful.

Sergio averted his gaze. He didn't trust himself to not stare. "Good morning," he croaked.

"Sleep well?"

He probed his face. His nose felt tender and puffy. "I could use a few more hours." He'd slept fitfully, his hyperactive brain at odds with his exhausted body. He wanted to go back to sleep, but didn't have that luxury. He needed to sort out the mess he was in. "Do you have any coffee?"

"Almost ready," she said as she disappeared into the kitchen.

Sergio looked under the blanket. He wore a T-shirt and boxer shorts.

His jeans were draped over the armchair across the room. He sat up and pulled the blanket across his lap. He stretched his arms skyward and swiveled his head in a slow deliberate motion as he looked around the cozy room. A large statue of the Indian elephant-headed god Ganesh stood prominently in one corner. Paintings from China, batiks from Indonesia, and a collection of wooden masks, probably from Africa, hung from the walls. A bookshelf covered the wall to the left of the sofa. Soft sunlight infused the room, the stillness disrupted only by the TV anchorman's bobbing head.

Malina came out of the kitchen with two mugs of coffee and a bag of ice. She set the tray on the coffee table and bent over to take a closer look at Sergio's nose.

"How does it look?"

"You have some bruising under the eyes, but that's normal. There's not much you can do about it at this point. Does it hurt?"

"A little."

She handed him the bag of ice. "Here, use this. It'll help keep the swelling down."

He managed a soft smile. "Thank you." He pressed the ice against the puffy flesh around his left eye. The pressure hurt but the coolness felt good. "And thanks for last night. I'm sorry for putting all that on you."

She sat down in the armchair and reached for her coffee. "You needed help." She met his gaze. "So what are you going to do now?"

The anchorman faded to black and a ruggedly handsome man on horseback took over the TV. Snow-capped peaks rose in the distance.

Sergio shook his head. "Hell if I know. I have to figure out who that guy was last night and whether he's working for Ko. Then I need to find out what Ko is going to do with all those socialbots."

"What do you *think* he's going to do?"

Sergio shrugged. "Criminals use socialbots to scam and steal from our users. I'm guessing that whatever he's doing, it can't be good."

"Go to the police."

Sergio waved her off. "They're not going to take my word for it. Not if Circles is pressing charges. They're going to arrest me and hold me for the weekend until I can get bail. I won't be able to do anything about this from inside."

"If you don't go to the police, you could be dead by tomorrow."

He heard urgency in her voice but he pretended not to notice. "Not if he doesn't find me."

Malina pulled back, doubt and concern stamped on her face.

"No, no," he said. "I don't mean here. I'm not asking to stay here."

"What about your brother?"

Sergio shook his head. "He'd probably slam the door in my face."

She leaned in and whispered in a conspiratorial tone. "Somewhere abroad?"

Was she trying to help or get rid of him? "No. I can't take any chances crossing a border."

A beep sounded in the distance. Malina stood and moved through the dining room toward the kitchen. "Want some breakfast?" she called out over her shoulder.

"That would be great," he answered, thinking about the Reuben he never got to finish.

She disappeared into the kitchen and Sergio sunk back into the sofa, turning his head to the left to work out a kink in his neck. He scanned the novels and travel guides on the shelves, taking extra time to study a handful of framed photos propped up in front of the books. There was Malina in a warm embrace with a man, a significant other, no doubt. A couple of photos featured several elderly people, most likely her parents and a family friend or two. In the fourth frame was a college-aged woman with a fresh face and a purple streak in her long platinum hair. She sat in the driver's seat of a convertible Beetle, its top down, looking over her left shoulder and staring straight at the camera with a smile.

But her big brown eyes suggested a different story. Sergio twisted his body and leaned over the side of the sofa so he could study the photo more closely. He sensed an air of impatience, as if the young woman was merely trying to placate whoever was taking the picture. More powerful was the sadness—maybe even loneliness—that her eyes projected. Something about her gaze was disturbingly familiar, like he knew her somehow. Or maybe those sad eyes were a haunting reminder of his pain all those years ago.

The voice on TV pulled him from his reverie with two upsetting words: "George Verneek." Sergio spun around to the talking head, who now shared the screen with Circles' corporate logo in the top left corner. Sergio reached for the remote and turned up the volume.

". . . was killed last night in his garage. Now Circles is saying the crash might have been caused by an attack launched by Verneek and another Circles employee," the anchorman said. "And here is where the story really gets strange . . ."

Launched by Verneek?

Malina appeared in the kitchen door. "Do you want cereal? Eggs? Toast?"

Sergio lifted his head for a brief instant before footage of George's house flashed on the screen. It was dark and an ambulance stood in his driveway. Two paramedics wheeled a stretcher into the open garage. Last night. Sergio's stomach churned as he imagined George's bullet-riddled body. His face grew hot; someone at Circles wanted to pin the cyberattack on his friend—now conveniently dead and unable to defend himself. It was simply absurd. There was no way he'd launched the attack. *George deserved better than this.*

He looked to Malina. "Cereal is fine."

She nodded and slipped back into the kitchen. The anchorman reappeared. "CNN has learned that the other employee under investigation is Sergio Mansour." A photo of him filled the screen. It was the same picture on his ID badge. He felt his face go slack and his brain wobble. "Mansour and Verneek were senior executives at the company and had worked closely together for the past fifteen years. Authorities are trying to determine whether the cyberattack and Verneek's murder are related."

Malina called out something from the kitchen.

"Uh, sure," he mumbled.

The anchorman continued. "It is unclear what prompted Verneek and Mansour to allegedly attack Circles, although CNN has learned Mansour has links to Lebanon and recently made repeated trips to the Middle Eastern country." His mind reeled and his stomach felt queasy. "One source said law enforcement authorities would be looking into his background to determine whether Mansour had ties to any terrorist organizations. Mansour's whereabouts at this time are unknown . . ."

Sergio rose unsteadily to his feet and leaned toward the TV, waiting for the talking head to clarify—no, take back—his words. His achy head was now a throbbing mass of raw nerves that reached deep into his roiled-up gut. The anchorman kept talking but his remarks no longer registered. All Sergio heard, over and over, were those words echoing in his ears. *Ties to any terrorist organizations.*

Images of "enemy combatants" in orange jumpsuits filled his mind. They were shackled with chains, cut off from the world by blindfolds and earmuffs. He recalled footage of dark interrogation rooms at Guantanamo Bay, empty except for those solitary chairs surrounded by chains bolted to the floor. Loudspeakers cranking heavy metal. The waterboarding.

Malina returned carrying a tray of toast, peanut butter, and jam. "Here we . . ." She stopped in her tracks. "What's wrong?"

Sergio froze, awkwardly exposed, like someone had just cast a spotlight on him. Then he dropped to the sofa, lifted the blanket from the floor, and pulled it across his lap.

"You look like you've seen a ghost. Everything okay?"

Sergio stared at her—stared through her—as he fought to steady himself against the torrent of emotions pummeling him. Shock gave way to disbelief, which in turn quickly succumbed to anguish. But those were merely placeholders for the anger, outrage, and sheer terror that quickly gripped him. And through it all, he continued to stare at Malina. What was he supposed to say?

"They think I'm a terrorist," he said weakly, as he pointed to the TV.

Malina set the tray on the coffee table and turned to the TV just as the anchorman faded from the screen. A cheerful elderly woman appeared and took a long blissful sip from a Coke bottle before smiling into the camera.

"What?" asked Malina in an incredulous voice.

"They think I'm a terrorist."

She cocked her head and squinted. "*Who* thinks you're a terrorist?"

Sergio grappled with the question. Did the anchorman say the police were after him? Or was it the authorities? Maybe he just said the government. Sergio couldn't remember now. All he could be sure of was that chilling phrase: *Ties to any terrorist organizations.*

"I dunno," he mumbled. "The police."

"Wait, wait, wait. Why do the police think you are a terrorist?"

"I don't know," he said. "All I know is what I heard that guy just say." He pressed his hands to his face and tried to wipe away the mounting stress. Suspected terrorists had no rights before those all-powerful, yet highly secret, military tribunals. *I'll disappear down a dark hole if they ever catch me.* He turned his gaze to the TV. "They showed a picture of George. They said we sabotaged Circles and that I'm wanted for questioning in George's murder. Then they said I have ties to terrorist organizations."

"Why would they think that?"

"I don't know," he snapped, maybe a bit too defensively. He looked up at Malina hovering over him. "I'm not, you know."

"You're not what?"

"I'm not a terrorist." He pounded his knees with his fists. "Jesus Christ."

"Okay, okay." She eyed him cautiously as she sat down on the arm of the sofa. She reached for the remote control in his hands. "Let's see if the other stations have anything."

She began to flip through Saturday morning cartoons, infomercials, and college pre-game shows, stopping whenever a newscast came up. None of them had the story.

Sergio pressed his fingertips into his eye sockets. It was only a matter of time before the police triangulated his phone, searched his emails, and traced his bank account and credit cards. Agents would pore over his electronic address book and online profiles to identify friends and family he might turn to for help. They'd search for his car and splash his photo all over the news. He was pretty much fucked.

He stood and reached for his pants. "I need to get out of here, out of San Francisco, fast."

He pulled up his jeans and sat back down to slip on his shoes. "I need to borrow—no, buy—I'll buy your car. I'll get you a new one as soon as this is over. You can say I stole it if you need to."

She looked at him sideways. "Just like that? Give you my car?"

Sergio nodded.

"For what?"

"To stop him." He was back on his feet, looking for his jacket.

"Who? Ko?"

He nodded. "Yes, Ko. Or whoever else is behind this."

"What do you mean, stop him? How?"

"I don't know yet." He pulled on his jacket. "I don't know what's going on and I'm not sure exactly how George's murder is tied into all this. But I *do* know that Ko is behind all those socialbots." He moved to the window, peeled back the curtain, and scanned the quiet street. "So that's where I need to start."

"Maybe you should go to the media with all this." Her eyes lit up. "Tell them all about the socialbots."

"Maybe," he replied, a little too quickly. There had to be some other way to stop Ko without putting Circles, and his own personal fortune, at risk. He turned to face her. "I need some time to think about this first. Do you have any cash?"

Malina studied him silently and he met her gaze. *I'm the good guy,* he silently repeated to himself, hoping somehow to project this simple truth. He felt her piercing stare pore over his face, look into his eyes, and penetrate his soul. Then her eyes flashed as she pulled back her shoulders and lifted her chin. "A bit," she replied. "I keep about two thousand dollars on hand just in case of an earthquake. We can get more from an ATM."

"*We* are not doing anything." He peeled back the curtain again and surveyed the street. "I'm in big shit. I can't drag you into this."

"You won't be able to use your car, your cards, your phone. How are you going to get around without money? Where are you going to stay?"

"I'll figure something out." He glanced at the TV. Wile E. Coyote had just skidded off a towering cliff and come to a halt in midair. He looked to the audience for an impossibly long moment, his face the picture of consternation. And then with a puff of smoke, he was gone. "I'm in big trouble—and serious danger."

"You need my help—"

"They'll put two and two together and you'll be just as screwed as me."

"How are they going to know?" she demanded. "You said last night that you came here specifically because there's nothing to tie us together."

"Last night I was worried about Circles. Now I'm thinking about the police. One of the first things they're going to do is check my phone records and see that I called you at the hospital."

"The number on my card is the main ER number. We get thousands of calls a day and they get patched into dozens of extensions, many of which are accessible to probably a hundred doctors, nurses, and staffers at any given time. There's no way they'll know you called *me.*"

Sergio regarded her silently for a moment and then turned away, running his hand through his hair as his gaze darted around the room. Bolts of pain fired through his skull. Jumbled images of George flashed in his mind. The weight of despair pressed down on him until Sergio felt helpless and utterly alone.

He steadied himself against the bookcase for a few seconds. Maybe she *could* help him, give him a head start, get him out of the city. But that would be wrong. He gazed at the photos on the shelf; the people who knew her and loved her. He couldn't put her at risk. Sergio turned to face her. "I have to do this alone. Getting you involved doesn't make sense."

She shook her head vigorously. "Sense? Don't talk to me about making sense." Her eyes were full of defiance. "The most sensible thing I can do right now is call the cops."

Sergio recoiled from the suggestion. Why were they even having this discussion? Anyone else would have been running as far away from him as they could. Something wasn't right. "Why are you doing this?"

"Because Circles uses people. It sucks them in, exposes them, and puts them at risk, all for the sake of money." She challenged him with determined eyes. "The more people realize that the better. And there's no better person to prove it than someone like you."

Sergio massaged his temples. Didn't she understand what was going on here? This was no time for some stupid crusade. He bit his tongue, fearful he might say something he'd later regret. Their eyes met in a clash of wills, but as the seconds silently ticked by, Sergio began to understand the argument was already over.

"You need my help," she finally said, her voice cool and collected. "You don't get to set the terms."

Her words sucked out whatever resistance Sergio had left in him. He needed her help—her cash and car—and he needed it now. She was part of the bargain, whether he liked it or not. He could deal with her later, once they were out of San Francisco.

-25-

Jay Feeley strode across Circles' soaring atrium and approached reception. He was in his late thirties, but his boyish features, freckles, and short red hair made him look ten years younger. Clad in jeans, a T-shirt, and a soft shell jacket, he could easily have been mistaken for just another lanky twenty-something employee. He pulled up to the desk and flashed his FBI shield. "Special Agent Feeley. I'm here to see Prederick."

He was in a shitty mood. Plans for a long weekend in Tahoe had been dashed by a six a.m. phone call from Washington. There was trouble at Circles. The complaint initiated in DC and was pushed down to the San Francisco field office—all in a matter of hours. Cybercrime cases hardly ever started at the top and the agency almost never moved that quickly.

Based on the quick briefing Feeley had received, it sounded like one of the oddest cases to hit Silicon Valley since, well, ever. But Christ, he hated it when Washington took a keen interest in an investigation, particularly since that ass-kisser Preston Garrison had been promoted to run the Cyber Crime unit. Everyone knew Garrison had weaseled his way up the ranks, often taking credit for his colleagues' work. Feeley now did his best to steer clear of the division director as much as possible.

Making things worse, some asshole at Circles had leaked the story. It was already the top news item, and Feeley hadn't even met with the company. Garrison would be all over him to make sure the FBI didn't lose control of this one. Feeley's every move and decision would be scrutinized and possibly second-guessed by Garrison.

Feeley took the elevator to the second floor, where an assistant ushered him into Prederick's corner office. Prederick rose to shake Feeley's hand and offered him a chair.

"Thanks for coming, Jay," Prederick said.

The two men had met many times before, usually at meetings between top tech companies and law enforcement. The two sides regularly sat down to discuss strategies for defending the nation's critical infrastructure and share intelligence on the latest cyberthreats. Prederick made a point of showing up even though Circles also had a designated rep. This gesture was well received by agents in the FBI and other agencies.

Prederick motioned toward Ko seated on the sofa along the wall. "Do you know Victor Ko? He's our CTO and runs Labs."

Ko never bothered to attend meetings with law enforcement. He nodded at Feeley but didn't get up.

"I have to admit," said Prederick, anxiously rubbing his hands together, "I'm a bit surprised you made it so quickly."

"Apparently not quickly enough to prevent leaks."

"We didn't—"

Feeley held up his hand like a cop stopping traffic. "The FBI sure as hell didn't leak this. Hell, we haven't even started our investigation. You better find out who's talking and *shut them up.*"

Prederick acknowledged Feeley's point with a respectful nod but kept silent.

Feeley finally spoke again. "Okay, so start from the beginning."

Prederick detailed the previous day's events. He paused a couple of times, turning to Ko for confirmation of technical details before continuing his story. Feeley had seen this dynamic play out many times before, but there was something unusual about the body language between the two men. Technical experts, when given an opening, usually took the opportunity to expand upon their CEO's comments. It was often a point of pride, a moment to strut their stuff. Ko, however, didn't seem the least bit interested in contributing to the conversation. It was almost as if Prederick was trying to impress Ko.

"So what did the attackers get?"

Prederick shrugged. "All encrypted by the attacker. We can't be sure."

Feeley rolled his eyes. There was no way Prederick would have called Garrison in DC if he wasn't certain they'd suffered a grave loss, one that could cripple operations, expose them to legal liability, or give competitors a detailed look at critical intellectual property. Tech companies were loath to reveal secrets to anyone, even the FBI, and so the silly game had to be played out.

"What do you *fear* they might have stolen?" Feeley's voice carried a hint of exasperation. His wife and kids were probably halfway to Tahoe by now.

Ko lifted his lanky body from the couch. "As you know, we've been waging an arms race against socialbots. Hackers use these programs to create and control tens of thousands of fake Circles profiles. Much of it is nuisance stuff, but some sophisticated criminals have figured out how to use these fake profiles to scam real users."

Ko spoke in an erudite tone, setting context before shifting to the matter at hand. "So suppose we've been experimenting with our own socialbot software. The idea would be to get ahead of the bad guys and figure out how to protect our network from next-generation socialbots. But there was a problem, hypothetically. What if the socialbot software we came up with worked too well? What if it was so advanced that we were unable to develop defenses agile and quick enough to keep up with it?"

Feeley frowned. "You've created a monster you can't control?"

"That's not how I would put it," Ko replied. "But if something like that fell into the hands of a foreign government or a criminal gang, we'd have huge issues. They could use it to infiltrate our social network and target our users, potentially exposing them to hundreds of millions or even billions of dollars in scams."

Ko paced back and forth across the office, his hands cupped together as he spoke with the clipped tone of an impatient professor. "That would erode user confidence, spook advertisers, and devastate shareholders," he concluded.

"And the national security implications?" asked Feeley.

"Potentially numerous," continued Ko. "We know Al-Qaeda, Hezbollah, ISIS, and scores of other groups already control thousands of Circles accounts. It's not easy, but we manage to keep pretty good tabs on them based on IP subnets, behavioral patterns, and the like. That's today."

Ko stopped pacing and spun toward Feeley. His eyes lit up as he continued. "But suppose the bad guys used this software to create millions of fake accounts on Circles. As it stands, we'd have no idea those accounts were socialbots. The randomization algorithms in the software are that good. So not only would the FBI, CIA, or NSA have to somehow identify all those fake accounts, but because there'd be so many, you guys would have to decipher which of the millions were being used to actually send messages and which ones were decoys." Ko's eyebrows shot up and he rubbed his hands together. "You think there's a lot of background noise now?"

Feeley regarded Ko warily. He couldn't tell whether the CTO was proud of his software or anxious about its potential misuse. "If the intruder encrypted everything, what makes you so sure he got your socialbot software?"

Ko stepped forward. "The hacker got into our Labs servers when I was working on the software. It was unencrypted at the time. Bad luck."

Feeley couldn't keep a thin smile from slipping across his face. "They got into Labs?"

"Not so hard for an inside job," Ko replied in a stiff voice.

"Our initial report says Verneek downloaded the software onto a thumb drive." Feeley raised a single eyebrow. "Isn't that a surefire way to bring attention to oneself?"

Prederick removed his glasses. "Verneek disabled the alarms. I'm guessing he didn't figure on being audited."

"And the thumb drive?"

Prederick handed Feeley two eight-by-ten high-resolution photos. "We just got these stills, taken from our surveillance video in the security bunker."

Feeley glanced at an image of George Verneek with his hand in the bowl of M&M's. He flipped to the second photo—a shot of Sergio Mansour reaching into the same dish of candies.

"The video clearly shows Verneek burying the thumb drive in his M&M's," continued Prederick. "Mansour retrieved it several hours later. We'll give you the entire sequence, of course."

"Of course," said Feeley with a nod. "What about those emails?"

Prederick handed Feeley printed copies of two messages from the day before. They were flagged by a monitoring program that scanned Circles for suspicious emails, instant messages, profile updates, phone calls, or videos. Any communication that contained specific keywords, or moved among certain user profiles or email addresses was immediately flagged. In this case, it was the recipient's email address.

```
>>IP: 435.448.335

>>13:21:54

>>To: bijouniKR1@ajipar.com

>>From: sMansour@circles.com

>>Subject: Cmpltd. NRt.
```

Prederick gave Feeley just enough time to scan the message before continuing. "BijouniKR1 at ajipar.com is on the watch list."

Feeley recognized the address. The FBI, CIA, and NSA routinely provided Internet companies like Circles with a list of email addresses and social media accounts the agencies believed were linked to criminal and terrorist suspects. BijouniKR1 was an alias the CIA believed was used by the leadership of Hezbollah, the Lebanese terrorist group funded by Iran. The actual message was blank, but the subject line said it all: "Completed. En route."

Feeley pointed at the time stamp. "This went out early yesterday afternoon. Why are we only just hearing of it?"

"We're not sure," said Ko. "Our software is supposed to flag suspect traffic immediately, but this message wasn't caught until we compiled the usual end-of-day summary at midnight. Best guess, yesterday's attack may have somehow interfered with the flagging tool."

Feeley flipped to the second message.

```
>>IP: 435.448.335

>>12:32:51

>>To: bijouniKR1@ajipar.com

>>From: gVerneek@circles.com

>>Subject: Cmpltd.
```

It was the critical piece of evidence Feeley needed. Verneek's murder was being investigated by SFPD as a simple homicide case. But the surveillance video linking Mansour and Verneek to the stolen thumb drive and a known terrorist email address was all he needed to take over the entire case. Garrison would insist on it.

Feeley frowned. "Mansour and Verneek must have known we'd see these." There was much more that didn't make sense to Feeley. Not only was it unusual for someone of Mansour's background to consort with terrorists, but it was almost unheard of for two accomplished professionals to go down that road together.

"I've wondered about Sergio ever since I took over his job." It was as if Ko had read the skepticism on Feeley's face. "Dan thought I was being ridiculous, but people have egos and his was definitely bruised."

Feeley waited for him to continue.

"I told Dan to let him go, but he insisted Mansour's expertise was still worthy. Dan also thought pushing him out would be bad for company morale." Ko shot Prederick a snide look.

"That's not a good reason to sell out to fundamentalists," intoned Feeley. "What about Verneek?"

"Even less obvious," acknowledged Prederick.

Ko sat back down on the sofa. "I'm certain your investigation will turn up some sort of motive in due course." He pulled open a *New York Times* with a crisp snap. He laid it across his lap and eyed Feeley impatiently.

Feeley bit down hard on his jaw. Ko's arrogance was legendary and Feeley could now see why. He addressed Prederick. "Any idea where he might go? Family? Close friends?"

"His parents are dead, I think," Prederick replied. "Verneek was his only close friend that I know of. I seem to recall someone saying he made a lot of trips to Lebanon a few years back. I think he's part Arab or Muslim or something like that, but I didn't think much of it at the time."

-26-

Sinon lifted the mug to his nose and drew in the bracing aroma of coffee. He took a tentative sip—the coffee was freshly brewed—and set the mug down next to his keyboard. He clenched his jaw, fighting off a yawn until he could no longer. He'd slept four hours. Yesterday had been a long day.

He checked the clock. It was eight thirty in the morning and Circles' weekend employees were about to start showing up. He couldn't be sure whether Julian Cahill would come in this Saturday, but someone would be on hand to manage the network operations team's weekend crew. Sinon leaned into his computer and opened a new window. He punched in a series of pre-set commands and watched with relief as sixteen small images, laid out in four rows of four, flickered on his screen.

He took a sip of coffee, now at his preferred temperature, as he tapped the right arrow key and another thirteen images popped up on his monitor. Sinon smiled slyly as he scrutinized the real-time feeds from Circles' twenty-nine high-definition indoor security cameras. He clicked on them one by one, expanding each image to full screen size so he could read the text in the top right corner of each frame that identified the location of the camera. As he toggled through the feeds, Sinon made a note of camera #6 in the security bunker and then flipped to camera #8 in the network operations pod. Using his keyboard, Sinon aimed the camera at Cahill's desk in the center of the cluster. He zoomed in, isolating the workstation and then the desktop until Sinon could read the letters on Cahill's keyboard.

When Cahill, or whoever was duty manager, sat down at the center desk, he would be asked to type in his company ID number or, perhaps, the last four digits of his social security number. Once he did that, he would be asked to enter a new password. He would be encouraged to make his password as difficult as possible—upper and lower case letters, with at least one number and one symbol, the @ symbol perhaps. He'd have to type it twice; it was standard procedure. Only then would the network operations team leader—and Sinon—be able to get back to work.

-27-

Liu Ting Wei stepped through the front door of his penthouse apartment and moved directly to the liquor cabinet. He pulled out a bottle of Midleton Irish Whiskey and poured a generous serving into a tulip-shaped glass. He swirled the whiskey and brought the glass to his nose. It had a delicate aroma: earthy and slightly fruity. Then he savored a long sip. It had been a very tiring but worthwhile day. He deserved it.

He ambled into the living room, his cell phone in hand, and dialed a number very few people had. The international circuits clicked and rings filled the line. He hoped his timing would be right.

"Hello?"

"Good morning, Richard," said Liu, his accent still crisp some forty years after his studies in London.

"Ting Wei! What a great surprise. It is always a pleasure to hear your voice."

"Likewise, my friend, likewise. I've been watching your poll numbers. You look more unbeatable by the day."

"Be careful. You know what we say about chickens and eggs."

The two men shared a hearty long-distance laugh.

"Nonetheless, you must be feeling quite good about your chances," replied Liu. "How is Amy?"

"She's doing very well, holding up to the pressures of the campaign. I tell you, Ting Wei, I couldn't have done it without her. And how are Lihua and the kids?"

Liu stepped into the kitchen and found his wife pressed up against the doorframe in her nightgown. Her eyebrows arched expectantly; it was her way of asking whether he needed anything. Liu shook his head and gently nudged her toward the hall to the bedroom. She was a good wife and a wonderful mother to his girls.

"She is well and the kids, you should see them now. Mei Mei started her first year at Peking University and Ye Ying is getting ready for her exams next year."

"Excellent. Wonderful. So good to hear." There was a moment of silence, a break from the formalities. "So to what do I owe the pleasure of this call?"

Liu stepped to the sliding glass doors in the living room and beheld the lights far below. A brisk wind had pushed out the smog; he couldn't remember the last time he'd seen Baotou sparkle so vibrantly. Hidden among the lights were the city's tired buildings, its crumbling infrastructure, and the toxic industrial stew that poisoned the rivers and fouled the air. Baotou, for once, looked serene and beautiful, if just for a few hours. He cleared his throat.

"I've been following the campaign very closely, Richard," he said in a deliberate cadence. "Many of us in the Party are concerned by what we're hearing."

He did not need to explain. Diebolt was fully aware of Liu's party membership and of his close ties to China's elite.

"Rhetoric about China was bound to get more heated as the campaign intensified," replied Diebolt. "The concern about China among voters is palpable, Ting Wei. We cannot ignore it and neither should you."

"This has moved far beyond mere rhetoric, Richard," he said with an austere tone. "You have created such a panic among voters that the next president will have to act against China." He paused to let his words sink in. "I can't allow that."

The conversation fell into an uncomfortably long pause before Diebolt finally spoke, graciously but evasively. "Ting Wei, one of the reasons we've remained good friends all these years is that we have looked forward with a common vision. I will be counting on our friendship to help smooth things over between the US and China as we move on from the election."

Liu stepped away from the window with a smile. Diebolt was rattled, even if he wasn't showing it. "I look forward to that," replied Liu. "In fact, I would be honored to be there with you on Tuesday . . . if that doesn't present any problems for you."

The conversation skipped another beat.

"Of course," replied Diebolt. "I would love for you to attend. I owe you a great deal, Ting Wei, and I have not forgotten. Your presence would be most fitting. I'm only sorry I didn't think of it myself. I will make the appropriate arrangements."

"Excellent, Richard," replied Liu. "I wouldn't miss it for the world."

-28-

The garage door swung open and Malina eased her Tesla Cruiser into the crisp morning air. Sergio sat in the passenger seat, her oversized Prada sunglasses perched delicately across his nose. He hunched down as they scanned the quiet street for anything out of the ordinary.

"No cops," she said.

"No Chrysler," he replied. He waited for an approaching car to pass and waved her forward. "Looks clear."

They skirted the main Haight-Ashbury drag and drove into Golden Gate Park, taking a right on the quiet one-way road behind the Conservatory of Flowers. "Pull over here," he said. Sergio jumped out, looked around, and hurled his cell phone into the bushes. The cops would eventually track it down and recover it. They'd also know he spent the night somewhere in the Haight. In hindsight, he should have just left it in the Range Rover.

Five minutes later Malina pulled into a parking spot in front of a sandwich shop on Clement Street; the area was home to a mishmash of Asian restaurants, pizza parlors, coffeehouses, and stores in the city's Richmond district. He stayed in the car and watched her withdraw five hundred dollars from a Citibank ATM, the highest they dared go for fear of raising unwanted attention. Combined with her emergency cash from home and the few hundred dollars in his pocket, they had a total of two thousand, seven hundred and eighty-four dollars.

She strolled down the block and gave him a knowing look before stepping inside Bruno's Electronics, a small repair shop that also bought and sold used equipment. Bruno handled all deals and repairs himself. He dealt exclusively in cash and transactions were untraceable. It was just the kind of place Sergio needed right now.

Minutes slipped by as slowly as the people who ambled past on the sidewalk: Asian families, clusters of millennials, and elderly couples, all enjoying a leisurely Saturday morning on Clement. English, Chinese, a bit of Spanish, and a healthy dose of laughter spilled off the curb. Sergio might have mingled with them on any other day. But today he was a wanted man.

His face was hot, and his nose, still tender to the touch, felt puffier than when he woke up. He removed the bulbous Pradas, pulled down the visor, and studied himself in the mirror. His nose had swollen to twice its normal size and the bruising continued to spread so that it now encircled his eyes like a raccoon mask. He stared at the wounded, scared animal in the mirror for a long while until the anchorman's words came rushing back to him, over and over. *Ties to any terrorist organizations.* It was a ridiculous notion but someone had made the cops think that. His muscles quivered as he lowered his head and massaged his brow. *Could Ko have done this?*

Vivid snippets of the past twenty-four hours pounded his head; a riot of emotion churned his gut. There was the utter terror of the car chase, the empty agony of losing his best friend, those precious few hours of his date with Malina, and the unsettling sense that the past was about to catch up with him.

Sergio threw his head back and took a deep breath. His mind was cloudy from lack of sleep and his emotional compass was way out of whack. He needed to get a grip. He needed to think differently. He had to be paranoid, expect the worst. He could assume nothing anymore, nor trust anyone. Sergio looked to the empty seat next to him and the back of his neck tingled. Malina had been gone a good fifteen minutes. Or was it longer? What if she'd already called the cops? And if not, why not? *Ties to any terrorist organizations.*

It was suddenly and very urgently time to go. He scanned the dashboard and console for the electronic key fob, but Malina had taken it. His skin felt clammy; sweat beaded on his forehead as he cursed his oversight. He eyed the sandwich shop in front of the car and wondered if it had a rear exit. He could casually step inside, run out the back, and keep running. It had worked the night before and he'd be a fool to wait any longer. He took a deep breath, reached for the door handle, and stopped. Malina was back.

"We're in business," she said, as she slipped into the driver's seat and handed him a heavy plastic bag. "I can't believe how many people—" She gaped at him with alarm. "Are you okay?"

"Sure. Why?"

"You look awfully pale." She touched his forehead. "You're cold and sweaty. Do you have a headache?"

"I'm all right," he insisted. "Let's go."

"Sure? Concussions can take a few days to show up."

He waved her off. "We need to get going. Now."

She looked at him with questioning eyes for a moment and then pressed the ignition switch. Sergio scanned the street and the sidewalks as she backed up and pulled into traffic.

"Go that way," he said, pointing toward a side street. "Turn down there."

Sergio threw an arm over his headrest and looked out the rear window. Malina took the side street, made a left on Geary, and a right at the next intersection. "What's wrong?" she asked.

Sergio looked back at the empty street. "Nothing, I guess," he said, as he slipped back into his seat and studied Malina intently. "Just wanted to be sure."

He opened the bag and checked its contents: one refurbished Apple DuoPro II laptop computer and two unlocked smartphones. He pulled out the laptop and ran his hand along its sleek profile. "Did you make sure to ask for the dual-core 5.6 gigahertz processor and the DDR6 memory?"

"Yup, although I could tell he knew that I didn't have a clue what I was asking for." She skirted the edge of Golden Gate Park and turned east on Oak. "Who knows if that's what he really gave to me."

"He did. Bruno's cool." He slipped the computers and smartphones into his messenger bag.

She looked at him sideways. "So he's a friend?"

"Sort of. He's as nerdy as they come. I go in there whenever I'm in the neighborhood." He lowered his head to peek at the side mirror, half expecting to see a police cruiser following them. "That's why I didn't want to go in there, just in case he's seen the news."

"So what does that all mean anyway, the 5.6 gigaprocessors and the DDR stuff?"

"It means this computer is one of the fastest and most powerful laptops you can buy."

She looked at him out of the corner of her eye. "For seven hundred dollars?"

He grimaced. "Bruno has his ways."

Malina shook her head. "So where are we going?"

Sergio glanced at the battery gauge. The electric car was fully charged. He patted the dashboard. "How far can this go?"

Her eyes lit up. "Almost four hundred miles on a single charge. It has the new Lithium-air batteries. They store a lot more juice than the old ones."

"Good," he said, scanning the street ahead and behind them. "We're headed to LA. We're gonna need all the juice we can get."

-29-

Diebolt turned in the doorway of his campaign plane and waved good-bye to the thousands of Phoenix Republicans who had turned up for his early morning speech. The crowd roared as he waved absentmind-edly. Just a few more seconds and he'd be done with this.

An aide tapped him on the shoulder and he retreated into the Boeing 737, slipping into his usual seat. Campaign chief Nathan Aaron held out a sheet of paper as he dropped into the seat facing Diebolt. "These are your posts for today."

Diebolt pushed Aaron's arm away. "Just deal with it."

"You said you wanted approval on all of your Circles comments."

"Yeah, but this is insane. Who has time for all that social media stuff?"

Aaron extended his arm again and waited for Diebolt to grasp the page. "Just remember," he said, "if not for our Circles surge, you'd be sunk already."

Diebolt tore the sheet from Aaron's hand and read the comments out loud.

"Onward to Ohio. Looking forward to seeing all my Stark County supporters."

"A shout out to Lisa D. Thanks for the cookies."

"Check out this article at FreedomFare at www.ff.com. This is my kind of club."

Diebolt looked up from the page. "These are as pathetic as the last ones."

"They're safe," said Aaron, his lips taut. "And going into the final days with a lead, it's all about playing it safe."

Diebolt released the paper and let it fall to Aaron's feet. "Whatever," he said, turning to look out the window. The call from Liu had been on his mind all morning. He should have expected it, really, but it still unnerved him.

"What did Liu want?" asked Aaron.

Diebolt couldn't help but smile. Aaron seemed to have the uncanny ability to read his mind. "He's trying to assess how determined I am about standing up to China," said Diebolt. "They're nervous. He's nervous. He'll be screwed if the US gets serious about rare earths." He looked out the window and waved again for the crowd.

His friendship with Liu provided Diebolt with a better appreciation than most of just how critical rare earth minerals were to America's ability to compete in a twenty-first-century economy. A handful of lawmakers had tried several times over the past few years to fund surveys of US rare earth stocks and provide incentives to drive domestic production. But none of those bills ever stood a chance, not with Congress paralyzed by legislators who put partisan politics ahead of what was best for the country.

Then came the Modulo bankruptcy. The up-and-coming US smartphone maker had shut its doors a year ago because it could no longer secure a sufficient supply of neodymium to make speaker magnets, nor europium, a phosphor needed to make touch screens more vivid. Company officials blamed the shortage on China's stranglehold on the rare earth market and warned of more American bankruptcies to come. That was all it took to transform what would normally have been an obscure business item into a major geopolitical story. Lester was first to pick up the theme, but it was Diebolt's scare-mongering that turned China into the boogeyman that threatened America's way of life and future prosperity.

The plane shifted softly and Diebolt saw the terminal slip away from his window. A cheerful male voice welcomed everyone aboard.

"So where are we with the rare earth initiative?" asked Diebolt.

Aaron took a sip of water to prime his voice. "We've run the DoE's blueprint past the usual experts at RAND Corporation, Penn State, and Caltech. We doubled the size of the proposal like you asked and it was well received," he said. "We'll have a fully-baked bill, twenty billion dollars in total, ready to go by inauguration."

"Good," he replied. "No delays on this one. Let's get this done."

Diebolt knew the US could wait no longer, not since it would take a decade, possibly two, to find new rare earth deposits, conduct studies, obtain permits and financing, and develop the technology and infrastructure needed to mine and process the minerals. Failure to move quickly pointed to a future in which China so thoroughly dominated the industry that it could starve US high-tech manufacturers and military contractors of the key materials needed for their products. Diebolt allowed himself to smile. It certainly didn't hurt that Diebolt Incorporated, which knew more about processing rare earth minerals than any other company outside China, would be one of the biggest beneficiaries of the massive bill.

Diebolt looked down the aisle. The rest of the campaign team had hunkered down to work in seats scattered throughout the plane. Somewhere farther back, a detail of Secret Service agents sat out of earshot. He turned back to Aaron.

"By the way, Liu will be with us on election night. Make sure he's treated well."

Aaron shot him a look of surprise. "Is that wise?"

Diebolt shook his head. "But it's done."

"I could—"

"I said it's done." He shot Aaron an icy look and held it for a long moment before turning his attention to the strawberry blonde who stood in the aisle, holding a seat belt for the standard safety announcements.

The intercom blared again and he quickly tuned it out, his mind drifting back to that night two decades earlier, when he and Liu had reached an understanding that changed the course of their lives. They had known each other less than four months when they sat down in the terrace bar at the Peninsula Hotel in Beijing.

The air was warm, the vibe relaxed, and lovely women sat all around them. Liu did not know it, but Diebolt had come to say good-bye. He was returning to the US.

A waiter in a dark red jacket, black pants, and a bow tie appeared with a bottle of Macallan eighteen-year-old Sherry Oak single malt Scotch and two tulip-shaped glasses.

"You must try it," said Liu, before adding in a playful tone: "A little refinement never hurt anyone."

The waiter served them, and Liu quickly raised his glass toward Diebolt. "Tonight, we celebrate with a toast."

Diebolt pulled back in surprise. "What are we toasting?"

"The success of the Dongfang Diebolt Machinery Company." Liu paused for a long moment to let the words sink in. "I had a chat with a good friend at Industry and Commerce. He was very disappointed to learn of your troubles with Dongfang. He will talk to their chairman and I think you will find them far more amenable to working out your differences."

Diebolt sat stunned. The joint venture between his father's company and its Chinese partner had collapsed almost as soon as the ink had dried. Despite assurances, Dongfang had not been able to source local supplies cheaply. Laborers had demanded exorbitant raises and authorities had repeatedly cited the company for infractions common in every other factory in China. It hadn't taken the elder Diebolt long to conclude that Dongfang executives wanted to drive their new partner from China. By that point, the Dongfang crew already had their hands on Diebolt Incorporated's technology and capital.

"How can you be so sure?" asked the younger Diebolt.

Liu grinned. "They will not say 'no' to my friend."

Diebolt rubbed his chin, unable to fully comprehend what Liu was saying.

"But the sourcing issues, the fines—" he began.

"Richard," Liu said, holding up his hand to quiet his friend. "It will all be taken care of. You must learn to trust me."

Diebolt sat stunned a long moment. And then Liu announced his own good news. "I have been appointed to run Baotou Jingyuan." He beamed with pride.

Diebolt smiled even wider, not surprised at this one. He lifted his glass. "Then we have much to celebrate."

During the next hour Liu explained how Beijing had tasked him with doubling Baotou Jingyuan's rare earth output within a decade. Failure was not an option, and to achieve that goal, Liu needed the hardiest miners, the best scientists, the most capable engineers, and all the precision machinery Dongfang Diebolt could provide.

———————

The engines surged and the aircraft began taxiing to the runway. The captain's voice echoed through the cabin; Diebolt tried to tune him out. That night in Beijing had been a turning point for him and Liu. Diebolt's partners had welcomed him back with big smiles. With Baotou Jingyuan Rare Earth High-Tech Company as its top customer, it seemed Dongfang Diebolt couldn't manufacture mining machinery and high-tech processing equipment fast enough to meet Liu's insatiable demand.

That night had also solidified a friendship with Liu that would stand the test of time. Liu, some fifteen years his senior, helped Diebolt learn about a culture and society that thoroughly baffled him. Liu had also introduced Diebolt to top officials and given him crucial tips on how to navigate the halls of power—and when to avoid them.

Success all but assured, Diebolt had been quick to immerse himself in Beijing's surprisingly robust social scene. There was never a shortage of events, cocktail parties, and dinner gatherings attended by expats, government officials, well-connected businessmen, and of course, attractive young ladies looking to meet rich and powerful men. Booze was consumed copiously, sexual partners were plentiful, and the opium, once he figured out where to get it, was divine.

The big jet swung onto the runway and came to an expectant halt. Aaron pursed his lips as he quietly eyed Diebolt for a long moment. Then he spoke.

"I really think you should reconsider inviting Liu for election night. It *will* come back to haunt you. You won't get everything you want in the bill and the minute you agree to water it down, the media will start asking questions about Liu. You're opening yourself up to allegations that you did your Chinese buddy a favor."

"That's bullshit—" Diebolt stopped himself, teeth gritted and his temper simmering at a slow burn. Aaron was just doing his job—and doing it well—but he sure had a knack of doing it in a way that pushed his buttons.

Aaron leaned in. "He's trouble."

The first mate's voice readied the passengers for takeoff, but Diebolt wasn't paying attention. Aaron was right, in the strictest sense. But his relationship with Liu was more complex than Aaron could ever fathom. Liu's words ran through his mind, over and over. *You have created such a panic that the next president will have to act,* he'd said. *I can't allow that.* The engines roared to life and the jet began rolling down the runway.

"Perhaps," said Diebolt. "But I can handle it."

-30-

Ko marched into the executive suite, betraying none of the stress and sleeplessness that weighed so heavily on Prederick. He wondered how Ko could look so fresh when he felt so groggy. Ko took his usual spot on the sofa.

"China is not happy," he said in a tone more suitable for a conversation about the weather.

Prederick felt a shiver slice through his body. "Nothing has changed. We are still on track for the announcement Tuesday."

"Much has changed from their perspective," countered Ko. "Our system crashed, internal saboteurs have stolen the profiles, and now the FBI is involved. My friends feel this might not be the right time."

"What the hell does that mean?" asked Prederick, as he ran his fingers through his hair. "There was never going to be a perfect time. And why the hell should they care if any of this comes out? This is one of the world's most oppressive and unabashed totalitarian regimes. Everyone already knows they spy on people. If anyone has reason to worry, it's us. We're the ones sticking our necks out."

"You should be more respectful of our partners," chided Ko. "It's one thing for people to insinuate, and it's another thing entirely when embarrassing evidence comes to the fore. My friends do not wish to be embarrassed. They suggest we revisit this after a cooling-off period."

Prederick felt his dream slipping from his grasp. For fifty-four straight quarters, the social network had increased—and at times even doubled—its number of users. Such momentum gave Circles tremendous clout online, on Wall Street, and among government officials. But almost all of the company's growth now came from new markets, and failure to launch in China would bring the company's streak to an end within a year or so. Rumors that Circles had peaked would surely follow and the company would suddenly be on the defensive. Prederick understood Circles had already struck the best deal it was ever going to get from China.

He shook his head adamantly. "If we don't get this done now, it's not going to get done."

"My friends are asking: If you can't keep your own employees under control, how can you promise to stay on top of more than one billion Chinese Internet users?"

"That's a load of crap," bristled Prederick. "You know damn well those are two different issues."

"Perhaps . . ."

"I wouldn't be so blasé about the whole thing if I were you. The board will be very upset if you just sit by and let this agreement collapse."

Ko glowered at Prederick. "Threats are a sign of desperation, Dan."

Prederick closed his eyes and rubbed his temples.

Ko continued in a measured tone. "I'm just the messenger. They want this fiasco to end. They won't move forward with us until we get control of the situation."

-31-

Sergio burst through the metal door and ran into the steamy night air. Gravel crunched beneath his feet as he sprinted to the middle of the wide roof. He skidded to a halt, spun around, and froze in the darkness. A sticky heat pressed in on him, mugging his skin and suffocating his lungs. He crouched down so he wouldn't stick out against the backdrop of light all around him. There was nowhere else to hide.

The door swung open again and a colossal shadow squeezed through the opening. The man's silhouette revealed his massive physique; his movements suggested military precision. The warrior in black quickly zeroed in on Sergio and stormed forward, almost doubling in size as he neared. Sergio ran but his foe overtook him, pulling Sergio into his overpowering arms as he skidded to a stop. Sergio heard a faint chuckle; it was the sound of a tormentor relishing the moment.

The hulking shadow grasped Sergio by the collar and hoisted him off his feet, like a kitten carried by the scruff of its neck. His mind cloudy and his vision blurry, Sergio saw a haunting luminescence from the streets far below. He flailed in desperation, his blows glancing off the massive arm that held him aloft. The line between dark and light was now beneath Sergio as he drove his heels backward like a kicking horse.

He struck his attacker in the knee and the man roared in pain. Then he released his grip and Sergio fell into the void. There was little he could do but accept his fate and maybe say a prayer. As Sergio turned his gaze skyward, his attacker leaned forward and exposed himself to the city lights below. Looking up, Sergio saw a face more terrifying than death itself, a face he knew all too well. It was George.

Sergio screamed as he reached up in a final desperate attempt to save himself.

A soft voice broke through the terror. "You okay?"

Sergio opened his eyes to a blinding light. It was daytime. In the car. With Malina. His heart thumped against his ribcage and his windpipe wheezed. Drops of cool sweat ran down the back of his neck. He noted his outstretched arm and discovered his fingers curled around the sun visor over the windshield.

"Bad dream?" she asked.

He pressed his face into his hands to gather his thoughts. "It was George."

Malina drove on to the plucky strings of Vivaldi's *Winter* while Sergio tried to make sense of his nightmare. He was grateful for the space.

Finally, she placed her hand on his arm. "I'd be honored," she began, "if you wanted to tell me about George. It might help you just by talking about it. What was he like?"

Sergio considered the request. He ached for his friend, even as he couldn't yet bring himself to believe they would never go fishing again, enjoy a beer together, or chat up some impossibly gorgeous woman at The Ramp. He felt a smile sneak across his face, the kind of irrepressible grin that George always seemed to bring out of everyone.

"George was a brilliant man," he said, pausing to imagine the eulogy he hoped he'd have the chance to write for his best friend. "He could code better than anyone I've ever met. But what I loved most about him was that he was full of life and he loved to laugh. He was a total people person. He'd just strike up conversations in the most random situations. You know what I mean?" He paused, worried he might be getting carried away.

"He sounds like a great guy," she said with a reassuring smile. "I wish I could have met him."

He pushed away a knot in his throat and waited for his teary eyes to clear before he continued. "One time, in the early days, I was helping George upgrade our security system and I made a mistake when I typed in a line of code for the new program. It was a stupid mistake, but we'd been at it for about eighteen hours and I was fried. Long story short, we went live with the new software and the website crashed. Boom. Lights out. It was a disaster. Everyone was scrambling to figure out what had happened. The Internet was buzzing with rumors and complaints, reporters were calling left and right. Weiss, our boss at the time, was freaking out."

"So what happened?"

"George eventually found my mistake. It took four very long hours, but he fixed it and we were back in business. And then he did something that still amazes me to this day. He marched into Weiss' office and took the fall. Said he'd given me the wrong code to type in. I knew that wasn't true and I should have gone in and manned up, even though he kept insisting it was his fault. Then years later, over drinks, he finally came clean."

"What did he say?"

"I was in the running to become chief technology officer at the time and he didn't want the mistake to become a black mark on my performance record. George worked under a bit of a cloud for years after that, and I'm pretty sure he was passed over for promotion because of it. Still, he never once complained. So in some ways, he was a better friend to me than I was to him. "

Malina reached over the center console and placed her hand on his forearm. "I'm sorry about George," she said softly.

He nodded in gratitude as he took note for the first time of the wide-open space around them. "So where are we?"

"About halfway," she replied. The blacktop of Interstate 5 unfurled under a cloudless sky along the western edge of California's Central Valley. To his right stood the undulating golden hills that separated the valley from the Pacific coast. To his left lay a patchwork of fields that stretched seventy miles to the Sierra Nevada foothills in the east. Most of the time the land was rich with strawberries, lettuce, almonds, and tomatoes. Dotted among the fields were huge industrial ranches where tens of thousands of cattle were fattened up for slaughter each year. It was with good reason that some called the state's central valley "the food basket of the world."

But at the moment, many of the fields lay fallow and a low pall of dust hung in the air. The valley looked tired and smelled rotten. He hated that stench, a mixture of decay and manure. He closed his eyes and tried to ignore the sickly sensation in his stomach.

"God, I hate this place," he said.

Malina tilted her head toward Sergio. "What's so bad about the valley?"

"For my people, it's a barren wasteland of mind-numbing monotony, back-breaking work, and soul-searing heat."

"Your people?"

"Immigrants. From Mexico."

Malina looked left and then right. "I almost lived out here once."

Sergio turned to her and waited, his eyebrows raised.

"There was this guy, Barry." She studied him carefully, as if she was deciding how much to share. "He was a doctor at the hospital, a bit older than me, but I liked that. He was intelligent, funny, adventurous. I really fell for him."

Malina's face glowed in the sunlight and her eyes flashed vividly even as they betrayed a sense of vulnerability as she spoke.

"We were together for almost four years. It seemed perfect. We'd arrange our work schedules so we could travel all over the world. Trekking in Nepal—I saw Everest; sightseeing in Italy. We had an amazing time." Her voice drifted off and Sergio waited in silence as he secretly traced her body with his eyes. He wondered what it would feel like to stroke her auburn hair.

"Anyway, I guess all those trips helped me overlook some pretty big problems. Like we never actually lived together. Four years and he refused to give up his place or share it with me. Doesn't that seem odd?" she asked, not waiting for Sergio to answer. "I know that should have been a big red flag for me, but I guess you convince yourself to believe what you want to believe. Or at least I did."

"So what happened?" asked Sergio.

"His mother died. Pancreatic cancer. She was in her seventies but neither of us saw it coming. He took it really hard. It was the only time I ever saw him cry. He went into a shell for weeks and then one day he suddenly announced he was moving to his mother's old farmhouse down here in the valley. Just like that."

"And you didn't want to live here?"

"He didn't even ask me to go with him." The pitch of her voice rose half an octave. "Just like that, he made a decision and didn't give me any say in the matter." She paused and then spoke in a hushed voice. "If he'd at least done that, I could have accepted it."

"I'm sorry it didn't work out," he replied. "That must have been really hard." An awkward silence fell over them. Barry was a fool, but Sergio sensed those were not the right words to comfort her.

"So what about you?" Malina finally asked.

"What about me?"

"Why are you still single?"

Sergio stared out the windshield, softly shaking his head. "Oh, I dunno," he began. "I guess I've been too busy at work for too long. Then one day you look up and all those years have gone by."

"Don't tell me you are one of those geeks who sleeps under his desk." Her tone was mocking.

He chuckled. "I gave that up a long time ago. And hey," he said with a smile, "I asked you out, so there must be hope for me yet."

She looked at him sideways. "There must have been someone . . ."

Sergio flicked his eyebrows and sighed in capitulation. "I did get serious about one girl a few years ago. She was from my ancestral village in Lebanon. I met her when I went back to visit. We hit it off." He paused. "Okay, I was crazy about her, so I went back several times. I wanted her to come here, but her family wouldn't allow it without us getting married."

"Marriage isn't so bad, is it?"

"No," replied Sergio. "But I didn't know her well enough to take that plunge."

"I thought you were crazy about her."

"I was, but dating in Lebanon is definitely not the same as dating here. There are always chaperones and curfews. You never know . . ."

Sergio shifted in his seat, turning away from her, a not-so-subtle signal that he was done with the topic. They fell silent and Sergio was grateful that Malina didn't press the issue. Still, she kept looking over at him, a curious expression on her face, as her eyes darted back and forth between the road and Sergio. Then, softly, she asked: "What happened to your ear?"

Sergio's head snapped to the left and his eyes met hers for an instant before he looked down at his fidgety hands. His usual story, the one about a rugby injury, didn't feel right.

"It's okay," she said after a moment. "You don't have to—"

"My father," he began, surprised by his own words, "was one of the leaders of the United Farm Workers movement in the sixties and seventies." Sergio looked straight down the road. "He led strikes and boycotts to force the big growers to increase wages and improve working conditions. Some of the growers resisted and sent in goons to attack striking workers. There were shootings."

He glanced to his left. Malina's eyes were filled with worry.

"They killed my father," he said, releasing the words in a painful whisper. "And I saw it. And this," he said pointing to his missing earlobe, "was taken to make sure I understood what would happen to my mother, Emilio, and me if I said anything."

Malina put a hand to her mouth. "Oh my God."

He pressed his lips tightly together as he stared out at the wide flat valley stretching into the distance. Somewhere out there, to the southeast, was a lifetime of anguish, fear, and guilt. And his brother Emilio.

They drove in awkward silence until Malina spoke again. "I didn't mean to—"

"You couldn't have known." He shuffled in the seat, tilting his shoulders away from Malina. Maybe he should have gone with the rugby story.

"Did they ever catch the guy who did it?" she asked, with the tentative tone of someone who wasn't sure how far to push.

Sergio shook his head. An undertow of sadness pulled at him. He wasn't ready for the memories, not when he had so much else to deal with. He leaned against the door and stared off into the hills. Mile after mile passed, each of them lost in thought, until Malina fiddled with the buttons on the steering wheel and the music cut out. A faint whoosh of wind and the whine of tires seeped into the car. Then, in an uncertain voice that Sergio could hardly hear, she spoke. "Do you believe in evil?"

"Evil?" He stiffened in his seat and met her questioning gaze. "Do you mean like some cosmic force unleashed by the devil?"

"Yeah, something like that," she said, turning back to the road.

Sergio drifted back to that night four decades earlier, to the man with the empty black eyes, raspy voice, and yellow teeth. "Terrible things happen to people all the time," said Sergio. "But how do you know if it's fate, bad luck, or the work of evil forces?" A sudden chill swept his body. "Do you?"

"Doctors learn to think in terms of chemical imbalances and bad wiring. It's easier to explain the shootings, the stabbings, and the other horrible things we see as the work of people who aren't quite right. We have all sorts of names for it: sociopathy, narcissism, psychosis. But sometimes that isn't good enough." Her voice cracked and her eyes moistened. "All those clinical definitions seem woefully inadequate to explain the fear, pain, and anguish people inflict on others. How can people do those things to each other?"

"I was just a kid," he said. "I'd never known fear and suffering until that night, and I didn't really understand any of it. But when that bastard laughed as he sliced off my ear, it felt evil to me."

-32-

Special Agent Jay Feeley walked into the corner conference room on the twelfth floor of the bureau's downtown San Francisco office. Half the region's Joint Terrorist Task Force, which included agents from the ATF, Homeland Security, the California Highway Patrol, and the county sheriff's department, sat around the laminate-topped table, laptops at the ready. The rest of the nineteen-person team stood behind them against the walls. A projector in the center of the table splashed an image of Sergio Mansour onto the whiteboard on the wall.

Feeley recapped the case for the benefit of those who hadn't made it to the earlier briefing and then he turned to Patrick Quick, a rookie agent with a snub nose and curly black hair. "What do we have, Quick?"

Quick looked up from his laptop, cleared his throat, and began his rundown.

"We found Mansour's Range Rover parked in a lot at Stanyan and Beulah. Front right fender was smashed in. Witnesses identified it as the vehicle involved in a single car collision overnight. The driver of the SUV appears to have been Mansour. He drove up the 8th Street off-ramp onto I-80. Nearly collided with an exiting semi, but he got lucky. Witnesses said another man with a gun ran up the ramp just after

Mansour's collision but turned around and fled in a late-model sedan parked at the bottom of the ramp. We're working on the assumption they're connected."

"What about the interviews?" asked Feeley.

"We spoke with . . ." Quick looked down at his screen, "thirty-seven Circles employees, most of them executives, but also engineers who worked closest with Mansour and a few who said they considered him a personal friend. With one exception, they were very positive. Hard worker, extremely intelligent, helpful to others, that kind of stuff. They all said Verneek was his closest friend, at least that they knew of. None of them could see Mansour as a killer, let alone a guy who would torture and murder his best friend. The notion he could be involved with terrorists came as a complete shock. But the CTO, guy by the name of Ko, was less than enthusiastic about Mansour. Others were quick to point out that Ko and Mansour never hit it off."

Feeley groaned inwardly as he recalled Ko's contemptible attitude earlier that morning. "What specifically did Ko say?"

"That Mansour was difficult to work with and not fully committed to the company's new strategy, that he was duplicitous, as evidenced by his theft of company property. That kind of thing."

Feeley quietly noted the dismissive tone in Quick's voice. Even the greenest cop on the task force could see through Ko's lies. "Duly noted," said Feeley. "Thank you, Quick."

Feeley looked across the table and nodded to the next speaker. "Harris?"

"His parents emigrated from Mexico, and he grew up in Fresno. The father was murdered when he was eleven and his mother died of cancer about seven years later. His brother claims they haven't spoken in years. He has relatives in Mexico and distant family ties to Lebanon. Mansour is a bit of a loner. Lots of acquaintances through work, but few close friends outside. We've put surveillance on a few of their homes.

A couple of them have cabins up at Lake Tahoe and we've asked local officials to make regular passes just in case he shows up there."

Feeley shook his head in frustration. He'd forgotten to call his wife to tell her he wasn't going to get away at all this weekend. "Ziegler?"

The Homeland Security agent took a step away from the wall and cleared his throat. "Ports and airlines have been notified and Mansour has been added to the no-fly list. Mansour gets around. He frequents Alaska or British Columbia at least once every winter . . . heli-skiing, I'm guessing. And in the past five years he's spent time in Hawaii, Tahiti, Indonesia, Fiji, the Philippines, South Africa, and Costa Rica."

"Circles employees said he's a big surfer," said Quick.

Ziegler nodded and continued. "He also traveled to Lebanon five times over a two-year period. We're trying to trace his movements while he was over there, but that'll take time because his last trip was three years ago."

Feeley pointed to the far side of the conference table. "Solano?"

"NSA is compiling a dossier. Our guys are doing the same. We should have them shortly," he replied.

"Good," said Feeley, hiding his disappointment. The NSA's dossier would include a treasure trove of data on Mansour: the contents of every email he'd sent in the past decade, a record of every website he'd visited, transcripts of most, if not all, of his calls—any kind of electronic signal he'd left in the years since the agency turned its powerful ears inward on US citizens. The FBI's behavioral analysis team at Quantico would provide valuable insights into Mansour's personality, and with any luck, a key clue or two that might help them track Mansour down. Without those reports, Feeley might as well have been working with one hand tied behind his back.

"Does anyone have anything that would point to a motive?" Feeley scanned the room. "Why would a US-born-and-bred computer expert suddenly get into bed with one of the most vicious terrorist organizations on the planet? Is he a closet fundamentalist? Did he have any business dealings that went sour? Is he a gambler? Some kind of pervert who's being blackmailed?"

The agents looked around the room at each other, but no one spoke. Feeley nodded at Agent Denny Palmer. "Denny?"

Palmer leaned back in his chair and began speaking in his familiar slow drawl. "Mansour has resources, lots of them. SEC records show he's sold more than thirty-five million dollars worth of Circles shares over the past fifteen years, and he still owns more than seventy million worth. He's spread his accounts around, but as far as we know so far, they are all domestic. He hasn't tapped any accounts since Thursday night, when he withdrew five hundred bucks from an ATM at Polk and California. He used his Visa last night at a bar in the Tenderloin."

"Do you have a time on that?" asked Feeley.

Palmer pulled Sergio's Visa account up on his screen. "Transaction time was ten twenty-three at night. Seventy-eight bucks."

"An hour and a half after Verneek's estimated time of death," said Feeley. "He either had a serious case of nerves or he was with someone."

Palmer nodded. "The bar opens in a few hours. We'll send someone down there to see if anyone remembers him."

"No," said Feeley. "Find the manager and get a list of staffers who were working last night. Then send a team out to track them down . . . now." This could not wait, not with Garrison looking over his shoulder.

"Got it," said Palmer.

"What else?" continued Feeley.

"He turned off his phone at two ten this morning. That coincides with the coffee shop and pursuit. He had not powered it up as of the last twenty minutes. His call records were mostly normal—calls to Verneek, work associates, his health club, a couple of restaurants, all within his normal pattern. But one number stood out. He made two calls this week to the main number at SF General's emergency room. One of those calls was Thursday. The duty nurse said that phone rings off the hook night and day and calls are patched through to the entire staff. We already interviewed forty-two of the sixty-seven people on duty Thursday. Of the twenty-five we haven't tracked down yet, only six of them were also working at the time the first call was placed on Monday night." Palmer's voiced trailed off as he scrolled down the page on his computer screen.

"Five of them are scheduled for the night shift this evening. The sixth," he said, staring at his computer screen, "an emergency room doctor named Malina Olson, called in sick today. Her next shift is Monday. We already have a team on it."

"Good," said Feeley, as he stood back from the table. "No delays. We are more than halfway through the first twenty-four hours. Let's get back to work."

The task force filed out of the room under Feeley's watchful eye. All in all, not much to go on yet, but the trap was set. If Mansour tried to get money, use a credit card, make a phone call, or send an email, Feeley would know in seconds. If his suspect reached out to a friend or family member, or showed up at an airport, harbor, or border crossing, Feeley would know within minutes. It was only a matter of time before Mansour fucked up. He had probably already made his crucial mistake. All they had to do was figure out what that mistake was.

-33-

Malina steered the Tesla into an alley off South Hope Street in downtown Los Angeles. Sergio sat beside her, the DuoPro II she'd bought at Bruno's in his lap.

"Keep moving," he said, his eyes locked on the computer screen. "Slowly."

Malina eased the car farther into the utility lane, her focus divided between the warped pavement ahead and the computer in Sergio's lap. The hum of traffic from the street faded as they moved into the shadows between a modern high-rise and an aging brick office building. A few Dumpsters and a couple of prominent NO PARKING signs dotted the alley.

"Keep going . . . A little more. Stop!" Sergio couldn't believe his luck. "Perfect. Four bars." He looked up and pointed to an empty space alongside the brick wall between two garbage bins. "Pull in there."

Sergio's fingers burst into a flurry of activity, typing in commands and toggling back and forth among windows. He paused at intervals, scanning the screen as he pondered strategy.

"What are you doing?" she asked.

Sergio stopped typing and stared blankly through the windshield. He was about to commit a felony—in front of a witness. He shifted in his seat and eyeballed Malina. She could have easily called the police when she went to the store in San Francisco. He had no choice now but to trust her.

"I'm breaking into Buxton King & Greenberg." He pointed to the office building beside them and paused a moment to meet her silent stare.

"I'm guessing this is not legal," she finally said.

"Believe me," he replied slowly, "I don't make a habit of this." Sergio continued typing, but he could feel Malina's disapproving eyes burrow into him. "BK&G is Circles' outside counsel. We use them for everything. Lawsuits, patents, human resources cases, work visas, and acquisitions. They should have everything I want to know about Ko."

"Come again?"

Sergio kept typing as he spoke. "One of the first things Prederick did when he became CEO was bring in Ko. He's a brilliant Chinese coder who came to the US to go to Carnegie Mellon, one of the top computer science programs in the world. After he got his doctorate, he got offers from Google, Amazon, Yahoo, Microsoft, Oracle, you name it. There were even rumors that the top US defense and intelligence agencies tried to recruit him."

Sergio paused for a moment as he remembered how a young Dr. Ko had rebuffed his personal pitch to join Circles. "But he just disappeared. Poof," continued Sergio, his fists popping open like flowers blooming. "He didn't take any offers and everyone assumed he went back to China to work for the military or something. Then he turns up as founder of a small unknown R&D shop called ZGT Technologies here in Los Angeles. Word was they were doing pure research. ZGT didn't have any clients or revenues as far as anyone could tell, and no one knew where he got the money to operate. Then when Prederick took over Circles, he stunned everyone by buying ZGT. That's how Ko ended up here, and I'm guessing whatever he's up to, he developed it before Circles bought his company. There's a good chance we'll find a detailed description of his company's software in the legal documents from the acquisition. BK&G will have copies."

Malina turned away with a frown and fixed her gaze on the alley exit half a block away. Neither of them spoke for a minute, and the sound of Sergio's fingertips dancing across the keyboard filled the car.

"Don't they have passwords or something?" she finally asked.

He stopped typing. "Of course they do, but Wi-Fi is notoriously porous."

"What do you mean *porous*?"

"There are all sorts of bugs in WPA3. That's the Wi-Fi security standard almost everyone uses now. And these bugs make it pretty easy to crack encrypted passwords. All you need is the right software."

"So if there are all these bugs, why is everyone using this WPA3?"

"Nobody knew about them when WPA3 was introduced. It was supposed to be foolproof and it quickly became the standard. Then a hacker in Japan discovered a pretty major flaw, but by that point WPA3 was in hundreds of millions of Wi-Fi routers around the world."

"So what happened?"

"Absolutely nothing. Consumers and corporations simply ignored the risk and the companies that made routers weren't about to kill their golden goose. Everybody just sort of stuck their heads in the sand, and they've been hoping for the best ever since."

The pinched look on Malina's face suggested she was less than impressed with his display of hacking skills. Feeling oddly shameful, Sergio turned his attention back to the screen.

"I'm directing the Wi-Fi card on this computer to sniff the airwaves for any signals in the area, and then we're going to wait until someone at BK&G connects to the network." He tapped in a few final commands, hit ENTER, and leaned back into his seat. "Now we wait."

Malina remained quiet as she stared toward the end of the alley with a slight frown on her face. When she finally spoke, her voice had an edge. "Is this why we came down here? To break into this company's network? And why is Circles' law firm in LA, anyway?"

Sergio arched his eyebrows. He wasn't ready for the onslaught of questions.

"Silicon Valley's legal scene is incredibly small and incestuous. Retainers expire, allegiances shift, lawyers change firms. It's pretty much a given that some lawyer you've worked with closely in the past will eventually show up on the other side of the table, and he'll know more about your technologies, business strategies, even your personality traits, than you'd like. So we decided a long time ago that the only way to avoid these conflicts was to look outside the valley."

"So conflict of interest rules are—"

A high-pitched beep drew both their eyes down to the computer in Sergio's lap. "Got one," he crowed. "That was fast."

Malina leaned across the center console to survey the jumble of text strings and numbers scattered across the screen. Sergio pointed to two lines at the bottom of the page.

```
>> # BSSID ESSID Encryption
>> 1 00:14:6C:7E:40:80 BK&G WPA3
   (1 handshake)
```

"Now what?" she asked.

He pointed to the last line. "This is the handshake between the network and the computer that just logged on to it. These numbers contain the password; now all I have to do is crack it."

"How?"

Sergio toggled to another window on his computer. "This handy little piece of software is called AirCracker. I downloaded it when we stopped at Starbucks." Sergio spoke swiftly as he typed. He was relieved to see Malina's disapproval give way to curiosity. "AirCracker matches a long list of preselected passwords against the handshake. If those don't work, it will automatically start generating passwords to test. And if I have to, I'll start typing in the company name, employee names, and stuff. The software will riff off those to come up with even more possible passwords."

"How long will this take?"

"That depends on how security conscious BK&G is. If they're like most midsize firms, they used an IT consultant to set up their network. And if the IT guys were like all the rest, they set up a basic default password like *1234567* or *password*. I'd hope BK&G had the brains to change it, but you'd be surprised how even the most basic passwords turn up year after year on the lists of most commonly used passwords."

Sergio turned to Malina with a smirk on his face. Her eyes were locked on the rearview mirror and her face darkened into a scowl.

"What?" he asked.

"Cop car. Just pulled into the alley." Malina shifted in her seat and pulled him toward her, crushing the computer between them. She pressed her mouth to his, fiercely and urgently, a kiss full of intensity but devoid of passion. Out of the corner of his eye he spied the cruiser silently closing the distance between them.

"Still coming?" she asked.

"Uh-huh," he mumbled through their kiss.

The police car closed to within thirty feet as Sergio racked his brain to come up with a story to explain why a well-to-do adult couple would want to make out in a seedy Los Angeles alley. Cheating spouses? An urgent Viagra moment?

The cruiser's blue and red lights suddenly flashed to life, engulfing the Tesla in a swirl of color. Sergio stiffened in fear as the low roar of the cruiser's engine filled the alley. The patrol car raced past them to the far end of the lane before the driver activated the siren and turned the corner.

"Holy shit. I thought we were done for," he said, pulling away.

"Me too," she exhaled. "We can't stay here much longer."

Sergio grabbed the computer from between their bodies and glanced down at the screen. He smiled and cocked an eyebrow. "It looks like we don't have to." He turned the computer to Malina and proudly displayed the message on the screen.

```
>> AirCrack5.1

>> [00:00:00] 1432 keys tested
   (37.20 k/s)

>> KEY FOUND! [password1234]
```

-34-

Special Agent Feeley cringed when his cell phone screen lit up with an incoming call from Preston Garrison in Washington. He momentarily toyed with the idea of not answering, but understood that would only make things worse.

"Preston, thanks for checking in." Feeley walked out onto the private deck of Sergio Mansour's Russian Hill condo.

"I told you I wanted hourly updates, Feeley. It's been three. So what's the latest?"

Feeley looked back inside at Palmer and Quick, who were cataloging and boxing the computers, game consoles, phones, and flash memory drives they'd found in the condo. The rest of the team had already picked apart the furniture, rifled through the suspect's bookshelves, and searched his filing cabinet.

"We interviewed the waitress who served Mansour at the bar last night," said Feeley. "It was a positive identification. He was there from about eight to eleven o'clock with a woman. They left together."

"And?"

Feeley looked north across San Francisco Bay. Brisk and clear, it was the kind of day when everything looked magnified and the distant shorelines seemed close enough to touch. "For starters, it means he couldn't have killed Verneek, at least not personally."

"Who's the woman?" asked Garrison, his tone increasingly terse.

"We're fairly certain her name is Malina Olson, an emergency room doctor at SF General. Mansour called there twice in the last week. Other than that, they don't seem to have any history."

"So?"

"So Mansour dumped his car about three blocks from her house last night." Feeley ran his hand through his hair and brought it to rest, cupping the back of his neck. "It could just be a coincidence, of course . . ." He let Garrison reach the same obvious conclusion he'd made an hour earlier.

Garrison breathed heavily into the phone. "So what do we have on the woman?"

"She called in sick today, but she's not home. Her mother told us she went up to Tahoe with a girlfriend. We're pulling everything we can on her."

"Good. What else?"

"We're just wrapping up at Mansour's condo." Feeley turned away from the million-dollar view and moved back into the living room. He looked down at the stacks of computer manuals they'd pulled off the living room shelves. Feeley shook his head. Not a single novel, travel guide, or magazine in sight. "We'll see what we get off his computers," he said into the phone.

"Any leads on the mystery man on the ramp last night?"

"Not much. Witnesses said he pursued Mansour through SOMA and fired at least two shots. We found Mansour's Range Rover and recovered two slugs from it. They were too beat up to be of much use to ballistics." Feeley twirled his finger in the air, signaling to his team to wrap it up. "Witnesses said the shooter drove a gray Chrysler 300, but nobody got the plates. There are over fifty thousand gray Chrysler 300s in California."

"Make that a priority."

"I already have," replied Feeley.

"He could be the gunman in the Verneek slaying." Garrison's voice trembled with excitement. "Hell, he could be a direct link to Hezbollah. Either of them could. Do you know what that would mean for our careers?"

-35-

Late afternoon sunlight filtered through the motel room's faded yellow curtains. Sergio sat at a beat-up table in the corner, oblivious to everything but the computer screen in front of him. He'd started out poring over the documents he'd downloaded from Buxton King & Greenberg but got sidetracked when Malina went shopping.

Taking advantage of the solitude, he figured it'd be a good chance to learn a little bit more about her. He hadn't expected to find much on Malina, but he never anticipated so little. Other than a brief bio on San Francisco General's online staff directory, her license on the state medical board's website, and a few published research papers, it was almost as if Malina Olson didn't exist. She didn't have a Circles page, a Twitter account, or any other social media presence. There were no Yelp reviews on her, but that was probably not surprising for an emergency room doctor. He checked property records, court documents, political donation registries, and any other filings that he thought might possibly be in the public domain. He scanned the Harvard University website, browsed the *Crimson*'s newspaper archives and scoured the school research sites for any trace of Malina when she had attended medical school. Then he searched for her on Harvard's alumni association

website, the American Medical Association site, and a handful of medical chat rooms. Not a peep.

The good news was that it appeared Malina was who she said she
was. The bad news was that he didn't know much more than that.
Either she was hiding something or she was unusually paranoid. Sergio
couldn't explain why, but he had the uneasy feeling it was a little bit
of both.

A knock on the door startled him. He closed the browser window
on his computer and tiptoed to the peephole. Malina was back.

"That took a while," he said, as he pulled open the door. He looked
away, vaguely ashamed about how he'd spent the past half hour.

"You're lucky I'm back so quickly. There's an entire shopping mall
right over there," she said, pointing toward the back of the motel.

"How'd you make out?" she asked, as she inspected the garish room.
She was visibly unimpressed by the pastel polka-dotted bed covers and
the blue, black, and gray camouflage paint job on the walls.

"I made some headway on Ko," he replied. "But I still have to do
more research."

She looked down at the ample red stain in the carpet. It was only a
matter of time before she'd notice the flecks of dust and faint chemical
smell floating in the air.

Sergio had chosen carefully. The derelict Holloman Motel, on Sunset
Boulevard, was the kind of place frequented by prostitutes and junkies,
and manned by a desk attendant who knew better than to ask questions.
The two-story horseshoe-shaped structure wrapped around a parking lot,
leaving Malina's car shielded from the street. And it had free Wi-Fi, probably so the hookers could book their "dates" online.

Malina set three shopping bags down on the sagging bed and nodded at the coin slot attached to the headboard.

"Is that what I think it is?" she asked with a delighted grin.

"The one, the only, the amazing Vibro-matic," he said, with the lilt of a carnival barker. "I almost fed it a few quarters but it occurred to me it might pose a fire hazard." He turned to the bags on the bed. "What did you get?"

Malina unpacked five T-shirts, a hoodie, a pair of jeans, as well as socks, briefs, Maui Jim sunglasses, and three ball caps from the first two bags. She pulled out toiletries, makeup, and an electric hair clipper from the third. "Everything a fugitive could want."

"Excellent," he said, as he rifled through the merchandise. Her self-lessness only made him feel more guilty for what he was about to say. He pressed his hands into a steeple and brought his fingertips to his mouth. "I think it's best if we split up."

Malina pulled back with a squint, as if she couldn't be sure she'd heard him right. "You're trying to get rid of me? After I drove you all the way down here?"

His eyes found the floor. "I think it's best if you head back to San Francisco."

She shook her head, her expression morphing into steely anger.

"Look," he said with more resolve. "I appreciate your help, but you can't stay with me."

"The hell you say."

"Don't you realize I'm in really big shit?" he asked sharply, a hint of frustration in his voice. "Someone at work just killed my best friend and they want to kill me. They've also somehow managed to convince the cops that I'm a terrorist. And they are doing this so they can sabotage the company I spent fifteen years of my life building. I don't have a clue what they're up to, but the only way I can save myself is to figure it out—before someone kills me or arrests me for terrorism."

Malina opened her mouth to respond, but Sergio threw up his hand and cut her off. "If that cop had stopped us in the alley, we'd have both been screwed. It was selfish of me to bring you along."

"I didn't give you a choice, remember?"

"It doesn't matter. You've helped me get a head start. But that's it. You need to go back to San Francisco and pretend you never met me. No one will ever know."

"But I did meet you . . ." she said, her voice trailing off.

They locked eyes for a long moment, their silent standoff interrupted only by the clicking of high heels on the veranda outside the room. He waited until the stilettos moved out of earshot. "Don't you realize what they'd do to you if they caught you aiding and abetting a terrorist?"

Malina pursed her lips and put her hands on her hips. "You're not a terrorist."

He spun away, confused and torn by this woman who insisted on helping him. "How can you be so sure?"

"Sure?" she answered with a flash of confidence in her eyes. "I guess you can never be one hundred percent positive. But I've worked in the ER for ten years and I know enough to trust my gut. There's no other way you can function when you have to make life-or-death decisions in a split second."

She paused for a moment and cleared her throat. "Life in the ER also teaches you how to read people. I can spot a patient who is lying to me in an instant. I can tell how someone is going to react when I explain that we have to amputate. And I know who's going to lose it and who's going to suck it up when I tell them their child just died. It comes with the territory."

She lowered her head and looked to him under the fine line of her silky eyebrows. "I saw the look in your eyes last night," she said softly. "It was pure shock, confusion, and anguish. I don't know what you've stumbled into, but you're no coldhearted terrorist. Of that, I'm sure."

-36-

Dan Prederick waved Ethan Burrard into his office and motioned to the sofa. "Thanks for coming, Ethan," he said. "I'm glad we're finally getting a chance to chat."

"I was going to come in tonight anyways," said Burrard, perching himself on the edge of the couch.

Of course he was. How else would Circles' weird genius of the night spend his weekend? Prederick had never before noticed how Burrard's head was far too bulbous for his lanky body. The guy was downright strange.

"So, Ethan," he began, fidgeting. It was a hell of an occasion for their first one-on-one. "How are you getting along with your colleagues?"

Burrard fiddled with the circuit board pendant dangling around his neck.

"Do you like working with them?" asked Prederick.

Burrard focused on a spot somewhere to the left of Prederick's head. It was as if Burrard was looking, not quite *at* him, but *through* him.

Prederick pressed. "How are things going between you and Ko?"

A puzzled frown crept across Burrard's face. "What *things*?" he asked.

Prederick chuckled. It was true. Burrard took everything literally. "I want to offer you an opportunity."

Burrard's gaze floated to the opposite side of Prederick's head and his frown deepened.

"There have been decisions made in Labs, by Ko, that I was not aware of," continued Prederick. "That cannot continue. As CEO, I need to know—"

"You want me to spy on my boss," declared Burrard. A spasm jolted Burrard and his elbows flapped away from his body.

"*I* am your boss," countered Prederick. "And I'm asking you to help me manage the situation."

Burrard trembled with nervous energy.

"I'll make it worth your while," continued Prederick. "How about three hundred and fifty-five thousand restricted stock units?"

Burrard's errant eyes lit up. "That's the same amount I was promised when Circles bought ZGT."

"What happened then was between you and Ko."

"But you did nothing to right that wrong." Burrard's sharp but dispassionate voice cut through the office.

Prederick looked down. Arguing the point would get him nowhere. "So why did you stay?"

Burrard hesitated. His elbows spasmed and his frown returned.

"If you felt cheated, why didn't you quit?" insisted Prederick.

"Because I can do what I do best here and everyone leaves me alone."

"Good," answered Prederick. "Let's keep it that way."

Burrard cocked his head. "Keep it that way. How?"

Prederick resisted the urge to snap at Burrard. "You will tell me what Ko is doing, and we will leave you alone," he said evenly. "Understood?"

Burrard nodded quickly. "I understand." He stood up and took three steps for the door before stopping mid-stride. "I heard our China launch is on hold. Is there trouble?"

"That is true," said Prederick. "It seems the Chinese authorities are concerned about the stolen software. But don't worry, it will only be a short delay. The FBI has tracked Sergio to LA. It should be over quickly."

-37-

Special Agent Jay Feeley pulled into the Lincoln Elementary School parking lot, two blocks from the Holloman Motel. Two-and-a-half hours earlier, in San Francisco, he'd received call detail logs indicating Malina Olson's phone was pinging cell towers in Los Angeles. They couldn't get a precise fix on her device because Olson didn't use mobile apps and never activated her phone's GPS. Luckily for Feeley, Olson had a Tesla, one of the new breed of cars that broadcast a continuous stream of performance data so the manufacturer could monitor vehicles, update software, and advise owners of any imminent problems. All Feeley needed was a National Security Letter—he didn't even have to bother with a subpoena—to compel the carmaker to reveal that Olson's Tesla sat parked at the Holloman Motel on Sunset Boulevard. Feeley wouldn't have sworn on the Bible, but he would have bet his paycheck that Mansour was with her.

A large bull of a man stepped forward to greet Feeley as he stepped out of his car. "Special Agent Hunter Brustein," he said, extending his hand. He swung his arm toward six men gathered around the back end of a Crown Victoria.

Feeley studied the crew, part of the LA region's Joint Terrorism Task

Force. None of the agents, officers, and deputies were in their twenties. No rookies. Feeley liked that. Rookies made mistakes, and he preferred they fuck up when he wasn't around. The team was already suited up in body armor and carried ample firepower: Heckler & Koch MP5 submachine guns, and a Binelli shotgun. That would do.

"And the others?" he asked Brustein.

"We have two more out front of the motel and two snipers covering the courtyard from the roof next door."

"Good." Feeley had never worked with Brustein, but he was known as one of the toughest bastards in the Bureau, the kind of guy Feeley would happily go through a door with. Now that he ran takedowns, Brustein was highly regarded as a detail-oriented tactical planner. He had yet to lose an officer in a raid, and that was really all that mattered as far as Feeley was concerned.

"The hotel front desk says the suspect and the woman checked in about three hours ago," said Brustein. "We've had surveillance on site for the last thirty minutes. We also have a chopper on station."

Brustein took a step backward, Feeley's cue to address the team.

"Our suspect is Sergio Mansour," began Feeley, as he handed out a photo to each of the agents. "He's five-foot-ten, slim build. He's missing his left earlobe. No known tattoos. He's a computer geek. A top guy at Circles. He is wanted for data theft, but don't let that fool you. He's also wanted for questioning in the murder of his best friend. And he's been linked to Hezbollah, so we must consider him armed and dangerous. Let's do this right. People upstairs are very interested in this case."

Feeley nodded at Brustein, who stepped forward and laid out a Google Maps printout across the hood of his car. "Mansour is in room twenty-six, the third room from the corner here in the front," he said, pointing to a row of rooms fronting Sunset. "There are stairs here to access the front rooms, but the owner put a heavy steel gate on them to make sure 'hourly clients' came and went by the back stairs next to the office. It's a fire hazard, but that's an issue for another day and another department. The attendant doesn't have a key to the gate so we sent Estrada to take a close look at it. The gate is heavy, and there's no way we'd get through it without making a shitload of noise."

A murmur of groans rose up from the group.

"So, we go up these stairs," said Brustein, as he pointed to the back staircase next to the office, "and loop around the courtyard on the veranda. You will be exposed for five to ten seconds, but he won't be expecting us. Raymond has set up a sniper position here." Brustein pointed to the rooftop next to the motel. "He can cover the entire courtyard from there."

Brustein looked at each team member. This was their chance to ask questions or express concerns. No one spoke.

"Dunne, Estrada, Parker, Mitchell, you're the entry team. Stick formation. Estrada, you're point. Dunne, you have the ram. Zerounian and Collins are backup." Brustein looked somberly at the team. "Remember, once you get into the courtyard, you will be exposed. Move quickly and be safe," he concluded. "Let's move."

It was almost dark in the room when the silence imploded in a deep reverberating *thump-thump-thump.*

It was violent and loud, and Sergio felt sound waves pulse through his body. Malina burst from the bathroom. She was wrapped in a towel, her hair still wet from the shower. "Is it an earthquake?"

"No, but I'm sure the earth is moving . . . for them," he replied, tilting his head toward the room next door.

Thump-thump-thump.

She listened for a moment until she looked at the coin slot on the headboard. "I guess those things still work," she said with a smirk.

"Not for long I hope." He turned away, shaking his head in resignation. "Feel better?"

She nodded with a smile. "Deliciously hot water. Who would have thought?"

She returned to the bathroom and reemerged fully dressed a few minutes later. She grabbed the clippers from the bed and pulled a chair into the bathroom. "Okay," she said. "Time to take care of you."

Sergio nodded reluctantly as he made his way to the bathroom and sat down in front of the mirror. She covered his shoulders with a towel and tousled his hair. She switched on the clippers and a high-pitched buzz filled his ears as she ran the clipper straight down the middle of his scalp. "So have you found anything useful?" she asked.

"Yes and no." His soft chestnut hair fell away in clumps, leaving a trail of quarter-inch bristles in its place. "The purchase agreement that Circles signed with Ko's startup is shockingly sparse. We acquired the rights to all of ZGT's technologies and research, but the agreement doesn't detail what those are. Whatever Prederick agreed to buy, he didn't even want our lawyers to know."

Malina ran the clipper from front to back in parallel lines, each pass revealing more of Sergio's pale scalp. The skin on his head tingled and felt surprisingly chilled.

"The other thing that's really weird is that we paid Ko the entire two hundred million dollar purchase price."

"Wasn't it his company?" She guided the clipper in a graceful arc around his right ear.

"Technically, yes, but he must have had investors. He ran that company for almost eight years, paying salaries, renting a warehouse, buying equipment. It must have cost him, I dunno, five million or maybe even ten million dollars over that period. *Someone* must have given him the money."

She traced the hairline around his left ear. "So what's the good news?"

"I scanned Ko's doctoral papers and they are stunning." He'd never doubted that Ko's mind was first rate, but Sergio had not until that moment fully appreciated his capabilities.

She pushed his head forward to expose the back of his neck. "In what way?"

The vibrating clipper tickled his nape. "He was an expert at predictive research, a field of study aimed at developing software models or formulas that can predict the likelihood that something will happen in the future. Predictive research has many distinct strands. There's learning theory, mechanism design, predictive statistics . . ."

"Voilà," she cried. She lifted his head so he could examine himself. "I'd never recognize you now."

Sergio stared into the mirror. He'd never realized he had an egg-shaped head.

Malina popped open a compact of Clinique base makeup and dabbed it with a sponge. She held a finger under his chin to steady him. "Turn your head and close your eyes."

He complied, sitting patiently as she tenderly dabbed his bruises with the moist sponge.

"There," she finally said.

He opened his eyes and leaned toward the mirror. The black and purple bruises around his eyes now appeared to be the faint shadows of fatigue, as if he were someone who worked too hard and partied too much.

"What do you think?" she asked, holding out for a compliment.

"Anything is better than those raccoon eyes."

"Here." She placed a pair of wraparound Maui Jim sunglasses on his face. "Now you look like an aging skinhead punk, not a fugitive." She paused a moment to inspect his new look. "So, what were you saying?"

"The point I was trying to make is that not many people in the world can master any one of these strands of predictive research. Ko understood them all. And not only that, some of his papers posit theories about how we could bring together all these strands into a single unified field of study to fully unleash the power of predictive technologies. At the time, his ideas were highly theoretical and entirely aspirational. Or so we thought."

"What do you mean?"

"The socialbot program George discovered. If it can do half of what I think it can, it would still be among the most sophisticated things I've ever seen. And that suggests Ko managed to put the pieces together in a way no one else has."

"Okay," she said slowly, her eyes rolling upward in thought. "So he's a genius. But you already knew that, didn't you? It sounds like you aren't any closer to figuring out what he's up to."

"True," he said, surprised by her directness. He motioned her to follow him back to the table. "But this is even more interesting," he said, pointing to the computer screen. It was filled with text and a headshot of Ko that could have been taken yesterday. "This is an alumni interview in a six-year-old edition of the *Link*, the Carnegie Mellon computer science school's magazine."

Malina leaned in to read.

As one of our most heralded graduates in recent years, Victor Ko could have picked just about any job he wanted. But after turning down dozens of offers from Silicon Valley's top firms, he began blazing his own way forward. "I would have been honored to have taken one of those opportunities, but I wanted to be free to follow my own path and experiment with radically new concepts," he says.

Ko joined forces with Ethan Burrard (CS '05), Tong Ping Xue (CS '05) and Kevin Zachary (CS '03) to found a Los Angeles startup called ZGT Technologies to continue the research they had started at CMU.

A native of Beijing, Ko says he was attracted to CMU because of its professors and top-notch reputation. He says faculty and students more than lived up to his high hopes, in large part because they lived the school's motto: "My heart is in the work."

These days his heart and much of his time are invested in ZGT, but he also enjoys tennis and calligraphy in what little spare time he has.

"So?" She pulled back. "I don't get it."

"Nothing unusual," said Sergio, "except that there were *four*." He waved four fingers, his thumb pressed into his palm. "When Circles bought ZGT, the company got Ko, Burrard, and Tong in the deal. There wasn't anyone else."

"This Zachary guy?"

"Exactly."

"And?"

"If anyone knew what Ko was working on at ZGT, it'd be Zachary."

"What about the other two?"

"Tong died in a car accident over a year ago, and Burrard still works at Circles. Burrard is no fan of Ko, but going to him might be too risky, all things considered."

"So we need to find Zachary," she said, pursing her lips.

"Already did," he said. "While you were pampering yourself in the shower, I tracked him down online." He flashed a confident smile, even though he knew locating Zachary on the Internet and corralling him in person were two entirely different challenges.

"I have a feeling that once we find him, we'll get the answers were looking for." He paused. Malina looked dubious. "Don't worry," he continued. "It's going to be all right."

He looked to her with raised eyebrows, waiting for a smile or some kind of acknowledgement. She nodded.

"Good," he said. "Now, are you hungry?"

Malina nodded eagerly. "Starving."

"Let's get some food and then we'll go pay him a visit," he said, as he stepped into the bathroom and closed the door. He stood in front of the bathroom mirror, putting on and taking off the sunglasses. She was right. As long as he didn't get into anyone's face, chances were no one would notice anything unusual. He moved to the toilet and unzipped, just as an urgent cry sliced through the door.

"Sergio!"

He scrambled from the bathroom, his fly somewhere at half mast, and found Malina standing at the window, peeking through curtains. He reached her, just in time to see four gunmen in dark fatigues and full armor race up the stairs at the far end of the balcony. Another pair hunkered in position at the bottom of the stairs. Sergio's stomach turned over and tightened into a knot. Maybe this was just another bust in the seedy part of LA. He desperately wanted to believe that. But then one of the officers below turned his body ever so slightly, just enough to reveal three bright yellow letters on his back: FBI.

Feeley hung on the Crown Victoria's open door, leaning over Brustein in the driver's seat. A voice crackled on the radio. "Entry team in position."

Brustein spoke into the microphone. "Raymond, look good?"

"Area is clear," the sniper responded. "We're good to go."

"Entry team, go." Brustein looked up through the windshield. A black helicopter began to descend from the high perch it held prior to the start of the operation. "Task-Five-Niner, Task-Five-Niner, level off at two hundred feet."

The voice of the pilot crackled through the radio. "Roger that. Takin' 'er down to two hundred."

Feeley was twitchy. Even the best-laid plan could fall apart in a split second. Mansour might just happen to step outside the room to fill up his ice bucket at the very instant the entry team crossed the parking lot below. The element of surprise would be lost and the risk of danger would go way up. Ordering men with guns to arrest other men with guns was never a sure thing. People sometimes died.

Raymond kept Feeley and Brustein updated with a running commentary from his rooftop vantage point. "Entry team has reached the top of the stairs."

Feeley tried to imagine the team duckwalking in pairs as they looped around the courtyard on the second floor balcony. Estrada would be in front, moving purposely on the balls of his feet, knees slightly bent, and arms outstretched with his Glock 9mm aimed at room twenty-six. Behind him would be Parker, also in a crouch, with his right eye trained on the scope of his MP5 submachine gun. Behind him would be Mitchell and his Binelli, a shotgun so devastating that it could take down a wall. And finally came Dunne with the ram, a heavy battering tool that could bash through a door with a single blow.

Five years had passed since Feeley last took part in a takedown. Leadership had its perks, but he still missed the excitement and camaraderie of being on a team.

The radio sounded off. "They're at the last corner. Twenty feet from target." Three seconds passed and the radio buzzed again. "Entry team in position."

Feeley nodded with satisfaction. He could picture it: three men pressed against the wall next to Mansour's room. Dunne would be on point now, preparing to lead the assault with the ram. Estrada and Mitchell would be next in line, ready to enter once the door was breached. Parker would be crouched against the railing, his MP5 pointed at Mansour's door just in case the suspect engaged them before the assault began.

Brustein raised the microphone to his mouth. "Go!" he shouted. "Take him down."

―――――――――

Sergio had been a fugitive for about twelve hours, and until this moment he'd hoped he would somehow be able to explain it all away as a big mistake. The sight of the agents drove home the gravity of his situation.

Sergio turned off the table lamps and took another peek through the curtains. The four agents were out of sight now, but presumably at the end of the balcony. He and Malina didn't have much time before the FBI came crashing through the door. They might even shoot a suspected terrorist on sight.

"We need to get out of here, now!" he whispered fiercely.

He tossed his laptop into Malina's duffel bag, while she gathered up the new clothes. She stuffed them in the bag and lunged for her mobile phone on the dresser.

"Leave it," he commanded.

She turned to him, her eyes clouded by confusion.

"The only way they could have tracked us was your phone," he said. "Or your car. Either way, they know you're here."

He reached for her, but stopped cold, his arm still outstretched as an unnerving thought raced through his mind. Had she called the cops? He leveled his eyes at Malina. Her confusion had given way to fear and he recognized the instant for what it was: her moment of truth. He opened his hand, offering it to her. "This is your last chance to change your mind. You can tell them you didn't know."

She hesitated, just a split second, before placing her trembling hand in his.

Sergio pulled her into the bathroom, opened the window over the toilet, and scanned the pavement below. The distant whomp-whomp of a helicopter filled the air but no lights were visible in the evening sky above.

"Looks clear," he said as he pulled himself back inside.

With a precision and clear-headedness that surprised him, he stripped the bed and tied the sheets together to form a rope. Menacing shadows floated across the yellow curtains.

He tied one end of the sheet-rope around Malina's waist and nudged her to the bathroom window. She looked up to the window and hesitated, her lower lip trembling as her frightened eyes met his.

"I won't let you fall," he said firmly but softly. "I promise." He wrapped her in his arms and squeezed her tightly. "Okay, out you go."

Malina slipped through the window feet first as he sat on the toilet and braced his legs around the tank. He tucked the sheet-rope under his armpit and squeezed his arm against his body. Then grasping the sheet with both hands, he gave Malina a nod. She lowered herself until she dropped out of sight and the makeshift rope went taut. He peeked in the mirror. More shadows skimmed across the curtains. *Any second now.*

The sheet slipped through his hands. He wasn't lowering her as much as he was controlling her descent. Then the knot connecting the sheets ripped into his armpit and tore at his flesh. The pain surprised him, just enough that he instinctively relaxed his arm. The knot flew under his arm and burst through his fists. The sheet and Malina were in freefall.

"Fuck," he cried out, as he tried to estimate how far she'd drop. He clamped down on the last sheet, but it was already too late. The end of the sheet whipped from his hand and flew out the window. Her yelp and a thud rose up from the alley. He jumped to his feet and sprang to the window, afraid of what he might find. Below, Malina stood up slowly and dusted her butt with her hand. She looked up with a painful grimace. "I'm good!"

Sergio grabbed the duffel bag and dropped it out the window. Somewhere behind him a sharp crack echoed and a muffled voice called out: "FBI. Get down on the floor!"

-38-

Feeley turned away from the Crown Victoria, his head thrown back and his body tense with nervous energy as a loud crack blared from the police radio. The assault team had smashed in the flimsy motel room door, and voices, high pitched and urgent, yelled out commands as they moved into the room.

"FBI! Put your hands where we can see them. Get down on the floor."

An instant later a second distant voice called out: "Clear!" Feeley understood the bathroom was empty. A final call came across the radio—"site secured"—and Feeley relaxed a little, knowing the raid had gone off without gunfire.

Some ten seconds later Estrada's voice called out. "We have a negative on the suspect, I repeat, negative on the suspect. We have one civilian here. Male, mid-twenties. Blond. Blue. Looks pretty whacked out. I'm guessing it's meth."

"Son of a bitch!" roared Feeley as he slammed his palm on the car roof. He reached into the Crown Victoria and grabbed the microphone from Brustein's hand. "Confirm you are in room twenty-six, I repeat, confirm room twenty-six."

"Confirmed," replied Estrada, a hint of disdain in his voice.

Feeley felt his chest tighten. What had gone wrong? A chorus of voices filled the room as Dunne and Estrada questioned the suspect. Estrada's voice soon crackled over the radio once more.

"This guy says a woman gave him sixty bucks to get a room and then they swapped keys. He says he can't remember the other room number."

"Can't remember?" Feeley closed his eyes and shook his head. He pulled the microphone to his mouth. "Get the fuck down to the office and find out." Feeley double-clicked the transmit button. "Task-Five-Niner. See anything from up there?"

"Negative," came the reply from the helicopter. "I'm over the front of the motel. Hang on."

Several agonizing seconds passed before the pilot's voice crackled again. "There's a narrow alley at the back of the motel. More like a crawl space. It's closed off at either end with a chain link—Wait! I got something. There's an open window along the back of the hotel."

Brustein's mouth scrunched up in anger. He reached for the microphone. "Raymond, do you have a visual on the suspects?"

"Negative," came the sniper's reply. "Permission to reposition?"

"Granted. Move to the west side of your roof." Brustein released the transmit button and pressed it again quickly. "We need to set up a perimeter on the west side, and we need to get into that room. Collins and Zerounian, get around back. Raymond, you will cover them. Estrada, find out what room they were in and clear it. Then send Mitchell, Parker, and Dunne to support Collins and Zerounian." Brustein looked to the sky above the Holloman. "Task-Five-Niner, should they skirt building on north or south side?"

"Go north," came the reply. "That end connects to the Galleria loading bay."

Brustein let out a low groan.

"What?" asked Feeley.

Brustein gave Feeley a grim look. "The Galleria Mall has at least seven public entrances, three car ramps, and who knows how many emergency exits. It'll probably take the LAPD at least twenty minutes to set a perimeter around it."

"Son of a bitch," barked Feeley, as he pounded his fist into the roof of the car. If Mansour and Olson had any sense, they'd be long gone by then.

-39-

Richard Diebolt floated down the steps and immersed himself in a sea of faces. Most Stark County Republicans had probably heard his stump speech before, but that didn't seem to dampen their enthusiasm. As long as he fed them red meat, and used China to scare the shit out of them, they'd turn out in droves on election day. The throng was loud and boisterous and all around him now, kept at arm's length by four sturdy Secret Service agents who were supposed to take a bullet for him. This was a Republican county, but some liberal whack-job could have easily made the trek down from Cleveland just to take a shot at him.

Scores of well-wishers thrust their arms in among the agents. Some shouted words of encouragement, others cried out for his attention. The energy of the crowd amped him up and Diebolt made sure to respond to each individual with a solid handshake and an enthusiastic smile. The crush of bodies parted and someone handed him a baby in a pink jumper. Diebolt kissed her and lifted her for all to see before handing the little girl back to one of the agents. Slowly but inexorably, his entourage neared a solid wood door to the left side of the stage. When they reached it, the agents turned to face the swarm, forming a formidable barrier as the door swung open. Waiting for him inside was campaign director Nathan Aaron and communications manager Mark Quinlen, his phone to his ear and a look of concern in his eyes. The door swung shut and the cries of the supporters faded.

"We've got a problem." Quinlen hung up the phone. "Vignault at the *Times* just called to give me the heads up. They've found some people willing to talk—" Quinlen looked around, moved in closer, and continued in a whisper. "To talk about past drug use. They want a comment."

Diebolt stiffened, even as his gaze flittered across the sparsely furnished room. It had painted cinderblock, cheap commercial carpet, and a couple of sofas. A group of three campaign workers he'd never seen before were gathered around the tables with coffee and snacks. He called over to them with a friendly smile. "Excuse me. Can we get a little privacy, please?"

"Oh, sure, sorry," said one of the fresh-faced young men.

Diebolt loosened his tie and poured himself a mug of coffee while the trio slipped out the door. He'd expected stories like this, but much earlier in the campaign. Over the past month or so he had started to believe he might get away without having to deal with the issue. But for it to come out now? Three days before the election? The phony smile slipped from his face as he spun toward Quinlen and Aaron. "All right," he barked. "What does that fuckhead have?"

Quinlen cleared his throat. "Vignault was vague," he began unsteadily, "but the gist was that he has sources saying you were much more heavily involved in drugs than you've let on. He mentioned speed, coke, and opium."

"Opium?" Diebolt's skin crawled.

"That's what he said."

Diebolt felt the impulse surge from that dark place within, asserting control and quickly subsuming him. It filled him with passion, gave him strength, and provided singularity of purpose, its pressure building explosively until he hauled back like a pitcher winding up for his delivery. Diebolt understood it was too late. He couldn't have stopped himself even if he wanted. He hurled the mug toward the wall with all his strength. Hot coffee sprayed through the air and Quinlen and Aaron threw up their arms to shield their faces. An instant later, the mug exploded against the wall and ceramic shards flew across the room. "*Three days* before the election?" roared Diebolt. "Fucking cocksucker."

The room went quiet, save for Diebolt's ragged breaths. He trembled as he surveyed the mess he'd made. It had been years since he'd let go like that. And it felt good, if only for an instant. But it didn't change the facts. "Three days . . ." he muttered. His eyes dropped to the floor. "That bastard."

Quinlen perked up. "Come again?"

"Nothing," said Diebolt. He took a step, then two, before doubling back like a man under siege but unsure from what quarter. He gathered pace and spun around at the wall, his soles crushing ceramic slivers into the carpet. A last desperate attempt by Lester to swing the tide? On the very same day he'd heard from Liu? What had it been? Three years since they last spoke? Whoever it was, Diebolt wasn't surprised they went to Vignault, the most virulently liberal reporter at a paper full of them. He was the perfect lapdog for anyone out to torpedo a Republican.

He stopped in his tracks, decided. "Get me on the phone with Vignault—now," he commanded, his voice strained but deliberate. "I want to hear what he's got."

Quinlen stepped forward. "Is that wise, sir?" He glanced nervously at Aaron. "Perhaps one of us should hear him out first. That way he can't drop any surprises on you—and perhaps rattle you—while you're on the phone with him. Once we know what he's got, we'll put out a statement."

"No." Diebolt focused on Quinlen with razor-sharp intensity. "I want to hear exactly what he has." Once Diebolt knew that, he might be able to figure out who was fucking with him.

-40-

Sergio and Malina dropped down the stairs into the bowels of the Galleria's underground garage. If they were lucky, they'd have maybe ten minutes before the police surrounded the mall. It seemed like a reasonable gamble when they ran through the loading bay gate, but the farther they descended, the more Sergio felt trapped.

They burst through a fire door on the fourth level, drawing unwanted stares from a handful of shoppers waiting at the elevator bank. The heavy door slammed shut behind them as Sergio led Malina to a distant corner of the garage, all the while untwisting one of the metal coat hangers he'd snatched in the loading bay. A muted *ding* announced the arrival of the elevator, and within seconds, they were alone on the floor.

He stopped and pointed to a 1994 Honda Accord. "This one."

Sergio fashioned the hanger into a long stretch of wire with a small hook at one end. Some three minutes had passed since they ran through the loading bay. He folded another hanger in half, wedged it between the frame and window and slipped the hook through the gap. He looked at her with a satisfied smile. "I used to have one of these."

He jiggled the hanger and worked it into place until it looped around the lock latch. With one forceful tug, the latch gave way. "There's good reason these Accords were the most stolen vehicles back in the nineties. Mine was stolen three times during the six years I owned it."

Sergio opened the driver's door and pulled on the lever next to the seat. He raced to the rear and lifted the trunk. "Bingo," he cried, as he pulled out a small toolbox, dug around inside it, and held up a flat-head screwdriver and wire cutters. "We're going to need these."

"You gotta be kidding," she said, shaking her head. "You can hot-wire a car, too?"

"Too?"

"You hack into the law firm, and now you're stealing a car." Her uncertain tone suggested she was torn between disapproval and hopefulness. "I thought we were the good guys."

Sergio tried to hide his smirk as he slipped into the driver's seat and unscrewed the plastic cowling around the Accord's steering column. "We used to race junkers. A race called the 24 Hours of Lemons—"

"LeMans?" she asked with an exaggerated French accent.

"No," he laughed. "Lemons. Like the fruit. Or a defective car."

She looked at him dubiously.

"The rules were you had to buy a car worth less than five hundred dollars and race it around a track for twenty-four hours. Whichever team drove the most miles during that time won. When your car broke down during the race, you'd have to fix it, so we learned a lot about cars during that time."

"We?" she asked. Five minutes gone.

He pulled three wires out of the column, snipped them with the wire cutters, and stripped the plastic coating. "Me, George, and a couple of other engineers who used to work at Circles." He glanced at her. "It was a lot of fun."

A heavy *clank* reverberated through the garage. Sergio slumped in the seat and Malina dropped into a crouch between the Honda and the Toyota next to it. He peeked over the dashboard. "Security guard near the stairs," he whispered, as he slipped out the door and closed it. "Get to the back."

Waddling like ducks, they squeezed themselves between the bumper and the wall as an eerie squelching sound filled the fourth level. It repeated itself in a two-beat patter; one high squeak, a second lower squawk in rapid succession, then a pause before the first beat repeated. One-two. Left-right. Rubber-soled shoes on the polished cement floor, each step louder than the last. They squatted and held on to each other for support. Was the guard making his usual rounds? Or did he know there were a couple of fugitives on the loose? Most important, did this rent-a-cop have a gun?

The squelching security guard was close now, maybe a few cars away. The noise grated at Sergio, even if it was also oddly reassuring. Only an idiot security guard would wear shoes that announced themselves a hundred yards away. The guard stopped. Sergio's legs began to protest but he didn't dare move. Seven minutes gone.

Screeching radio chatter pierced the silence: a jumble of fuzzy words that made no sense. The call went unanswered and the garage went quiet once again, except for a soft rustling Sergio couldn't decipher. Then came the flinty *flick flick* of a lighter before the guard inhaled and released a deep satisfying breath. Malina rolled her eyes and shook her head. The guard took two or three more drags before moving on, his telltale squelch slower now as if he was making time to finish his smoke.

A cramp grabbed hold of Sergio's right leg and viciously tore at his hamstring. He shot upward, threw this leg out in front of him, and fell onto his butt as he lost balance. He lay still on the ground, his ears alert for any change in the guard's squeaky but now distant cadence. The guard kept moving away and Sergio regained his feet, just enough to spot the security guard on the other side of the garage, doubling back to the stairs. The distant fire door opened and slammed shut with a thunderous clang.

"Sheesh," said Malina, wiping her fingers across her brow in obvious relief. "Talk about freaky."

"Are you okay?" he asked, as he straightened up and stretched his legs.

"Yeah, but I've had enough drama for today."

Sergio dropped into the driver's seat and reached for the steering column. He twisted the battery wire and ignition wires together, bringing the warning lights on the dash to life. Then he delicately touched the remaining wire to the first two and the engine came alive.

"That's it?

"Not quite." He got out of the car and motioned for her to stand beside him. "Now we need to break the steering column lock."

Together they reached into the open driver's door, grabbed the top of the steering wheel and pulled on it in unison. "Rinse and repeat," he said, heaving on the wheel once again. They yanked for a third, then fourth time and they soon had the Accord rocking from side to side as they built up momentum with each pull. At least eight minutes by now, maybe more. Then a metallic crack filled the car. "That's the pin." A proud smile spread across his face. "Now we're good to go."

-41-

Damon Graves dropped down for his forty-third push-up. He felt strong, resolute, and angry, a potent combination to fuel his superset workout: seventy-five pull-ups, seventy-five sit-ups, seventy-five push-ups, and seventy-five squats, all without a break, followed by three sets of eighty-pound bicep curls. It was brutal, far tougher than his usual workout—punishment for a job poorly done.

. . . forty-four, forty-five, forty-six . . .

Last night's mistakes were unacceptable. It wasn't his fault Verneek didn't have the thumb drive, but Graves had failed to persuade him to reveal where it was. Worse was the Mansour thing. How the fuck had the guy spotted him outside the coffee shop? Graves pushed harder, faster, practically driving himself into the air on each upstroke.

. . . sixty, sixty-one, sixty-two . . .

He had to grudgingly admit he'd underestimated the techie. There would be no assumptions next time. Whatever game these people were playing, they were all fucking dirty. He'd put at least three bullets in Mansour's car and nearly drove him into a head-on with a semi and still the guy didn't go to the police. Fucking dirty, for sure.

. . . seventy-three, seventy-four, seventy-five.

He stood up and strapped on a training vest stuffed with sixty-five pounds of weight. Then with his feet shoulder-width apart, he dropped down into a deep squat and rose up once again. He repeated the squat in a fluid and steady motion.

. . . two, three, four . . .

He wanted another shot at Mansour. No fucking way would some punk-ass techie, a civilian, embarrass him like that. Graves had a reputation, and a business, to protect. Just one more chance. That's all he'd need. Mansour was gonna die ugly, painfully.

. . . nineteen, twenty, twenty-one . . .

The phone rang—the white phone on the dresser. It was his client. No one else had that number. He rose from his squat and pressed ANSWER. "Yes?"

"We cannot tolerate any more mistakes," said the caller.

"It will not happen again," replied Graves, making sure to voice just the right amount of contrition.

"Are you ready to finish the job?"

His client was mocking him. "Yes," he replied through gritted teeth.

"Good," came the reply. "Because I think I know where you'll find Mansour."

-42-

Cool ocean air wafted through the Honda's open windows as Sergio turned off the Pacific Coast Highway and headed into the hills above Malibu, an hour outside Los Angeles. Coral Canyon Road snaked left and right as they gained elevation, leaving the well-traveled coastal highway behind. There would be no cops up here.

They drove silently into a dark void illuminated only by the Honda's high beams and scattered lights from the homes on the mountainside above. Sergio tried to rehearse what he'd say to Zachary, but his mind refused to let go of the narrow escape from the hotel.

"How old were you?" asked Malina, her quiet voice ripping him away from his thoughts.

"Huh?"

"Your father. How old were you when he died?"

"Eleven," he replied.

Malina waited for him to continue. He wasn't used to sharing this part of himself.

"We lived in the fields, at the end of a dirt road," he began, unsure of his own words. "It was sunset and we were almost home when a group of men in pickup trucks cut us off and forced my father to stop. He pushed me down to the floor of our pickup so the men wouldn't see me. Then he got out."

Sergio's stomach tightened, just like it did at the first hint of trouble all those years before. "At first I heard angry voices, and then they started beating him. He cried out, pleading with them to stop. I wanted to help him, but I was so scared. Then I heard a gunshot. I looked over the dash and saw my father lying motionless in the dirt road surrounded by six men. That's when I screamed. I couldn't help myself."

Malina reached for his shoulder and squeezed tightly.

"The men yanked me from the truck and dragged me to the man who shot Papá. I'll never forget those black eyes. He had a pockmarked face and a scratchy voice that didn't sound quite human." Sergio forced an oversized lump back down his throat. "The man leaned into my face," he said, holding his hand a few inches from his swollen nose. "I can still smell that awful reek of alcohol. That's when he said he'd come back for all of us if I ever said anything about that night to anyone. He yelled it, over and over again. And then," he added, touching his left ear, "he pulled out a big Bowie knife and sliced off my earlobe."

Sergio's eyes watered as he relived the fear of that night. "I'm sorry," he said. "I didn't mean—"

"No," she said. "Don't be sorry. It's not your fault. "

Malina turned in her seat and stroked the back of his bristly head. "You know," she began, "when we were at the bar having drinks, I sensed a deep sadness in you. I felt it when you talked about your family. I knew there was something there."

"It wasn't all bad you know, my childhood," he said, as he stoically guided the Honda up the hill. "But when I think of what happened, it's my chance to remember him, honor him, to let him know I haven't forgotten."

"'The wound is the place where the Light enters you.'"

"Huh?"

"It's a saying by Rumi, the thirteenth-century Persian mystic and poet."

Sergio pursed his lips as he tried to recall any mention of Rumi in high school or college, but the only books that came to mind were the tech manuals lining his living room shelves, organized by subject, and alphabetized for easy reference. "I think maybe this Rumi guy had a point," he said.

A short while later, Sergio turned onto Seaview Drive and coasted slowly as he followed the bend in the quiet street. He passed a couple of parked cars and pulled to the edge of the pavement a few houses past number thirty-eight, Kevin Zachary's address.

Finding Zachary had been easy, especially with a name like that. It didn't hurt that a guy in business for himself had his own website. The hard part was about to begin. Sergio pulled apart the ignition wires and the low drone of the engine gave way to a whispering wind floating up from the sea one thousand feet below. They sat silently in the Honda for a while, letting Seaview Drive reveal itself to them. Lights flickered on and off inside homes. Shadows glided past closed curtains. A car passed and disappeared into a driveway down the street. An elderly couple looked down from their perch on the veranda of the house across the road.

Zachary's house was a sizeable Mediterranean, probably worth a couple of million dollars, and it stood out against the more modest homes on Seaview Drive. The shades in all of his windows were drawn and no lights were visible inside. The garage door was closed, the yard was scraggly, and the mailbox was so stuffed with envelopes that the lid would not close.

"Stay here for now," Sergio said, as he stepped from the car.

He strolled briskly to Zachary's front door and gave it a couple of sharp raps. He waited half a minute and knocked again, this time pressing his ear to the door. A sound, maybe. He couldn't be sure. He knocked again, if only to demonstrate that he wasn't going away. Another minute passed before he knocked again, louder than before. Arm cocked, he was poised to pound on it with his fist when the rattle of locks stopped him.

The door swung open a few inches until a chain snapped taut across the opening. Sergio stared into empty space for a second until a man in a wheelchair rolled into sight. His legs flopped to one side but his upper body sat ramrod straight. He was mid-forties with a round face, unruly shoulder-length hair, and penetrating blue eyes. He held a gun in his lap. It was pointed toward Sergio's knees.

His stomach tightened. "Kevin Zachary?"

The man squeezed the pistol grip, raised his chin, and waited for Sergio to continue.

"I'm Sergio Mansour," he stammered. "I work at Circles."

Zachary lifted the gun an inch off his lap and wiggled the barrel. "A lot of people are looking for you," he said in a gravelly voice.

The words sucked the air out of Sergio's lungs. He pried his eyes from the pistol. "You used to work with Victor Ko. I need your help."

A flash of anger streaked across Zachary's face. And just as quickly, it was gone. "Haven't seen Ko in years," he said tersely.

"Something has gone terribly wrong at Circles," blurted Sergio. "Our chief security officer has been killed. He was my friend. Now they're trying to kill me."

"So go to the police." Zachary reached for the door and started to push it closed. Sergio jammed his foot into the gap between the door and frame and squeezed his face into the narrow space. He locked eyes with Zachary. "Just a few questions and then I'll be gone," he pleaded, trying to suppress his fear and desperation. *"Please."*

"Not my problem," replied Zachary. He lifted the gun from his lap and pointed it at Sergio's face.

Sergio's heart fluttered as he stared into the inky black barrel. For a terrifying split second, he was sure it was the last thing he'd ever see. But as the instant stretched into seconds, he came to understand he'd already be dead if Zachary wanted to shoot him. He drew in a deep, grateful breath. "I think it *is* your problem."

Zachary pulled the gun back and lifted his chin once again. "Why's that?"

"Because I think you have unfinished business with Ko."

-43-

Zachary led Sergio and Malina into a sitting room next to the kitchen in the rear of the house. It should have been the dining room, but Zachary had furnished it with an oversized sofa and a couple of well-worn armchairs. Heaps of books and papers filled the shelves; stacks of magazines were piled in one corner. A thick layer of dust had settled over everything in the room. Heavy curtains were drawn tight over every window. The stuffy air smelled of mold and fast food.

Sergio pushed aside a pile of clothes to make room for Malina and him on the sofa. Zachary parked his wheelchair in front of the doorway, blocking their way out. The gun was still in his lap. "Now who are you?" he asked Malina.

"She's with me," replied Sergio.

Zachary kept his focus on Malina. "Abetting a fugitive?" he asked. "Are you really sure you want to take a fall for this man?" He nodded at Mansour.

"Nobody's going to take a fall, not if you help us," she said.

Zachary scoffed and Sergio leaned forward from his seat. "I told you, she's—"

"I wasn't speaking to you," Zachary said sharply. "You've dragged this woman into a real mess. She has no idea what she's involved in."

Sergio tilted his head thoughtfully. "What exactly are we involved in?"

Zachary arched an eyebrow and flashed an impish grin. "So what happened to you?"

Sergio reached for his face, self-consciously. "I told you. They tried to kill me." His nose felt as crooked and puffy as it did in the motel room.

"Well, *they* sure made a mess of your nose." Zachary's eyes narrowed and his smile tightened into a grimace. "So tell me, what did you mean when you said I have unfinished business with Ko?"

"Why did you leave ZGT?"

Zachary's expression darkened. "I get to ask the questions," he said, flicking his wrist just enough to make the gun twitch in his lap. "And you get to answer them. Now, what did you mean?"

Sergio's mind raced into overdrive, searching for, grasping at, and testing any answers that came to mind. He'd bluffed his way into the house and now he was being called. Rattled by Zachary's withering gaze, Sergio had the sinking feeling he'd made a mistake coming here. His shoulders sagged and his mouth went dry as it occurred to him, for the very first time, that Zachary and Ko could be best buds, for all he knew. He hesitated and then slowly brought his fingertips together, like he was about to pray, before pressing them to his lips.

"Please, would you put the gun away?" he asked, his voice cracking. "So we can talk?"

"About what?"

"About what Ko is doing at Circles."

Zachary leaned forward and zeroed in on Sergio. "What's he doing?"

"Please. The gun."

Zachary mulled the request with pursed lips. After a moment that dragged on far too long for Sergio, Zachary flicked the gun's safety switch with his thumb and wedged the pistol between his right leg and the side of his wheelchair. He set his elbows on the armrests and slowly stroked his chin as he leveled his eyes at Sergio. "Start talking."

Sergio began at the start, right from the moment George had called him in the lab. Slowly and meticulously, Sergio unpacked the past twenty-four hours and laid it out for Zachary, who pulled out a steno pad to take notes and draw bubbles connected by scratchy lines that linked the people and events in Sergio's tale.

Sergio pulled the thumb drive from his pocket and told Zachary about the Chinese profiles he'd discovered in the café. Sergio ruefully noted that George would almost surely be alive if he hadn't found and copied them. Sergio still couldn't understand why the hacker had carefully encrypted all the data he was stealing, except for the fake user profiles. "It was almost as if the intruder wanted the profiles to be found," he concluded.

Zachary fell silent. He looked down at the carpet as he lifted his hand and softly pinched his lower lip. Then he looked up. "Did you find a signature?"

Sergio nodded, surprised by the question. "It was an odd one," he replied. "Capital S, dot dot dot, capital N."

Zachary's blue eyes twinkled and a mischievous smile slipped across his face.

"Do you know who that is?" asked Sergio.

Zachary nodded. "That's Sinon. I'm surprised you haven't heard of him. Sinon doesn't make mistakes. He didn't encrypt the profiles because he *wanted* them to be found."

"How can you be so sure?"

Zachary looked to Sergio and then Malina, indecision now etched all over his face. He reached between the armrest and his left leg, fumbling around for an instant until he withdrew his clenched fist. Slowly, he began kneading a red rubber ball, squeezing it over and over until he finally said: "Because I'm Sinon and that was my attack."

-44-

Sergio couldn't decide if he should be angry or relieved. The master hacker who'd caused so much grief wheeled his way onto a metal platform at the top of the basement stairs. Sergio wanted to lash out, but instead he stood quietly as Zachary flipped a switch that sent the platform sliding down a set of rails. Following closely behind with Malina, Sergio sensed that answers to his many questions were near at hand.

"I met Ko in my third year at Carnegie Mellon," Zachary said, looking over his shoulder. "We were both young, eager PhD students. He was, *is,* exceedingly bright, as you already know, and I was no slouch myself. I guess that's why we got along."

The platform settled on the basement landing, a door to either side. Zachary raised the safety arm and led Sergio and Malina into a chilly room lit only by the faint glow of screen-saver software. The fragrant aroma of coffee rushed up Sergio's battered nose and the distinctive whir of servers filled his ears.

"A lot of the other students didn't like him." Zachary rolled across the polished concrete floor and flicked on a lamp hanging over his desk. "As you've surely noticed, he has a way of pissing off people who don't agree with him."

He nudged his ergonomic keyboard and two large flat-screen monitors came to life. They were plugged into a DuoPro II laptop, which was in turn connected to a desktop computer at his feet. Sergio didn't have to check to know those computers were networked to a rack of servers stacked against the wall to Zachary's right.

"He was usually right, of course, but he just never seemed to master that delicate art of telling other people why they were wrong," said Zachary with a chuckle. He motioned to the frayed loveseat near the door. Malina sank into the cushions. Sergio took an armrest.

"It didn't bother me," continued Zachary. "I never saw that side of him because we kept up with each other. There aren't many people I can say that about." He hesitated before flashing Sergio an appreciative smile. "I imagine you know that feeling, too."

Sergio stammered, unsure what to say. He hated being put on the spot like that. It was pure awkwardness. "What did you work on together?"

"We overlapped on a few projects at school, but we didn't really start working together until Ko offered me a position at his startup. He was very persuasive. He told me I could work on whatever I wanted and that I'd get a cut—not a one-time bonus, we're talking royalties here—from anything I developed that had commercial applications."

"Who funded it?" said Sergio.

"Family money, or so he said. Almost fifty million dollars. He showed me the accounts."

A long low whistle escaped Sergio lips. "So I'm guessing you were hooked."

"How could I not be? He gave me absolute freedom, a great salary, and the chance to pocket millions if we scored a hit. There was no downside."

"Except you know what they say," said Malina. "If it's too good to be true . . ."

Zachary nodded reluctantly. "At first it was great. There were four of us working our asses off, writing code. I stuck to security. I had a lot of fun working on stuff like post-password authentication and strategies to thwart state-sponsored espionage. Ko focused on hard-core machine learning theory, things like multiagent systems, computational social choice and preference handling, mechanism design and fair division, decision making under uncertainty . . ." Zachary glanced at Malina. "Oh, sorry. Am I getting carried away?"

"No," she insisted. "Well, maybe a little. What's machine learning?"

"It's a field of study that aims to develop algorithms, theories, and statistical methods that enable computers to learn from data, not only so machines can recognize previously learned data, but also to antici-pate events and patterns not yet seen."

Malina looked to Sergio, her eyes full of doubt. Zachary plowed ahead.

"Humans do this all the time. Imagine you are in the woods at night and you hear a loud grunt, unlike anything you've ever heard before. Seconds later you run into a big furry creature you've never seen before. Your first reaction would be to run away. Why? Because your mind will instantly process everything you've learned about similar sit-uations. You know the woods can be dangerous. You know that other big furry creatures have sharp teeth and claws and they are much stron-ger than you. And you know that some big furry creatures eat people. So your brain processes all that information and formulates the most appropriate response to a situation you have never encountered before. Then you get home, you Google the creature and discover that it was indeed dangerous. That confirms your response was appropriate. And from then on your brain will be forever wired to react when you hear that distinctive grunt."

A satisfied smile spread across Zachary's face. "Until relatively recently, computers could only do exactly what they were programmed to do. They could not make leaps of logic like our frightened hiker."

"So what you're saying," began Malina, "is that computers are becom-ing . . . maybe not self-aware, but eerily prescient. Kind of like the creepy stuff that Google guy said a few years back, something to the effect that your computer will know what you want before you even know it."

"Sort of," replied Zachary. He continued talking, no doubt explaining how the latest algorithms enabled computers to predict events, patterns, or behaviors that would have been impossible just a few years earlier. Sergio heard none of it as his eyes drifted around the room. Two rectangular windows hung high on the wall over the desk. They were covered on the inside by thick steel louvers locked with sliding surface bolts. A worktable on the opposite wall was covered with monitors, spare computer parts, and a tangle of cables and wires. A stack of discarded machines in the corner stood near a door to a back room. The unfinished basement had a slightly disheveled feel to it, but Sergio felt certain Zachary knew exactly where everything was.

"So what about Burrard and Tong?" asked Sergio.

Zachary quickly changed gears. "Burrard spent most of his time working on filtering software that could identify, track, and delete content from web pages based on a wide variety of parameters. Write a swear word on your page? It will be there for all to see, except for kids, say, under the age of twelve . . ."

"Auto-censoring," said Sergio.

"So you've seen it?"

Sergio nodded. "We'll be seeing a lot more of it soon enough. What about Tong?"

"Tong was into socialbots." Zachary put his hands on the armrests of his wheelchair and pushed himself up, shifting his body as he lowered himself back into his seat. Then he readjusted his legs so that they leaned to the left rather than the right. "He became an expert in building massive socialbot networks that could fool the most sophisticated defenses. Remember, this was when US Cyber Command started using socialbots to infiltrate terror networks. Tong figured he could do much better, especially if they incorporated Ko's prediction models. And he did."

"So what happened?" asked Sergio.

"Over time, I grew very uncomfortable with what Ko and Tong were doing. It was way more advanced than anything counterintelligence was doing at the time, and I didn't know who we were working for." Zachary sighed, the weight of frustration evident in his voice. "One of the investors—Ko's uncle, or so we were told—would come around every now and then. He was all business, not very friendly, but really interested in our work. Burrard used to joke that he was a Chinese spy. I didn't think that was so funny and I tried to get it out of Ko, but the more I pressed the more he pushed me aside. Eventually, I had to leave."

"Too good to be true," said Sergio, nodding toward Malina.

"I was the lucky one," said Zachary. "Ko wrote me a big check to go away and keep my mouth shut. I later heard he shafted Tong and Burrard when he sold to Circles. Promises weren't kept."

Malina leaned forward on the sofa. "It's scary to think that someone so ruthless and nasty like Ko has control over billions of people's most sensitive information." She challenged Sergio with a peevish stare. "And all these big Internet companies have the gall to insist that we should trust them."

Sergio held his tongue. There was nothing he could say to change Malina's opinion. Besides, there were more important things to consider at the moment. "So what did you do?" he asked Zachary.

"I went to work for InTEK Systems as an intelligence contractor for the military's information warfare effort. I didn't think much more about ZGT until a few years later when I read Circles had bought them. That's when I started to get worried."

"Worried? Why?" asked Sergio.

"You remember the headlines," said Zachary, spreading his hands in the air like a movie star imagining his name on a marquee. "Circles supposedly bought ZGT for its machine-learning expertise. The wave of the future. But most of what Ko and Tong were doing was designed to compromise social networks, not protect them." He paused, studying them both carefully. "I probably shouldn't tell you this, but while I was still at ZGT, I copied their socialbot code and brought it home. It struck me as a bit obsessive at the time, but I was so unnerved by the situation that I felt compelled to do it. And when Circles took over ZGT, I decided to break into Circles to figure out what they were doing with Tong's socialbots."

"Wait, wait." Malina stood up and waved her hands. "Wait a sec. Before you go on, there's just one thing I don't get about all this social-bot stuff. The only way they work is if people agree to become buddies with them, right? So why do people do that when the socialbot perso-nas are obviously complete strangers?"

Sergio and Zachary looked at each other, waiting for the other to respond. Sergio was certain he saw his own impatience mirrored in Zachary's eyes. Finally, Zachary held out his hand to Sergio. "After you," he said.

"It's been a huge problem for us." Sergio stood up and approached the coffeemaker on the workbench. "We did a survey a few years back and found that almost forty percent of Circles users had accepted requests from strangers who claimed they shared a mutual friend." The coffeepot was cool and half full, but the condensation dripping down the sides of the glass suggested it was, in relative terms, freshly brewed. He held up the pot to his companions.

"Be my guest," replied Zachary.

Malina quickly shook her head.

"So," he continued, as he looked for a clean cup, "pretty much every Circles user has received those requests—someone who claims to be a friend of a friend, or someone they went to school with, or some-one who works at the same company. Typically, the greater the number of connections people had, the more likely they were to link up with strangers. Not surprisingly, our study showed requests from socialbots purporting to be attractive females were far more likely to be accepted—at least by men."

He picked a blue cup with an InTEK Systems logo and filled it with coffee. "And once you become buddies with a socialbot, it has access to a list of all your friends. Then it sends out connection requests to them. A network can grow very quickly."

He brought the cup to his lips and winced at the acidic, bitter taste.

Zachary grinned. "The important thing to understand is that there is a massive socialbot network thriving on Circles, and it's downright scary."

"And because this one is an inside job, Circles' defenses are useless against it," she said, looking to them for confirmation.

"Correct." Zachary sat up in his chair, his blue eyes heavy with concern. "And it's very sophisticated. It targets real people based on the school they went to, the jobs they've held, their favorite teams, hobbies, club memberships, you name it. But that's not all," he continued. "These socialbots use predictive algorithms to shape their interactions with users."

Malina cocked her head at Sergio. "Predictive algorithms. Isn't that what you were explaining in the hotel room?"

"Yes," he replied, his mind racing to piece together Zachary's words. "Except that when you run people's Circles profiles through predictive algorithms, things get a lot creepier. Just about every website on the Internet, including Circles, plants tracking cookies on people's computers when they visit a site. Some people delete them, but most don't bother, and those cookies help us track everything a person does on the Internet."

Zachary nodded, confirming to Sergio he was going in the right direction. "Circles has compiled detailed user profiles based on what people like to say, write, read, watch, play, and buy on the web. In some cases we have fifteen years of data on people."

Zachary let Malina absorb Sergio's words before picking up the thread. "Running such detailed profiles through advanced predictive algorithms is pretty Big Brotherish. If you know in advance how people will respond to specific stimuli, it's pretty easy to nudge them in a predetermined direction."

Sergio looked to Zachary. "And if I'm getting your drift, you're saying there are thousands of socialbots running loose on Circles and they are capable of convincing people to behave in certain ways."

"That's exactly my drift," he replied.

"But why would somebody at Circles go to all this trouble to brainwash a bunch of Chinese Internet users?" Malina asked. "That doesn't make any sense."

Sergio winced at the question. Malina wasn't going to like the answer. "We are about to launch in China and—"

Zachary cut him off. "It's not China I'm worried about."

Sergio drew back in surprise. "What are you talking about?"

"The Chinese bots are a sideshow."

"A sideshow?" Sergio was totally lost.

"Whoever created those Chinese bots also created at least fifty thousand bogus American profiles," he said, curling his fingers into quotation marks to highlight the fictional nature of the Circles accounts. "At first I was stumped, too, but I've gotten plenty familiar with them over the past few weeks and I think I have a pretty good idea what they're up to." He abruptly spun his chair around and sidled up to his workstation. "And you're not going to believe it unless I show you."

Zachary tapped his keyboard and pulled up the staff portal for the University of California at Los Angeles. He typed in a user name and password. The screen twitched.

>> WELCOME CHARLES!

"Charles?" asked Malina.

Zachary glanced over his shoulder, a sly grin on his face. "Charles runs UCLA's entire network. Of course, UCLA doesn't know that." He dragged the cursor over a series of menus and clicked on a raft of folders that eventually landed him on the "special projects" folder. "Special projects is mine. I've buried it so deep in the network that no one's ever going to find it. But if by some chance someone stumbled upon it, they wouldn't have the password or the encryption keys."

"Doesn't breaking into UCLA's network increase your chances of getting caught?" asked Malina.

"Technically speaking, yes. But university security is awful, just like at most companies." He gave Sergio an apologetic smile. "I'd rather not do it this way, but I've downloaded so much data from Circles that I can't store it all here."

He turned back to his keyboard. "So while we've been talking, and for the past several weeks actually, UCLA computers have been unlocking Circles' most carefully guarded secrets."

"Hold on," interjected Sergio. "Are you saying you cracked our encryption?"

"I didn't need to. I stole the encryption keys from Circles' key vault. All the UCLA machines had to do is figure out which keys worked with which files and bingo," replied Zachary.

A shiver ran up Sergio's spine. Zachary had stripped him bare. The security system Sergio and George had built was designed to bend but not break. It had multiple layers of defense, with the encryption keys stored in the digital equivalent of a massive steel vault protected by dozens of locked doors, building walls, and an outer fence. A hacker might get through some of the layers, but no one before Zachary had ever penetrated Circles to the core. It didn't matter that it was within the theoretical realm of possibility. It wasn't supposed to happen. Sergio folded his arms across his chest, mortified and unsure what to say.

"Don't take it so hard. I'm a Defense Department security contractor. I've seen shit you wouldn't believe." Zachary paused. "By the way," he added quietly, "I'm back in."

Sergio swallowed hard, nearly choking on the knot in his throat. "Back in?"

"Yeah. After Circles cut me off and clamped down, I got back in." He beamed with pride. "With full admin rights."

Sergio glanced at Malina, embarrassed to ask his next question. "How?"

Sergio pressed his fingers to his eyelids and massaged them with long, weary strokes, as Zachary explained how he had taken control of Circles' security cameras. They'd specifically locked down the surveillance system to guard against something like this. What had they missed? He could feel Malina's gaze on him. He could almost hear her say: I told you so.

"Look." Zachary pointed to a Circles profile on his computer screen. "This is Brian Wallace, a student at the University of Missouri."

A handsome, blonde-haired, blue-eyed youngster with a lean athletic build peeked out from the page.

"Communications major. Phi Kappa Epsilon. Drama club. An all around All-American kid." Zachary looked over his shoulder. "Except he's not real."

Sergio's shoulders sagged and his jaw fell slack as Zachary flipped through a series of profiles. The faces on the screen were radiant and cheerful, even as the poses seemed unusually stiff. It was as if Sergio were back in the coffee shop twenty-four hours earlier, stunned by the discovery that had killed his best friend and moments later sent him running for his own life. Doubts and questions gnawed at him.

"What I don't understand is why you didn't encrypt the list of social-bots that George discovered. It was the only data you didn't bother to encrypt."

"Everything I took from Labs servers was already encrypted, except for that list. I found it on Ko's computer." He shifted his gaze from Sergio to Malina. "Engineers have to decrypt files before they can use them. I must have hit his machine just as he was working on them."

"So," he continued, "I figured I'd leave it in readable format in hopes someone like George would find it and start asking questions, you know, shake things up a little."

"And why did you suddenly ratchet up your attack? We probably wouldn't have noticed if you hadn't done that," said Sergio.

"I ran out of time." Zachary puffed up his cheeks and released a rush of air. "If I'm right, we have two days to stop this."

"Stop *what?*" asked Sergio.

"The election," cried Malina. Her eyes wandered in a moment of doubt before focusing once again. "The election is in two days."

Zachary nodded excitedly. "Exactly," he said. "And if we can't figure this out by then, Richard Diebolt is going to pull off one of the most outrageous conspiracies in history."

"What the hell are you talking about?" asked Sergio.

Zachary nodded toward the profile on his screen. "I'm pretty sure these socialbots have been specifically built to tilt the election in Diebolt's favor." His gaze shifted between his two guests. "I think somebody at Circles," he said slowly, "is helping Diebolt steal the election."

Zachary's words sliced through Sergio like a blast of icy wind. A gasp escaped Malina's open lips as she raised a hand to cover her mouth.

"You can *prove* this?" asked Sergio, trembling from the chilling implications of Zachary's claim.

Zachary nodded. "Sort of," he began, "but I haven't been able to figure out who is—"

Zachary's head snapped to attention and his eyes grew wide with alarm. He lifted one ear toward the ceiling and raised an index finger to his puckered lips. *Shsssssh.*

The three of them remained frozen in place for what seemed like minutes, tilting their ears toward the ceiling, straining to hear something . . . *anything.* Sergio racked his brain; no one had followed them and nobody could know where they were. He opened his mouth, ready to chalk it up to Zachary's overactive imagination. And then he heard it—a muffled *creeeak*, just for an instant.

Zachary urgently jabbed his finger at the ceiling and then swung his hand to mimic the motion of a door. His message was obvious. There was an intruder at the top of the basement stairs. He reached between his leg and the armrest of his chair, pulled out his pistol, and flipped the gun's safety.

Malina grabbed Sergio's hand and squeezed tightly. She trembled in his grip as he tried to meet Malina's frightened gaze with as much confidence as he could muster.

"That won't be the cops," whispered Zachary urgently. His wide eyes darted around the room, as if the key to their salvation was hidden somewhere in the shadows. Then he looked to Sergio. "What's your phone number?"

-45-

Graves froze at the top of the steps, his silenced Sig Sauer in his right hand. The quiet drone of voices below fell silent and the light floating up the stairs suddenly went dark. *Fuck.* One loose floorboard had just cost him the element of surprise. He stood motionless for a minute, maybe two, his ears pricked for sound—any hint that would lead him to Mansour and Zachary. They could move around the dark basement, but Graves was confident they wouldn't do it quietly.

Sure enough, a whisper soon floated up the basement stairs. The downstairs door on the right—that's where he'd find Mansour and Zachary. There was just one more thing Graves needed to know. He backed away from the top of the stairs, careful to avoid the soft spot in the floor, and stepped onto the hard tile in the kitchen. He followed a light to a sitting room piled high with magazines and books.

Moments later, he crouched at the top of the stairwell, a stack of hardcover books in his arm. Feet scampered across a smooth floor below, a whisper, and the clack of a keyboard. Then a click and a whomp, probably the furnace igniting. He grabbed a book and dropped it on the second step. Then he tossed the others, one-by-one in rapid succession, each book landing farther down the staircase like a man bounding down the steps, two at a time.

The right wall of the stairwell erupted in a fusillade of tiny flashes. Bullets flew across the opening and pierced the opposite wall. One round zinged off a metal rail and ricocheted dangerously in the darkness. At least one of them had a gun. It was a small caliber, maybe a 9mm, but more than enough to complicate things. If only he had a couple of grenades.

A gravelly voice rose out of the darkness. "What do you want?"

Graves stayed silent.

The voice called out again. "If I'd have hit you, you'd have rolled down the stairs. Now, what do you want?"

A soft glow escaped from the doorway to the room at the right of the bottom of the stairs. Thin rays of light, about waist high, streaked though bullet holes in the wall and shot across the dark stairwell, a testament to the deadly firepower his targets could use against him. Graves squinted into the dimly lit stairwell. A wheelchair lift sat at the bottom of the stairs and there was another open door on the left side of the basement corridor. The light faded.

"Give me Mansour and I'll let you go," he called out.

A second voice, one not quite as confident as the first, filtered up from the basement. "Who are you?" Graves knew instantly it was Mansour.

Graves slowly dropped to the floor, lowered his Sig Sauer into the stairwell and fired five shots into the wall. The bullets cut through the drywall with ease: Several smacked into walls or furniture; a couple more skipped off the floor and ricocheted around the room. A woman yelped.

He was in luck. Leverage. "You're willing to risk your lady friend's life, too?"

A barrage of bullets roared through the drywall in response. Graves felt two rounds strike the wood studs directly beneath him. He backed away from the door and waited in a crouch until the basement went quiet again. There were no good options. He couldn't wait them out. And arson was risky; there would be too much left to chance. He could—

A series of sharp electronic tones pierced the silence. Someone was dialing a mobile phone. Graves shook his head in frustration. The smart move was to retreat and fight another day. The slugs from his gun were untraceable and no one could identify him. But then came silence, as if the caller hadn't bothered to complete the call. If they'd dialed 911 and hung up, protocol would require the operator to dispatch a patrol to this location. It'd taken him a good fifteen minutes to drive up from the coast, so odds were that it would take the cops at least that long to get here from Malibu. He wouldn't go back empty-handed again. It was time to finish the job.

Graves flicked the safety switch on his pistol and tucked it inside the collar of his compression shirt, right below the nape of his neck. He pulled his sheepskin tactical gloves tight around his wrist, lowered himself onto his hands and knees, and pushed headfirst into the stairwell. Drywall dust and acrid gunpowder tickled his nostrils as he sunk into the darkness like a cat, head low and haunches high, stalking his prey. He moved slowly, painstakingly placing each hand and foot silently, distributing his weight and minimizing the risk that the steps might groan under his heft. And if he did make a noise, chances were he'd slip under the barrage of gunfire that was almost certain to rip through the wall. Five steps. The muscles in his arms, shoulders, and buttocks moved with strength and precision as the ambient light from upstairs faded behind him. Ten steps. Almost there. Eleven.

His gloved hands pressed down on hard metal. The lift at the bottom of the stairs. His heart thumped in his chest and his soft breaths seemed to scream in his ears. His muscles couldn't withstand the strain forever. He made for the doorway on the left, relying on memory from that one fleeting glimpse to negotiate an opening he couldn't quite see. His fingers found the open door and he pulled himself forward, twisting his frame as he crawled into the room. It was a high-risk move, one that exposed him to the open door across the corridor where Mansour, Zachary, and the woman lay in wait. The furnace roared more loudly now. Sometimes sound was good.

He was almost inside the room when his right foot slipped off the last step and scraped the metal lift. A half second passed before the basement erupted in bursts of light and angry cracks as bullets flew over Graves' head. He scrambled into the room and pressed himself to the cool floor as round after round smacked into the walls above him. The click of an empty magazine brought an end to the fusillade. It would be easy enough to rush them now—if he could be sure they had only one gun.

Graves reached behind his neck. The Sig Sauer was still there, tucked inside his top, ready for that moment when he'd need to draw his weapon and fire in an instant. He lifted himself off the smooth concrete, a half push-up, and turned to face the door he'd just crawled through. He stuck his nose into the corridor and a soft breeze brushed his face. Three feet of blackness separated him from the room where Mansour was hiding. Graves pressed forward on fingers and toes, his body just inches above the wheelchair platform, pausing every step to control his breathing and listen for theirs. He needed to keep moving, just in case the cops were coming, but he wouldn't be rushed into carelessness. A full minute passed before he felt the other edge of the metal platform, just inches from the door. They didn't know they were already dead.

A loud *pffft* echoed through the basement and the house went eerily quiet. Arms and legs locked in place, it took him a second to realize the furnace had gone off. A wisp of air brushed his face, and with it came the stench of stale coffee.

Then he saw a glowing red dot at ground level, most likely from a power strip on the floor. A green LED light floated in the darkness; it was probably from a computer against the far wall. They were the only specks of light in the room and they were not enough, at least not yet.

He lowered himself onto his belly to wait. Either his eyes would adjust to the darkness or one of his targets would eventually scratch an itch or swallow too hard. It was only a matter of time now.

Graves reached over his head to the back of his neck, his arm moving an inch every second or two. From somewhere in the blackness came a raspy gush of air; the sound of someone who'd held their breath too long and let it out too quickly. Or maybe the stress was simply too much. It was impossible to panic silently.

Graves slipped the gun from his shirt, drew it over his head, and brought his outstretched arm to the ground, ready to fire. There. A second red glow and another green dot, this time closer together in the middle of the room. These dots were dimmer, more diffuse, like they weren't really there. Reflections, and then movement, maybe an arm swinging. He aimed and fired, spitting bullets in a tight circular pattern between the faint dots of light.

A voice cried out as two quick bursts of gunfire raked the ceiling. A low groan rose up and a gun clattered to the floor. Graves fired three more rounds at the wounded man, each bullet sinking into him with a wet thud.

-46-

Sergio gunned the Accord and sped off on Seaview Drive, Malina shaken but safe at his side. Zachary had bought them enough time to unlatch one of the louvered windows in the basement and crawl to freedom. Sergio had needed to get Malina out of there, but he could not outrun a screaming sense of guilt as he turned onto Coral Canyon Road and headed down the mountain. He'd barely gone a quarter of a mile before he turned into a side street, rounded a curve, and pulled over to the side of the road.

"I need to go back," he said, as he killed the lights and unhooked the ignition wires.

"Are you crazy?" Malina glared at him in wide-eyed panic. "That guy wants to kill you."

"You don't think that made an impression on me, too?" He gripped the top of the steering wheel and pressed his forehead into the back of his hands. He struggled to summon the courage he demanded of himself.

"And what are you going to do if he's still there?" she asked in a tone that was more warning than question. "You don't even have a gun."

"I shouldn't have left him like that, but I had to get you out of there." He opened the driver's door, handing Malina one of the prepaid smartphones. "Just stay down and you'll be safe here. If I'm not back in twenty minutes, call the police, and tell them everything."

He was running before she could argue. He darted from tree to bush to parked car, worried that the gunman—it had to be the guy from last night, didn't it?—would pass this way as he fled Zachary's house. Sergio's senses were on full alert, his eyes scanning the empty road and ears pricked for any sounds. He was halfway across Coral Canyon Drive when a distant pair of headlights pulled out of Seaview Drive up ahead. He flattened himself alongside a row of bushes as a gray Chrysler 300 roared past, revealing the silhouette of a man with a crew cut.

Sergio stared in disbelief; it had to be the same guy from the night before, but how had the gunman known where to find him? He waited a full minute after the Chrysler disappeared down the mountain, and then he took off in a sprint, cut between two houses, and approached Zachary's place from behind. Ahead of him was the black hole of the open window through which they'd escaped. He dropped to the grass and crawled the last forty feet so his profile did not stand out against the starry sky. He pulled up within a foot from the opening and listened for any sound from within. He counted to sixty.

"Zachary?" he whispered urgently. *"Kevin."*

Sergio lay motionless for another long moment, hoping against hope for a sign that it was safe to enter the basement. The more he waited, the more he was certain the silence could only mean one thing—somewhere down there in the dark, Kevin Zachary was dead. Just like his father, years ago. Despair and emptiness pressed down. Sergio wasn't sure he could face this again.

He rolled sideways and pulled himself up against the side of the house. He leaned his head back and scanned the crisp night sky. A million stars met his gaze and he struggled to reconcile their wondrous grandeur with a terrifying sense of his utter insignificance. He locked on the distinctive hourglass shape of Orion, the hunter's waist cinched tightly by the three stars of his belt. Below them hung the stars of his sword.

He stared transfixed at the constellation for a long while, trying to draw strength from the mythical hunter. Sergio had never been able to shake the belief that he was supposed to believe in something greater than himself, greater than all humanity. Maybe Orion was a symbol of that greater spiritual power. Or maybe it was simply that Orion, unlike God or Allah or Yahweh, was real and tangible. He couldn't be sure. All he knew was the giant hunter in the sky was always there to comfort, guide, and protect him in those moments he needed it most. And that was usually enough.

He pivoted, threw his feet through the black window, and dropped into the dark basement. His feet landed with a slap against the smooth concrete floor. Anyone already down there would hear him coming. He advanced in a crouch until he bumped into a wall and found a doorframe. He pressed his ear to the door and held his breath, begging, maybe even praying, for some reassuring sound from the other side. Or maybe a warning. He gripped the doorknob and turned it slowly until the latch bolt cleared the doorjamb. He pulled the door open a few inches and the stench of gunpowder poured through the opening. He cautiously reached into the room and brushed the light switch. He hesitated, still hoping for a sound that might tell him it was okay—or not—to turn on the light. Silence.

He flicked his finger and the room lit up. Sergio drew in a sharp breath. Zachary sat slumped in his chair facing away from him. His head was thrown back and a chunk of his skull was gone, torn away by a bullet. The wall beside him was splattered red. Sergio's stomach heaved and a desperate retching sound escaped his throat. He steadied himself against the doorframe and took a deep breath. Lowering his gaze, he circled around Zachary. The gun that had so paralyzed Sergio a short while earlier now lay uselessly on the floor, spent shells scattered around it. He forced himself to look up. Zachary's chest was chewed up by a cluster of bloody bullet holes. Crimson spittle oozed from his open mouth and his vacant blue eyes had rolled upward, as if to inspect the gaping hole in his head.

Sergio turned away, dropped to his knees, and vomited, over and over until there was nothing left to throw up but bitter bile. Waves of nausea racked his weakened, shuddering body, but he knew he couldn't give in to his terror. Not now. He sucked in several deep breaths and tried to put his screaming abdominal muscles out of his mind.

Wobbling to his feet, he looked away from the gruesome sight and stumbled to the desk. He looked for Zachary's laptop, but it was gone. So was the computer on the floor. He spun to the rack of servers on the opposite wall. They were smashed beyond repair. Next to them on the ground, in jagged pieces, were Zachary's computers. A sledgehammer lay on the floor.

He stared blankly at his feet, trying to make sense of the scene. Zachary was dead and the man who'd killed him had also destroyed his computers—and with them the evidence that could help Sergio clear his name. He pulled his fists to his chest, threw his head back, and let out a primal roar of frustration, anger, and grief.

Zachary's last jittery words then came to him, as if the dead man spoke from the other side. *Here's what we're going to do*, he'd said. Malina had to be saved and Sergio needed to go with her. They'd escaped with a name and an address.

Sergio started for the window when something stopped him. Unfinished business. He forced himself to look back at Zachary's lifeless body. A life snuffed out, abruptly and violently, just like George. Sergio inched closer, his gaze focused on Zachary's cold blue eyes, not the grotesque wound inches above them. He reached out and softly swept his palm over the dead man's face, pulling closed his eyelids.

"Sorry, my friend."

-47-

Graves raced down Coral Canyon Road, looking for a glimpse of red taillights below. He couldn't be sure how much of a head start they had. One minute? Maybe five. The only certainty was that Mansour and the woman were in the Accord. It was there when he'd arrived and gone when he left. The other cars on the street hadn't moved.

Hope and desperation mounted as the Chrysler leaned into each corner, tires screeching against the pavement. A tunnel of light stretched before him, the mountain on one side and a black void on the other. No lights moved below and doubt crept into his mind. Had he guessed wrong when he chose to go down instead of farther up the mountain? It was a fifty-fifty gamble and his odds would be again cut in half if he didn't catch them before they reached the Pacific Coast Highway. He flew down the mountain, arms clamped on the steering wheel and tires protesting the tight corners as he pushed forward with singular focus.

It took eight minutes to reach the stop sign at the coast. He came to a sharp halt, looking north and then south along the nearly deserted highway. A few cars slipped past, but the Accord was nowhere in sight.

They were either way ahead of him or they had gone up the hill. It didn't matter; they were long gone. He slammed his palm against the steering wheel.

"Fuck!"

-48-

Sergio coaxed Zachary's van up sinewy Coral Canyon Road in silence as the first hint of dawn seeped into the eastern sky. It took all his focus to force Zachary from his mind so he could concentrate on manipulating the hand controls mounted on the steering column. The push-to-brake, pull-to-accelerate lever at his fingertips was simple enough, but he quickly discovered that operating the sensitive control demanded a certain degree of finesse. He practically slammed on the brakes each time he approached a curve, and then threw Malina back into her seat as he accelerated out of the bend. The pattern repeated itself each time the road doubled back on itself as it climbed from ridge to ridge thousands of feet above the Pacific. Even worse, the wheel felt wobbly in his hands, as if the steering column was dangerously loose. He brought the van to a full stop in the middle of the road and sudden flashes of skull fragments, brain matter, and splattered blood tore through his mind. His hands and arms still trembled.

"Are you okay?" Malina asked softly.

Sergio nudged the van forward, slowly guiding it through a series of sharp curves. "Yeah, I guess."

"That look in your eyes, I've seen it a lot in my job."

Sergio kept driving, vaguely aware of the ribbon of asphalt directly in front of the van. Powerful recollections pressed into his consciousness, memories lost to him for decades. Malina spoke again, but her words didn't register.

"I ran home that night," he said suddenly. The images in his mind started as halting snippets, just like a streaming Internet video that hasn't finished buffering. "I was terrified and I ran as fast as I could."

He pulled up to a stop sign and looked left, then right. There was nothing but empty road surrounded by thousands of acres of chaparral and sage scrub, washed steel gray in the predawn light. Then the memory was complete, playing itself for the first time in living color. Tears flowed as new details from that night came rushing back to him. He gunned the engine and turned right.

"I was covered in my father's blood. It was warm and gooey at first, but by the time I reached the irrigation canal, it had dried into a cool, sticky film. I could feel it all over my hands and face. My T-shirt and jeans were smeared red." The road was wider and flatter, making it easier to navigate. "I remember diving into the canal and tearing off my clothes. They floated away with the current. I almost rubbed myself raw to get that blood off me. I had to get if off me. Otherwise, everyone would know I was there, that I knew what had happened. And then that man would kill us."

The van crested the range and Sergio pulled into a gravel turnout on the side of the road. His hands trembled on the steering wheel as he looked toward the eastern horizon. The sky was painted in bright orange and blue hues, almost like the sunset just before those men had come for his father.

"I must have been in the water for at least an hour." He closed his eyes, succumbing to the now-vivid memory. "I stayed there until it was too cold. I got out, shivering, my teeth chattering. I ran home, barefoot on the dirt road. I was just about dry when I ran up to our house naked, in a daze, still shivering and shaking."

He leaned on the steering wheel and took a deep breath, pushing the air through his cheeks with a rush. "It's funny," he said with no hint of humor. "I'd totally forgotten that. But I never forgot the look on Mamá's face when I got home." Sergio lifted his head and gazed out the windshield. "She was frantic, trying to figure out what had happened to me and Papá. They found him on the road a short while later and there were cops everywhere. They questioned me over and over. I told them I didn't see anything and that I sliced my ear on a barbwire fence when I was running away. They didn't believe me, but I never broke down. I was terrified they'd come for the rest of us. So I never spoke about what happened that night, not to the police anyway."

"Who *did* you tell?"

Sergio dropped his head. "Emilio. Years later when I thought he was old enough to understand."

"And?"

"And he went ballistic." Sergio pointed his index finger skyward. "He was furious that I hadn't said anything earlier."

"Did he go to the police?"

"I never told him who it was."

"Is that why you two haven't talked in all these years?"

Sergio nodded. "He called me a coward, said I betrayed our father by not speaking out and bringing his killer to justice. And maybe he was right. I don't know if I've ever forgiven myself for that." Sergio looked to Malina, hoping for some signal of understanding. "But Emilio wasn't there that night. He didn't look into that man's eyes. The way he looked at me . . ."

Malina reached for Sergio and pulled him into her arms. "You were just a boy," she whispered. "A very scared boy."

He squeezed her tightly, taking comfort in her warmth, her smell, and the tickle of her hair against his cheek. He felt safe and strong in her embrace. "It felt like I lost my entire family that night—first my father, then my mother. She was never the same after that. And then Emilio. I haven't seen him in more than twenty-five years."

"It's never too late."

He shook his head. "No, it *is* too late. The man who killed my father died in a car accident about five years later."

Malina squeezed him tightly. "I mean Emilio. It's not too late for you and him. He *will* forgive you. You know that, don't you?"

He pulled back and shook his head. "I don't think so . . ."

She hooked his chin with her finger and turned his face until their eyes met. "Gandhi once said 'forgiveness is the attribute of the strong.' And if Emilio is anything like you, he will come to realize that you had your reasons—even if he didn't understand them at the time."

-49-

DIEBOLT USED HARD DRUGS IN HIS YOUTH,
SOURCES SAY

By Alan Vignault

Republican presidential candidate Richard Diebolt's
well-known brushes with substance abuse weren't
limited to marijuana and alcohol, according to several
sources interviewed by the *New York Times*, who claim
he was a "frequent user" of speed, cocaine, and opium
during his twenties and early thirties.

The revelations, which suggest Diebolt managed to
hide his use of hard drugs for more than two decades,
threaten to turn the presidential race upside down just
two days before Americans vote.

Diebolt, who holds a two-to-five-point lead in the polls
over Democrat Ian Lester, has openly acknowledged he
had an alcohol addiction during the period in question.

But he claimed he stopped drinking after becoming a born-again Christian in 1997, soon after his return from China, where he ran his family's business in that country for five years. He has never denied reports that he also experimented with marijuana during his youth, but this is the first time anyone has made allegations of more serious drug abuse.

Each of the four sources spoke on the condition of anonymity, saying they were concerned that going public could impact their careers or prompt retribution from Diebolt's supporters.

The Diebolt campaign dismissed the allegations as an ill-advised political hatchet job designed to provide a last-minute boost to Lester's campaign.

"We denounce this kind of character assassination from anonymous sources," said Diebolt campaign manager Nathan Aaron. "These are outrageous and unsubstantiated allegations by unnamed sources. The fact that the paper would be willing to publish this story—two days before the election—is the height of irresponsibility."

The *New York Times* interviewed several other people who said . . .

-50-

Richard Diebolt stood backstage at the edge of the curtain, his eyes closed as he steeled himself for the most important appearance of his campaign. Aaron came up next to him and patted him on the back. "It's going to be fine," the campaign chief said. "Just remember, humility is what plays today."

Diebolt nodded quickly as he tugged on his charcoal gray sleeves and fidgeted with his red silk tie. The story in Sunday's *New York Times* was not the total disaster he'd feared. He hadn't anticipated there would be four sources; that was bad on a couple of levels. It was harder to credibly refute the allegations and almost impossible to pinpoint the source. On the other hand, none of the sources had been willing to go on the record, a critical detail he intended to fully exploit.

On stage, a booming voice sounded his cue, ". . . please give a warm welcome to Richard Diebolt!"

An audience of thousands erupted in applause as Diebolt emerged from behind the curtain and strode confidently across the stage. Televangelist Tyler Mulchane awaited him atop a carpeted dais furnished with two brown armchairs. Diebolt shook hands with his old acquaintance, who then turned to the audience to coax more applause from them. The clapping subsided and the two men settled into their arm-chairs, angled to face each other even as they looked out to the crowd. Diebolt was calm; he had made the right decision.

Mulchane was the latest in a long line of Christian ministers who'd carved out niches ministering to their flock on TV. Handsome, intelligent, and soft-spoken, he was widely admired within his ministry and respected from without because of the understated manner in which he questioned—he never criticized—those who lived their lives in a more liberal fashion. And he did it with an understanding, caring, and non-judgmental air.

Preaching from his pulpit in what was once a small movie theater, he came across as someone neither interested in nor burdened by material wealth. Mulchane's ability to connect emotionally and fiscally with his congregation had turned him into the most popular evangelist on TV. No rival could match his influence among social conservatives, the very voters who would most likely withdraw support for Diebolt following the drug story. If Diebolt had to respond to the *Times'* drug story, and it was clear that he must, then he wanted to make sure to do so on the most favorable terms possible.

"Welcome, Richard, and thank you for coming today. We're very happy you've joined us."

"Thanks for having me, Tyler. I'm just so happy our schedules have finally meshed. Running for president, as you may imagine, is extremely time-consuming. I always make time for the Lord, and I'm excited to share this moment with all of you," he said as he motioned to the audience, "this fine morning."

Mulchane waited for another round of applause to die down before jumping into a prearranged series of questions. Who are your greatest heroes? What are America's greatest challenges? Is there a point at which a person is too rich? What was your most difficult decision? Diebolt rattled through the answers in a humble and conversational tone. All the while he scanned the audience, making eye contact with those closest to the stage, striking a rapport before things got serious.

Returning from a second commercial break, Mulchane leaned forward on the edge of his seat and clasped his hands. He hesitated, as if to show reluctance, before nudging the conversation toward its inevitable conclusion. "What has been your greatest moral failing?" he asked.

Diebolt nodded slowly and respectfully, his show of contrition. "I'd love to say I didn't have one," he said, pausing for the audience to chuckle. "But the truth is that I've struggled at times, like we all struggle every now and then, with my faith. I grew up Christian, went to church and Sunday school all through my youth. And then as you grow older, you begin to realize that the world is a tough place. People get hurt, sick, die. Other people do evil things. Life isn't fair. So I began to question all that in my twenties. I began to wonder what life was all about."

Diebolt pressed a clenched fist to his lips and bowed his head. "Everyone knows I had a substance abuse problem back then. For a while, alcohol took control of my life. I think there were times I didn't treat people with the respect they deserved." He stopped again, letting his mea culpa sink in. He focused on a woman in the front row who was close to fifty, probably a mom, with a kind and wholesome face. He smiled at her and she nodded back. "But slowly I came to see that I was not happy, not productive, and not proud of myself. I realized that all the time I spent questioning my faith was wasted time. In doing so, I had rejected God and denied myself his love and guidance. As you know, Tyler, I've since accepted the Lord Jesus Christ into my heart and I live God's word every second of every minute of every hour of the day." He made another dramatic pause. "But that period of uncertainty, when I questioned our Lord, that was my greatest moral failing."

The audience erupted into applause. He was close to sealing the deal.

"And what about these latest revelations in the *New York Times*, that you abused not just alcohol, but hard drugs as well? Is any of that true?"

The audience held its collective breath. This was the moment that would play and replay itself across the nation, repeated endlessly on Internet and TV for the next hours and days to come.

"Tyler, I was really disappointed in that story." Diebolt brought his hands together and held them over his heart. "When the *Times* told me they were going to run that piece based entirely on unnamed sources, I was saddened. The fact that none of their sources were willing to identify themselves should set off alarm bells. Now, I've already told you I've made mistakes, but I need to point out that the story is full of inaccuracies. And to run it just before the election . . ." He shook his head in a display of solemn disappointment. "This is how bad things have become between the right and left."

"But let me say this," he continued, raising his index finger to make a point. "Even if that story were one hundred percent true, it wouldn't change anything I've already said. I was once a lost soul, unsure about my direction in life, wondering what it was all about. And then I found my way, thanks to my relationship with God. I've never looked back. I've said many times before that I believe in redemption. I'm living proof that we can all rebuild our lives, whether you call it a second chance, atonement, or being born again."

Diebolt slowly leaned back into his chair and the audience stood in unison to applaud once again. The woman in the front row rose to her feet, too, nodding approval and fighting back tears. He'd nailed it. Aaron's advice was masterful. He never denied it. Hell, he'd practically admitted it was true. But this was no longer a devastating story about drug use; he'd just turned it into a powerful tale of redemption.

Now he just had to get through two more days without any other shoes dropping.

-51-

Sergio and Malina drove north, skirting the massive San Fernando Valley; they made sure to signal every lane change and assiduously stayed within the speed limit, anything to avoid unwanted attention. Malina eventually dozed off, leaving Sergio alone with his unsettling memories and painful emotions as he eased on to Interstate 5, climbed over the Tejon Pass, and dropped down almost four thousand feet into the dusty Central Valley.

He pulled down the sun visor and studied his face in the mirror. The puffiness was subsiding but that only served to accentuate the crooked bridge of his once-straight nose. Even worse, the makeup around his eyes had started to cake and his face was a splotchy pattern of black, purple, and mocha-pink powder base. He inhaled deeply. At least he could still breathe.

He glanced right. Malina slept peacefully, slumped against the door. The corners of her mouth were curled ever so slightly, as if she were lost in a wonderful dream. He didn't get how she could sleep so soundly at a moment like this. Maybe it was all that medical training, those years of residency when young doctors on long shifts learn to get their sleep whenever and wherever they can.

He wondered what he'd done to deserve her—and why she'd stuck by him, especially since she'd made no attempt to hide her scorn for Circles. How had she put it? *"Circles uses people,"* she said in her apartment. *"It sucks them in, exposes them, and puts them at risk, all for the sake of money."* Maybe he had underestimated the conviction behind her words. Maybe there was much more going on here than she was letting on. He glanced right again. There would be time for that later. What mattered now was that she'd stuck by him and almost been killed. Sergio couldn't let that guy chasing them have another shot at her. George, Ko, and Circles would have to wait.

"Sorry," he whispered in her direction.

Malina's eyes popped open. She bolted upright, stifling a yawn as she scanned her surroundings. "Did you say something?"

"Nah," he replied. "Just talking to myself."

"Where are we?"

"About halfway back to San Francisco."

"We're going back to San Francisco?"

"Nope. I know this guy who has a cabin up in Humboldt County, a friend of George's brother-in-law. We were up there a couple of years ago. It's way off the beaten track, in pot country." He arched his eyebrows. "They don't like cops up there."

"But we can't just hide out, can we? Knowing what we now know?"

"I'm not going to hide out there. You are." He glanced sideways at Malina. "We need to find a safe place for you to stay until this is over."

Malina drew a quick breath and held it for a moment. She shook her head, almost imperceptibly at first, and then with ever more conviction. "No. If Zachary is right, then this is so much bigger than either of us ever imagined. The public deserves to know the truth."

Sergio frowned. It was an odd choice of words. "What exactly were you imagining?"

"That's not the point," she shot back. "What matters—"

"What matters," he began, his voice stressed, "is that we could've ended up like Zachary." He paused to let his words sink in. "You are not safe with me, not as long as that guy is chasing me. I should never have sucked you into this."

Malina shot him a flinty stare. "You didn't ask me, remember?" she said. "And it's too late for regrets now."

He shook his head in frustration. "You're not listening to me—"

"You're right, I'm not," she said, as she crossed her arms and looked off to the right.

Sergio's hands tightened around the steering wheel. He opened his mouth to speak, but stopped himself. They fell silent, their words replaced by the reverberating *thunk-thunk* of the joints connecting the highway's concrete slabs, each cycle ticking off distance in twenty-foot increments. A limitless parade of overpasses soon marked their progress in miles and the thinning traffic confirmed that they'd left Los Angeles far behind them.

Malina's words echoed loudly in his mind. *If Zachary is right.* Sergio went on autopilot, driving but not really focused on the road as he grappled to get his head around Zachary's hypothesis. It was easy enough to manipulate people through social media, and it would be theoretically possible to affect the outcome of an election. But it was one thing to dream up something like this; doing it on the sly on the world's biggest social network was an entirely different matter. An icy chill spread through his body. If someone could pull this off—

"Sergio," cried Malina as she thrust her arm forward and jabbed at the windshield. Her eyes grew wide and her mouth dropped open. *"Look!"*

He glanced back and forth among the vehicles closest to them before scouring the roadway ahead. "Where?" he asked urgently.

"Up *there.*" She stabbed the top of the windshield.

Sergio followed her motion to a digital road sign, its amber message flashing brightly over the road.

White Chevy Express
Lic CA 8SDS290

He didn't need to check the registration to know that Zachary's plates matched the number on the sign. The police had found Zachary's body far sooner than he'd expected. One of his neighbors must have heard something. "We have to get off this highway," he said.

Sergio moved to the right lane, pulling in front of a beat-up Toyota. He readjusted the rearview mirror. The long-haired kid behind him looked thoroughly uninterested in his surroundings and took no note of the wanted van. The guy in the pickup truck ahead wasn't paying them any attention either, and the elderly couple motoring alongside in their Buick was absorbed in conversation. Just behind the Buick was a family of four, all of them wearing glazed-over expressions. A sign announced the next exit was one mile ahead, one minute in which Sergio could do nothing but hope no one noticed them.

An overpass came into view, slicing across the Interstate at an angle. *Thunk-thunk.* Roughly five thousand three hundred feet in a mile, divided by twenty. Less than two hundred seams and counting. He pulled into the left lane and gently pulled on the accelerator lever, speeding up the pace at which the seams slipped under the tires. *Thunk-thunk.* He reached eighty, the average speed in the passing lane, and he kept on accelerating. All that mattered was reaching that exit. *Thunk-thunk.*

He pulled into the exit lane and eased off the gas as the van rolled smoothly up the off-ramp. No one followed them. He surveyed the brown landscape all around them. To the east lay the agricultural heart of the valley; to the west rose the low-slung hills that separated central California from the Pacific. He came to a smooth stop at the top of the ramp and the rush of wind disappeared. In its stead came the distant wail of a siren. Off to the right, a cruiser flashing bright lights came roaring down the side road toward the Interstate.

Within seconds the cruiser was nearly upon them, slowing down as it climbed to the overpass. Sergio raced through his options, quickly concluding that moving in any direction would only invite attention. The cruiser skimmed past and continued over the Interstate before braking sharply and careening onto the southbound on-ramp. The cop car accelerated down the ramp with a low roar and raced into traffic behind them.

Malina let out a deep breath. "Holy shit, my heart's in my throat."

Sergio nodded vigorously and realized he had been holding his breath as well. His mind raced. Humboldt County was still a good six hours away, all but impossible in these circumstances. "We need to dump this van," he said, watching a car glide up the ramp behind them.

"Have we passed Coalinga?" she asked.

"I don't think so." He handed her a road map from the door panel and turned onto the overpass. "This is Twisselman Road."

She studied the map for a moment. "I'm guessing it's about an hour if we stick to side roads. I've only been there a couple of times, but I'm pretty sure I can find Barry's place."

"Barry?"

"My ex. I told you about him on the way down."

He nodded in recognition. "Is that a good idea?"

"Do you have a better one?" she asked.

Sergio knew she wasn't expecting an answer.

-52-

Dan Prederick negotiated the twin steel doors into Circles Labs and poked his head into Victor Ko's office. "That FBI agent wants to talk again."

Ko looked up from his computer. "When?"

"Right now." Prederick closed Ko's door and dialed his mobile phone. Special Agent Jay Feeley picked up on the first ring.

"I have Ko with me," said Prederick. He turned on the speaker and placed the mobile on the desk between them.

"Good," came the reply. "Mr. Ko, tell me about Kevin Zachary."

Ko's face soured as he eyeballed the phone for several seconds. "Why do you ask?"

"We found his body a few hours ago," said Feeley. "He was killed at his house outside Malibu. Mansour's fingerprints are all over the place."

Ko's brows twitched, almost imperceptibly. "He used to work for me until about three years ago. I haven't seen or spoken to him since."

"Did Mansour and Zachary know each other?"

"It seems they did, based on what you just said," answered Ko.

The connection went quiet. Prederick could almost see the FBI agent on the other end of the line sneer into the phone. Ko had that effect on people.

After a short pause, Feeley patiently resumed the conversation. "Were you aware of any prior relationship between them?"

"No."

Prederick fumed silently as Ko responded to Feeley's questions. Maybe it was Ko's standoffish demeanor or perhaps his own distrust of Ko, but Prederick had the distinct impression his subordinate was holding out on the agent.

After a few minutes, Ko leaned over the phone and turned the tables on Feeley. "Are you saying Mansour killed Zachary?"

There was a pause before Feeley's voice crackled over the phone. "That is one possibility."

"You just said his prints were all over the place."

"That is true," replied Feeley.

Ko pressed. "Do you have any theories about what Mansour and Zachary were up to?"

"It's too early. Zachary's computers, servers, hard drives, and phones were trashed. We're taking them to our forensics lab and we're auditing his network activity."

"You know . . ." Ko looked at Prederick and then back to the phone. "If anyone could have pulled off Friday's attack on Circles, Zachary's the guy."

Feeley hesitated for a long while before finally responding. "Do you have any reason to believe he'd be motivated to attack Circles? Maybe a personal vendetta?"

"No. Just thinking out loud," answered Ko. "You never really know what people are capable of."

"Prederick?"

"I'm here."

"Anything to add about Zachary?"

"I'd never heard of him before."

"Okay," said Feeley. "We'll be in—"

"Do you have any idea where he is now?" asked Ko.

"Mansour? No."

Prederick leaned over the desk. "Thank you, Agent Feeley. Let us know if we can be of more help."

The line went dead and Prederick glared at Ko. "Why haven't I heard of this guy Zachary before?"

Ko shrugged. "Because he was irrelevant," he said.

Prederick looked sideways and his gaze fell upon Ko's ceremonial tea set. None of this felt right. Another dead body. Secrets from the past. The situation had spun out of control and the China launch looked more dubious by the hour. All Prederick knew for sure was that he could not trust Ko.

Jaw clenched, Prederick retreated from Ko's office. He pulled the door shut behind him, spun around, and froze. A few feet away stood Burrard, his head tilted to the right, as if cocking his ear to Ko's door.

Prederick looked at Burrard; Burrard looked past him. Slowly, Prederick lifted his index finger to his lips—*ssshhhh*—before touching the corner of his eye and then his ear. Burrard nodded and Prederick turned for the heavy steel doors at the entrance to Labs.

-53-

Sergio followed a thin strip of pavement about half an hour northwest of Coalinga. They had escaped the arid valley and were now surrounded by rugged and austere hills flecked with tangled chaparral, hardy oak, and the occasional pine. It was the kind of place that might not see a cop for weeks.

"Here," cried Malina. "This is it."

He jammed the hand lever forward and brought Zachary's white van screeching to a halt in front of a dirt driveway. He turned off the road, squeezed through the open gate, and plunged into an overgrown gully that seemed to swallow up the lane. As they rounded a bend half a mile from the main road, a stately Queen Anne Victorian came into view. The yellow two-story house, topped with a turret, a steep roof, and an ornate chimney, stood proudly in a wide open hollow between the hills. A row of towering eucalyptus trees lined the narrow lane as it disappeared into an open field behind the house.

Sergio pulled the van up to an ornate carriage house alongside the Queen Anne. An imposing man stepped from the front door of the house and moved to the edge of the wraparound porch. Dressed in a cowboy shirt, jeans, and boots, he stood at the top of the steps with a rifle cradled under his arm. Sergio nodded toward the porch. "Is that Barry?"

Malina nodded as she reached for the door handle. "Stay here for a minute."

Sergio saw a flicker of recognition in Barry's eyes as she stepped from the van, though the man seemed neither happy nor upset to see her. She stopped at the bottom of the steps, her hands tucked in her back pockets, breaking the ice with Barry, just out of earshot. Barry looked to the van with a nod, as if to ask: "Who's that?" They spoke a while longer until he lowered the rifle to his side.

Sergio stepped out and walked toward them, extending his hand to Barry as he approached. When they shook, Barry's stare was at once challenging and curious.

"Sorry to drop in on you like this," said Sergio. "Malina mentioned she hadn't seen you in some time."

"Not at all," he replied, his gaze focused squarely on Sergio's nose. "Are you all right?"

"Oh, you mean this?" Sergio pointed to his face. "I had a little accident with a surfboard." He tilted his head to Malina. "But I'm in good hands."

"Of course," said Barry. He jiggled the rifle, calling attention to it. "Sorry if I scared you. Out here, you have to be prepared."

The three of them shared an uncomfortable laugh.

"You've painted the house," Malina offered. "It looks great."

"I never thought I'd end up living on the ranch. But life is funny that way."

Sergio nodded sympathetically and looked to Malina to drive the conversation.

"Barry," she began, "we need a favor."

Barry registered no surprise, as if he knew Malina hadn't simply dropped by—with another man—to say hello after all these years. "I'll do what I can."

"Thank you," said Sergio. "There's an emergency at work and I need to get online. I might have to stay online for quite a few hours, maybe through the night. Do you have broadband?"

Barry frowned. "There are lots of places you can do that."

"We need privacy," she countered.

Barry looked at them coldly. "Must be some emergency."

Sergio jumped in. "Maybe not the life and death emergencies you used to handle in the ER, but this affects millions of people."

Barry raised his chin. "Who do you work for?" he asked.

"Pony Networks," replied Sergio. The name just popped into his brain and it was too late to change it now. "We make sure Internet traffic gets to where it needs to go."

Barry's eyebrows came together in doubt. "Never heard of it."

Sergio forced a chuckle. "You will if we don't get this problem fixed soon."

Barry shifted on his feet as he pinched his lower lip between his fingers. Malina stepped onto the porch and looked to her old lover with beseeching eyes. "Barry, please."

Barry held her gaze for a long moment, the two of them communicating silently, a test of wills that Sergio could not handicap. Their only hope was that she still had some sort of hold over her ex. With a nod and a sigh of resignation, Barry finally spoke.

"All right," he said as he cracked half a smile. "Just let it be known that I did my bit for humanity, at least the part of it that can't survive without the Internet."

Barry ushered them into an entry hall with a grand staircase featuring an ornate wooden banister. The house had high ceilings, parquet floors, large fireplaces in the formal parlor and dining room, and a kitchen that looked right out of the 1920s. They walked down a hall past the back staircase before reaching a study in the rear of the house. It had a desk against one wall, a bookshelf and filing cabinets on another, and a sofa sat beneath one of the windows.

Barry cleared a bunch of books and papers from the desk and piled them in a corner on the floor. "You can plug in here," he said, as he disconnected the Ethernet cable from his laptop and slung it under his arm. He motioned to the couch. "That's a sofa bed. I'll get some sheets later." Then he looked at Malina. "There's a room upstairs, if you like."

She looked away in obvious discomfort, and Barry smiled dryly at Sergio as he left the room.

She sat down on the couch, pulled her clenched fists to her chest, and rocked forward on the balls of her feet. "This was a mistake. I thought I could handle this."

"You *can* handle this. You have to," he said in the most reassuring tone he could muster. "I need you to keep him occupied. You have to make sure he doesn't watch TV or read any news."

Malina looked dubious.

"You have to," he coaxed. "Besides, I need to work and there's nothing you can do to help me with that."

She nodded reluctantly.

"Go," he urged. "Hang out with him. Make him feel at ease."

He watched silently as she walked out and closed the door behind her. An unexpected pang of jealousy quivered within. He hoped he wasn't helping rekindle a flame that had fizzled but perhaps not gone totally cold. Still, he resisted the urge to call her back. He had work to do—and maybe, if Zachary was right, an election to save.

He booted up the DuoPro II and closed his eyes as he tried to recall Zachary's final words. Zachary and the gunman had just exchanged a fierce volley of gunfire through the wall and an acrid cloud of gunpowder filled the darkened room. Then Sergio rummaged through his bag until he found one of the prepaid smartphones Malina had bought the day before at Bruno's. Sergio whispered the number on his screen and watched Zachary punch it into his cell phone. The ridges and curves of Zachary's face were exaggerated by the faint glow of the screen and, for a brief instant, he looked like some hideous zombie in a black-and-white horror movie. Then he looked up from the phone and spoke softly: "Tristan dot Cormac dot Moriarty at Gmail dot com."

Sergio pulled back, unsure what Zachary meant.

"Got that?" whispered Zachary urgently. "Tristan dot Cormac dot Moriarty at Gmail dot com." He paused a second. "Password is Sunspot33." He held up the phone. "And watch for the Two-F-A."

Sergio nodded. Zachary was directing him to an email account that was protected by two passwords, the second of which would be delivered by phone. Zachary spoke again. "And remember to transpose the entire alphabet." He'd spun his chair, pulled himself to his keyboard, and shot Sergio one last glance. "Now go."

Sergio opened his eyes and returned to the present. He pulled up Gmail's sign-on page, logged in as Tristan.Cormac.Moriarty@gmail.com, and typed the password Zachary had given him. Then he turned on the same prepaid phone he'd pulled out the night before in Zachary's basement. Two-F-A was shorthand for two-factor authentication, which meant he should quickly receive a text message containing the one-time verification code he needed to finish logging in to the email account.

He stared at the smartphone's screen as the seconds ticked by. It was roaming, with one bar of reception. If the message with the code didn't come through, he'd be dead in the water—unable to follow the trail Zachary had laid out for him. He tried to remember the last cell phone tower they'd passed before getting to Barry's. It might have been about three or four miles back, which in theory was well within range for a cell site in such hilly terrain. But all the usual bets were off if that cell site had a weak transmitter or one of its antennae was misaligned. And the real wild card was the narrow valley they were in, a location that was prone to poor reception.

"Come on, come on," he whispered, as he rocked back and forth in his chair, bouncing his foot nervously under the desk.

The phone lit up and a soft chime announced an incoming text message. He closed his eyes and tilted his head up, his own private "thank you" prayer. Then he copied the verification code and finished logging into Tristan Cormac Moriarty's account. A single email was waiting in the inbox.

He opened it and read: "Staff portal. C. Wilkensen." Attached to the email was a compressed text file containing a long string of random letters, numbers, and symbols, over ten thousand characters in all. An encryption key. He covered his face with both hands. An encryption key for C. Wilkensen's staff portal? Who was C. Wilkensen? Sergio leaned forward, his elbows on the arms of the chair, and pressed his fingertips to his temples. He closed his eyes and massaged his head as he replayed Zachary's final words, over and over again. Nothing Zachary said—

Then it hit Sergio like a bolt from the sky. *Welcome Charles!* C. Wilkensen was Charles, Zachary's alter ego at UCLA. Sergio looked again at the random string of letters and numbers on the screen. It was the key to unlock Charles Wilkensen's account at UCLA's staff portal. It was the key to everything Zachary had taken from Circles, and nobody could use it unless they knew what Zachary had told Sergio—the entire alphabet had been transposed so that A became Z, B became Y, and so on. It was crude and simple security, but given the terrible pressure Zachary was under at the time, it was good enough.

Sergio downloaded the key and quickly wrote a simple command to transpose all the letters:

```
>>TR ABCDEFGHIJKLMNOPQRSTUVWXYZ
   ZYXWVUTSRQPONMLKJIHGFEDCBA
```

He called up UCLA's staff portal and, like Zachary the previous night, signed in as Charles Wilkensen. The screen immediately filled with an index of files containing petabytes of data, far more than he could ever get through in two months let alone two days. He picked his way through the folders, most of which were labeled in familiar Circles nomenclature. The folders he didn't recognize attracted his attention, as well as the ones that had been most recently opened.

Within half an hour, he'd isolated all the socialbot files Zachary had zeroed in on. With a deep breath, Sergio plunged into the files one after another, just like he had done two nights earlier in the coffee shop. This time, however, the phony personas were not Chinese; the "people" on screen were as American as they come. Hour by hour, he pored over the profiles, fighting tedium and fatigue as he tried to discern the pattern Zachary had been seconds away from revealing.

His eyelids sagged. It was four in the afternoon, some thirty-two hours since he'd woken up at Malina's. And that was after pulling his all-nighter in the lab. All told, he'd slept five hours in the past seventy-eight. His head bobbed and slipped sideways, carrying his entire frame with it until his body jolted abruptly as his internal gyroscope warned of imminent collapse. His eyes snapped open and he pulled himself erect. Beverly Tustin, a twenty-seven-year-old paralegal from Miami, smiled back at him from the screen. She was cute, but not real. His eyelids drooped once again. He needed a break, just a short power nap. Then he'd be as good as new. He leaned back in the chair, closed his eyes, and let his mind slip into darkness.

-54-

Liu Ting Wei shuffled uncomfortably in his seat. The private lounge in Baotou's airport was blissfully quiet but the boxy lounge chairs were too small for someone of his girth. His foot bounced with nervous energy as he opened the *New York Times* website and read the Diebolt drug story. Speed, cocaine, opium; it was all there, just as Liu had seen all those years before. The knives were coming out for his friend. Liu then read about Diebolt's turn on the minister's show. He'd been brilliant. The candidate had practically admitted the story was true and yet he still came off as some sort of spiritual icon. Diebolt was, as they used to say in the US, like Teflon.

Liu dug up a couple of instant polls on the Web. Though not statistically valid, they still showed most people were unmoved by the drug story. Diebolt continued to hold a narrow lead two days before voting. Liu bit his lower lip and marveled at how his old friend always managed to skate through such trouble practically unfazed. His thoughts drifted back two decades, to the first trip he and Richard had taken to the Philippines.

———————

Disco lights flashed through the smoke as the slim Filipina waitress guided them to a table next to the stage. "First class all the way," said Diebolt, as they sank into their seats and ogled a naked girl twirling around a brass pole.

More young ladies in miniskirts and bikini tops paraded past their table, making eye contact as they moved their lithe bodies to the deep pulsing techno music that filled the club. Most of them could have been eighteen, some not quite.

The plan was to pick a couple of women and pay the bouncer about one hundred and twenty-five dollars per girl to take them traveling. Then they'd spend seven wonderful days drinking, snorting, and fucking at the beach.

"Which one do you like, Ting Wei?" Diebolt slurred his words. He'd been drinking for hours.

Liu singled out an impossibly cute girl with perky breasts, golden skin, and a beautiful tight ass. She was fresh faced and tantalizingly innocent. Then another one took the stage and his mouth fell open. Just as sexy as the first, the second stripper appeared to be in her late twenties and something about her told Liu she knew exactly how to please a man.

"Too many choices, Richard," he said with a laugh. "I might have to get them both."

Diebolt nodded toward a girl seated with a Filipino man in a booth against the wall. "I like that one."

"She's busy right now," Liu replied.

"Yeah, I know," he brooded. "Fucking guy is taking forever, too."

Then the Filipino customer lifted his arm and signaled to a burly man next to the bar. The customer had made his selection. The big man lifted a finger and nodded in acknowledgement.

"You're too late," quipped Liu. "How about the one on stage?"

Diebolt grasped the corners of the table and leaned forward, his head hung low and his eyes riveted on the girl in the booth. "The hell with that," he said as he rose to his feet.

Diebolt stomped over to the booth and began yammering at the Filipino customer. Liu strained to hear his friend but the heavy beat drowned out Diebolt's words. The Filipino customer looked annoyed as he shook his head and wrapped his arm around the girl's shoulder. Diebolt pulled a wad of cash from his pocket and waved it in the man's face, enticingly at first and then more aggressively as the customer's expression darkened. Finally, the man stood to meet Diebolt's challenge.

Then it happened. Diebolt slapped the cash on the table, grabbed the customer's beer, and smashed the bottle against his head. The blow knocked the man to the floor in a shower of glass and blood and Diebolt pounced again. Screams rose above the music and a two-hundred-and-fifty-pound bouncer darted across the floor with surprising speed.

Liu rose to his feet and tried to intercept the bouncer. But it was too late. Before he could reach them the massive bouncer seized Diebolt from behind and threw him to the floor. A second bouncer appeared out of nowhere and pressed his knees into the small of Diebolt's back, pinning him down. Beside them, the dazed Filipino customer clutched his bloodied head as he rolled on the floor.

Eyes raging, Diebolt struggled to free himself. "You're all a bunch of assholes! That guy started it," he yelled, craning his neck to look up. "Get off me, you fucking gorilla."

Liu knelt down beside his friend. "Richard," he yelled. "Let me deal with this."

Liu then went into damage-control mode, apologizing to the bouncers and explaining that his American friend was simply drunk, horny, and overly excited about his first trip to Manila. It was really just a big misunderstanding, fueled by too much booze. They were ready to leave quietly and there would be no more trouble.

The bouncer shook his head. Minutes later a trio of Manila policemen entered the club. They nodded familiarly to the staff and chatted to a grandmotherly woman behind the bar. She pointed at Diebolt several times as she complained to the officers. Ten minutes later, Diebolt and Liu sat locked inside a dank and crowded holding cell at a Manila police station just down the road from the city's red light district.

A young female attendant stepped in front of Liu and pulled him back to the present. She bowed to him and smiled demurely. "Your jet is ready," she said.

Liu rose to his feet and followed her down a corridor to the gate, pulling his roller bag behind him. Twenty years earlier, he and Richard had taken a similar walk through Manila's international terminal, determined to get on the first flight out of the country before the city's chief of police decided he could squeeze a bigger bribe out of them.

Diebolt's meltdown had shocked Liu, but he had quickly concluded the episode should not derail their thriving business relationship. And then there was the not insignificant matter of Diebolt's impressive pedigree. He was a Harvard MBA, the heir to an industrial empire, and a scion of a politically well-connected family—an American with access to the corridors of power, a future leader, and a once-in-a-lifetime connection that Liu was eager to cultivate.

-55-

Time evaporated as Sergio surrendered to the billions of bits floating through his head. Zachary had stashed away a huge amount of code, raw data at the heart of the massive artificial organism that Sergio, George, and many other veterans had created during their time at Circles. It should have been a familiar exercise, like greeting an old friend, but as his brain picked through all the data Zachary had siphoned from Circles, Sergio quickly discovered the software wasn't acting normally. Before long he came across unfamiliar code—a parasite that had infected his perfect creation and turned it into some sort of mutant that talked, acted, and thought in ways Sergio had never before seen. At first he was mystified, but little by little he dissected the invasive code, visualizing its behavior until new connections clicked in his brain and secrets revealed themselves, some so incredible and disturbing that it was no wonder Zachary needed to be sure.

A soft voice shattered the silence. "How do you do that?"

Sergio pulled himself away from the screen. The desk lamp's incandescent bulb had warmed his face. Outside the cozy ring of light, the room was dark and a draft of chilly air tickled the short bristles on his head. "Do what?" he asked, turning in his chair.

"Stare at the screen like that." Malina sat up on the sofa, her auburn hair lit by an argent sliver of moonlight. She rubbed the sleep from her eyes. "It looks like you haven't moved for hours."

Sergio felt warm inside. "It's what I do," he said with a shrug. "Kind of the way you pull iron rods out of people's necks. No way I could do that."

Malina smiled.

"How do you feel?" he asked.

"Better. You must be exhausted." She looked at her watch. "It's two thirty."

He shook his head. "I'm wide awake."

His short power nap had turned into a three-hour respite, interrupted only when Malina had come to see if he was hungry. Their hastily arranged dinner of pasta and bottled marinara sauce had been awkward. Barry couldn't understand why it was taking Sergio so long to sort out his emergency.

"Have you heard Barry?" she asked, looking up to the ceiling.

"Not a peep." He threw his arm over the backrest. "Thanks for keeping him busy this afternoon. I'm guessing that wasn't easy."

"We had a lot to rehash."

"Good," he lied. That was not the answer he'd wanted to hear.

She moved behind him and leaned over his shoulder. "Find anything?"

"Too much," he said. The past five hours had gone by like mere minutes.

Malina arched a single eyebrow and waited for him to continue.

He tilted his head back. "Zachary was right," he said, a hint of resignation in his voice.

Malina's mouth fell open. "You mean someone *is* trying to steal the election?"

"In a sense, yes. But this is far more subtle than stuffing ballot boxes or misreporting results. Someone has gone to a lot of trouble to influence Circles users to vote a certain way. And they are using their personal data against them to do it."

She peered at the computer screen. "But isn't that what campaigns have been doing since Obama's first run?"

"Not like this," he said. "Over the years both parties have built massive national voter databases that contain public data collected from local, state, and federal records—stuff like party registration, voting history, political donations, and property records. On top of that, they added things like magazine subscription records, credit histories, and even grocery club-card purchases to create fairly detailed voter profiles."

"Things took a radical step forward during the Obama era. His team encouraged supporters to become buddies with him on Circles. This gave him access to his supporters' profiles, everything he could possibly hope to know about his base, almost like a diary on some of their most personal opinions and beliefs. In short, Obama was able to build the largest, most detailed, and powerful voter database in the history of political campaigns. It seems obvious in hindsight, but it was a stroke of genius at the time." Sergio paused to catch his breath. "But there was a key shortcoming to this approach—"

Malina jumped in. "Voters who became buddies with Obama were already in the candidate's camp."

"Right," he said. "That was good for a number of reasons—the Obama team could target voters with the very issues they most cared about, it could encourage supporters to pull their friends into Obama's circle, and it could help get supporters to the polls on voting day. But this strategy didn't help them reach out to independent or undecided voters, who often don't decide who they'll vote for until the last few days. And because of the divided state of our electorate, middle-of-the-road voters hold the balance of almost every election in their hands."

"So how do they get around that problem?"

"They haven't, really. Both parties came to us quietly, numerous times, asking for our user data. They tried all sorts of pitches. They wanted to buy our data, but we said no. Then they wanted to rent it," he said, crooking his fingers to draw air quotes. "And when that didn't work, they asked to borrow it or exchange it. They would have done just about anything we wanted, paid any price, to get their hands on our data. But Johnny Weiss and the collective brain trust were dead set against it."

"So you think Circles is doing that now?" she asked.

"Not exactly." Sergio wondered how best to explain it to Malina. "Remember when Zachary said he found a bunch of fake American profiles, like the Chinese ones George found?"

Malina nodded.

"And remember we told you about the program Ko and Tong built to create and control those profiles?"

Malina nodded again, and Sergio's hands flew into a frenzy, his fingers gliding effortlessly over the keyboard. Within seconds, the screen filled with line upon line of code.

"See these lines?" he asked, pointing at the screen. "This is that program and it's running live at Circles right now. It's not supposed to be."

Malina looked at him blankly.

"Remember how Zachary said he got back into Circles after they'd kicked him out?" Sergio didn't wait for her answer. "I followed his tracks and this program is just as scary as Zachary thought. See this?" he asked, scrolling down the computer screen until he settled on another set of codified gobbledygook.

"This is an opinion-mining algorithm inside the socialbot program. It detects a person's thoughts or opinions based on what they write in their posts. So if someone writes, 'I hate felines,' the socialbot will know that person doesn't like cats. And if the socialbot is programmed to look for cat lovers, the socialbot will ignore the cat hater and move on to the next person."

Malina nodded as if she followed Sergio's train of thought. The puzzled expression on her face suggested otherwise. "But this doesn't explain why these socialbots are going through all this trouble."

"We're getting to that. So the socialbot identifies someone who loves cats. Its next task is to engage the cat lover based on a list of pre-programmed commands it can execute. It can send a 'happy face' icon, write a note bragging about its own not-so-real cat, or it could even send a fake photo. It might even criticize dog lovers, just for the fun of it. And here is where things start to get really interesting," he said, again pointing to the screen. "This chunk of code here is a sentiment-analysis algorithm. It measures a person's mood. Let's say the socialbot writes an anti-dog post and two real people respond. One writes, 'Dogs are too messy,' and the other says, 'I wanna take my neighbor's dog out behind the woodshed!' Both are anti-dog posts, but the sentiments are significantly different. This socialbot can distinguish between the fastidious person and the angry person, and makes adjustments so its next comments to each person are compatible with the moods they have expressed."

"What makes these socialbots even more insidious is that they tap into affinity groups—" He stopped himself. "These are all the alumni organizations, professional associations, and fan clubs on our network, groups that bring millions of like-minded people together, even if they don't know each other well. So the socialbots identify targets and then join their groups. Once the socialbots establish a friendly presence within the group, they start engaging their targets individually and expanding the nature of their, um, opinions."

"So each person thinks they've encountered some kind of kindred spirit," Malina interjected.

"Exactly," he said. "And remember all that stuff about machine learning? There are reams of code in here that enable this socialbot to self-learn. So if it makes a mistake with one person, the socialbot will make adjustments the next time it interacts with a user."

Malina closed her eyes as she tried to absorb everything he'd just explained. "So what you are saying is that people who are targeted by these socialbots can be seduced, influenced, cajoled—whatever you want to call it—and they have no way of understanding what's happening."

He nodded somberly. "The socialbot program is so sophisticated that it can spoon-feed people information tailored to their moods, biases, idiosyncrasies, grievances, and soft spots. And it raises a very disturbing question: If you make a decision that was almost a foregone conclusion because of the stream of information you've been fed, have you really exercised free will?"

"Holy shit," she said breathlessly. "And this has nothing to do with cats and dogs."

"No," he said quietly. "Zachary was right. It's about Richard Diebolt."

Sergio tapped quickly on the keyboard and brought up the Circles profile page of a blond woman in her late twenties. "Meet Beverly Tustin," he announced. "To the average user, she's an attractive single woman from Miami. Successful paralegal. Almost three hundred friends, all of whom she met through our Naturalist group, several legal association pages, the Red Cross fan club, and other groups on Circles."

As he spoke, Sergio flipped through Tustin's photos, her biographical information, and a sampling of her comments. "She seems like a thoroughly likeable person. Intelligent, caring, funny, and entirely middle of the road. There is nothing in her profile that suggests she leans toward one party or the other. The only problem with Tustin is that she doesn't really exist."

Malina tapped his shoulder. "Diebolt . . ." she said impatiently.

"So I scrolled through Tustin's buddy list and as I suspected, not one of them identifies with either party. Every single one of her Circles buddies is self-declared independent." He tried to suppress a self-satisfied grin. "I'm no statistician, but I can assure you the odds of having more than three hundred friends, none of whom is a Democrat or Republican, well, let's say the odds are astronomical."

Malina opened her mouth to speak but Sergio couldn't stop himself. "Let's take a closer look at some of her political comments. Here are a couple from last week."

"*Saw Diebolt on* 60 Minutes *last night. I'm starting to like the guy!*"

"*Can't believe all this dirt. There ought to be a law against this kind of negative campaigning. They are both guilty, but Lester seems a tad more desperate.*"

"Here's another," he said.

"*Awesome debate last night. Diebolt nailed it. Don't you just love a hunky man with brains?*"

Sergio continued to scroll through Tustin's comments, stopping every few posts to read them out to Malina.

"*Lester will say anything to get elected. I don't always agree with Diebolt, but at least he makes sound arguments to back up his positions. What a breath of fresh air!*"

"*Glad to see Diebolt standing up to China. It's about time someone did. I might have to vote R this time.*"

Malina leaned in. "She seems very reasonable, doesn't she?" she said. "Intelligent, witty, and colorful—not even close to extreme or inflammatory. It's like Tustin had thought long and hard about the election and made a well-considered decision to back Diebolt."

"Exactly," replied Sergio. "Then I stumbled across something truly sinister. As I checked Tustin's friends, the real people the socialbot is connected to, I noticed a piece of code in their profile templates that I didn't recognize. That's not entirely unusual. Our engineers rewrite and tidy up code all the time. But this isn't just any old time, so I checked and discovered the code created a surreptitious link to Labs servers, a direct access link that shouldn't be there under any circumstance."

Malina's eyes grew wide in anticipation. "And?"

"All of Tustin's friends are being blocked from seeing comments, videos, and media reports that are favorable to Lester. They are being spoon-fed a steady diet of Diebolt propaganda and starved of anything positive about Lester."

"How can they do that?"

"Censoring software. Labs has been testing automated censoring software that we're going to roll out when we launch in China. This was one of the projects Ko has been working on. I was dead set against it, but I'm not the boss."

Malina's eyebrows came together in disapproval. "Wait a minute. You're saying someone has set it up so that Circles is secretly censoring American voters' accounts?" Her jaw tightened and her eyes narrowed. "How can someone just do that? Doesn't Circles have systems in place to prevent employees from acting on their own?"

"Technically, we do. The rule of thumb is 'two sets of eyes,' which means a second person has to sign off on any changes introduced. And for the most part it works. But in Labs, we don't always do that before signing off on a colleague's work. We're the company's most trusted and capable engineers. And we're busy. Things would get bogged down if we spent hours going over each other's work."

Malina gave him a flinty look. "So there are more profiles like Tustin?" she asked.

"This socialbot software has generated more than fifty thousand fake profiles. While you were sleeping I wrote some code to slice and dice them. It turns out they have a lot in common. For starters, these people," he said, drawing imaginary quotes, "are all decidedly middle income and hold respectable jobs, people like firemen, policemen, nurses, and teachers. They are not lawyers, doctors, CEOs, and the like—the kind of people that other people love to hate. No, these people are the salt of the earth that everyone can identify with."

He looked up at Malina. "Then I wondered who these socialbots were targeting. So I compiled a data set of all the real people that these socialbots have fooled and befriended. There were close to eight million in all, some of whom appeared multiple times, and all of them live here . . ."

Sergio tapped in a few keystrokes and brought up a map of the US featuring clusters of tiny red dots in Ohio, Virginia, Pennsylvania, Missouri, Florida, and Colorado.

"The swing states," she said.

"Exactly," he said. "The states where presidential elections are ultimately decided."

He pulled up a three-bar chart onto the screen. The blue bar on the left and the red bar on the right were barely visible, while the white bar in the middle soared to the top of the graph. "This blue blip shows the tiny faction of those eight million voters who are Democrats. The red one on the right is for Republicans, and the middle bar represents all the undeclared voters that the Tustinbot and all the others have targeted. Some ninety-eight percent of all those voters."

Malina whistled softly. "That's insane!"

"But true."

"But how do you know that this is actually making a difference?" asked Malina.

"Ah! So I created a timeline," he replied, as his fingers danced effortlessly across the keyboard. "The socialbots started propagating about six months ago. They spread slowly at first and some were detected and deleted. But most of them eventually built sizeable networks of friends and then friends of friends."

He nodded to another graphic on the monitor. A thin green line emerged from the bottom left corner, spiking and dropping erratically as it moved across the screen. About halfway across, the line suddenly surged upward and continued climbing dramatically as it moved to the right.

"This line represents the amount of activity these fifty thousand social bots were engaged in. To put it another way, it shows them getting down to the business of influencing voters and this, right here," he said, pointing to the spot where the line jumped upward, "is late July. It just so happens to correspond to the moment when Diebolt began to surge in the polls."

Malina flashed a sour smile. "And with such a polarized electorate, all it will take is a shift of a few percentage points and—voilà—the election is transformed."

"Exactly," he said with a nod. "It's not that hard if you know what you're doing."

"Why don't we just take this to the FBI?"

"For starters, I'm not so sure it's illegal, at least not if Circles is behind it," he said.

"You can't be serious."

"Ah, but I am," he replied. "Circles' terms of use explicitly state that we can conduct all sorts of experiments using our users' data. Everyone agrees to be a subject when they click on the 'agree' box at sign up."

"We've . . ." Sergio stopped himself, unsure whether he still could, whether he wanted to, refer to himself as a Circles insider. "We do this sort of thing all the time—tweak what people see—but only with the goal of improving our service, as far as I was aware. So if someone like Prederick or Ko billed this as an experiment, then, technically, Circles might not be breaking any laws."

A frown clouded Malina's face. "But isn't Diebolt behind all this?"

He shrugged. "Hard to say for sure. All I know for certain is that someone at Circles is making this happen."

"Ko?"

Sergio grimaced as he scratched his head. "He's the obvious one, but I have trouble seeing him help Diebolt, who's done nothing but criticize and threaten Ko's homeland." Sergio shook his head. "I don't know. I have no idea what motivates Ko."

"What about the CEO?" she countered. "What's his name again? Prederick?"

He pursed his lips. "Could be, but the only thing Prederick cares about is money, and I can't see Diebolt paying him enough to put the company—and his stock grants—at such great risk."

"So this is a dead end?"

"No. This is where it gets interesting," he said with a grin. "According to the company's network map, all this rogue software is running on a computer connected to Labs' private subnet. That limits our list of suspects to fourteen guys, thirteen if you will agree I'm not involved."

"I guess I can grant you that," she said.

"So I ran the MAC address of the computer—" He stopped himself. "Sorry, not MAC as in Apple. Every computer, smartphone, and router in the world has a unique MAC address. It's like a special barcode, except it's a string of numbers. So I ran this computer's MAC address against Circles' master list and discovered it's not a company machine. The socialbot network is being controlled from a non-company computer plugged into one of our network servers."

"So we don't know who it is?"

"The only way to figure it out is to physically follow the cable that runs from the server to the computer."

"So . . ."

"So, I need to go back there."

"Back to Circles?" Malina looked at him dubiously. "You really think that's a good idea?"

He offered her a reluctant smile. "Do you have a better one?"

-56-

Barry turned on the night-light and swung his legs over the side of the bed. He sat naked and motionless, hands on the edge of the mattress, staring down at his bony feet. The chilly night air sent a shiver through his body.

He replayed his afternoon with Malina, an interlude at once wonderful and agonizing. They'd talked about old friends, laughed about their ER antics, and relived some of the good times, like the diving trip to Palau.

But there was a distance to her, an aloofness that pained him. Quite happy to rehash the past, she quickly shut him off every time he tried to move into the present. She had ripped apart the emotional cocoon he'd built over the last few years and she seemed content to let the wound fester. He threw himself back onto the mattress. His eyes traced the fissures in the ceiling, hairline cracks he'd never noticed before. Why had she come? What did she want? Was this some sort of revenge, served exceptionally chilled?

That awful possibility muddled his mind and roiled his soul. Why else would she appear on his doorstep, intruding without warning, accompanied by a man who maybe was or wasn't her lover? Barry sensed an intimacy between them, and yet . . . He reared up and threw the pillow at the wall. Then he slid off the mattress and fitfully paced the room. Or maybe she'd come back to see him again, to see if there was anything left that they could salvage. He looked to the door but stopped himself. In his agitated state, it would be a mistake to confront Malina.

Resigned to a sleepless night, he slipped on a pair of shorts and a fleece pullover, and made his way along the upstairs hall to the TV room at the top of the front staircase. He picked up the remote and flipped through the channels, more than a hundred stations of infomercials, reruns, sports, and news. Boring. He really ought to upgrade his cable package so he could watch movies—

What the fuck? Barry could hardly believe his eyes. On screen were two photos: one of Malina and the other of a handsome Latino. The caption read: *"Murder suspect and accomplice."* He studied the man's picture as he fumbled with the volume. The male suspect had a full head of hair and a straight nose, but it didn't require much imagination to see it was Sergio.

". . . their last-known whereabouts were in Malibu, early Sunday morning. Anyone with information about these two suspects should call 911."

And then they were gone, replaced by a late night pitchman selling cheap kitchen utensils. His mind reeling, Barry frantically flipped through the channels, trying to find another news station that could fill in the blanks. *A murderer?* How could Malina have gotten herself involved with this guy?

None of the other channels had the story, at least not until the top of the hour. He collapsed on the sofa and stared at the phone, hesitating until he could justify it no longer. He picked up the receiver and dialed 911.

The emergency operator took his details and put him on hold. He bounced from one operator to another until a groggy FBI duty agent came on the line. "Mr. Neff? I understand you have information about Sergio Mansour and Malina Olson. Is that correct?"

"He's here, in my house. I just met him today. I didn't realize who he was until I saw the news." The receiver shook in Barry's hand, whether out of nervousness or anger he wasn't sure.

"Is there anyone with him, a woman?" the agent asked.

"No," he replied as he wiped his damp forehead. He'd never broken the law before.

"Where is Mansour now?"

"Downstairs, sleeping."

"Good. Mr. Neff, are you in any danger?"

"No. I don't think so," he said, struggling to remain calm.

"Are there any weapons in the house?"

"Yes, I have several rifles, shotguns, and handguns."

"Does the suspect have any weapons?"

Barry seized up. He hadn't even considered that possibility. "Not that I've seen."

"Very well. Are you able to get out of the house without waking the suspect?"

"Yeah, I think so."

"Good. Are you calling from a landline or a cell phone?"

"A landline."

"Do you have a cell phone?" asked the agent.

Barry paused. His cell phone was charging on the night table next to his bed. If he said yes, the agent would ask him to call back on the mobile and stay on the line until he was out of danger. "I think I left it in my truck," he replied.

"Okay, can you reach your truck safely? And do you have a neighbor where you can go?"

"Yes, and yes. The Handelmans live just down the road."

"Very well, Mr. Neff. Call back on your cell phone the minute you get to your truck. Go to the Handleman residence. It might be a little while, but we'll send a local patrol as quickly as we can."

Barry hung up. He didn't have much time. Somehow, some way, he needed to get Malina away from Mansour and out of the house before the cops showed up.

-57-

The lights were off and the laptop was powered down, but Barry's office was illuminated by a slash of silver light from the rising moon. Sergio and Malina lay pressed together on the couch, a wool blanket covering their fully clothed bodies. He was on his back, his left arm around Malina as she snuggled next to him, her breathing deep and steady.

He should have been sleeping, but he couldn't stop his mind from turning over and over, like it was running on an endless hamster wheel. His distress was compounded by the torment of emotions swirling within. He was impressed and enthralled by the sophisticated social-bots he'd seen. A small part of him, the competitive coder part, wished he'd come up with it himself. But most of all, he was horrified by what Ko, or whoever it was, was doing with his baby, the network he'd helped build. And then there was Zachary, who'd outmaneuvered him, laid bare the lies that Sergio had convinced himself were true. He felt like a prizefighter who'd been dropped to the canvas for the very first time. Defeated. His weaknesses exposed. He released a deep sigh.

"What's wrong?" asked Malina.

He rolled his head away from her. "I was just thinking about Zachary."

"It wasn't your fault."

"No," he interrupted. "Not that. I was thinking about how he penetrated Circles and UCLA, almost at will. It's got me all freaked out. At first I was really pissed off at him. I mean, who the fuck did he think he was to hack into Circles?"

Malina said nothing.

"But then I realized I was also mad at myself . . . and George, I guess, because we couldn't stop him. We let him in." He stared at the ceiling. "We were so damn sure of ourselves, so damn sure we'd built the world's most impregnable fortress. Some hackers have gotten past our outer defenses, but we've always been able to cut them off before they did any real damage. At least, that's what we always thought. But Zachary got into our most secret and secure sub-net. If we can't protect Labs, then everything we've been telling ourselves is total bullshit."

Malina freed herself from his arms and sat up. "So you're gonna start feeling sorry for yourself now? Is that it?" Her voice had an edge that surprised him. "You got beat by an expert." She shook her head as she looked down on him. "You heard him. He worked for the fucking CIA or the NSA or whatever. Did you really think you were unbeatable? *The* very best?" Her eyes were full of judgment and scorn, practically daring him to respond. "Grow up," she snapped, as she lifted herself from the couch.

Sergio sat up, stunned by her antagonism. She parked herself at the window, facing away from him, her feet apart and arms crossed as she looked out to the moonlit hills. He groped for words but something in the way she stood there—rigid, emotionally charged, and defiant—told him to remain quiet.

A long moment passed, the silence broken only by occasional creaks and groans from the aging Queen Anne. Little by little, Sergio sensed Malina's stiff legs relax, the sharpness of her shoulders soften, and her resolve weaken. She bowed her head and her frame quivered, almost imperceptibly. Seconds later, she put her hand over her mouth and a soft sob escaped her lips.

"Are you okay?" he asked.

Malina straightened herself and pivoted quickly. "Don't you people understand what you're doing?" she asked with anguish in her voice. "You get young kids to expose themselves to the whole fucking world and you promise you'll protect them from bad people. Well, you can't do that, can you?"

Sergio looked down to escape Malina's challenging stare.

"You can't live up to your bullshit promises or your inflated sense of self," she said, her voice rising in pitch and volume. "Frankly, I'm glad—no, ecstatic—that Zachary ripped your security to shreds, and I'm delighted you were there to see just how easy it was. I doubt he's the only expert out there who . . ." Malina's voice cracked with emotion and she turned back to the window.

He sat frozen on the edge of the sofa, his mouth open but unable to form words. He didn't know this woman and didn't know what to say to her. Wind whispered through the eucalyptus trees behind the house, and at long last, after the silence in the room became unbearable, he forced himself to speak.

"Where's this coming from?"

"From my sister," she said, her plaintiff words caressing the window. She took a deep breath. "My younger sister was in college when she was raped and killed by some sick fuck who stalked her through Circles." She turned and faced him. She was once again the Malina he knew, even if her eyes were glazed and shell-shocked, as if she were a long way away from Barry's den. "She wrote an update saying she was on her way to meet some friends up at Lake Berryessa and this guy went up there and lay in wait for her."

A horrifying chill swept Sergio's body and the photo of the young woman on Malina's bookshelf flashed through his mind. "Oh my God." He stood up on trembling legs. "You're Hannah Birch's sister . . ."

The Hannah Birch incident, as it came to be known within Circles, was the most distressing moment of his professional life and the biggest crisis Circles had ever faced. News of the brutal crime went national and Circles came under intense pressure to tighten up its privacy policies. Johnny Weiss took most of the heat, but Sergio, George, and other senior managers were all stung by the widespread public rebuke that followed.

"So you remember her name," she said with resignation. "Hannah, like a lot of other people, had no idea how Circles really worked. All those privacy settings for different parts of your profile. Hell, I had a hard time figuring it out." Her voice turned brittle as she crossed her arms protectively, each hand on the opposite shoulder. "And the settings seemed to change every month, as if you were trying to make it as confusing as possible for the rest of us. And so, this guy she didn't even know was somehow able to stalk her without her having a clue . . ." Her words dissolved into a great heaving sob.

Fear and anger jolted Sergio to the core; a million questions collided in his head. This relationship, or partnership, or whatever it was . . . He felt like he was on one of those spinning carnival rides that always made him sick to his stomach. He squeezed his eyes shut and pressed his balled-up hands into his face. His father was there with him, smiling on one of those happy days. Sergio tried to latch on to the memory, but it quickly slipped away.

A painful sob filled the void. At first, he thought it was his own cries from that distant night, but then he heard a whimper and finally a squall of anguished cries. Malina. She stood hunched over, her arms pulled into her body as if she was protecting herself from the painful blows of the past. She needed him. There would be time later for explanations. He stepped toward her, ready to throw his arms around her and comfort her—to tell her he was sorry.

She saw him coming and backed away, thrusting her open palm straight out to warn him off. "Just, just . . . don't," she commanded, her voice fiercely defensive.

She stood in the moonlight, tears streaming down her cheeks, defiant and broken all at once. He wanted to tell her how sorry he was, how he and George and the rest of the Circles team had done everything they could to prevent something like that from happening again. But he knew more than ever that none of it mattered—not to her and no longer to him. It was as if the present and the past were closing in on him.

She moved to the door, opened it, and stepped into the hallway. Leaning back for the doorknob, she lifted her haunted eyes to his, just for an instant. Then she pulled the door shut.

-58-

Barry tiptoed down the front stairs, crossed the grand lobby, and padded his way into the library. He opened the gun case, broke his 12-gauge shotgun in half, and made sure both barrels were loaded. He put four more shells in his pocket. One would be enough to deal with Sergio if it came to that, but there was nothing wrong with a little insurance.

He considered the agent's question. Surprise was critical. Sergio might be armed and Barry couldn't afford to give him any opportunity. Stick the shotgun in his sleepy face and get Malina out of there. He wasn't sure what he'd do with her after that; he hadn't gotten that far. He puffed up his cheeks and exhaled. He'd figure that out later.

Barry skittered across the lobby and skulked through the parlor. He'd almost reached the kitchen when he heard the jiggle of a doorknob, a creaky hinge, and the sound of a door closing. He crouched behind a camelback sofa and propped the twin barrels across the backrest. He ran his finger along the shotgun's trigger as footsteps moved up the hall.

A shadow swept past the parlor doors. A gasp, maybe a sob, a wisp of moonlit hair. Then she was gone. Barry jumped to his feet and followed the sound of her footsteps to the front of the house. He was almost to the foyer when the front door swung open and was pulled shut.

Barry stepped out to the front porch and ran after her. A rising half-moon lit the cool breezy night. "Malina!" he cried in a half whisper. "It's me."

She spun around, her beautiful face contorted in anguish. He reached her and wrapped his arms around her as she collapsed into his chest. He held her tightly, at once fearful for the woman he still loved and grateful that fate had delivered her into his arms once again. Little by little, Malina's sobs ebbed until all emotion drained from her body. "I'm sorry." She pulled back and wiped away a tear hanging from the corner of her eye.

"Are you okay? What's wrong?"

She shivered in his arms. "It's Hannah. I kind of melted down."

Painful memories rushed back to him. He said nothing. It had all been said many times before. Five years had passed since Hannah's murder; it had been the beginning of the end for their relationship. He gave Malina a moment to regain her composure before walking her to the parked vehicles. Comfortable he'd put enough distance between them and the house, he leaned the shotgun against the white van.

"Do you know who that guy is?" he asked, pointing back to the house.

Malina regarded him silently.

"He's a fugitive, wanted for murder, and the cops are looking for him." He paused to let the information sink in. "They're also looking for you, by the way. What the hell are you doing with this guy?"

"He's *not* a murderer," she shot back. "None of that is true."

"You *knew* this? You're *with* him? Don't tell me you are part of this . . ." He raised his palm to his forehead. "This is crazy. What the hell happened to you?"

"I know what they are saying, but you have to believe me," she pleaded. "He's discovered a plot to steal the election and they're trying to pin the blame on him."

"Steal the election?" He couldn't quite believe what he was hearing. It was crazy talk, right up there with some of the bizarre shit he used to hear from meth addicts in the ER. "That's insane. Who told you this? Sergio?"

Malina's eyes flashed anger, but Barry didn't care. He'd gladly absorb a thousand angry stares if he could save her from Sergio. Barry gripped her by the arms and shook her lightly. "Get a hold of yourself," he said sternly. "That man is dangerous."

"No, he's not. He's *in* danger."

"You're the one in danger," he said, wondering how she'd become so angry, desperate, and confused. It was so unlike her. Always in control, she had veered wildly off course.

He pulled her close and softened his tone. "Okay, okay," he whispered. "I'm sorry. You were always looking for the good in people, even when you had to force yourself to overlook the bad."

She pulled against him but was no match for his strong arms. He caressed her gently, stroking her hair. God, he'd missed her. He'd been a fool to take her for granted. The tension in her body dissipated, her resistance ebbed, and she allowed him to press her head against his chest, just like she used to do. His world suddenly felt right again.

"Don't worry," he whispered. "You're safe now."

Her muscles relaxed and her breathing deepened, just like he knew they would. There'd been many problems in their relationship, but never lack of passion. It was only a matter of time before she'd slip into one of her trance-like spells.

"You can stay here with me. I'll protect you, no matter what," he whispered in her ear. He released one arm and kneaded the nape of her neck. She'd always liked that. "Don't worry, it'll all be over in the next half hour or so."

Malina snapped to attention and spun away from his grasp. "Over?" She glared at him. "What do you mean over?"

"The cops," he said, looking at his watch. "They're probably at the gate already."

-59-

Sergio sat sprawled on the sofa, a tumult of emotions pressing down on him. It was as if someone had poured all his shock, guilt, loneliness, anger, and desire into a heavy black cauldron and lowered it on his chest. A throbbing ache squeezed his frontal lobe as a million thoughts ripped through his mind. He wanted to rub his temples but his arms felt too heavy to move.

Eventually, a singular question pushed its way to the forefront: after all that had happened to Hannah, why had Malina helped him? Why had she risked everything? He churned through the possibilities quickly; there weren't many and there were even fewer that made sense. He bolted upright. In the end, only one answer seemed compelling enough—revenge. But against whom? Or what?

He moved to the window, unsure of what to do next. The towering eucalyptus trees blocked out most of the view. Orion the Hunter was up there somewhere, although Sergio couldn't see him in the little slice of visible sky. He stood motionless. Should he go after her? Escape on his own?

The wind picked up and the trees swayed freely as the moon peeked through the branches. Then he heard it. A call of some sort, maybe a cry. It came louder next time, more defined, like an animal in distress. He instantly knew.

Sergio bolted from the room and ran through the house, dodging furniture as he scoured the ground floor. "Malina!" He stopped at the bottom of the stairs and looked up into the darkness. He took two steps and heard it again, a shriek that seemed to float on the wind. She was outside. He swung open the front door and a blast of cool air whipped his body. There in the moonlight, halfway between the house and the vehicles, she struggled to free herself from Barry's grasp.

Sergio ran down the steps and charged, vaguely aware that his bare feet were no match for the gravel and dirt pathway. Malina twisted her body and kicked at Barry, though it was obvious she wasn't strong enough to fight him off. Barry wrapped one arm around her torso and covered her mouth with the other. He started to drag her back toward the van, her heels scraping along the dirt.

"Let her go!" yelled Sergio, as he closed the distance between him and Barry.

Barry released Malina and dropped into a crouch, his legs ready to spring and his raised fists poised to strike. Sergio came within ten feet of Barry and stopped. Malina circled behind Sergio as the two men squared off, eyeing each other warily. Barry was younger, bigger, and undoubtedly stronger.

"Malina says you're innocent," taunted Barry. "So why are you running from the police?"

Barry took one step back and to the side, and Sergio expected him to rush from an angle. Instead, the hulking man kept moving away, cautiously at first but increasing his pace as the gap widened. Something wasn't right. *Why is he backing away?*

"Sergio!" cried Malina, pointing to the vehicles. "The gun."

And then he saw it: the shotgun propped up against the van thirty feet away. Sergio sprang into action, his legs pumping furiously as his mind focused on one existential thought. He would die if Barry beat him to the shotgun.

Barry pivoted toward the van, but he stumbled and his momentum faltered. Charging at a full run, Sergio lowered his shoulder and drove himself into Barry's ribs with a forceful crunch. A blast of air rushed out from Barry's chest with a heavy grunt as the two men fell to the ground. Sergio leapt to his feet and jumped on Barry, driving a knee into the man's chest. He cocked his fist and readied himself to rain blows down on Barry.

Barry crossed his arms in front of his face. "Wait! Stop!" he pleaded.

Sergio hesitated, his fist still cocked as he looked down upon his helpless rival.

"Thank you," said Barry, as his arms dropped to the ground.

Sergio's brain registered the blur of movement a split second before he could react. From down in the dirt, next to his left leg, Barry's arm was coming back at him. Sergio started to turn away just as a cloud of gritty dirt pelted his face and stabbed his eyes. Searing pain rushed up his optical nerve and exploded in his brain. He cried out and reached for his face, exposing himself to Barry's counterattack. A fist slammed into the side of Sergio's head and sent him sprawling sideways to the ground. For a terrifying instant, he imagined his father, in the dirt, absorbing boot after boot with his savaged torso. Sergio rolled and lifted himself to his hands and knees. Dirt and grit caked his eyes and scraped his corneas; bolts of excruciating pain ripped through his head. Barry was surely on his feet by now, panting and grunting as he readied the next blow. Somewhere in the blackness, Malina screamed: "No, Barry, no!"

Instinct took over and Sergio pulled his arms in to his ribs to protect himself, just as Barry's foot slammed into his side with tremendous force. Air whooshed out of Sergio's lungs. He was certain the kick had rearranged his internal organs. But it was Barry who yelled in pain. "Arrrgh! My foot," he cried. "Fuck!"

Only then did Sergio realize the bony point of his elbow had absorbed the brunt of Barry's kick. With any luck the top of Barry's foot had shattered. Malina screamed at her ex, buying Sergio precious seconds. He stood and tried to pry open his eyelids with his fingers. Malina shrieked again, her screams louder and more guttural, as if she was engaged in a desperate struggle with Barry.

"Get off me," he yelled at her. "Are you nuts?" A deep smack, the sound of a fist landing a forceful blow, brought silence.

"Malina!" called Sergio, as he spun toward the sounds and forced open his eyes. More jagged pain, but this time accompanied by a flash of light. He fluttered his eyelids over and over, praying that his tears of pain would wash away the dirt. His left eye gummed up shut, but his right eye spied a flash of light—the moon. His right eye would have to do.

Even with blurry vision, in the moonlight, he could distinguish between the two hazy figures in front of him. The much smaller Malina was on the ground, Barry towering over her.

Sergio lowered his shoulder and charged, swiftly and silently. Barry heard him and spun around at the last minute, exposing himself to the full force of Sergio's bull-like attack. He slammed his shoulder into Barry's abdomen and drove him to the dirt, his head snapping backward against the ground with a hollow thud. Barry gasped for breath. Sergio felt no pity this time. He raised himself up and pummeled Barry's unprotected face. The first blows tore at Sergio's knuckles as they connected with Barry's chin and teeth, but fury and fear took over and the punches no longer hurt his hands.

A hand grabbed his arm. "Enough!" yelled Malina. "That's enough!"

Sergio looked up, shaken and confused, as Barry rolled over in the dirt. Malina pulled Sergio to his feet and they fell into a desperate, trembling embrace. His abdomen ached. His hands hurt. And his eyes still screamed. He stepped back in a daze, spread his fingers, and held his bruised and bloodied hands in front of his face.

At his feet, Barry moaned in pain, his right eye swollen shut, the skin over his left cheekbone split wide open. A couple of his front teeth were cracked. As Sergio looked down at the ghastly scene through his one good eye, he couldn't decide whether he felt pride or shame.

-60-

Special Agent Jay Feeley slapped at the rearview mirror, throwing it off kilter to escape the glare of the bright morning sun directly behind him. It was quarter after six in the morning, almost forty-eight hours since he'd kissed his wife and kids good-bye and sent them off to Tahoe. It felt more like weeks.

He'd been on the road for two hours and fifteen minutes, probably an all-time record between Burbank and Coalinga, although starting out at four in the morning certainly didn't hurt. He'd spent most of the drive on the phone, coordinating the takedown with various agencies. Detaining Mansour should have been straightforward, but his hopes of getting it done began slipping away when the caller went missing. No one had seen or heard from Barry Neff since he'd placed his 911 call almost three hours ago. Officers at the scene didn't know if he had escaped the house and driven off, or maybe fled into the hills. But if the caller had remained in the house with Mansour, then they were looking at a potential armed gunman with a hostage. And that meant calling in the county SWAT team from Paso Robles, more than an hour away.

Mansour had surprised him in more ways than Feeley could have imagined. The guy's resourcefulness and tech savvy was to be expected, but Feeley figured someone like Mansour would have buckled at the first sign of police pressure. Instead he'd run, and now there was a good chance he had actually killed someone. The bureau's evidence response team had found three sets of fingerprints from the Zachary murder scene—the victim's, Mansour's, and Olson's. That didn't necessarily mean Mansour or Olson had done it, but they were now the prime suspects.

Feeley's phone rang. It was Garrison again.

"And?" said the unit director.

"Not yet," replied Feeley.

"Jesus Christ," complained Garrison. "What the hell are you guys doing out there? I swear to God, Feeley, if this guy gets away again . . ."

"If you want to authorize a hostage operation without a negotiator and SWAT team, then go ahead."

Garrison didn't answer, just as Feeley expected. Garrison was quite happy to take credit when one of his agents notched a good operation, but he never stuck his neck out when cases demanded tough calls.

Feeley swung around a curve and slowed down for a police roadblock up ahead. "I'll keep you posted," he said before hanging up.

He flashed his badge at the roadblock and soon after rolled up to a fleet of local police cruisers, California Highway Patrol cars, and the SWAT team's armored vehicle scattered alongside the road outside Barry Neff's private lane. It was almost six thirty in the morning.

Feeley stepped out and introduced himself to the group of local and county law officers milling around the SWAT truck. Lieutenant Michael Rodriguez of the San Luis Obispo County SWAT team came forward to shake hands.

"Still no word on the caller?" asked Feeley.

"Negative," replied Rodriguez. "A Coalinga patrol car got out here and blocked the driveway at about four thirty, and we put a sniper up on the ridge half an hour ago." He pointed to a hill towering over the dirt lane. "The suspect's white van is parked next to the house, but we've seen no activity at all since we set up."

"Do you have infrared?" asked Feeley. Heat signatures would have quickly told them how many people were in the house.

Rodriguez shook his head, his face pinched with frustration. "Budget cuts."

Feeley winced. "How long before we can move?"

"We're about ready to start calling," said Rodriguez, who then briefed Feeley on the tactical plan.

The hostage negotiator tried calling Barry Neff, first on his landline and then cell phone. Feeley rushed to his trunk, where he put on a bulletproof vest with bright yellow FBI letters emblazoned on the back. Then he loaded his Colt close-quarters assault rifle and was back at the SWAT truck by the time the negotiator hung up, shaking his head. It was time.

Two minutes later, four vehicles rolled out in a column spearheaded by the armored SWAT truck. It moved slowly up the dirt lane, followed by two police cruisers and Feeley's Crown Vic. The house came into view half a mile up the gully and the armored vehicle accelerated in a straight line to the front porch. The cruisers peeled off from the column and bolted past the Queen Anne to take up perimeter positions about fifty yards beyond the house. Feeley stayed tucked in behind the SWAT vehicle as it stopped five feet short of the house. The armored car's rear doors swung open and eight officers in tactical gear burst from the back and took cover behind the vehicles. Rodriguez lifted a bullhorn and called on Mansour to surrender. He waited fifteen seconds and repeated the call.

Then, with a quick nod from Rodriguez, the SWAT team was on the move, bolting onto the porch in pairs. One foursome smashed in the front door; the other group skirted around back. Feeley listened on the radio as they moved from room to room, clearing the ground floor and upstairs within forty-five seconds. Then came the words Feeley feared. "The house is clear. There's nobody here."

Feeley shook his head in disgust as he marched to the carriage house and flung open its double doors. Inside were two parking spots and one silver Ford F-150. Feeley brought his radio to his mouth and called out to anyone who was listening. "How many vehicles registered at this address?"

There was a long pause before one of the local officers responded. "There are two vehicles registered. A silver 2013 Ford F-150 and a granite 2005 Jeep Grand Cherokee."

Feeley pressed his fingers to his temple while his mind churned through the calculations. Mansour had as much as a two-hour head start. He'd most likely used slower back roads as much as possible. Best guess: he was probably a good hundred miles from the ranch by now. Sergio Mansour—data thief, possible terrorist, murder suspect, and now a likely kidnapper—was starting to get under Feeley's skin.

Feeley approached the house, wondering what to tell Garrison. Rodriguez, his phone to his ear, intercepted Feeley. The lieutenant's eyebrows shot up and he pulled the phone from his face. "We found Barry Neff."

-61-

Malina guided Barry's Grand Cherokee down from the hills into a wide valley west of Hollister, a small agricultural town about two hours shy of San Francisco. Sergio sat in the passenger seat, his left eye covered by a patch fashioned with gauze and tape. His good eye focused on the second of the two untraceable smartphones Malina had bought at Bruno's. His right hand was grotesquely swollen and starting to curl up like an eagle's claw. Barry's face had been as hard as it looked.

"This road will take us around Hollister and up toward Gilroy," he said, after consulting the map on the tiny screen. "There we can catch a road up into the Santa Cruz Mountains and follow the ridgeline most of the way back to the city."

Almost two hours had passed since they'd hogtied Barry, loaded him into the Jeep, and set off into the open field behind the Queen Anne. They zigzagged across rolling hills, dodging rocks, avoiding crevices, and skirting clumps of hardy oak trees in the predawn darkness until they reached a narrow county road. There they released Barry, by then fully conscious and armed with a bottle of Perrier from his fridge. It'd take him at least a couple of hours to walk back to the ranch. A few minutes later, Sergio had tossed the first phone, just in case. Then they drove north, relying on the light of dawn and Sergio's innate sense of direction to guide them through the hilly terrain. Other than the words necessary to pull off their escape, they'd not spoken since Malina had left the back room at the farmhouse.

Sergio surveyed the wide-open valley around them. A handful of weather-beaten houses dotted the landscape and distant tractors floated on a sea of dirt. It was straight out of his childhood, and the awful memory of his father was present and all too raw. So, too, was a heavy weight of despair for Malina and her sister.

He peeked at Malina sideways. She was lost in thought and her far-off gaze seemed to barely register the road ahead of them. The silence in the Jeep grew more oppressive with each passing mile; he felt as if he were standing at the edge of a cliff, and he couldn't be sure if Malina was about to pull him to safety or push him over the side.

When he could no longer stand the tension, he set the phone in his lap and cleared his throat. "I know I can never change what happened to your sister," he said somberly. "But I just want to say that I'm really sorry."

Malina tightened her grip on the steering wheel but didn't flinch otherwise. The drone of the highway filled the Jeep until she finally looked at him with heavy eyes. "I know you are."

He'd seen that same lonely gaze only days ago. "That's Hannah in the photo on your bookshelf. Isn't it?"

She nodded, almost imperceptibly, and wiped a hint of moisture from the corner of her eye. "That was the last photo of her." She stopped to take in a deep breath. "I took it just as she was leaving for the lake the day she was killed. I didn't want her to go up there alone and I was being a pain-in-the-ass big sister. But she wanted to be one of the popular kids. She assured me she knew where she'd find her friends and that everything would be fine."

He remembered the studio portrait of Hannah that went viral after she was murdered. It had probably been taken a few years before she died. Her face was a bit fuller and her long platinum hair was shorter and more of a sandy blonde back then. No wonder he hadn't made the connection. "But why is she Birch and you Olson?"

"She's technically my half sister, from my stepdad." Her eyes were misty. "But I never thought of her that way."

"All this time," he began, his voice barely a whisper, "and you never said anything."

"I didn't want you to know." She glanced at Sergio and turned back to the road. "I wasn't sure how you'd react."

"How *I'd* react?"

She took in another deep breath and collected herself, wiping a tear with the back of her hand. "Peter Dixon killed my sister. I'll never forget the way he sneered at our parents in court, with that awful self-satisfied smile, taunting us, making fun of our loss. It was chilling. It was pure evil." She grasped the steering wheel, leaned into it, and stared down the road for a long while.

"But for a long, long time I also blamed Circles for being so casual about people's lives and their private information, for making it so easy for a predator like Peter Dixon to stalk Hannah."

Sergio focused on his hands in his lap, unable to look at Malina and afraid to interrupt.

"And then I just couldn't do it anymore," she continued. "I got to the point that I had to let go of my anger. I had to forgive, you know, so I could move on." She cleared her throat, like she was trying to swallow her sadness. "And that's where I was when you just happened to walk up to me at the movies. You were so nice and funny and I was charmed right away. When I found out you worked at Circles, I thought God was playing some sick joke on me. But then I realized that this was an opportunity, a chance to forgive, to find some peace. As much as I loved Hannah, I knew I had to let it go."

The drone of the Jeep's tires on the pavement filled the void until she continued. "And then you came to me with this scary story about

George, the socialbots, and your boss Ko. It stirred everything up again." She hesitated. "I know it sounds crazy, but it seemed like a chance to expose Circles for what it is—a company that manipulates people into sharing their most secret desires, wants, and needs, and then turns around and sells their data to the highest bidder." She became more animated as she talked, and Sergio wondered if she was really ready to forgive.

"It's destroyed our notion of privacy," she continued, "and leaves unsuspecting users vulnerable to stalkers, trolls, and online criminals. And based on what you've just discovered, that's only the half of it."

She shook her head slowly. "I don't know. Maybe it's too late to change anything. Maybe we're all like little frogs, being slowly boiled alive without even realizing it." She paused. "And then one day we'll wake up and realize we've been stripped of our privacy, our identity, and our self-determination." She looked squarely at Sergio. "You're an insider. You have credibility. People will listen to you."

Sergio felt the weight of overwhelming expectation press down upon him. "But that's not what I set out to do," he protested. Sergio could almost hear the ding of the opening bell on the New York Stock Exchange from the day he and Johnny Weiss and the rest of the Circles team became wildly rich. "I was trying to protect Circles from Ko. I was trying to make sure he didn't destroy the company."

"Maybe," she said, focusing once again on the road ahead. "But I'm a doctor, remember?"

He turned to her, his eyebrows crunched in confusion.

"I told you," she said. "I'm pretty good at reading people. And I knew you'd do the right thing, even if it meant exposing the manipulative power of the company you helped build."

"So that was the deal? You help me and I go public?"

Malina shrugged, then nodded. "If that's the way you want to put it."

"And when were you going to tell me about this . . . deal?"

"I didn't think it'd be necessary."

"And if I wasn't willing to go public?"

Malina scrunched up her face but said nothing. Sergio nodded soberly. He didn't need to know the answer; and he didn't really want to. Deep down, a part of him knew this would all have to come out, right from the moment he discovered the socialbots on George's thumb drive.

The silence returned, but the tension that earlier had filled the Jeep was gone; in its place was sadness and reflection. Malina, in a very roundabout way, had just forgiven him for Hannah's death. He wondered if he could have ever forgiven the man with the vicious black eyes. Malina came to a stop at a T junction. They looked left and right down a desolate straightaway that cut through miles of fields. There were no cars in sight in any direction.

"How's your eye?" she asked.

"It hurts like hell."

She nudged the Jeep over to a dirt pull-out next to an irrigation canal. She patted her lap. "Let me take another look."

Sergio lay across the seats, his head in her lap, facing up, vulnerable and childlike. She peeled away the bandage and inspected his injured eye once again.

"What do you think?" he asked.

"Your cornea is pretty scratched up but I don't think it's serious." She pulled a bottle of eyedrops she'd taken from Barry's medicine cabinet and flooded his eye. Then she covered his good eye with her hand. "How does it look?"

"A little blurry, but basically okay," he said, lifting his battered right hand up to his face.

"Let me take a look at that." She probed the knuckles and bones along the back of his hand until Sergio pulled it away.

"Ouch!" he cried as he sat up. "Careful, Doc."

"Looks like you've broken your fourth and fifth metacarpals," she said, tracing two lines along the back of her hand between her wrist and the two outer knuckles. She rummaged through the back seat and sat down with one of the T-shirts she'd bought the day before. She tore at it with her teeth, pulled it apart in strips, and wrapped his hand.

"We need to keep going," he said. "There's a good chance they've found Barry by now." He checked the map on the phone. "This way," he said pointing west. "It'll take us up into the hills so we can skirt San Jose."

"You're not really serious about going back to Circles, are you?"

Sergio nodded. He could see her fear.

"Don't you think it's time to go to the police? We know what's going on. We can prove it now."

"There will be time for that. At this point, it can't end any other way. You will get what you want," he said. "But we're not going to change the outcome of the election if we go to the police now."

"You really think you can change the election?" she asked with a disbelieving grimace.

He shrugged. It was a great question.

"It's too risky," she complained. "I mean, the cops are looking for us and this Jeep sticks out like a sore thumb. Some guy is trying to kill us. We have no place to go and we're almost out of money. And, now," she said as she threw her hands up, "you want to break into Circles?"

"Who said anything about *breaking* into Circles?"

She looked at him dubiously.

"Don't worry. It's going to be all right," he said, trying to believe his own words. It was not lost on him that he'd said the very same thing two days earlier, just before they'd been cornered by the police, hunted by a killer, and betrayed by her ex-boyfriend.

-62-

Liu Ting Wei rolled over and faced the shuttered window. The Gulfstream's sleeper seats were softer and more spacious than ever before, but they didn't help him sleep any better, not with the drone of engines in his ears and the dry air parching his throat. He glanced at his Patek Philippe with weary eyes. Four more hours to go.

Slowly and reluctantly, Liu eased his seat to a more upright setting. He switched on the overhead light and fumbled through the magazines and newspapers stashed into the tray by his feet. He flipped on his video screen, but nothing interested him.

Liu crossed his ankles and pulled his legs against his seat so that his knees fell below the height of his buttocks and his spine stood ramrod straight. He placed his hands atop his thighs, palms up, and closed his eyes. Then he took deep, long breaths and allowed his mind to wander. When he was at ease and merely tired, his mind would go blank. But within seconds Liu recognized the edginess in his soul. Eight months of planning and searching within himself. Here he was, the hard part done. The plan would work. He could not waver. His moment was coming.

It was on a crisp March day eight months earlier that Liu had stood by the edge of Yuyuan Pond, in central Beijing. Office workers on lunch breaks filled the pathways around the small basin, doing their best to ignore the hum of traffic and blaring horns that floated across the water from busy Third Ring Road. The city's space-age Central Radio and TV Tower rose a few blocks away to dominate the horizon. An ageless stand of willow trees was among the last links to the past, a distant era when the pond was a favorite fishing spot of Chinese emperors.

Fong Shiaoshi, China's minister of science and technology, arrived a few minutes later in a chauffeur-driven black Audi. He was in his late fifties, but his perfectly coifed hair remained as black as night. He wore a dark suit, a conservative red tie, glasses, and a serious mien, just like every other Party mandarin. The two men greeted each other with the casual familiarity of old acquaintances before they set off for a stroll through the willows. They exchanged the usual pleasantries and the requisite questions about each other's families before Fong got to the point.

"You have heard of Tian Youkang," the minister began. "He wrote that paper on the Lithium Chloride-Potassium Chloride vacuum distillation process."

"Indeed, I have. It's very impressive." Liu plastered a smile on his face to hide his concern. His team at Baotou Jingyuan had already tried and failed to produce purer rare earth metals using similar methods.

"Tian," continued the minister, "is eager to test his research on an industrial scale." Fong let his words hang in the air for a moment. "We are, too."

Liu held his smile despite the alarm bells sounding in his head. Tian was a rising star, much like Liu was all those years ago. Both had earned their PhDs at Peking University's Laboratory of Rare Earth Materials Chemistry and Applications, the nation's top program. But Tian had an advantage Liu never did: the youngster was well-connected to the upper echelons of power.

"Tian's theories are very innovative and require that we follow up his research with great enthusiasm," said Liu, as he leaned forward obsequiously. "In due course, we will have a much better sense of—"

"I'm most gratified to hear you agree," interjected Fong. "If we can replicate his results at scale, we may be able to boost our output of dysprosium, gadolinium, and europium by as much as forty percent."

"Yes. Very impressive," said Liu, his curled lips still frozen in place. China not only sat on the world's biggest rare earth deposits, it was the indisputable leader in the complex and costly processes necessary to refine rare earth minerals into strategic metals. And after more than two decades at the forefront of the industry, no one knew as much about rare earth refining as Liu. He stopped in front of a row of cherry blossom trees at the opposite end of the pond. "But you know as well as anyone, Minister Fong, how long these technologies take to perfect."

Fong leveled his eyes at Liu. "That's why Tian will be joining you at Baotou Jingyuan. The generals are determined to ramp up even faster. We have received new intelligence about the US rare earth plan. It's a much bigger threat than we anticipated."

Liu's phony smile fell from his face as he turned to walk again. The country's top military officers were keen to maximize China's strategic advantage in rare earths. They wanted ever more sophisticated weapons, and it was his job to meet their needs. If he couldn't, someone else would, someone like Tian. "What are they telling you?"

"Intelligence tells us the American energy department has drawn up a ten-year plan to kickstart the country's rare earth industry. They've budgeted ten billion dollars for new exploration and to train a new generation of scientists. They will also provide financial assistance for US companies to acquire deposits in Greenland, Kenya, or Australia. And they will establish a strategic stockpile to meet the country's rare earth needs for the next twenty years. If they succeed, our control of the industry, the very foundation of our economic might, will be severely undermined."

"The US Congress will never pass it," Liu said. "They can't agree on anything."

Fong shook his head. "You are wrong, Ting Wei. US public opinion has been aroused by the Modulo debacle and the Americans are uniting around this issue. You overplayed your hand."

Liu grit his teeth and looked away to hide his anger. It would do him no good to point out that he had driven up prices for the fledgling smartphone maker under pressure from General Jiang Tao, a member of the powerful Central Military Commission and an investor in a Chinese competitor. Now they were trying to cram this kid Tian down his throat. Undoubtedly bright, Tian also happened to be the son of a commander in the People's Liberation Army and grandson of one of the vice-chairmen of the Central Military Commission. Liu's key role in the nation's high-tech industry afforded him an influential seat on the Communist Party's prestigious Central Committee, but it provided no protection from the nation's powerful military brass. Liu, like anyone else in China, was one political misstep away from winding up in a cell in Qincheng Prison.

Liu carefully studied Fong's uneasy expression as he weighed his next question. "Is this your final decision?" Liu finally asked.

"My decisions are always final," said Fong, as he searched Liu's eyes. He turned to walk again. "Even if some decisions are more heartfelt than others."

Liu fell in step with Fong and they walked silently for a few moments. "I have kept us on top," Liu said.

"You have performed admirably," agreed Fong.

"Output is twelve times higher than when I took over."

Fong nodded.

"We've gained control over Vietnam's rare earths, increased our leverage in Brazil, and put Kenya in a state of turmoil. It'll be decades, if ever, before they get their industry off the ground."

Fong stopped and turned to Liu with a look of concern on his face. "Work with Tian. Don't fight him." Fong's tone was decisive and curt. "If you do, you will lose."

Liu waved for a flight attendant and asked for a Macallan 18. The memory of that meeting still riled him up. He'd been shown the future, and he was yesterday's man. Worst of all, they were asking him to coddle the youngster who would replace him. If history was any guide, Tian's apprenticeship would be on an accelerated curve. This was always the way with the children of the powerful. At best, Liu would be cast aside in five years, perhaps sooner.

By the time he'd returned home from that meeting, he had decided. They were not going to push him from the company—the industry— he'd worked all his life to build. He'd seen them do it too many times to count. They'd destroyed his father during the Cultural Revolution, but they wouldn't do it to him—not if he and he alone could stop the Americans.

A trim attendant handed him a snifter with a generous pour. He swirled the Scotch in his glass and savored its aroma. Then he enjoyed a delicate sip and sank back into his seat. He looked at his watch. Three hours until arrival.

-63-

Sergio adjusted his Maui Jim sunglasses, pulled his Los Angeles Dodgers cap down, and slung the duffel bag over his shoulder. Beside him, Malina tucked her hair under an Anaheim Ducks hat. They stood just inside the entrance to the underground garage at the Van Ness Cineplex in central San Francisco.

"Ready?" he asked, not waiting for an answer before stepping into the bright midday sunlight.

They headed east into the heart of the Tenderloin district, a few blocks from where they'd shared life stories and tequila a few days earlier. All around them were the commuters, city workers, and street people who crowded the neighborhood by day. He wondered what would draw more stares, his Dodgers cap or the eye patch, crooked nose, and bandaged hand he held gingerly against his ribs. Either way, he felt safer now that they had ditched the Jeep in the garage.

Five minutes later, they turned on to Taylor Street, where he knocked on a large wooden door at the side of Shine Memorial Church. Home to a shelter, a food kitchen, and rehab programs, the church was the neighborhood's heart and soul.

A plump elderly woman with an apron and a well-worn face opened the door. She wore the benign smile of someone greeting a stranger.

"Juanita," he said, taking off his hat and peeling away the glasses. *"Soy yo."*

The woman's rheumy eyes flashed with recognition. "Sergio, you're hurt," she said.

"It's nothing serious."

Juanita regarded Malina with an uncertain gaze, like she couldn't quite place her. Then she surveyed the street and stepped back from the door to let them inside. "I've been reading about you, Sergio," she said, with a tiny trace of an accent. "You are in a lot of trouble."

He reached for her right hand and took it with his left. "I know what they're saying, but none of it is true."

The old woman studied Sergio for a long time before granting him a perfunctory nod of support. She turned her attention to Malina and that look of consternation returned.

Malina took a half step forward. "Juanita, it's me," she said, pressing her hands to her chest. *"La Doctora Malina."*

Juanita burst into a smile and cried out in joy as she wrapped her arms around Malina. *"Doctora! Que sorpresa.* What a surprise." Juanita pulled back to look at the woman who'd saved her life.

She gave Malina another hearty squeeze before releasing her. Then, her lower lip quivering, she addressed them both. "What do you need?"

"Is the Deacon back?" asked Sergio, his eyes involuntarily drifting to the scar on her neck.

She shook her head. "He's still abroad."

"We need a place to sleep for a few hours. Then we'll leave."

"You could bring us a lot of trouble, Sergio." She looked at both of her unexpected guests as she pulled her upper lip between her teeth.

Sergio started to speak but she quickly put up her hand to stop him. "Are you hungry?" she asked.

Sergio looked to Malina and she nodded eagerly.

Juanita led them into the Deacon's kitchen and sat them down at the breakfast table. She rummaged through the fridge for some leftover lasagna, blasted it in the microwave, and served it to them steaming hot. Malina beamed with delight. "Oh my God. I didn't realize how hungry I was," she mumbled, shoveling the pasta into her mouth.

Sergio took one bite and set down his fork. "Have people been here looking for me?"

Juanita set a bottle of red wine and two glasses on the table. "An FBI agent was here two days ago, but there was nothing for me to say."

Sergio reached for the bottle and poured the wine. "Good. I can't imagine why they'd come back."

Juanita placed her hand on Sergio's shoulder and looked down at him with a worried face. "Would you like me to go with you to the police?"

"Maybe tomorrow," he said, as he shot Malina a furtive glance. "There's something we need to do first."

After lunch, Juanita led them upstairs. "You are safe here in the Deacon's residence." She paused in front of the first door on the left and nodded to Malina. "This will be your room." Then she continued down the hall to the last room on the right. She showed Sergio in and turned back down the hall.

"I'll be downstairs if you need anything," she called out, as she started down the first step.

Malina and Sergio stood in their respective doorways, gazing at each other for a long while.

"This might be an odd thing to say right now," he said, "but I feel very lucky."

She smiled and he could not miss the yearning in her eye. Hopefully, there would be a time and place for that later. "Get some sleep," he said, retiring to his room.

-64-

Richard Diebolt stepped from the elevator on the fifth floor of the Marriott Des Moines, his Secret Service detail in tow. They walked to the stairwell at the end of the hall and climbed to the floor above.

"Wait here," he said to the agent, as they stepped into the sixth-floor corridor. Diebolt continued another thirty feet and stopped abruptly in front of room 610. He double-checked the hall to make sure it was clear and knocked on the door.

The door swung open seconds later and Eric Bellarmine, the chief financial officer at Diebolt Incorporated, ushered him inside.

Diebolt strolled to the window and pulled the curtains closed. He spun around, loosening his tie as he looked at Bellarmine's sunglasses on the king-size bed. "It's a little late for shades," he said. "Are you sure no one recognized you?"

Bellarmine nodded as he laid his briefcase on the table and snapped the latch. He opened the case and pulled out a bottle of eighteen-year-old Macallan. He set it on the table and pulled the stopper. Bellarmine had bad news.

"Just a short one," said Diebolt.

Diebolt had almost not come. He and Bellarmine were not to communicate with each other, at least not like this, in private, where they could discuss business. It was all part of the blind trust dog-and-pony show required of candidates. Diebolt was to have no control over his assets, nor any communications with company executives in order to avoid even the appearance of conflict of interest.

Bellarmine unwrapped two hotel glasses and poured a finger of Scotch into each one. He handed a glass to his boss.

Diebolt took a quick sip, not bothering with a toast. "So?"

"We've got a problem," the finance chief said. "Vickers-Healy found out you're planning to double the size of the rare earth initiative to twenty billion dollars."

"Motherfucker," Diebolt muttered, as he closed his eyes and shook his head in disgust. Bellarmine had taken more than six months to strike a deal to buy Diebolt Incorporated's biggest rival—an agreement in principle that had not yet been signed. The sale was suddenly in jeopardy now that Vickers-Healy knew of Diebolt's plan to double the rare earth initiative. He glared at Bellarmine. "Can't anyone keep a secret in DC?"

"Whoever leaked it, it had to be high up in DoE."

Diebolt's brain churned through all the possible permutations. One stuck out—if this had leaked to Vickers-Healy, then Liu almost certainly knew as well. Diebolt would deal with that later. "Did Vickers counteroffer?"

Bellarmine nodded. "Six hundred and forty-five. But tha—"

"Son of a bitch." Diebolt spun away as he fought to quell a storm of anger rising within. Six hundred and forty-five million dollars was almost double the agreed-upon purchase price. He took a deep breath. Then another. There was too much at stake to let anger sway his reaction. He knew the math and while six hundred and forty-five was an enormous amount of money, it was still a reasonable price to take command of the US market for rare earth mining and processing equipment.

With national security the raison d'être for the rare earth initiative, US miners, as well as those doing business with the US, would be forbidden to buy Chinese equipment, meaning Diebolt Incorporated would pretty much dominate the market. Even at that price, Diebolt would still make a killing on his investment once federal subsidies kicked in.

Diebolt turned to address Bellarmine. "Think we can knock them down a bit?"

"Richard, we need to . . . *you* need to be careful here." Bellarmine took a gulp of his Scotch. "There will be all sorts of questions if I agree to pay double Vickers' market value. Everyone will know that I knew everything about your rare earth initiative."

Diebolt massaged his temples. "We've been over this, too many times," he said, the frustration evident in his voice. "This deal will give us a thirty-seven percent share of the overall mining machinery market. There's no way they'll do a merger review."

"The Federal Trade Commission can review any deal it wants," said Bellarmine, his teeth clenched. "This was supposed to be a two-step. Get the deal done before you take office. Then you push the initiative. But now we have some DoE official blabbing about your twenty-billion-dollar rare earth bill." He slammed his glass on the table. "At best, it stinks worse than a Mexican whorehouse. Worst case, the authorities will come down on you, and me, hard."

Diebolt paced the room, trying to suppress his temper. "This was supposed to be done a month ago."

"It was, just about." Bellarmine ran his hand through his hair. "Then came the DoE leak, about two weeks ago."

Diebolt came to a stop, his face a foot from Bellarmine's. "You just close the deal," he said, jabbing a crooked finger at Bellarmine. "How low do you think you can push Vickers-Healy?"

"We might get them down to five and a half, but at this—"

"Get it done." Diebolt retreated, his anger easing as if some escape valve had popped open to release the pressure. "In the meantime, I'll have a chat with Gwynne," he said, referring to the chairman of the FTC. "He owes us and I think it's time we settle up, just in case it gets to that point."

Bellarmine nodded, but his eyes looked doubtful. "Even if this goes through, the optics still look—"

"The optics," blurted Diebolt, "will be that we are saving the US. The optics will be that the country needs us. I've got everyone so freaked out about China right now that they'll believe and accept anything." He poured another shot and threw it back. "This isn't about right and wrong, or left and right. This is about national security, what we need to do to survive as a nation. And if you and I are the means to that end, then all the more power to us."

Bellarmine's shoulders drooped.

Diebolt thumped his glass on the table. "Now let's get the hell out of here," he said. It was time to head home to Tucson. Voting was only hours away.

The sun was setting and a thick layer of marine fog had descended on the city by the time the limo carrying Liu Ting Wei skirted along the shore of San Francisco Bay.

Liu glanced at his watch. He was more than two hours behind, thanks to the customs agents who pulled him into an interrogation room and demanded to inspect his computer. Not only was he president of a company that had national security implications for both countries, Liu had close ties to the highest echelons of the Chinese Communist Party. The US had stepped up the frequency of these searches, particularly when it came to the Chinese elite. He could hardly blame the Americans, given all the corporate and government espionage they'd been subjected to over the years. Hell, it was an obvious step to take, in his opinion.

But they'd taken much longer than he'd anticipated, particularly since the laptop they inspected was the brand new—and completely empty—Lenovo computer Liu had pulled from its box at the warehouse at Shanghai's airport. The only computer that mattered—the laptop that would put Liu on top of the world—was waiting for him at Circles.

Exhausted, Liu dialed his phone and pressed it to his ear.

A half-ring, a click, and then a voice. "Hello?"

"I have arrived," said Liu.

"I was expecting you earlier. How was your flight?" came the reply.

"Long and tiring. And that was before I got to customs," Liu said wearily. "The Americans trust no one anymore, it seems."

The voice on the other end of the line chuckled. "One cannot have a heart that doesn't guard against anyone. Isn't that what you say in China?"

"That is what *we* say." Liu grit his teeth. "You have been here too long. You are forgetting your roots, your proud Chinese heritage."

"Not again, uncle," came the tired refrain. "Always about the past."

Liu ignored the jab. His nephew, who now preferred his American name, Victor Ko, was slipping away. He had forsaken family responsibilities and lost his sense of loyalty. But Liu didn't have the energy for another argument.

"My body demands rest now. A few hours. But I would like to see Circles before I fly to Tucson tomorrow." The cab crested a rise and darted into a spaghetti bowl of highways at the southern edge of the city. "Can we meet later tonight? I'm sure I'll be wide awake by then."

"I will be here whenever you are ready." Ko paused for a moment. "Did you talk to your friends?"

"I did," lied Liu. "The ministry has made its decision."

"Did they say how long?" asked his nephew.

"They will revisit the Circles file when the time is right," said Liu, purposely vague to maximize his nephew's angst. Liu had clout within the Ministry of Industry and Information Technology, home to China's Internet watchdogs. But he wasn't prepared to call in any favors to help his nephew, not after Victor had defied him.

"Is there anyone else you can speak with, uncle?"

Liu expected the question; his nephew always demanded more. Liu had raised him after his parents died, put him through eight years of the best higher education money could buy. And then Liu had cobbled together financing for ZGT. It had turned out to be a lucrative investment, a tenfold return on his money. But that wasn't the issue. When it had come time for Liu to call in his chits, Victor had balked.

"There is no one else, Victor." Liu looked out from the elevated freeway. The city's famous skyline, punctuated by the iconic Transamerica pyramid, towered directly ahead. Off to the right in the distance, in the heart of the Mission Bay district, rose a glass building with a giant *C* etched on one side. "Any news of the employee yet?"

"Not yet," said Ko.

"The sooner—"

"I'm aware of that, uncle," said Ko. "All too aware of it."

-66-

Sergio and Malina darted across an open lawn and found cover at the corner of a small office complex. Across the street stood Circles' massive southern wing, still just a skeleton of concrete floor slabs and pillars with no outer skin. It now rose five stories, right on schedule. To its right stood the company's headquarters, half lit up against the night sky. A handful of cars remained in the employee parking lot in front of the building. It was typically quiet for a late Monday night, unlike those frenetic early years when the lot was crammed at all hours.

"We're early," he said, as his one good eye scanned windows and surrounding rooftops. The vision in his other eye had improved, but every blink still hurt. He tried clenching his right fist. The drugstore wrist splint helped but the hand was basically useless. A car passed, and then another, their headlights flickering along the building behind them.

Directly in front of them was a chain-link fence that separated the two Circles structures. At the far end of the fence, in the gap between the two buildings, was Circles' loading dock. He pointed to two trucks backed into the service bays. "Let's get across to those trucks," he said. "They'll give us much better cover until it's time."

He adjusted his messenger bag so that it hung down his back; then he tightened the strap to make sure the computer inside would not bounce around as he ran. It was his Circles computer, the one he'd last used at the coffee shop Friday night. The machine they'd bought at Bruno's had been left with Juanita. "If we don't come back," he told her, "give this to the FBI." It would be too late to salvage the election by then, but with a little luck the Bureau might eventually piece together the entire story.

They dashed across the brightly lit four-lane street and crouched down between the fence and a tree at the outer corner of the parking lot. It was a good forty yards to the trucks, with only two small trees for cover along the way. He scanned the parking lot once more, took Malina's hand, and pulled her forward along the fence.

They were halfway to the next tree when a car came around the north corner of the building and stopped in front of Circles' main entrance, about seventy-five yards away. They crouched down at the next tree, hoping their shadows would blend in against the black mesh lining attached to the nine-foot fence ringing the construction site.

A large man dressed in black stepped out of the car's passenger door and walked up the stairs to Circles' main entry. The car eased forward, advancing directly toward them as it moved into the parking lot. It turned into the first row and Sergio's heart thumped in protest. It was the gray Chrysler 300.

He sank to the ground and pulled Malina with him. They were completely exposed, but there was nowhere to run without attracting attention. The Chrysler slowed as it passed a cluster of parked cars and then sped up toward another group in the middle of the lot. It eased by the second group of cars and moved toward the loading bay, making slow meandering turns so that its headlights swept across the parking lot like a pair of searchlights. Suddenly, the car veered sharply toward them and its high beams flicked on, blasting them with light. That sickening fear from Zachary's basement was back.

The Chrysler's engine roared as the killer charged toward them. Sergio jumped to his feet, pulled on Malina's arm, and pushed her toward the fence. "Go!"

She ran three steps and jumped, latching on to the fence about a foot from the top. He landed on the fence a second later, causing it to sway as they scrambled upward. Pain ripped through his right hand as he clawed at the fence, pulling himself up with his good hand and holding on with his injured one. The rumble of the Chrysler's engine grew louder and the glare of headlights lit them up like it was daytime. His fingers found the horizontal steel pole at the top of the fence and he threw himself over in tandem with Malina. They tumbled to the dirt as the Chrysler came screeching to a halt a few yards away. The opaque black mesh on the fence turned bright white under the glare of headlights. "Run!" he yelled, scrambling to his feet.

Silent bullets pierced the black mesh and whizzed past as they ran into the shadows of the concrete skeleton. Sergio led the way up a dimly lit staircase beside the elevator bank at the near end of the building. As they climbed, he visualized the blueprints he'd eagerly perused more times than he could count. There were two more elevator banks and stairwells: one in the middle and the other at the far end of the building, about one hundred yards away. One of them was their escape route. They reached the fourth floor landing; a metal barrier blocked access to the fifth and newest level.

"Look," cried Malina, as she pointed to the stairs they'd just climbed. Their footprints were clearly visible in the thin film of concrete dust that had settled in the stairwell. The patter of footsteps filtered up from below.

Sergio pulled Malina through the open door to the fourth floor, where they were swallowed up in a forest of metal shoring posts holding up the floor above. The posts stood in neatly arranged rows, like a series of tubular dominos that stretched the length and width of the building. A string of bare lightbulbs running down the center of the floor threw off dim light and erratic shadows. They cut to the left—moving as far from the light as they could—and ran for their lives to the far end of the floor. Behind them the footsteps grew louder.

Sergio and Malina were panting by the time they dropped into crouch positions near the far corner of the building. The gunman was out there somewhere, hidden in the thicket of shoring posts. They needed to get away from the edge, where they stood out against the light from adjacent buildings. It was only a matter of time before their hunter saw their silhouettes.

"That's the south stairwell." He pointed to a cinderblock structure rising up the side of the building. "I think they've already installed the stairs."

Sergio dropped to his hands and knees and crawled along the edge of the building. The rough concrete dug into his knees as he cautiously moved between the rows. Somewhere in the metal forest was that man with his gun, hunting them. Sergio silently scolded himself for not having taken Zachary's pistol. Sweat beaded on his forehead.

They crawled through a door into the stairwell. The unfinished landing, about the size of a parking spot, was crammed with tools and supplies. To his right, a flight of stairs dropped to the third floor; the steps to the fifth level were not yet installed. To his left stood the wall of the elevator shaft and directly in front was the open edge of the building, guarded only by a temporary wooden safety rail. Above, Sergio saw Orion.

The landing served as a staging point for construction crews. It was crammed with rebar, welding equipment, a rolling tool chest the size of a coffin, and a coil of rope. He crouched against the heavy tool chest and pulled Malina down to him.

"What are we waiting for? Let's go," she whispered, her eyes fixed on the stairs.

Sergio did not budge. "No," he said. At some point in the last few minutes, as he was running for his life, fear had turned into anger. And now crouched among the tools and supplies, anger morphed into resolve.

The gunman was advancing on their hiding spot and that gave Sergio and Malina a small advantage, perhaps the only edge he'd ever get against a hit man with a gun. He scanned the landing again and reached for the coil. "We need to end this now." He rose to a low crouch. "Here, give me a hand with this rope."

Graves moved along the left side of the building, checking his sightlines as he passed every post. He'd covered about two-thirds of the floor when he heard it. Soft scraping sounds swirled through the thicket of metal. They came from everywhere and nowhere in particular. He crouched and spun around in a tight circle to make sure no one had snuck up on him. A city bus passed in the street below, drowning out all sound and robbing Graves of his most critical warning system. By the time it was gone, the scratchy noises had faded. He allowed the stillness to settle in again and slowly rose to his feet.

He moved forward until a squeak pierced the silence. This time it came from the far end of the building. Another muffled sound bounced off the concrete and steel. Graves moved quickly now, his gritty footsteps betraying his approach. He was the hunter and he had the advantage. He couldn't afford to waste it. He cut diagonally across the rows, homing in on each new hint, like a sonar operator. He was somewhere along the centerline of the building when he heard whispers. They were close.

Graves drew himself into a crouch and peeked into the next row. Then he saw it—a silhouette at the end of the building. He retreated, moving three rows sideways before cutting once again toward the end of the building, confident the posts would shield him until he drew close enough to strike. He inched forward, his eyes locked on the row ahead of him, even as he watched for peripheral threats. Closing to within thirty feet of the building's edge, he sidestepped across two rows and lined himself up with the silhouette. As he leveled his gun, the crouching silhouette moved sideways and the shapes around him shifted in unison. Even as Graves lined up his target and squeezed the trigger, he sensed something was wrong. Something slithered beneath him, like a snake coiled at his feet.

Graves fired twice, but he'd already lowered his gun. The rope on the floor snapped taut and his ears filled with a terrifying screech, one he instantly understood was the sound of shoring posts scraping across the concrete floor. The metal columns around him quivered until row by row, the steel posts gave way, some fifteen deep and eight across, tumbling in unison under the irresistible pull of the rope at his feet. Graves rushed toward his shadowy prey as the posts closed in on him, clanking angrily against each other and crashing to the hard floor. He closed to within a few feet of the stairwell landing when a post slammed into his chest. A second one shattered his leg and sent him tumbling to the concrete. More posts pummeled him like battering rams, cracking his ribs and breaking his arms as he tried to fend off blows to his head. He tried to curl up to protect himself, his screams for a moment rising above the clamor until they were drowned out by a heaving groan that thundered from above. Within seconds it all went black.

———————————

A tremendous crash rang out as Sergio bolted down the stairs. The angry shriek of posts and the tortured roar of uncured concrete and rebar buckling under its own weight sounded like an earthquake ripping apart his world. He reached the U-turn in the stairwell when two shoring posts flew toward him like javelins. Sergio dodged and threw himself headfirst down the stairs. Another column whizzed past and pierced the cinderblock beside him. Heavy clods of wet concrete walloped him as he slammed onto the third floor landing. He rolled quickly, sprang to his feet, and launched himself down the next flight of stairs just as three more posts crashed down behind him.

Then it was quiet, the stillness of the night absorbing the terrible sounds of calamity. Sergio carefully lifted himself off the floor. His arms were scraped and bruised, his knees were banged up, and his rib cage hurt. But he was okay.

He peered over the edge of the third floor landing. Outside in the dirt below lay the giant toolbox, its lid ripped open by the force of the impact. Scattered around it were an assortment of tools, several shoring posts, and the coil of rope, one end still tied to the box.

Malina raced up to meet him. "Sergio!" she cried as they embraced. "I thought that was you screaming." She pulled back to look at him. "Are you hurt?"

He shook his head. "You?"

Malina held him tightly. "I'm fine."

He stroked her hair. "I need to go back up there—to make sure."

He pushed a couple of shoring posts to the side and squeezed his way through a thicket of tangled steel, crushed cinderblock, and wet cement. They moved slowly upward, careful not to touch anything. He couldn't be sure which post might bring the entire three-dimensional maze crashing down on them.

The knot of steel thickened until they reached the fourth floor landing and they could go no farther. Malina pointed down. "Look."

Sergio squinted in the dim light, into a bramble of mangled posts, following Malina's outstretched arm until he saw it. Sticking out from a thick mound of wet concrete and metal rods was a gloved hand, still gripping a black semiautomatic pistol.

-67-

"In here," whispered Sergio. He pulled Malina behind a parked truck outside Circles' loading bay. They dropped into a crouch and he tapped out a text message on the prepaid phone. One word: "Here."

"Someone got out of the killer's car before he came after us. Whoever it was went inside Circles," she said, still panting from their dash across the construction site.

"I saw that too. Big guy," said Sergio. "I couldn't really see him, but he didn't look like anyone I know."

The damp ocean air chilled his shaved skull. He spied the battery of closed-circuit security cameras aimed at the loading bay; everything they did until they got into Labs would be recorded and scrutinized later.

He watched the phone's screen. Nothing yet.

A siren wailed in the distance. Then a second joined it, each growing louder as emergency vehicles closed in. They'd find the killer's body soon enough and then eventually notice the Chrysler 300, still running with its door ajar next to the chain-link fence.

"C'mon, damn it," he whispered at the phone.

A police cruiser raced past the parking lot toward the far end of the construction site. Malina squeezed his arm. "We can't stay—"

The door next to the loading bay gate swung open with a groan and a tall figure with a tuft of wispy hair emerged. Sergio whistled and Ethan Burrard waved him in.

"You're early," said Burrard, as they approached the door. He had on an open zip-front hoodie and a Nine Inch Nails T-shirt, and looked like he hadn't slept in days. He stared at Malina. "Who is that?"

"This is Malina."

Burrard threw up his hands on either side of his head, palms outward. "Stop," he said, filling up the doorway. "You didn't tell me you were bringing someone with you."

"She's with me and I'm not leaving her out here."

Burrard's gaze fell to the floor as he gnawed on his lower lip. After a few seconds he lowered his arms and spun around. "Stay right behind me."

Burrard led them along the edge of the company's bright warehouse, using forklifts and crates for cover. They climbed the back stairs and hurried across the seventh floor to the entrance to Labs. Burrard appeared to have misgivings as he swiped his access card to release the magnetic lock. Sergio turned his face from the security camera as he stepped into the passage between the double doors. The outer portal slammed shut. Burrard swiped his card again and punched in his password to release the inner door. Sergio stepped into the lab, relieved to be away from those all-seeing cameras. He was close, so close his hands shook. It would all be over soon.

Just inside the door, Burrard spun around and took two steps backward, creating a buffer zone between them. He looked past Sergio's shoulder. "You need to explain yourself," he said. "All this stuff about the election."

Sergio stepped around Burrard and headed for his office, one of the small suites along the side wall. "I need to inspect one of our servers," he said, without looking back.

"Wait," cried Burrard, as he chased after Sergio. "You said you had proof. What have you found and what are you looking for? You can't just—"

Sergio pivoted and glared at Burrard. "There's no time right now."

Burrard's elbows flapped at his side. "Well, I'm in no hurry."

Sergio hated Burrard's stubborn streak. Once he set his mind to something, he never let go. And if he had an anxiety attack, that would only slow things down. "Okay," said Sergio, trying to sound as soothing as he could. "Just get me into the system, and I'll explain as we go."

Burrard cocked his head sideways. "This better be quick," he said, as he retreated to his office. Sergio leaned in while Burrard logged on to his computer and pulled up the Labs network infrastructure database. "What are we looking for, Sergio?"

Sergio reached into his messenger bag, pulled out a slip of paper, and called out the IP address of the suspect server.

Burrard didn't move. "What's so important about this server?"

"There's a rogue computer connected to it."

"A rogue computer?" Burrard wheeled in his chair. "You know as well as anyone that we don't have rogue computers." He grew visibly agitated as his words spilled from his mouth at an ever-faster pace. "The alarms would go off. And you know—"

"Ethan, Ethan," said Sergio in a firm but hushed tone. "It's okay, it's okay." It was the best way to calm Burrard before he got on one of his rolls. "Just punch it in."

Burrard clasped his hands tightly for several seconds. Then he took off his glasses and wiped them on the bottom of his hoodie. He turned back to his keyboard and typed in the IP address. "It's server CL134. Rack fifteen, in the back row." He glanced over his shoulder. "Do you have a MAC address for this rogue computer?"

Sergio read off the MAC address he'd pulled from the network map the previous night at the farmhouse, and Burrard tried to match it to Circles' master list. "Nope. That MAC is not one of ours."

Sergio rolled his eyes. "That's what I've been trying—"

Burrard cut him off. "And I don't see that computer anywhere on our network," he said with a hint of I-told-you-so righteousness.

Sergio stopped breathing, hoping Burrard had made a mistake. "Not on the network?" He peered over Burrard's shoulder. The network map on the screen showed ports one through nine on server CL134 were connected to terminals throughout the lab. When Sergio had hacked into the network from the farmhouse the night before, all ten ports on CL134 had been connected.

He bolted from the office and burst into the cooling room, Malina and Burrard close behind him. Sergio scanned racks of humming machines until he located the one labeled CL134. He clenched his good fist in elation. Someone had unplugged the computer that was connected to port ten, but had left the cable in place. Sergio tapped the blue Ethernet cable sticking out of port ten.

"How much do you want to bet the other end of this cable is in Ko's office?" he asked. He was close, very close.

"What are you talking about?" Burrard's elbows lurched outward and his hands trembled at his side.

Sergio began summarizing the events of the past few days as he traced the blue wire with his fingers until it merged into a large bundle of cables and disappeared into the crawl space above the ceiling panels. He stepped up on a chair and pushed aside the ceiling panel where the cables disappeared. Above, stuffed into the eighteen-inch gap between the false ceiling and the concrete above, a mass of wires, cables, and pipes ran in all directions.

"Wait," cried Burrard, his hands still twitching. "What are you doing?"

Sergio looked at Malina and pointed to another chair. She nodded and within seconds was standing on the chair beside him. "We're going to see where this cable goes," he said.

They worked feverishly in tandem, Sergio punching out ceiling panels with his one good hand while Malina followed behind him, isolating the blue cable from port ten as it slipped through the palm of her closed fist. Every few feet they stepped down and slid the chairs across the floor.

"You can't do this," cried Burrard, his staccato voice thick with anxiety. "You're destroying the lab. You told me you had proof. You told me—"

"Stay here," said Sergio to Malina as he bumped against the wall. He ran into the main lab and ripped out more ceiling panels on the other side. His hand met Malina's in the hollow space above the wall and she handed off the blue wire to him. Within seconds, she was at his side again and they were back at it, moving across the main lab as Sergio recounted how Zachary had helped him discover the socialbots. He clutched the blue cable and looked down at Burrard. "The last piece of the puzzle is at the other end of this line."

Burrard paced back and forth at Sergio's feet. "Zachary was an asshole. You shouldn't have listened to him."

By the time Sergio neared the offices along the edge of the R&D lab, his left arm and shoulder were killing him. He stopped to rest, flexing his bicep as he described the powerful socialbots roaming the Circles network.

"The election?" asked Burrard. "How? Who?"

"Diebolt," replied Sergio, stepping down and sliding the chair to within a few feet of Ko's office. He stepped up and pulled down the last panel between him and Ko's door. The cable wasn't there. Sergio stuck his arm into the crawl space and discovered the cable made a sudden right angle turn. He popped three more panels, moving away from Ko's door. The blue wire changed course once again and crossed into one of the offices. Confused, he looked back toward Ko's suite when Malina tugged on his arm.

"Sergio," she whispered.

"Hold on," he said, as he studied the gaping hole in the ceiling.

"*Sergio.*"

This time her sharp tone got his attention. He turned to her and followed her frightened gaze downward. Burrard stood beneath them, his shaky hand holding a gun pointed at Sergio's chest. Burrard's gaze shifted from the floor to the ceiling, pausing ever so briefly to make contact with Sergio. It was the first time Burrard had looked him straight in the eye.

-68-

Special Agent Jay Feeley pulled up to the hulking concrete frame and parked next to a dozen or so police cars, fire trucks, and ambulances that had responded to the call. A body at a construction site wasn't all that uncommon, but the odds of it happening randomly at this project in the midst of the Mansour case were a little too long for his liking. This had something to do with Mansour. He could feel it.

Feeley flashed his ID and ducked under the yellow police tape surrounding the scene. Quick was already there and greeted Feeley with a mock, but respectful, two-fingered salute. Then he tilted his head toward the construction worker beside him. "This is Don Trenault, the site foreman."

The foreman nodded quietly. The shock on his face was apparent even in the night light. He cleared his throat. "Part of the fifth floor collapsed. We poured the concrete this afternoon and it was held up by shoring posts." The foreman pointed to the building behind him as he struggled to compose himself. "We went up to investigate and that's when we discovered the body."

Feeley looked up at the five-story shell. A section of the top level had been gouged out, as if someone had taken a giant bite out of the unfinished building.

"Any chance this was an accident?" Feeley asked.

The foreman shook his head. "Someone tied a rope to that," he said, pointing to a large tool chest at the base of the building. "Then they pushed it over the edge to pull down several dozen shoring posts." He allowed Feeley a moment to visualize the scene. "This was deliberate."

"Thanks for your time," said Feeley. He turned with Quick and walked toward the building. Portable floodlights shone brightly up on the fourth floor, where construction workers, police officers, and evidence response technicians tried to stay out of each other's way.

A uniformed San Francisco Police Department officer stepped forward to intercept them. "I'm sorry, sir, I can't let you inside."

Feeley nodded. "Who's in charge?"

"Inspector Ralston."

Good news. Feeley and Ralston had a cordial and professional relationship—almost bordering on friendly—after years of dealing with each other. Neither of them had time for the petty interagency rivalries that often got in the way of good police work. Minutes later, Ralston stepped from the building and greeted the two agents.

"You know the drill, Jay," began Ralston. "I can't let you contaminate the scene. But how can I help? What's so interesting about this one?"

"Just a hunch," replied Feeley. "I'm working the Mansour case and it seems odd to have a body show up here, right next to his office. That's all. What have you got?"

"The victim was most likely crushed and or suffocated after the roof collapsed," said Ralston, handing over a digital camera.

Feeley flipped through a series of photos on the LCD screen. Thousands of pounds of wet concrete, rebar, and shoring posts—and an arm sticking out from under it all. "The foreman says this wasn't an accident."

"He's right," replied Ralston.

"Have you ID'd him yet?"

Ralston shook his head. "It took the construction crew a while to stabilize the site. We sent in the deceased's fingerprints; we're still waiting to hear if there's a match." Ralston paused. "One other thing. The stiff glued his fingertips."

Feeley snapped to attention. Savvy perps smeared glue on their fingers to make sure they didn't leave any prints behind. Of course, that trick wasn't much good if the cops could peel the glue off a dead man's fingers. "So he was a pro," Feeley said evenly, trying to hide his mounting excitement.

Ralston nodded.

"Anything else?"

"Footprints suggest three people came over the fence from the parking lot, climbed the north end stairwell and crossed the fourth floor to this end," said Ralston, pointing to the collapsed section.

Feeley perked up. "Three people? Any chance one of them was female?"

"Yeah," replied Ralston. "One set of prints was likely female."

Feeley nodded knowingly, now quite confident this wasn't a mere coincidence. "I'd like to know the minute you get an ID on the corpse." He looked at the building. "How long does concrete take to set?"

"It's about ninety-five percent cured in the first twenty-four hours, or something like that." Ralston pointed to the collapsed section. "This south end of the floor was poured in late afternoon. Another few hours and that stiff would probably still be alive."

"So they knew what they were doing," mused Feeley.

A detective approached them and addressed Ralston. "We've gone over the car—"

"What car?" interrupted Feeley.

"There's a gray Chrysler 300 in the Circles parking lot on the other side of the fence. We found several shells in the parking lot. Shots were fired toward this building. The door was left open, like the driver got out quickly. There are several weapons inside."

Feeley smiled at Quick. "Our missing gray Chrysler," he said.

Sergio stood frozen on the chair and looked down the barrel of Burrard's gun. It was a singularly binary moment—alive one second, maybe dead the next. He wouldn't even know it.

Burrard wagged the pistol, instructing Sergio to step down. "Don't look so surprised," he said. "It's insulting."

Sergio dropped to the floor, reached for Malina's hand, and pulled her with him as he backed away from Burrard. He scanned the lab for anything he could use as a weapon—a stray golf club or a souvenir baseball bat—but nothing within reach could challenge the gun in Burrard's hand.

"Now what?" asked Sergio, as he pulled Malina behind him.

"It would be a good question if the answer wasn't so obvious." The fingers of Burrard's left hand trembled. The gun quivered in his right. It was as if his jittery hands had taken on a life of their own.

"You can't just shoot us," Malina cried over Sergio's shoulder.

"Yes, I can."

"You'll never get away with it in here. The three of us are all over the surveillance videos," countered Sergio.

A crooked grin slipped across Burrard's face as he looked past them. "You had this gun in your pocket when you arrived. You threatened me. The video will show that." He raised his hands to the sides of his head, just like he had at the loading bay door. "You forced me to bring you up here. There was a struggle. I was the lucky one and two wanted fugitives were killed."

"You're crazy," said Malina.

His brow furrowed and his jaw tightened, Burrard focused on his unruly hands, as if struggling for control. After several seconds that seemed like minutes, Burrard's jittery hands settled down. He tilted his head to the right. "I need you," he said to Malina, "to move out where I can see you."

Sergio reached behind him to hold her in place. He needed to buy time, to distract Burrard—maybe even talk their way out of this. "I left proof with someone," he called out in a shaky voice. "They have instructions to turn it all over to the FBI if we don't come back."

"Bullshit." Burrard's staccato voice sliced through the lab. "You came here looking for proof," he insisted. "That's clear to me now."

"That's why you let us in here? To see what we knew?"

"You weren't supposed to get this far, but when you did, I had little choice."

Sergio's mind whirled in confusion, as if a trillion synapses in his brain short-circuited all at once. Not supposed to get this far? He grappled with the words, trying to make sense of what Burrard was saying. In the end, only one answer fit.

"You mean," Sergio began, "that guy outside, the killer who's been chasing us . . . He's with you?"

Burrard said nothing, but his silence spoke the truth. The gun in his hand looked twice as big. Sergio had to keep him talking. "How did you know we were at Zachary's?"

"Easy enough. The police tracked you down in LA. You could have gone anywhere. But you went to LA, downtown LA." He was jabbering now. "At first I was puzzled, but then I remembered our law firm. But why go there?" continued Burrard, the words spilling out of his mouth almost too fast for Sergio to keep up. "I knew you'd discovered the socialbots, so the obvious answer was that you were trying to investigate Ko and ZGT, learn more about what we worked on before joining Circles. That's what I would have done if I'd been in your shoes. And if you got that far, then Zachary was the next logical step."

"But why are you doing this?" asked Sergio. "Who is paying you?"

"I can't tell you that," answered Burrard. "But that's beside the point. I'm doing it because I can. Because this is my chance to break new ground—to write code that fundamentally transforms the way we harness big data. This is what I do. This is what *we* do, Sergio."

Sergio shook his head. "Not me. Not Circles. We don't—"

"Fuck Circles. I don't care about Circles." Burrard's elbows jerked at his side and his fingers trembled anew. "I care about the ideas. Ideas matter, they stand on their own. You know that as well as anyone, Sergio. Ideas always win out."

Malina stepped from behind Sergio. "But you're sabotaging the election, everything this country stands for. You're willing to sacrifice all that just to satisfy your ego?" she asked.

"As if it matters who wins the election," he shot back. "And it's not about ego. If I didn't do this, someone else would. The technology is here and we can't go backward. It's too late for that."

Sergio's mind reeled. None of this could be happening and yet here he stood, watching an insanely brilliant man self-destruct to defend his crazy notion of progress. He had no doubt Burrard would kill them if necessary. He'd all but pulled the trigger on George and Zachary. Sergio couldn't let him get Malina.

A muffled buzz filled Labs, a quiet hum he'd heard thousands of times before. The magnetic lock on the lab's outer security door had just disengaged. Within seconds, the inner door to Circles Labs swung open. Prederick entered the room first, his forward progress cut short when he noticed the gaping holes in the ceiling. Behind him walked Ko, his eyes immediately drawn to Sergio. Ko then fixed his withering gaze on Burrard while pointing at Sergio. "How the hell did *he* get in here?"

Burrard stood motionless, his mouth wide open in surprise, the gun lowered to his side. Sergio had never before seen his fast-talking colleague at a loss for words.

A portly Chinese man moved through the door. He had a haughty demeanor and a black suit that looked too formal for Silicon Valley. Outsiders were not allowed into Labs, and yet here was this big—

The realization hit Sergio like a punch in the gut. He'd seen this man before. It had to be him, the man in black who'd stepped out of the gray Chrysler 300. Sergio's mind raced to pull the pieces together. If this stranger knew the hit man then he had to be working with Burrard. And if Ko was involved too, only one question remained. Sergio looked at Prederick and pointed to the gun hanging at Burrard's side. "Are you part of this too, Dan?"

Prederick's eyebrows came together and pushed up his forehead as he noticed the gun in Burrard's shaky hand. His confusion was instant and genuine. "What the hell is going on?"

Sergio pointed at Burrard and Ko. "They built a massive socialbot network, running right now on Circles. They built it to swing the election for Diebolt." He had no reason to hold anything back. "That's what George discovered and that's why he is dead. I've seen it."

Sergio's words hung in the air as the five men and Malina sized each other up. Ko was the first to react, his head swiveling back and forth between the stranger and Burrard. Ko's trademark haughtiness had been stripped away; instead, in its place, he wore an expression that suggested he was both flustered and disoriented. Before long, he focused on the stranger. The glazed look in Ko's eyes crystalized and his jaw slipped open, as if he couldn't believe the answers forming in his head.

"Uncle, what have you done?"

"Quiet," hissed the smartly dressed stranger.

Ko's jawline tightened and he glanced once more to Burrard. Ko glowered with resolve, as if he was more confident about his conclusion. "Tell me you didn't—"

The stranger snapped at Ko. "This is not the time."

Ko took a step toward his uncle, his jaw taut and his eyes on fire. "You went behind my back like that? After I said no?"

"You ungrateful little . . ." the elderly man exploded with rage. "Did you really think all that money was free? You should have done this, not him," he said, tilting his head toward Burrard.

Liu and Ko glared at each other with an intensity Sergio could fathom but not understand.

"Do what?" yelled Prederick at Burrard. "What the hell did you do?"

Burrard puffed up with pride. "Just like Sergio says. Tomorrow, my socialbots will deliver the presidency to Richard Diebolt. It is without doubt the most sophisticated piece of social engineering the world has ever seen."

"Are you crazy?" shouted Ko. "Don't you see what's going to happen?"

"You've been quite happy to give our socialbots to China," countered Burrard. His jittery hands floated up in front of him, the right one again pointing the gun toward Sergio and Malina.

"China is different," insisted Ko. "We're working *with* the government. It's low risk, high reward." He put one hand on his hip and ran the other one through his widow's peak. "Doing it here is way too dangerous," he added, his voice thick with exasperation. "We'll all lose."

Sergio tucked Malina behind him, shielding her from Burrard. He could do nothing more to protect her.

"There's no reason for anyone to find out." Burrard's gaze darted around the room. "It's in nobody's interest. We all lose if this comes out. Our jobs, our stock, our reputations. We all lose."

Prederick shook his head and pointed to Malina. "What about her?"

Malina pressed against Sergio's back, her hands clutching his shoulders. He felt her tremble.

"What about her?" Burrard asked as he wagged the gun.

Ko's eyes bulged. "Have you lost your mind?"

"Do you have a better solution?" Burrard spoke with eerie calm.

Ko looked to his uncle. "Stop him. This is crazy."

The old Chinese man blinked casually, as if he had little interest in the test of wills unfolding around him. He had the hard mien of a man ruthless enough to kill, but who was too old and soft to do it himself. He met his nephew's gaze with stoicism and a shrug. Who was this man?

Sergio leaned back against Malina, nudging her with his shoulder—once, twice, until she dropped one hand and slipped it between their bodies.

Ko appealed to Prederick. "Dan?"

Prederick's eyes shifted back and forth among the others, as if considering his options.

"Dan, this is not you," urged Sergio. "He's not going to get away with this."

"Of course we will," said Burrard. "It'll be two dead fugitives and four witnesses, all corroborating what happened. You attacked us, Sergio."

Sergio felt Malina tug on the bag hanging off his back, teasing the zipper so that each plastic tooth released with a whispery *click* . . . *click* . . . *click*.

The shock and confusion had faded from Prederick's face. He now reflected a grim resolve that sent Sergio's heart into overdrive. The CEO was allowing himself to be pulled along.

Burrard looked at Prederick as he raised the gun toward Sergio. "Well?"

Malina stopped tugging on the bag.

"Wait," commanded Liu. "Give me the computer and I shall be gone. Then you can do what must be done."

Liu's words sucked the air out of Sergio's lungs. His face felt hot and his scalp prickled. Malina eased back and wedged her hand into the messenger bag. A moment later she squeezed his shoulder.

"Here," said Burrard, digging into his pocket and pulling out a key. "It's in the top drawer of my filing cabinet." He spun around to point out his office.

The scratchy rustle of nylon filled the room as Malina ripped her hand from Sergio's bag. Burrard reacted, pivoting toward them, his arm swinging the gun in their direction. Malina thrust the killer's pistol, its silencer still attached, out in front of Sergio's face as she pulled the trigger. The gun hissed, spitting out three rounds. Two of them slammed into Burrard's chest. He cried out and fell. He was dead before he hit the floor.

-70-

Feeley leaned on Ralston's open car door and looked over his shoulder as the inspector pulled up the deceased's file on his car's console computer.

"The prints belong to Damon Graves. This is the most recent photo we have. He'd be thirty-four now," said Ralston. They studied a Defense Department headshot of a twenty-something soldier with a chiseled face, deep-set eyes, and closely cropped hair. "He was Marine Recon. Saw action in Iraq and Afghanistan. Left the service in 2006. Worked two years for Black Shield as a military contractor. And then nothing. No driver's licenses, vehicle registrations, or credit history. He went completely off the grid."

Feeley pressed his fingers to his forehead and rubbed gently. "Exactly what you'd expect from a professional."

Ralston nodded and typed in another name. "The Chrysler was rented to Jack Smith." The screen flashed and Smith's driver's license appeared. On it was a photo of the same chiseled face from Graves' military file, only this face looked several years older. Ralston glanced over his shoulder. "You think he was working with your suspect?"

"Could be," mused Feeley. Graves' background raised all sorts of possibilities. "But everything seems to suggest Graves was trying to take Mansour out."

Feeley turned to the half-lit Circles building at the far end of the construction site. There was so much about this case that didn't make sense, starting with the fact that no one could find any motive to explain why a well-respected Silicon Valley engineer would suddenly throw in with Middle Eastern terrorists. Mansour more than anyone would have known to stay off the Internet. But the FBI computer forensic technicians who had descended on Neff's ranch discovered he'd hacked into Circles' network. Mansour clearly had unfinished business at Circles. And now there was a dead body outside the company's headquarters.

Feeley zeroed in on the top floor, home to the secretive research unit where Mansour worked. Mansour was there. He'd come back for something. Feeley could feel it. But what? The crackle of Ralston's radio pierced his thoughts. "All units. Ten twenty-nine. All units. Ten twenty-nine," cried the dispatcher's voice. "Fugitive Sergio Mansour has been sighted at three Circular Way. I repeat, three Circular Way."

Feeley fought to suppress a thin self-satisfied grin. His instincts were still sharp.

71

Sergio pressed his hand against his ear as a tiny puff of white smoke curled from the gun barrel only inches away from this head. He spun toward Malina, who stood frozen, her shell-shocked eyes and the gun-man's pistol now trained on Prederick, Liu, and Ko. Sergio looked down at Burrard's lifeless body and back to Malina. He couldn't decide if he was grateful for what she'd done or sickened that she'd been forced to take a life.

"You okay?" he asked her.

She nodded, a little too emphatically. "Get the gun," she said, nodding toward Burrard.

Sergio dropped to his knees next to Burrard, and for the second time that night pried a pistol from a dead man's hand. He stared at Burrard's lifeless eyes, trying to summon anger and hatred for the man who'd helped, in some way, to kill George and Zachary. Maybe it was shock or maybe he was all wrung out after four intense days, but Sergio felt nothing. He cradled the gun in his injured hand, pulled the key from Burrard's fist, and stepped over him to get to his office.

Sergio slipped the key into the lock of Burrard's filing cabinet and pulled it open. Inside was a black Lenovo laptop. An invigorating tingle ran up Sergio's spine. Labs didn't use Lenovo computers. They were almost exclusively bought for the company's finance department. There was no reason for it to be in Burrard's office. He allowed himself a celebratory whoop as he retrieved the machine from the drawer. This was the rogue machine he'd come looking for; the computer at the other end of the blue cable, the very machine that powered all those insidious socialbots. It had to be.

He carried the black laptop back to his workbench and booted it up. The screen flickered through its usual startup process until a single prompt challenged him. He looked at Liu: "Password?"

Liu shrugged.

Sergio held Burrard's gun with his left hand and aimed it at the Chinese man. "You said it was your computer. And that means it's your password."

A muted ring filled the room, drawing everyone's attention to the phone on Sergio's workbench. He peeked at the phone and did a double take; the call came from the administrative assistant's extension on the other side of the double steel doors. Someone knew he was here. Time was short.

Liu smirked. "Aren't you going to answer?"

The anger Sergio only moments before could not muster now erupted from within. This arrogant fuck might not have pulled the trigger, but he bore ultimate responsibility for George's death. And Zachary's. Sergio stepped forward and swung his arm, slamming the butt of the gun into Liu's forehead. Liu stumbled backward and Sergio closed the gap, waving the gun in his face. "I want that password."

Liu steadied himself and dabbed at his wound as the phone kept ringing. He fixed his dark searching eyes on Sergio, as if trying to decide whether Sergio had the guts to shoot an unarmed man. The phone went quiet. Liu pulled his shoulders back, lifted his chin, and tilted his head ever so slightly. A thin snarky smile snaked across his face, a silent challenge to Sergio.

"Last chance," said Sergio, trying to control the outrage and bitterness that threatened to consume him. Flashes of Zachary's spattered brains turned Sergio's stomach. If he didn't stop this evil man, there was no telling what he might do, who he might hurt next. "The password."

"Last chance?" Liu replied with a chuckle. "You are in no position to make de—"

Sergio couldn't be sure he made a conscious decision to fire. All he knew was that he aimed at Liu's leg and then the gun exploded in his hand. The bullet smashed into Liu's right knee and blood spurted everywhere. Liu tumbled to the ground, grabbing his leg as he screamed.

Sergio recoiled from the force and noise of the gun, but he kept the pistol pointed at Liu. *Am I really doing this?* He eyed Liu's mangled knee and took note of the fear on his face.

Eyes wide with alarm, Ko dropped down next to his uncle. He reached for Liu's knee, but he froze when he came face to face with the bloodied mess of shattered bone and flesh. Malina stepped forward and, gun still at the ready, told Ko to pull off Liu's tie. Then she instructed Ko how to wrap it around Liu's leg, just above the wound, and run a pen through the knot. Pale and sweaty, Liu breathed quickly and shallowly as he watched Ko fashion the makeshift tourniquet. "Not too tight," she said. "Just enough to stem the blood."

Malina leaned close to Sergio. "He needs to get to a hospital," she said in a calm but urgent whisper. "He doesn't have a lot of time."

"Neither do we," Sergio replied quietly. He jabbed the gun toward Liu and raised his voice. "What's the password? You don't have much time."

Liu gawked at his shattered knee and the pool of blood seeping outward across the floor. Then he looked up to Sergio. "Please," he croaked, "call an ambulance."

Sergio snorted. He felt little compassion for Liu at that moment. "The password."

"It's Diebolt," Liu said, his face a picture of resignation. "D-I-E-B-O-L-T."

Sergio raised both eyebrows. "Diebolt?" It couldn't be mere coincidence.

Sergio placed the gun on his workbench, next to the black Lenovo. He scanned the laptop's directories but found nothing other than standard programs that come preloaded on every new computer. Then he pulled up the machine's hidden files, standard system files that are not displayed to keep clutter to a minimum. He scanned the list of files, relying on his memory to flag anything out of the ordinary. Nothing popped out at him, nothing that could command an elaborate network of social-bots. Either Burrard had already wiped this computer clean or this was a brand new laptop. A whisper of doubt fluttered through Sergio's mind.

"What's wrong?" asked Malina.

Sergio winced as he ran his hand through his hair. "Just about everything at this point," he replied.

72

Feeley hunched over a desk just outside the red steel doors to Labs. Two San Francisco Police Department patrolmen stood next to him, their guns drawn just in case the Labs doors suddenly opened. In front of him, a Circles security guard played back a closed-circuit security video on the computer monitor he'd commandeered. The sequence showed an employee with a badge escorting a man and a woman through the double steel doors into Labs.

"At first I didn't realize who it was and I didn't think much about it," said the guard as he looked up over his shoulder. "But then our CEO and a couple of other people went inside and all that activity, well, it's pretty unusual at this time of night. So out of curiosity, I played back the video and . . . right . . . there. You see?" His voice rose as he pointed to a frozen screen shot showing the man's face. "It's definitely Sergio Mansour." The guard smiled with satisfaction. "That's when I called you guys."

Feeley stared at the man looking into the camera. He was practically bald, his face bruised and swollen, but he was still a dead ringer for Sergio Mansour's Circles ID photo. The woman wore a ball cap, but she otherwise matched the photos of Malina Olson. "Well done," he said, patting the guard on the shoulder.

"There's more," said the guard as he played footage from the loading bay showing the employee sticking up his hands. "You think Mansour has a gun in his jacket?"

Feeley shook his head. "Could be, but you'd think he'd have his hand on it, right?"

The guard shrugged.

"Do you have a PA system?" asked Feeley. "There might still be a way to talk Mansour down."

"Our PA system doesn't work in Labs," said the guard. "Their networks are separate. I can call though."

"Call Mansour's number," said Feeley.

The guard dialed and handed over the receiver. Feeley listened as digital rings filtered through the earpiece. After fifteen rings, he handed the phone back to the rent-a-cop. "Try again."

The guard started dialing when Feeley's cell phone came alive. Another call from Garrison in Washington. Feeley rolled his eyes at Quick and lifted the phone to his ear. "This is Feeley."

"Where the fuck have you been?" Garrison was in a pissy mood. "There's a report that Mansour's been spotted at Circles."

"I'm *at* Circles," Feeley said.

"Ah, good," replied Garrison, his tone suddenly less aggressive. "What's the situation?"

Feeley gave him the rundown; he could practically hear Garrison licking his chops on the other end of the line.

"You know what this means, don't you?" Garrison paused. "Damn. A terrorist. We haven't had high-profile collar like that in years."

Feeley hesitated. "I think we need to tread carefully here."

"What the hell are you talking about?" demanded Garrison.

"Things aren't adding up."

"What things?"

"Mansour. He's not acting like you'd expect a murder suspect or a terrorist to act." Feeley explained his reservations, starting with the lack of motive and the hit man who was apparently chasing Mansour, to the fact that he'd left tracks all over the Internet and had now come back to Circles.

"Jesus Christ, Feeley," roared Garrison. "Did it ever occur to you that he might have come back to blow the whole fucking place up?"

Feeley pulled the phone away from his ear as Garrison yelled out his orders. Mansour was to be taken down, and he didn't care if Mansour was taken dead or alive. Then the line went dead.

Feeley tucked the phone into his pocket and smiled at Quick. "He's gonna make Director someday."

The guard held up the landline. "It's been ringing. No answer."

Feeley collected his thoughts. There had to be some way to get through to Mansour. He looked down at the guard. "Call him—"

A muffled crack rippled through the room.

Quick snapped to attention. "Was that a gunshot?"

Feeley held his breath, waiting for the muted sound to repeat. After a few seconds, he looked at the men around him. "Whatever it was, it sounded like it was a mile away."

"It's probably the soundproofing," offered the guard. "If that was a shot, then I'm surprised you'd even hear it through those walls."

Feeley nodded and turned to Quick. "Are we sure that's what we heard?"

"I think we need to assume so," said a somber Quick.

"Understood," replied Feeley. He couldn't afford to assume anything else at this point. "Then we need to declare an active shooter."

An active shooter situation changed the dynamics radically. Mansour was not behaving like any fugitive Feeley had ever chased before, but the time for questions had passed. He had no choice now but to proceed with all necessary force. Garrison would have his ass if he didn't.

He turned to the security guard. "Do you have access?"

The guard shook his head, a downbeat expression on his face. "None of us have clearance. Only Labs employees can get in. And the CEO. That's it."

"Are there any nearby rooftops that would give us a vantage point to see what's going on in there?" asked Feeley.

"It won't do you any good," replied the guard. "The windows in Labs are one-way. They can see out but no one can see in. They're pretty serious about security here."

Feeley rubbed his forehead before turning to the patrolman beside him. "How long for the SWAT team?"

"Radio is saying ten to twelve minutes."

Feeley cursed. They'd never get past those steel doors until the SWAT team showed up. And by that point, there was no telling who they'd find alive.

-73-

Sergio commanded the black Lenovo laptop to reveal its logs, the computer's record of activity. He discovered a single action, five days earlier. Someone added what appeared to be a system file, a line of software important to the computer's operating system. Sergio toggled back to the hidden files, found the suspect file, and clicked on it.

The computer's hard drive whirred into action and a video player filled the screen, followed a second later by a pop-up window prompt that read:

```
>>Key: _____
```

A video player? Sergio had never seen one disguised as a systems file. He looked down at Liu. "The key," he commanded.

Liu's shoulders slumped. Sergio reached for the gun. "Are we going to do this again?"

"Okay, okay," he moaned. "Baotou1997."

Sergio tapped the keyboard with his good hand and the video player loaded a grainy image of an empty room. Sergio turned the computer in Malina's direction and clicked PLAY. The black-and-white scene fluttered and the video began rolling. Liu's breathing was ragged, his mouth twisted. He slumped back against a workbench.

On screen, a door opened and a small Asian girl in a short dress entered the dim bedroom. Then came a dark-haired Caucasian man who towered over her. The young girl led him to the heart-shaped bed before stepping to the minibar to prepare a drink. The mood was accentuated by burning candles and wall hangings depicting erotic scenes from ancient dynasties. Sergio had never been to a brothel, but if he had to guess, it would look something like the room on the screen.

The young girl turned to speak to the man, but her words were lost on the silent video. "What would you like to drink?" she must have asked. The man got up, swaying like he didn't need another drink. He walked to the bar and eased the young woman aside, turning toward the camera as he did. At that instant, Sergio was sure. The man was younger, thinner, and had a fuller head of hair, but there could be no doubt it was Richard Diebolt.

"What the hell is this?" he said, turning to Liu. "A sex video?"

Liu didn't react. He'd sunk into his own world of pain and, Sergio hoped, enforced remorse.

Diebolt downed three quick shots and snorted a couple of lines of white powder off the dresser. The girl slipped between his legs and loosened his belt. Sergio couldn't quite believe what he was seeing. How could all of this be about a sex video? And what had happened to the socialbot software? He glanced at Malina and looked down at Burrard's body. And then came a moment of clarity: The computer he was looking for, the one he had expected to find at the end of the blue cable, had been running the socialbot command-and-control software last night. If this Lenovo was that computer, someone had to have wiped it clean and restored the laptop's factory settings in the twenty-odd hours since they'd left Barry's farm. Otherwise there would be telltale signs of activity all over the machine's logs. It didn't make sense, then, that the logs on the Lenovo recorded the moment someone hid the sex video in the computer's operating system—five days ago. There was only one logi-cal conclusion.

He bolted toward Burrard's office. "That's not the computer we're looking for," he called out to Malina. "Keep an eye on them."

Sergio leapt over Burrard's body and pulled a chair into the office. He jumped up and started punching out ceiling panels with his left hand. The blue cable from port ten crossed Burrard's office and slipped down a conduit to the back of his desk. Sergio pulled the desk away from the wall and his heartbeat spiked. The blue cable disappeared into a small hole in the back of the desk. Sergio opened the top drawer of Burrard's desk and inspected its contents. Then he checked the middle one before yanking on the bottom drawer. It was locked.

He fumbled with Burrard's filing cabinet key, but it didn't fit the lock. Then he searched the desk, even as he knew Burrard would not have left it lying around. Sergio stepped out into the main lab and dug into Burrard's pockets. Empty. Fuck.

He hovered over Burrard, his eyes drawn to the outline of Burrard's pendant pressed up against the inside of his bloody T-shirt. Three inches lower were two round holes where the bullets had ripped into his chest. They were identical to the neat wounds in Zachary's chest—both men had been killed by the same gun. Maybe Burrard had been right. Maybe karma really was a bitch.

The phone on Sergio's desk rang again, drowning out Liu's quiet sobs. Someone definitely knew he was in the lab. Each successive ring seemed to get louder. Or was he just imagining it? One person was dead, another gravely wounded, and he had nothing to show for it. Where had he gone wrong? He looked at Liu and back at Burrard. Then he shut his eyes. He needed to think like Burrard: alone, stubborn, self-reliant, no-nonsense. He had to have the key. But where?

He opened his eyes and it was suddenly clear. The circuit board pendant. Burrard never wore it under his shirt. Sergio pulled on Bur-rard's bloody collar and tore the chain from his neck. The pendant snapped free along with a single small key that flew into the air and clattered across the floor. Sergio stared at the key for a long moment, stunned by his discovery. Then he grabbed it, raced back to the office, and dropped to his knees in front of Burrard's desk. Sergio's hands shook as he inserted the key. The lock clicked and he pulled the bottom drawer open. Inside he found a silver Apple laptop. He desperately wanted to believe this was the computer with the socialbot software. After all, how many locked laptops could Burrard have? This had to be the one—but there was only one way to know for sure.

"Oh my God." Malina's breathless whisper floated across the lab.

Sergio spun, ready to race to Malina's rescue. She stood right where he'd left her, still pointing the gun at the three men. Her wide eyes were locked on the video and her free hand covered her mouth.

"What's wrong?" he called out, as he ran from the office.

He reached the workbench and glanced at the screen. Diebolt had pinned the young girl on the bed, their naked bodies straining against each other as she clawed and scratched at his face. Diebolt rose up and slammed his fist into her face. Sergio's stomach turned as Malina looked away from the screen. "I can't watch this," she whimpered.

Sergio looked down at Liu, now dangerously pale.

Diebolt punched and slapped the girl as he wedged his knee between her legs, prying them open so he could move between them. She fought fiercely until his blows sapped her strength. Diebolt drove into her and the girl's face contorted in pain and her mouth opened wide; maybe she was screaming. Waves of revulsion rose from Sergio's stomach. Diebolt covered the girl's mouth with one hand and grabbed her throat with the other, one moment pushing her into the bed, then shaking her violently the next. All the while he continued to fuck her with fury, his aggression mounting with each thrust. The girl's resistance ebbed with each blow and thrust, until she eventually went limp. Minutes passed and his frenzied strokes only grew more urgent until he threw his head back and rolled off the unresponsive girl. He sat on the edge of the bed, oblivious to the still body of the young girl next to him. The video faded to black.

Tears clouded Sergio's eyes. None of the last seventy-two hours had prepared him for this. He was sickened, not only by Diebolt's savage assault, but also by Liu's callous disregard for that poor girl two decades ago. How it was that Diebolt had never answered for that crime, Sergio would never know, but his gut told him Liu had something to do with it.

Malina turned away, her watery eyes wide with shock. "What kind of monster does something like that?" she asked no one in particular.

Sergio stopped to consider the question. "Are you talking about the man who's about to become our next president?" He looked down at Liu. "Or the man who wants to blackmail him?"

-74-

Sergio looked at the clock. It was just past midnight. The first voters in New Hampshire had already gone to the polls. The rest of the East Coast would begin casting ballots in less than five hours. He pulled his work laptop from the messenger bag, booted it up, and connected it to the 3-D camera that four days earlier had captured his eureka moment. He pointed the camera at himself and began pecking at the keyboard with his good hand.

"I thought your account was suspended," said Malina, still holding the gun on Liu, Ko, and Prederick.

"It is, but I'm using one of our admin accounts within Labs' firewall. I commandeered it a while back to test my new retina scanner. Admin rights are powerful."

He clicked the mouse and the computer captured an image of his eye. Almost eight agonizing seconds later, the message appeared:

>>BETA USER

>>IDENTITY APPROVED

He was in. Just a few more commands and . . .

A sharp blast rattled the heavy steel doors connecting Labs to the rest of Circles; a concussive rush of air ripped through Sergio's body.

Urgent but muffled voices cried out from the other side of the inner door. *They've blown the outside door. They're coming for me.*

Sergio pulled up the beta user account's video page, plugged Liu's computer into his, and began transferring the video. A dialogue box popped up, asking permission to reformat the video. Damn!

He slapped the ENTER key and a scrolling bar appeared on screen, slowly inching its way across. A counter kept tabs on its progress. Fifty-two percent, fifty-seven. Then sixty-three percent. *It was moving too slowly.* It was only a matter of seconds before they blew the inner door, too.

Prederick and Ko crouched down next to Liu, taking cover behind the workbench next to Sergio's. Prederick was close, too close for comfort, but they were under control as long as Malina kept her cool. Something clanged against the red steel door, probably the explosive charge that would blow it down. Seventy-eight percent.

Sergio looked at Malina. Her face was smeared with grime, her hair disheveled, and her hands and clothes splattered with blood. Her eyes, intense with fear, somehow looked as radiantly beautiful as the first night they had met.

A faint voice from outside the door broke the moment. "Fire in the hole!"

Words popped up on the screen:

>>CONVERSION COMPLETE

He pecked out more commands, first saving the video and then asserting his admin privileges to upload the clip to Circles' massive user database. Almost there.

A concussive blast shook the room and tossed Sergio from his stool. Malina shrieked as she disappeared in the thick cloud of white smoke that filled the lab. Somehow, amidst all the noise, Sergio heard the distinctive clatter of Burrard's gun falling to the floor.

He rolled on the linoleum tile, stunned by the force of the explosion. He needed to find Malina and he needed to get up, to finish what he started. The shouts from outside were louder now; the door was down. He'd sat up when something rattled along the floor toward him and a second blast rocked the room, this one far more immediate and powerful. The explosion blinded Sergio and threw him on his back. Thick smoke from the concussion grenade choked him and his ears screeched in pain. The piercing fire alarm sliced through the lab, but Sergio could barely distinguish it from the ringing in his ears.

"Malina!" he cried out. He could hardly hear his own voice.

Sergio rolled to his knees and tried to find his way back to the computer. He bumped against someone heavy—a man, but he couldn't tell who it was. He crawled in a daze and his hand found the gun. He gripped it tightly.

Voices struggled to be heard over the earsplitting alarm. "Police. Get down. Down on the floor."

They were inside the room. Sergio wobbled to his feet and pushed forward, his mind focused on a single objective.

———

Special Agent Feeley peeled off the wall and pushed past the blown doors. Second man in, he pressed his assault weapon into his shoulder and lined up his eye to the gunsight. On any other day, he'd have let the SWAT team do its thing. But he insisted on suiting up for this takedown; no one else was going to give Mansour any chance.

The point man cleared the door and veered right to cover his quadrant. Feeley continued straight ahead, his eyes straining to penetrate the smoke, acquire targets, and make instant friend-foe decisions. He moved steadily, his years of training overriding the fidgety nerves firing in his body. Cries and groans competed with the fierce alarm; Feeley couldn't get a fix on them through the haze. A cough over on the right. That was the point man's job.

Feeley heard a voice cry out, dead ahead. He pressed forward. More coughing and then someone over to the right cried out: "Down here. Don't shoot." Feeley's senses went into overdrive as he advanced. There! Directly in front, thirty feet or so. A shadow in the thick smoke. A shape.

"Down on the floor!" he called out. "FBI."

Feeley zeroed in on the nebulous form, who was half-doubled over behind a row of workbenches. The figure stumbled, as if still disoriented by the force of the concussion grenade. Feeley couldn't make out if the silhouette was facing toward him or moving away. The gauzy shape rose up. Gun in one hand, his arms flailed at his sides, like a blind man trying to get his bearings. It looked like . . . Feeley squinted through his sight; he had to be sure. He took two quick steps. The target came into focus. It was definitely Mansour.

"Mansour!" yelled Feeley. It was his final warning. "Get down!"

Mansour's head snapped up; his eyes were wild with confusion and panic. Feeley hesitated, just a second, hoping Mansour would drop to the floor. But when Mansour lurched forward, Feeley no longer had a choice. He squeezed the trigger and Sergio Mansour fell to the floor.

The men in cowboy boots drove off, leaving Sergio in a cloud of dust, alone with his badly injured father. Sergio moved haltingly around Daniel Mansour's curled-up body, choking back tears as he circled. His father's eyes were closed and his hands were pulled up to the gunshot wound in his chest. Or had he brought his hands together to pray?

Sergio dropped to his knees with tears streaming down his cheeks. His father's face was lacerated and grotesquely swollen, his breathing ragged and soggy. Daniel let out a low groan. He wasn't dead yet, but would be soon.

"Papá, please wake up," young Sergio cried softly, tenderly stroking the back of his father's head. "Papá . . ."

Papá's eyelids fluttered and his mouth quivered. "Sergio . . ." he murmured in a scratchy voice. A wet cough escaped his father's lips and his eyes popped open. "Your mother . . . Emilio . . ." His voice faltered, drowned out by heavy gurgling. "Take care of them." Then his eyes froze and he spoke no more.

Sergio awoke to a world of white: an alabaster ceiling, ivory-colored curtains, and bright light from the window. He might have been in heaven if not for the searing pain in his chest, which felt like someone had run a samurai sword right through him, just before bowling him over with a car. His right hand throbbed, as if it'd been smashed with a hammer.

Malina's face floated above.

"Hey there," she said, as she looked down at him. "How are you feeling?"

"Malina . . ." he croaked. His mouth was dry as sand and his head felt groggy. His stomach curdled and his ears ached. "I saw my father . . ."

Slowly, taking long pauses to fight back the pain, he recounted his flashback, sharing every vivid detail and terrifying sensation. When he finished, Malina softly stroked the bristles on his head. "You did exactly what your father asked you to do," she said. "That little boy protected his mother and brother in the only way he knew how. You honored his dying wish."

Sergio stared at the ceiling with watery eyes and tried to absorb the meaning of Malina's words. The constant *beep beep beep* of a heart monitor seeped into his consciousness. His father's dying wish. "You think?"

Malina leaned over him and nodded.

Sergio closed his eyes and tried to draw in a deep breath, only to cry out as the imaginary samurai twisted the blade slicing through his chest. "Why does it hurt so much?"

"You were shot by the police. You had the gun and they thought you were a threat."

From somewhere in the room came the low squawk of a TV. His stomach churned again, like he wanted to throw up. "I feel awful."

"You were lucky." She pressed her palm to his cheek. "The bullet punctured a lung and hit the pulmonary artery. You lost a lot of blood."

He fought off another spasm of pain. "What time is it?"

"It's Thursday morning," she replied. "You've been out for almost sixty hours."

The fog lifted and a million questions rushed into his head. "The election," he said. "What happened with the election?"

Malina stepped away and pulled back the curtain surrounding his bed. A uniformed police officer stood outside the open door. She pointed to the TV hanging high on the opposite wall. On screen, Richard Diebolt stood surrounded by an entourage of police. The station cut to the video of the brutal beating of the girl, only this time blurred to obscure the graphic sex scenes. Mug shots of Prederick, Burrard, and Liu appeared on the television. Sergio couldn't hear the voice-over, but he didn't need to.

"The video went out to everyone on Diebolt's buddy list, just as you intended," said Malina. "There were lots of reporters on the list so it was all over the news by the time the East Coast woke up. Diebolt claims the video is doctored, but I think everybody knows what they saw is real. The amazing thing is, some people still voted for him. He got almost twenty-five percent of the vote."

"But I didn't . . ." He racked his brain, trying to remember those last chaotic moments in Labs. He'd pulled himself to his feet. Voices screaming over the alarm. The last desperate lunge for the workstation. And then blackness. "I didn't push enter. I never sent it."

"No," she said. "But when you got shot, you kept saying 'press enter, press enter.' So I did."

An official standing in front of a dais bearing an FBI logo took over the TV screen. Animated and self-important, he beamed for the camera as he took reporters' questions. The on-screen caption identified him as Preston Garrison, Assistant Director, Cyber Crime unit. Behind him were roughly a dozen agents, all wearing glazed-over looks.

"That's him!" cried Malina, pointing to the TV. "The guy at the back on the right," she said, singling out a boyish-looking agent with short red hair. "Agent Feeley. He's the one who shot you. He also interviewed me."

Sergio stared at the screen for a long while. He wanted to be angry at Feeley, but he didn't have the energy. Sergio looked away and drew in a deep breath, gritting his teeth as the pain attacked. "What about the others?"

"They're in custody, all except Ko." She walked to the window and lowered the blinds. "He's going to testify against the others. I don't think he was involved. Do you?"

Sergio tried to shake his head, but couldn't. "No."

"I still shudder every time I think how the other guys were going to let Burrard kill us," she said.

"The Chinese guy was part of it all the way," he replied. A stand-up reporter popped up on TV. Behind him stood Circles' headquarters and the damaged concrete structure where they had set their trap for the gunman. "What about that guy who chased us?" He fought for a deep breath. "Did they figure out who he was?"

Malina nodded. "A professional killer, someone the Chinese guy—Liu is his name—hired to eliminate rivals and deal with problems like you. The FBI believes he might be involved in murders in Australia, Greenland, Kenya, and Asia—anywhere there are rare earth deposits and dead bodies."

"Rare earths?" asked Sergio.

"They're these very unusual—"

"I know about rare earth minerals."

"Oh. Of course you would," she said, gazing down on him with tender eyes. "Liu isn't talking, but the FBI says he's the world's top rare earth producer, and he wanted to make sure the US couldn't catch up with China."

She offered him a sip of water. It felt cool and fresh down his throat. "So this Liu guy wanted to make sure Diebolt was elected so Liu could blackmail the next president and kill any policy or legislation that could challenge China's rare earths monopoly?"

Malina nodded. "The FBI thinks Liu and Burrard panicked when George discovered the socialbots. They couldn't afford to have either of you digging around."

A new thought crowded his brain. "Wait, what about the computer in Burrard's bottom drawer? Was it really—"

Sergio never finished as Malina pressed her finger to his lips. A delicate hint of jasmine floated in the air. "You need to remain calm," she whispered. "Okay? It's not good for you to get worked up right now."

He nodded.

"Okay," she said, stroking his short prickly hair. "The computer in Burrard's desk was the one you were looking for. It had the socialbot command-and-control software."

Sergio closed his eyes and grappled to make sense of it all. Diebolt. Burrard. Rare earths. Socialbots. And George. The pain in his chest rippled through his body. "What a waste."

Footsteps in the hallway drew their attention and Sergio nodded toward the policeman outside the door.

"Why is he here?" he whispered.

"To protect you, that's all," she said. "You're in the clear. Circles dropped the data-theft charges and the FBI concluded that you didn't send the emails."

"What emails?"

"Burrard spoofed emails to make it look like you were communicating with terrorists." A frown came over her face. "I'm not sure I understand how that works . . ."

"Easy," he said, ignoring the pain as he struggled to form words. "Write an email, put a fake time stamp on it, and insert it into the daily logs. Admin rights are powerful."

"It seems so incredible," she mused. "I mean, I saw it all with my own eyes and I still have a hard time believing what just happened." Her words lingered as she and Sergio lost themselves in their own thoughts. After a while, she cleared her throat.

"I told the media everything," she said, her eyes at once defiant and yet searching for his reaction. "They know all about the socialbots and the election scheme. And it's all over the place."

Sergio nodded. No way this could remain a secret. There was no way it should. He said nothing until curiosity got the best of him.

"Circles . . ." He swallowed painfully. "How is Circles doing?"

"They say traffic is down a bit, but not much."

Sergio closed his eyes, unsure how he felt about that. He squeezed her hand and offered a melancholy smile. "Part of me is relieved. The other part is sad. What does it mean if people just ignore this?"

"It means people already depend too much on Circles," she replied. "There's no way they're going to give it up."

Sergio managed a weak smile. "So you were right about the boiling frogs; is that what you're saying?"

Malina leaned in until their noses touched. "I'm usually right, you know." She kissed him softly on the lips and pulled back just enough so he could revel in her sparkling eyes.

The spell was broken by the footsteps of someone entering the room. The visitor paused behind the partially drawn curtain and a rich baritone voice filled the room. "Miss Malina?"

She looked beyond the curtain and her eyes lit up. She nodded and held up a finger, as if to say, "Wait a second." Then she leaned over Sergio to whisper in his ear. "There's someone to see you. Are you up for it?"

"Should I be?"

"I think so." She waved the visitor forward.

A darkly tanned man with a full face, pug nose, and hopeful eyes stepped from behind the curtain. Sergio stared dumbfounded for a long moment. It was a face weathered by many years under the hot Central Valley sun, but one he knew all too well. Tears surged from deep within and spilled freely down his cheeks.

"*Hermanito,*" whispered Sergio in a choked voice. Little brother. "I've missed you."

ACKNOWLEDGEMENTS

Many people deserve credit for helping make this book possible. I thank Nino Walker, Anil Pal, Vincent Lo, and Jonathan Altman for selflessly sharing as much technical information as my brain could absorb. Jennifer Grayzar, Dave Putnam, Roland Salvato, Marty Smith, Judith Hammerman, Amanda Enayati, and Victoria Bruce stepped up at critical moments when I needed a helping hand. I simply would not have reached the finish line without the generosity and commitment of my writing group: Cathy Bator, Fred Campagnoli, Michelle Kicherer, Peter O'Donnell, Audrey Tran, and Pat Griffith. Countless friends and family members, including Pat and Chuck Gerhan, offered me more support and encouragement than I could have ever reasonably expected. Special kudos go out to Sugeet Manchanda-Madan and Laetitia Mailhes for simultaneously picking apart my manuscript and urging me to continue. I am particularly grateful for those long bike rides with Jeff Davis, who managed to convince me that suffering for one's art is a good thing. My agent Brandi Bowles took me on long before I was ready and helped shepherd me through many rewrites and that gut-wrenching process known as 'finding a publisher.' Thanks to Kjersti Egerdahl at Amazon Publishing for taking a chance on this story and to Charlotte Herscher for her superb edits. None of this would have been possible without the love, support and sacrifices of my parents, Bruce and Cristina. Most of all, I owe a special debt of gratitude to my wife, Martha, who believed in this story—at times more than I did.

ABOUT THE AUTHOR

Photo © 2015 Jeffrey Davis

Scott Allan Morrison was a journalist for almost twenty years, covering politics, business, and technology in Mexico, Canada, and the United States. Morrison arrived in Silicon Valley as a reporter for the *Financial Times* during the darkest days of the dot-com crash. He later covered the Web 2.0 boom for Dow Jones Newswires and the *Wall Street Journal*. Over the course of a decade, Morrison covered most of the world's top tech companies and chronicled many of Silicon Valley's greatest stories, including the rise of Internet insecurity and the explosion of social media. Before setting his sights on journalism, he spent four years teaching English and traveling in Southeast Asia. He speaks fluent Spanish and very rusty Mandarin. He lives in Northern California with his wife and his hockey sticks.

Visit the author's website at www.scottallanmorrison.com.